DREAM
SKY

PRAISE FOR THE PROJECT EDEN THRILLERS

"Sick didn't just hook me. It hit me with a devastating uppercut on every primal level—as a parent, a father, and a human being."—**Blake Crouch**, best selling author of Run

"...a gem of an outbreak story that unfolds like a thriller movie and never lets up, all the way to the last page. Absolutely my favorite kind of story!"—**John Maberry**, *New York Times* bestselling author

"...not only grabs you by the throat, but by the heart and gut as well, and by the time you finish you feel as if you've just taken a runaway train through dangerous territory. Buy these books now. You won't regret it."—**Robert Browne**, best selling author of Trial Junkies

"You think Battles was badass before? He just cranked it up to 500 joules. CLEAR!"—**PopCultureNerd.com**

"Brett Battles at his best, a thriller that also chills, with a secret at its core that's almost too scary to be contained within the covers of a book."—**Tim Hallinan**, author of the Edgar-nominated The Queen of Patpong

ALSO BY BRETT BATTLES

DREAM SKY

SKY

Brett Battles

A PROJECT EDEN THRILLER

Book 6

What Came Before

THOSE WHO HAD survived the initial outbreak of the Sage Flu were relieved when they saw and heard the message from the secretary general of the United Nations telling them a vaccine was available. But the message was merely a means to lure the living to Project Eden's holding facilities, where individual judgments could be made on whether or not the survivors were valuable enough to keep alive.

After Ben Bowerman buried his family in a San Mateo, California, cemetery, he headed south to find his girlfriend Martina. He stopped first in Santa Cruz, where he'd been attending college, to pick up a present he'd purchased for Martina. While there, he discovered Iris Carlson locked in a basement, unaware of what had been going on. He took her with him, but when he woke the next morning, he discovered she'd stolen his Jeep and most of his things.

In Ridgecrest, California, Martina Gable's band of friends decided to leave their hometown and travel to the survival station in Los Angeles. Martina had different plans. Three of her friends stayed with her, and together they went in search of Martina's boyfriend, Ben. What Martina found was Ben's Jeep being driven by someone she didn't know, someone who told her Ben was dead.

In Mumbai, Sanjay and Kusum investigated the survival station, suspecting it wasn't what it claimed to be. Their observations confirmed their suspicions, but in the process,

Kusum and a few of the couple's colleagues were taken prisoner by Project Eden. Sanjay mounted a rescue operation, not only for his friends but also the others being held. He and Kusum then went back in to steal as much vaccine as they could find.

The survivors on Isabella Island anxiously awaited the return of the UN. When a plane carrying medical personnel finally landed, the island occupants received their inoculations. Afterward, Robert and a few others met with the people from the plane and learned they weren't from the UN, that the UN message was a lie. The plane then left, but Rich "Pax" Paxton stayed behind to help convince the rest of the island residents that the trouble was not over. He was proven right when another plane approached and sprayed the island with Sage Flu instead of landing. Through Pax's quick action, everyone took cover inside the resort.

Outside Washington DC, Tamara Costello and Bobby Lion located an NSA communications facility, and set to work finding a way to use the equipment to replace the fake UN message, which continued to play over the airwaves, with one of their own. After several obstacles, Bobby was able to get the system to work, but they couldn't play their prerecorded message and Tamara had to convey it live, over and over.

The Resistance had split into two groups. The larger group traveled from the Ranch in Montana to the Resistance's alternate base at Ward Mountain North, Nevada. The smaller group, led by Matt Hamilton, the leader of the Resistance, waited a few days for Daniel Ash to recover from his wounds, until a storm forced them to leave. But Matt did not lead his band of people directly to Nevada. Instead, they headed south to New Mexico. Matt had received a message from a contact, known as C8, inside Project Eden, informing him that the Project's principal director was at the Project Eden base outside Las Cruces, New Mexico. When his team arrived in the southern New Mexican town, Matt headed to the base alone, rendezvousing with C8. Inside the base, Matt and C8 placed sarin gas dispensers throughout the facility. Matt also set up remote-controlled explosives near the central elevator. The plan was to wait for a meeting the principal director was scheduled to attend, but before the meeting happened, Tamara Costello's live broadcasts appeared, replacing the fake UN message. Realizing he couldn't wait any longer, Matt set off the explosives and the gas. Once the way was clear, he headed to the principal director's office, where he found the man and his assistant still alive. Matt killed the principal director and left. But before he could reach the stairs that would take him outside, he was shot by the principal director's dying assistant.

Ash rushed toward the burning Project Eden facility, hoping Matt had been able to escape. When he saw his friend standing outside the building, he was momentarily relieved. But then Matt fell to the ground. Kneeling at his side, Ash saw his friend's wounds were grave, but the leader of the Resistance was determined to pass on some information.

"Augustine...green...sky," Matt whispered.

"What?" Ash asked.

"You...need to...know..."

"Augustine green sky?"

"Dream," Matt corrected him. "Dream sky."

Ash asked what the message meant, but Matt Hamilton was dead.

January 3rd

World Population
918,992,056

1

"THE TIME IS four p.m., GMT. Shall we begin?"

As expected, there was no dissent.

"It has now been over ten hours since our last communication with NB219 or Principal Director Perez," Celeste Johnson told the others partaking in the video conference. "Due to this silence, and per Project guidelines, this emergency meeting of the directorate has been called."

The irony that this was the first meeting of the directorate since Perez had taken charge of the Project was not lost on them. He had turned the group into merely an advisory council—one he had yet to call on—and the members had little doubt he had been planning on disbanding them completely.

The current group was actually the second incarnation of the directorate, since the members of the pre-pandemic board had all been killed at Bluebird on Implementation Day. Out of that initial post-KV-27a-release directorate, only two members remained: Dr. Henry Lassiter, stationed at NB772 in southern France; and Erik Halversen at NB405 on the outskirts of Hamburg, Germany. The rest had all been appointed to their positions by Director Perez: Johannes Yeager at NB338 outside Rio de Janeiro, Brazil; Kim Woo-Jin at NB202 near Seoul, Korea; Parkash Mahajan at NB551 in Jaipur, India; and Celeste at NB016 in New York City, USA.

"If I may," Dr. Lassiter said from his monitor.

"Go ahead, Doctor," Celeste said.

"As ranking Project member, I believe the role of principal director falls to me. I suggest we all agree to that immediately so we can move on to more important matters."

Celeste looked at the different screens in front of her. Yeager, Kim, and Mahajan were all trying very hard to keep their faces neutral. Halversen, on the other hand, was nodding in agreement.

"I understand your thoughts on the manner," Celeste said. "As we all do."

"Excellent. Then we're agreed."

"No," Kim said. "We are not."

The doctor looked surprised. "Mr. Kim, we can work out a solution to whatever problem you're—"

"Dr. Lassiter," Celeste said. "Mr. Kim is not the only one who has an issue with your suggestion. I believe you will find that Mr. Yeager and Mr. Mahajan share a similar point of view."

"For God's sake," Lassiter said, "this is not the time for infighting. We are at a critical point in the plan, yet for the second time in two weeks we have lost our leader. We need a smooth transition to someone familiar with how things work at the top. What we don't need is a split vote."

"Split vote?" Celeste said. "I think you've misunderstood. I would not vote for your ascension to principal director, either."

"No. Absolutely not. You four are only on the directorate because Perez needed bodies in seats so that the membership felt everything was fine. You wouldn't even be on this call otherwise."

"The fact is, we *are* on this call," Yeager said. "Whether we should be here or not is no longer an issue."

"Doctor," Celeste said, "we may not have been on this board very long, but, if I may remind you, that means we were not part of the directorate that allowed Perez to take full control."

"You're saying that like Erik and I had a choice," Lassiter said.

"There is always a choice," she said. "And you two made

the wrong one. You went against the best interests of the membership and allowed Perez to become the dictator. If he hadn't been eliminated, I don't even want to imagine what would have happened to the Project."

"I think you are being a little premature there," Halversen said. "We do not even know what happened. It is very possible he is still in charge. We should *all* remember that."

"Principal Director Perez is dead," Celeste said.

"And how could you possibly know that?" Lassiter asked. "We have not heard back from the investigation team yet."

"Actually, we have. I spoke to them thirty minutes ago."

"We've received no report of this," Lassiter said, waving his arm to indicate the other directorate members. "Any information should be shared immediately."

"It was shared," she said. "Mr. Yeager, Mr. Kim, and Mr. Mahajan have all received a full briefing."

Lassiter's face turned red. "This is out—"

"Principal Director Perez and all those stationed at NB219 are dead. Not only were the central elevators destroyed, and everything up to and including the ground-level warehouse completely burned, it appears that some kind of poisonous gas was released within the base itself." She pushed a button on her keyboard, and the feed from her camera was replaced by a picture of Perez lying on the floor of his office, surrounded by a pool of blood. "As you can see, in addition to whatever effects the gas may have had on him, he was shot."

Lassiter remained silent as he watched the footage. When it was over, he said, "I can't say I'm not glad he's dead, but this is something you should have shared with Erik and me immediately."

"You clearly don't understand what's going on here, Dr. Lassiter." She leaned back. "I'd like to vote on the first motion."

"What motion?" Lassiter said.

"What are you talking about?" Halversen said.

"Item A: the removal of Dr. Henry Lassiter and Erik Halversen from the directorate. All in favor?"

A chorus of four yeas.

"What the hell is this? You can't remove us!"

"I believe we just did."

"For what cause?" Halversen asked.

"Dereliction of duty. Endangering the Project. Inaction resulting in the deaths of the personnel assigned to NB219. Shall I go on?"

"This is absurd," Lassiter said. "You are all to confine yourself to your quarters. You are relieved of your duties and no longer a part of the directorate."

"We're not the ones who let the Project down," Celeste said. "And I think you'll find that the membership agrees with me."

"The membership doesn't care. They will follow what I say." He reached forward to disconnect the call.

"I wouldn't do that if I were you."

He snickered but pulled his hand back a few inches. "Oh, really? You think anything you say is going to change my opinion?"

"We don't care about your opinion. We just want to watch what's going to happen."

Lassiter's brow furrowed. "What are you talking about?" As he finished asking the question, he turned toward a noise off camera. "I'm in the middle of something right now. Whatever you need can wait."

Someone out of sight said something the microphone didn't pick up.

"Get out!" Lassiter said. "All of you!"

"Dr. Lassiter," Celeste said calmly. "There's something I probably should have mentioned right at the beginning of our meeting. I took the liberty of broadcasting our discussion live to all Project facilities. I believe you'll find that those there at NB772 will be more than happy to escort *you* to your quarters, where you will await trial."

Several people moved into the picture behind Lassiter.

"Get out of here! Leave me alone! You don't

understand!"

Men on either side grabbed his arms. He tried unsuccessfully to shake them free as they lifted him out of the chair and carried him out of the frame. In the feed from NB405, Halversen had been joined by his own group of self-appointed deputies, but, in contrast to the doctor, he went quietly.

Celeste killed the two feeds, looked directly into her camera, and said, "Members of Project Eden, we have all been through some unexpected bumps since Implementation Day. To keep that from happening again, Mr. Yeager, Mr. Kim, Mr. Mahajan, and I have agreed to split the responsibility of principal director, so that no one person will have ultimate power. Project Eden has never been about that. We are about creating a sustainable, successful human society free of the old world's problems. Thanks to your support, we are back on track."

2

CURTIS WICKS HAD watched his friend die from the cover of the arroyo as the blaze lit up the night and consumed NB219.

Though he didn't know it, there was nothing he could have done. Matt Hamilton had been fatally shot before he stumbled out of the emergency tunnel doorway. Wicks could tell his friend was hurt, though, and knew he should have left his hiding place to see if he could've helped in some way. But no, he had stayed in the arroyo even as Matt fell to the ground. Others— members of the Resistance—moved in quickly, but their efforts had been for naught.

Wicks could have gone over to them then, could have grieved at his friend's side—should have done both—but instead he watched as Matt was carried to a vehicle and driven away.

The flames burned for hours, working their way through the thousands of tons of supplies that had been stored at the base. Finally, as the sun rose and dissolved the shadows, Wicks crawled out of the crease in the land and forced himself to walk over to what was left of the facility.

The warehouse was gone, piles of burnt wreckage surrounding a gaping hole in the center, where the elevator shaft had been. Scattered outside were the bodies of security personnel killed by the Resistance, and a few Project personnel who'd apparently been close enough to one of the exits to get outside, but not close enough to avoid breathing in smoke or the poison gas. Though Wicks didn't want to, he checked each for a pulse and found none.

He, Curtis Wicks—Project Eden member and Resistance informant known as C8—was the sole survivor of the destruction of NB219.

There was no question of reporting to another Project facility. Given his still-healthy status, he would forever—and rightly—be suspected of participating in the assassination of Principal Director Perez and the murders of hundreds of Project members.

As he surveyed the destruction, he wondered if the remaining Project Eden leadership already knew something had happened. Chances were, after failing to establish communications with the base, teams were already on the way.

He couldn't help looking at the skies.

They were empty, but for how long?

He needed to get out of there. Now.

He went half a mile before he found a car with keys still in the ignition. He pulled out the body in the driver's seat, rolled down the windows to counteract as much of the smell as he could, and then went in search of an auto dealership where he could find a vehicle free of any rotting corpses.

He spotted a Ford lot, and liked the looks of the F-150 trucks out front. After dumping the temporary car at the curb, he headed for the sales office to find the keys to the vehicles. But before he reached the door, a speck in the eastern sky caught his attention.

A plane.

Project Eden was coming to town.

He could hardly breathe as he realized he'd waited too long to leave. Taking a truck was out of the question now. They would spot it in no time. Hell, they'd spot anything.

Plan B, then—collect some supplies and find an out-of-the-way place he could hide in until the plane was gone. There was a market several blocks back. He could probably find everything he needed there.

He ran, afraid to drive even that short distance. Two blocks from the store, he slowed when he glanced down a side street and spotted something that was potentially even better than hiding.

A motorcycle, parked in a driveway.

He should have thought of that first. A motorbike had a much smaller profile than an F-150.

He switched course.

The bike was old, its chrome and paint dulled from years on the road, but otherwise it looked in pretty good shape. The tank was near full, but the keys were missing. He glanced at the house, steeled himself, and ran up to the door.

It was locked. He looked around and spotted a weathered garden gnome tucked between two leafless bushes. He used it to smash through the living-room window.

Wicks jumped through the opening and began his search. In addition to the keys that he located in a cabinet near the door, he found a helmet, a pair of riding gloves, a scarf, and a winter jacket that was about his size and would help keep him from freezing to death.

It had been years since he was last on a motorcycle, so it took him six attempts to get the engine started. When he finally did, he checked the sky again.

The plane was low now, maybe five miles out of town. The only consolation was that it was a small jet that probably held no more than ten people.

He considered heading right out, but knew the smart play was to wait a bit.

As the aircraft drew closer, it adjusted its course to the north, putting it on a direct path for NB219. Though Wicks couldn't see the base from where he was, the column of smoke rising above it was clearly visible.

When the plane neared the plume, it began circling the base.

Again, the urge to run hit him, but he remained where he was.

After a third go-around, the plane lowered its landing gear and flew toward the nearby airport.

Wait, Wicks told himself.

The plane was only a few hundred feet above the ground now.

Wait.

Five stories up.

Wait.

Tree level.

Wait.

Down.

Go!

He twisted the accelerator and almost fell off the bike as he shot out of the driveway, but he didn't slow down. With the plane barely on the ground, it was his best—perhaps only—opportunity to get out of there. Not only would they be unable to see him, but the plane's engine would drown out the initial burst from the motorcycle.

He took the southbound ramp onto the I-25 and sped out of town.

When he hit the I-10, he continued south, every few minutes sneaking a peek over his shoulder at the sky and the highway, sure he would see people coming after him. It wasn't until he was somewhere in the vast nothingness of west Texas that he started to think maybe he was going to be okay.

He spent that first night in Abilene, and began considering his next move. If he avoided Project Eden locations, most of which he knew about, nearly the whole world was open to him. Finding a place where he could live out his life undetected shouldn't be that hard.

A voice woke him at four a.m.

What choice do we have? We're the only ones who can do anything about it.

Matt's voice. The words from so many years earlier, before Matt had faked his death and left to form the Resistance. And though the Resistance may have failed at its main objective, it hadn't failed completely.

The original directorate was dead. And now the new principal director, Perez, was also dead. Project Eden may have unleashed its unholy hell, but the organization had been rocked, too. And if there was any chance of keeping the Project from controlling the resurrection of mankind, it had to be rocked again, in as big a way as possible.

The urge to pull the blanket over his head and hide from everything was so strong that Wicks's hands trembled. The weak part of his mind said, "You've already done your part. Find a beautiful beach or a cabin by a lake. Anywhere. You have your pick. For you, the fight is over."

But the blanket remained under his chin. The fight was *not* over.

"Do I really need to do this?" he whispered.

Matt's words again. *Yes. You do.*

January 5th

World Population
862,727,366

3

A COLD WIND blew down the barren mountain, passing through skin like water through cloth and chilling the bones beneath. Teeth chattered, hands were stuffed in pockets, necks were buried under scarves, but no one said a word in complaint.

The grave was dug on high ground, well away from the flash-flood channels and dry riverbeds that latticed the area. The coffin was a pine box hauled in from a mortuary in Ely. A fancier one, with metal handles and ornate scroll work, could've been chosen, but Rachel Hamilton had said Matt would have wanted things simple.

All but the most essential personnel had made their way out of the warren of rooms and tunnels that made up the Resistance's base, and trekked the quarter mile to the gravesite. Despite the frigid air, there was no snow, only the dirt and the shrubs and the wide-open sky playing home to a tiny, distant sun.

Ash glanced at Rachel. Her eyes were locked on the pine box that held her brother. Ash let her mourn in silence for several more seconds, and then moved to the head of the grave.

"As you can imagine, I've thought long and hard about what I was going to say here today, but I realized no matter what words I chose, they would be inadequate. To say Matt has been an essential element of our cause would not do him justice. Matt was the embodiment of why we are all here. Without him, it's doubtful any of us would be alive today. He was our leader. Our friend." He looked at Rachel. "Our brother." He paused. "It would be easy to say we are now lost without his guidance, that our only choice is to give up. But if we are going to truly honor Matt's memory, then we can never give up. We *must* fight on." A silent beat. "I will miss him every minute of every day."

He nodded to the men standing next to the coffin. They moved the box over the hole, using cloth slings, and gently lowered it inside.

"If anyone has anything they'd like to say, please step forward," Ash said.

One by one, people shared their stories and thoughts and wishes. When the last finished, Ash caught Chloe's attention, silently asking if she wanted to take a turn. For a moment, he thought she was going to say something, but then she shook her head.

"Go in peace, my friend," he said, looking down into the hole. "We'll take it from here."

Slowly the mourners began to drift back to the base. Once most were gone, the men who had lowered the coffin picked up shovels and started to fill in the grave.

Ash walked over to Rachel and put an arm around her shoulder. "We should go back."

"Not yet," she said.

He could feel her shiver.

"You're going to get sick if you stay out here any longer," he told her.

"Not yet."

As he started to take a step back to give her privacy, she touched his arm.

"No. Stay."

Ash caught Chloe's attention, and motioned with his eyes toward where his children were waiting with Ginny Thorton. Chloe nodded, collected the kids, and led them toward the base.

Soon, the only ones left by the grave were Rachel, Ash,

and the four men burying the casket.

"Walk with me," Rachel said.

She started down a path leading away from the base into the empty desert, Ash walking at her side.

"I can't do this," she said after they were out of earshot of the others.

Ash said nothing.

"I'm serious. I'm not qualified. I don't know what he knew, I didn't have his experience. I can't…it's too much."

"None of us is qualified," he said.

She turned to him. "You are. You have a military background. You should take his place."

"No one is going to take Matt's place."

"But that's what everyone's expecting *me* to do."

"No, they're not. They are expecting you to lead us, yes, but they know you're not Matt."

"It's the same thing."

"It's not." He paused. "The people here look up to you. They always have. They wouldn't accept anyone else in charge but you."

"But I can't do what my brother did! I wasn't inside the Project. I don't know what he knew."

"I don't, either. And neither does Pax or Chloe or anyone else. That's something we'll have to move forward without."

"But Matt always knew what to do."

"Just because you're in charge doesn't mean you have to lead the same way he did. You can rely on others to advise you and help decide courses of action."

She turned back to the desert. In a near whisper, she said, "I don't know. I just don't know."

CHLOE WAS WAITING near the entrance when Ash escorted Rachel inside thirty minutes later. She was pretending to inspect some equipment, but he knew she was waiting for him.

"Where would you like to go?" he asked Rachel. "Your room?"

Rachel thought for a moment, and then nodded. "Please."

As they headed toward the tunnel leading to the residential sections, Ash caught Chloe's eye and patted the air with his hand, telling her to stay. She frowned, but he knew she would do as he asked.

The few people he and Rachel passed on the way to her quarters moved quickly to the side, muttering their condolences. Rachel greeted the first two with a "thank you," but seemed to lose steam after that so Ash took up the task.

When they finally reached her room, he said, "If you need anything at all, want to talk or whatever, have someone find me and I'll come right away."

She put a weak hand on his arm. "I know you will, and I appreciate it." She opened her door and disappeared inside.

The moment the latch slipped into place, he headed back the way they'd come.

As soon as Chloe saw him, she said, "Okay?"

He nodded.

But before they could leave, they heard steps coming toward them from one of the other hallways. They held their position and were joined a few seconds later by two men from engineering, toting tool boxes and dressed for the outside.

"Captain," the lead man said. "Chloe."

His partner nodded.

"Morning, Caleb," Ash said. "Problems?"

Caleb Matthews stopped next to the outside door and adjusted his scarf. "Stupid solar panels," he said. "One of them decided it didn't want to work today."

He opened the door and let a blast of cold air into the room.

"This is going to be fun," the other man—Devin—said as he pulled his hood over his head.

"This is not my definition of fun," Caleb shot back.

"Hello, it was a joke," Devin said.

"Not a funny one."

"Be careful out there," Ash said.

"Oh, I'll be fine," Caleb replied. "Devin's doing all the work."

"I don't think so," Devin said as they stepped outside.

Caleb said something back but it was lost behind the shutting of the door.

"Come on," Ash said to Chloe.

They returned to the residential section and stopped in front of Matt's room.

Until that morning, it had been where their friend's body was kept. As a show of respect, members of the Resistance had taken turns sitting watch. All very thoughtful and good, except it meant the room had not been vacant since Ash, Chloe, and the others had brought Matt to Ward Mountain.

Augustine. Dream. Sky.

Those had been nearly the last words Matt had spoken before he died. He had been desperate for Ash to remember them, but had failed to explain their significance.

During the journey back to Nevada, Chloe was the only one Ash told about the words, but she'd had no more ideas than he did about their meaning. What they did know was that the words were important or Matt wouldn't have wasted his last breaths passing them on. And since he'd kept them secret, they agreed to be careful about who they asked about the words' significance.

Rachel was the obvious one to talk to, but she had been in a deep depression since they'd radioed ahead about her brother's death and was having a hard time focusing on anything. So Ash had been reluctant to approach her and had even considered putting it off. It was Chloe who finally convinced him it was not something that could wait. With her help, he'd arranged a few moments alone with Rachel the day before.

"I don't mean to bother you," he'd said, "but I need to ask you something."

It took her a moment to look at him, as if his words were traveling at a fraction of the speed of sound.

"What?" she asked, even that single word a struggle.

"Matt said something to me before he died."

She looked confused.

"I didn't understand what he meant, but thought maybe

you would."

"What did he say?"

"Augustine dream sky."

A blank stare, then, "Sounds like gibberish to me."

"He was very insistent. Wanted me to remember."

"I have no idea what he meant," she said, her face hardening. "If it's not gibberish, then it's probably something that will get our people killed. Forget it. Forget he said anything."

"I thought it might be good if we—"

"I said forget it."

He should have waited, he realized, let a few days pass, maybe a week or two. Her brother's death was still too fresh. He could see all she wanted to do was curl up in a corner and he couldn't blame her for that. But he couldn't ignore Matt's message, and a delay of a week or two could very well be too long.

The only other person who might've known something was Rich Paxton. But while Ash was relieved to hear Pax was alive and had returned from northern Canada, Matt's old right-hand man had left for Latin America to help a group of survivors, so a private conversation with him was currently impossible.

The only option left was for Chloe and Ash to check through Matt's things to see if they could find an answer.

Obtaining a key to Matt's room had not been a problem. With Rachel overwhelmed by her brother's death, and Pax off site, Ash had been seen as the next in command. No one noticed when he kept one of Matt's keys.

The hallway empty, they slipped inside the room and closed the door.

The bed where Matt's body had lain was rumpled, the top cover off center from when the pallbearers had come to carry him out to the casket. Piled against the back wall were the four boxes and two large duffel bags containing all his personal possessions from the Ranch, waiting to be unpacked. Though in death Matt had occupied the room, he had never lived there.

Working silently so as not to disturb Rachel in her suite next door, Ash and Chloe started going through the boxes. Sweaters, long underwear, socks, T-shirts, buttoned shirts, pants, and shoes—all four boxes full of clothes.

They carefully taped the boxes back up and moved on to the duffel bags. The heavy one was stuffed with books—a survivalist's how-to treasure trove of instructions on how to do everything from simple farming to advanced electronics. Ash could imagine Matt sitting up late reading through them.

The lighter bag held a box of photos, a few pictures in frames, and several journals, each tied closed by strings. Chloe pulled the top one out, untied it, and opened the cover. On the front page was a thirteen-month date range from several years earlier.

Ash motioned for Chloe to flip through the book.

Every single page was filled with handwriting they recognized as Matt's. She randomly stopped at one of the pages and held the book out so they could both read.

Monday, Sept. 23rd

Prep for winter almost complete. Have left most of those details in Rachel's hands. Heard from G1 this morning. No real news, which I guess is good. Pax is still out on the recruiting run. When we spoke, he said things with the group in Singapore looked promising. If he's able to bring them aboard, that'll up our organization by another thirty-seven. They will also hold a strategic position that we desperately need. I stressed to him how important it is that he succeeds.

At the end of the entry were several numbers, in distinct sets.

A quick glance at some of the previous entries revealed a few of them also ended with numbers. Ash could discern no obvious meaning, so told Chloe they could figure out later if the numbers were important or not.

They quickly went through the rest of the books, eight in all. Each was filled front to back like the first.

"We're missing one," Chloe whispered.

Ash nodded. He'd noticed it, too. The journal covering the last four months wasn't there.

He stepped over to the pack Matt had taken with him on the trip south to New Mexico, and searched through the pockets. He found the journal wrapped in a shirt at the very bottom of the main section.

"Done here," he whispered, showing her the book.

They closed the duffel bags and arranged them and the boxes exactly as they had been before. At the door, they paused to make sure the corridor was quiet before leaving with their old friend's journals.

4

"HOW YOU FEELING?" Robert asked, raising his voice enough for it to carry through the wall into the next room.

"No change," Renee's muffled reply came back.

Though he was still pissed off at her, his anger was far outweighed by the relief he felt from her response.

Twenty-four hours earlier—two days after Isabella Island had been doused with the Sage Flu virus by an organization apparently known as Project Eden—Renee had walked outside.

While Robert knew that eventually someone would have to test the effectiveness of the vaccine they'd been given, he'd fully intended to be the one leaving the confines of the dining room where everyone had holed up. Leave it to Renee to sneak away and do it herself. When Robert found out, it took Rich Paxton, Estella, and several of the others to keep him from running out after her.

"We only need one guinea pig," Pax had said.

Renee had stayed outside and exposed herself to the virus for several hours before moving into the restaurant manager's office on the other side of the wall. Robert had yelled at her at first, but soon tempered his emotions when he finally accepted that what was done was done. Since then, he had spent most of his hours leaning against the wall, talking to her and checking on her, and sometimes not saying anything at all.

DREAM SKY

Pax had told them it could be anywhere from a few hours to a couple of days before she'd show signs of infection, but given the concentration of the virus she'd been exposed to, he was leaning more toward the former than the latter. Robert's own experience with the Sage Flu was minimal. Dominic was the only one he'd watched die, and it hadn't been much more than a day before his friend had shown signs. Surely Renee would have come down with it by now.

"No sniffles? Fever?" he asked. "You don't feel tired?"

"No change means no change, Robert. I feel fine. Can we talk about something else?"

"Uh, sure. What do you want to talk about?"

"I don't care. Anything."

Robert was saved from having to come up with a subject by Estella's arrival.

"Pax would like to talk to you," she said.

"About what?"

She shrugged. "He was on the phone to his people, then he wanted you. That is all I know."

"Hey, you still there?" Renee asked.

"Go," Estella said. "I will keep her company."

Robert found Pax across the room. "You were looking for me?"

Pax nodded toward the buffer room and headed over. The area next to it was a quiet place to meet, most people not wanting to get so close to what was right on the other side.

"The arrangements are set," Pax said. "But we've got a bit of a time crunch so we need to start getting things moving."

The island—coated now with the virus—was no longer a safe place to stay, even for the inoculated, so Pax had been working on a way to get them all off.

"When will the planes be here?" Robert asked.

"That's part of the problem. They can't come here exactly. If we had enough seaplanes, maybe, but with only one or two, it would take far too long to get everyone off. They're sending a passenger jet. It'll land at the airport over in Limón tonight. So that means we have to get ourselves over there."

"But we don't have enough boats," Robert said. The resort had only a few speedboats and some diving boats. "Even if we overloaded them, it'll take at least two trips to get everyone across. And if the water's at all rough, I don't want to think about how dangerous that'll be."

"We'll take them all at once," Pax said.

"And how the hell are we supposed to do that?"

"A ferry."

"But the ferry is at the coast."

"Which is why," Pax said, "you and I are going to go get it."

"WE'LL BLOW THE horn as soon as we reach the bay," Robert said after he explained to everyone what he and Pax were going to do. "That'll be your signal to head for the dock. Until then, stay in here."

"Are you sure it's okay to leave?" someone asked.

"Renee has shown no signs of the flu," Robert said.

"Doesn't mean she won't," someone else countered.

"What about our stuff?" a man near the back asked. "Do we grab that on our way out?"

"If there is something vital you need to bring, then you can get it. But no suitcases, no clothes, nothing bulky. They'll take up too much room."

"What's the hurry?" a woman asked. "Isn't it safer if we just stay here?"

"I'll take this one," Pax said. He stepped forward. "In all likelihood, your system is now as immune to the Sage Flu as it's going to get. So, from that point of view, staying in here or leaving would be the same."

"Are you a doctor?"

"No, I'm not."

"Then how can you know that?"

"Because I've been dealing with this a lot longer than you." His words came out sympathetic, but firm. "There is a very good reason not to stay here, though. The people from

Project Eden will be back soon. It's a pattern my people have seen elsewhere. They're going to want to make sure the disease they dumped on the resort took hold. They'll expect to see a quiet island with perhaps a few bodies spread around. If they don't, they'll very likely send in a squad of armed personnel to see what happened. From our observations, this can take place anytime from now through the next few days. So, no, it's not safe. And, yes, we *are* in a hurry."

Several people shouted at once.

"Listen to me," Pax said loudly enough to cut through the clatter. "I would love to stand around and answer all of your questions, but every minute Robert and I delay our departure is another minute closer to their return. You can argue all you want with each other, but we're leaving now."

He started toward the buffer room. Robert stood there a moment longer, feeling the need to reassure everyone.

"Are you coming?" Pax asked, looking back from halfway across the room.

Robert turned to the group of residents. "We'll be back as quickly as we can," he said, then headed after Pax.

Two steps into the crowd he felt a hand on his arm.

"Be careful," Estella whispered. She kissed him on the cheek before letting go.

"Make sure everyone's ready," he said.

"I will."

He doubled his pace and met Pax at the plastic flap that served as the buffer's door.

"They'll be fine," Pax said, giving him a reassuring smile.

"I know."

The older man pulled the flap back enough to duck through. As soon as the way was clear, Robert followed.

Renee was waiting for them as they stepped outside. "What the hell is going on? I could hear people shouting, but I couldn't hear what anyone was saying."

Robert quickly explained the plan.

"You're taking me with you, right?" she said.

"One of us has to stay here," he said. As she opened her

mouth to argue, he added, "If we don't come back, you need to use what we have here and get everyone off, no matter how many trips it takes."

She frowned as she closed her mouth, but didn't fight him.

"Keep an eye out for us," Robert said. "If you see us coming before we get into the bay, you can get the others started."

She shook her head. "I make the sacrifice, you get the glory. Typical."

He winked at her. "I'll make sure they put an asterisk by your name in the history books."

"Get out of here before I throw you off the deck."

Heading down the stairs, Robert couldn't miss the spots of residue along the railings and on the steps. He wanted to pull away from them but the gunk was everywhere.

When they reached the sand, he moved in front of Pax and led them down the path to the dock. One speedboat was tied to a buoy in the bay, while the other—Robert's preferred boat—was at the dock.

While he started the engine, Pax untied the mooring ropes, and within moments they were moving across the bay toward the channel that led to the sea.

"How long is it going to take?" Pax asked.

"In this, not more than an hour, less if the sea's calm."

He slowed as they turned into the channel, and slowed again as they exited the other side. The sea was choppy but not too bad. He didn't open the engine all they way up, though, until they circled around to the side of the island that faced Costa Rica.

"You might want to hang on," he said, and then pushed the throttle forward.

THE TOWN OF Limón was located on a little bump of land along the Caribbean side of Costa Rica. With the exception of a few scattered villages, it was the only real civilization on the country's entire eastern seaboard, and the only place able to accommodate the ferry that had shuttled guests to and from Isabella Island.

The first indication that Robert and Pax were getting close was the sight of red and white antenna towers peeking above the horizon. Soon after, the buildings that crowded the coast came into view. From the sea, the town looked to Robert like it always did. It wasn't until he and Pax were closer that he could see the roads were empty and there were no people about.

Robert tried not to think about it as he guided the boat around the southern end of the land bump to where the main port was located. As soon as it came into view, he stared in surprise.

Limón had always been a stop for cruise ships touring the Caribbean. In the past, Robert had never seen more than one docked at the pier at a time, each ship usually staying only a few hours before heading back to sea. Now, however, three giant vessels were in the harbor—two on either side of the main pier, and the third tied to the ship on the east side.

Robert wondered if the flu had broken out on board the ships first, or if the vessels had rushed to shore upon hearing news of the outbreak. As the speedboat neared the docks, he was able to get a better look at the third ship. It appeared it hadn't pulled up next to the other one, but had crashed against it, buckling metal and scraping off long streaks of paint. He could see hastily rigged gangways between the two vessels, apparently so that passengers could cross onto the ship at the pier and then to shore.

Jesus. They must have been in full-on panic.

"Where's the ferry?" Pax asked.

The haphazardly docked third ship was blocking their view of the dock where the *Albino Mer* was normally tied up.

"Should be on the other side," Robert said, hoping the bigger vessel hadn't clipped the ferry, too. If so, the *Albino Mer* wouldn't have suffered a few dents and some lost paint. It would be on the harbor floor.

He exhaled a deep, long sigh of relief as they came around and saw the *Albino Mer* tied to the next dock, pretty as a picture.

He maneuvered alongside it, and after their boat was tied to the ferry, they climbed on board. First stop was the engine, accessed through floor panels near the rear of the boat, where Robert checked the tank.

"Almost empty," he said. "It don't think there's enough to make it back."

"Where do we fill up?" Pax asked.

Robert stood up and scanned the port. "I'm not sure. I never even thought about it before."

"I don't see any pumping stations."

"Me, neither. But they had to fill up all the time so there's got to be a way."

They hurried down the dock to shore and took another look around.

Robert's gaze stopped on a pickup truck with a large tank permanently affixed to its bed. It was parked in the shadows, next to one of the buildings fronting the piers. He pointed and said, "Maybe that."

As they jogged over, they were enveloped by the strong smell of fuel before they reached the truck. A quick peek into the top of the tank showed it was nearly full.

They found the vehicle's keys under the front seat. Its engine wasn't happy about being started again, but after a few sputters, it rumbled to life.

"How long's the trip back going to take us?" Pax asked as they drove toward the ferry

"About twice as long as the speedboat took, give or take."

Pax frowned. "By the time we get to the island, get everyone on board, and head back, it's going to be close to sundown. I had hoped to locate a few buses before we returned so they'd be here waiting, but that'll waste even more time."

Robert slowed as he turned onto the pier. When they were as close as they could get to the boat's engine, he engaged the parking brake and turned off the truck.

"It'll take me at least fifteen minutes to fill up," he said.

43

"Gotta be some buses parked nearby, if you want to take a quick look."

"Not a bad idea."

While Robert ran the fuel line to the ship's tank, Pax jogged back to shore. The next time Robert looked up, Pax had just reached the buildings and within seconds disappeared between them.

Robert opened the valve and let the fuel flow out. As the ferry's tank filled, he entered the covered passenger section and walked over to the small corner that served as the snack bar. There he found a couple dozen Cokes in a cooler. The ice that had kept them cold was now a puddle of water at the bottom. He grabbed a can and popped the top. The liquid was lukewarm—not ideal, but drinkable. From under the counter, he snagged a bag of spicy chips and a chocolate bar and headed back to the tank.

A few more minutes passed before he heard the fuel sloshing near the top. He backed the valve down, slowing the flow, and cut it off completely as the tank reached its maximum. The ferry had more than enough fuel now to get them to the island and back and then some.

Once he recoiled the hose onto the back of the truck, he moved down the pier toward shore, searching for Pax, but except for a few birds, the area was empty. He checked his watch. The fifteen minutes he had given Pax were verging on twenty.

He walked to the end of the pier, cupped his mouth, and yelled, "Pax!"

Several of the birds fluttered into the air.

"Pax!"

Surely Pax wouldn't be so far away that he couldn't hear Robert. He was the one wanting to leave for the island right away after all.

"Pax! We're ready to go!"

He scanned the buildings and roads that ran in front of the docks, but he was the only one there.

What if Pax had been hurt? Maybe twisted an ankle or something and was having a hard time getting back?

Robert tried to remember the exact buildings Pax had passed between. He crossed over to them and entered the passageway.

"Pax!"

Receiving no response, he raced out the other end and didn't pause until he reached the edge of a four-lane divided road. He checked both ways for movement, but saw none.

What the hell? Pax shouldn't have gone any farther than this.

"Pax! Shout if you can hear me!"

Not a damn thing.

He decided to cross the road and keep going north for a few blocks. If that didn't work, he'd try east and west.

"Pax! Can you hear me? Pax!"

All remained silent, until he neared the point where he'd planned to turn back.

It wasn't a voice he heard, not even something rapping against the ground to get his attention. It was an engine, and by the sound of it, one belonging to a large vehicle, like a…

…bus.

Relieved, he started jogging back down the street. He was still a good half block from the divided road when a tour bus came speeding through the intersection. He slowed, surprised. While he had clearly seen Pax behind the wheel, the older man had not been alone.

The people Pax worked with must've shown up early, Robert decided.

He sprinted back to the buildings in front of the port, and reached the ocean-side corner of the passageway moments after the bus pulled to a stop. He was just about to step into the clear when the vehicle's door opened and Pax stumbled out.

Robert paused, still mostly hidden behind the building.

The second person to exit was a man carrying a rifle. He shoved the weapon's stock into Pax's back, prodding him forward. Four more people piled off—two men and two women. The men and the younger woman were similarly armed.

DREAM SKY

They had a desperate look to them as they conferenced at the end of the dock. The talk seemed heated, one of the men gesturing angrily at Pax. Then a man and the armed woman ran down the dock and disappeared onto the ferry. Robert could see them moving quickly through the boat, and knew they had to have been looking for him. When they returned to where the others waited, the man shook his head and the woman said something.

The guy who'd shoved Pax shouted a curse and turned Pax away from the water, not quite angled at Robert, but close enough.

"I know you're out there!" the man yelled. "I saw you and your buddy come in! So you might as well show yourself."

Robert didn't move.

"Here's the thing," the man continued after a moment. "We're taking your boat. Now your friend says he can drive it for us, but you were the one behind the wheel of the one you two came in on, so I'm thinking you're the pilot. Or captain. Whatever. I think your buddy here is useless. So, unless you want to watch me kill him, I need to see you walking over here."

What the hell was wrong with these people? They didn't look sick. Shouldn't they have been happy to find others alive?

"Thirty seconds," the man announced, "or I swear to God I will shoot him in the back of the head, and we'll try to figure out how to sail this thing ourselves."

"I told you I can do it," Pax said, his voice not quite as loud as the other man's. "My friend's long gone by now. He's not coming back."

"Is that right?" The response was yelled so Robert could hear it. "You the kind of person who will just leave your friend to die?"

Robert didn't know what to do. He didn't want Pax to get hurt, but who was to say these people wouldn't kill both him and Pax if he did as they asked? Robert's main responsibility was to those still on Isabella Island. Without him, they would never get off. Of course, without the ferry, getting everyone to the mainland would become infinitely harder.

"Goddammit! Where the hell are you?" the man screamed. He grabbed the back of Pax's shirt and shoved the end of the rifle into Pax's neck. "I'm fucking serious! Show yourself!"

One of the man's companions came up and said something Robert couldn't make out.

"I know what I'm doing!" the agitated man shouted. "I know what I'm doing!"

"I can pilot the boat for you," Pax said, his voice surprisingly even.

"Jacob, his buddy's obviously not coming back," the man who'd walked up said, his voice louder now. "We need to let this one try. What other choice do we have?"

"Come on! Where are you?" the man holding the rifle—Jacob—yelled.

"Let's just go," the other man said. "He's not coming. We're wasting time."

Jacob grunted in frustration and then lowered his rifle. After twisting Pax around, another conversation ensued, again too low for Robert to hear. When it ended, Jacob shoved Pax toward the *Albino Mer*.

The only time in his life Robert had felt more helpless was when he realized Dominic had contracted the Sage Flu. From his hiding spot, he watched as Jacob led Pax onto the boat, while the other four retrieved several suitcases from the bus and carried them to the ferry.

As the two women untied the lines holding the boat to the pier, the engine kicked to life. For a few moments, the *Albino Mer* simply drifted in place. Finally, the rumble of the motor increased and the ferry pulled slowly away.

Robert noticed activity along the opposite side of the boat. He couldn't tell what was going on at first, but when the ferry cleared the end of the dock and turned to the northeast, he saw two of the kidnappers repositioning the speedboat he and Pax had arrived in so that it could be towed behind them.

DREAM SKY

Robert waited until the ferry disappeared behind the cruise ships before stepping out from the building. If he didn't already have proof the world had changed, he had it now.

Pax's kidnappers had made a serious mistake, though.

They had taken the boat Robert needed to help his people.

Perhaps old-world Robert—the one who had to worry only about himself—would have done nothing.

But, like the changing world, he wasn't the same anymore, either.

5

SINCE MY LAST entry yesterday evening, three more people have been added to our waiting area. This is the fewest new arrivals since I got here. I'm not sure if that means there's just no one else alive or what. Still, three more adds to our strain. There are already too many survivors here for the bunks we've been given. Noah pointed this out to one of the guards, but they basically told him to shut up.

I don't know how many additional arrivals may have been added to the other area. I tried to get a count, but since most everyone over there seems to be sick, they pretty much go straight inside their dormitory and only a few come back out. There were at least four, though. Could have been double that, I guess.

It's strange listening to the new people. They're all excited and relieved. They can't believe they made it. I remember feeling that way just a few days ago. How quickly things change, huh?

The question they all ask is how long until they get vaccinated? They can't believe it when we tell them that none of us has received the shot. They make up the same excuses we all have—that the vaccine hasn't arrived at the station yet, or the supply is limited so the UN wants to make sure we're healthy first to prevent wasting any on someone it won't help.

I still want to believe it's one of these things, but it's becoming harder and harder. Those who have been here longer than me have completely given up hope.

This morning we had something new thrown into our usually dull days. As we were given our breakfast, we were each handed a packet. Inside were about twenty sheets of paper stapled together, a pencil, and a Scantron card like something one of my college professors would use for tests. Printed at the top of each page of the packet was SURVIVOR SURVEY, and below were several multiple-choice questions.

The questions seem to be aimed at finding out about our backgrounds and skills. The multiple-choice aspect makes it a bit limiting, though, not letting you explain or elaborate on anything.

For example, here's one that annoys me. The question is, Which of the following do you consider best describes you? The choices (we're only allowed to pick one) are: A. Broad technical knowledge, B. Focused technical knowledge, C. Non-technical. I mean, come on. There's a whole range of possibilities between B and C. And then there are follow-ups, very specific questions, like if you answered A, please answer questions 14-19, if you answered B, please answer questions 20-27, and if you answered C, continue on to question 28. The specific questions are clearly meant to zero in on the exact nature of the test taker's knowledge.

There are more questions like that, all focusing on tangible skills like engineering and science and medicine. I get it. The world's a different place now, and people with those kinds of abilities are going to be in high demand, but the rest of us are still useful. My writing skills are useful, for God's sake. Someone has to record what's going on, don't they?

Be right back.

Okay, this is not *good. I heard some raised voices outside and went to check what was going on. It seems another five people were just put in with us. Noah and two other guys tried to block the gate so they couldn't get in. The shouting I heard was them yelling at the guards that until we got some more beds, the UN needed to find some other place for the survivors.*

What happened next took us all by surprise. While the new survivors were held back, seven guards moved into our holding area and knocked Noah and the other two men to the ground. And by knocked to the ground, I mean they smacked the butts of their rifles into the men. The guy who hit Noah knocked him on the side of the head. Noah wasn't exactly unconscious but he was dazed for sure, and there was blood all over his face.

I was too far away to do anything, but a few of those closer rushed over to try to help him up. Before they could reach him, though, the guard flipped his rifle around and pointed it at them, telling them to get back.

The guards then picked up the three men and carried them out the gate. I'm assuming they're taking them to get medical attention but I'm worried that they aren't. Needless to say, the new survivors were ushered in before the gates were closed again.

I can't lie and say no part of me wishes I had stayed back in Madison. I guess I could write everything off as tension created by the pandemic. I mean, how can anyone be expected to act normal?

But as much as I'd like not to believe it, something feels wrong. Very, very wrong.

CAMBRIA, CALIFORNIA
11:10 AM PST

NOREEN DROVE HER motorcycle slowly down Moonstone Beach Drive, looking into the motel parking lots that lined the right side of the road. To her left, she could hear the waves crashing on the beach just below the short bluff.

Noreen, Riley, and Craig had been searching for Martina for three days now. When their friend had sped off in pursuit of the red Jeep, Noreen, the closest one to Martina at the time, had immediately followed. For over an hour, she was able to keep Martina in view, but ten miles north of Paso Robles, her bike began to sputter as it used up the last of her gas. Rolling to a stop, she had watched her best friend disappear around a bend a half mile south.

When Riley and Craig showed up ten minutes later, she sent Craig after Martina while she and Riley refueled Noreen's bike. They found Craig on the bridge just north of Santa Maria waiting for them. He had never even caught a glimpse of Martina and wasn't sure she had come that way. They had continued south, though, thinking that staying on the 101 made the most sense.

When they reached Santa Barbara, they finally stopped. Any farther south and they would be encroaching on Los Angeles, where there would be a near infinite amount of routes Martina could have taken, and an equal amount of odds against them finding her. They decided their best course would be to check everywhere between Santa Barbara and where they had lost sight of her. That was what they had been doing.

"Noreen?" It was Riley, her voice coming over the CB radio they had installed on their bikes the day before. Each came complete with a new helmet that had an embedded microphone and speaker.

Noreen keyed the talk button. "I've got nothing over here."

"East end of town is clear, too," Riley said.

"Let's check out the west end, then."

"Meet you there."

Cambria was a quaint tourist town along Highway 1 on the California coast. It was divided into several different areas, with most businesses either in east village or west village. Noreen entered west village from the ocean end and slowed again. Stores and restaurants occupied both sides of the street—gift shops and candy shops and antique marts and a barbecue place and a bar and grill. As she passed them, she had the sudden memory of being on this street before. It had been with her parents, some weekend trip God only knew how long ago, before high school, for sure, maybe even back when she went to Faller Elementary. They'd been in a magic shop, and she remembered being in awe of everything. But the shop seemed to be gone now.

She pushed the mic button, not wanting to think about the past. "Where are you guys? I don't see you."

"Not there yet," Riley whispered back.

Noreen stopped in the middle of the road. "Something wrong?"

"There's a grocery store between the east and west ends. We stopped to check it out."

"Yeah? So?"

"Someone's there."

"Martina?"

"Not Martina."

"Who is it?" she asked.

"We've seen two people, but there's got to be more,"

Riley said. "They've got a pickup truck and at least two motorcycles. And they don't look friendly."

Immediately, the memory of the guy who had shot at them in the hills a few days earlier came back to Noreen. "They haven't seen you, have they?"

"Uh-uh. We parked our bikes on Main Street and snuck up the hill. Hiding behind a delivery van someone left here."

"Enough talking," Craig broke in. "They're going to hear us."

"You guys should get out of there," Noreen said. "We don't need to make any new friends."

"We're okay here," Riley said. "They can't—oh, God."

"What is it?"

"Shhh," either Riley or Craig whispered.

Noreen killed the engine to her motorcycle and wheeled it onto a side road, parking it at the curb.

"What's going on?" she said.

She heard nothing, not even static.

"Hello? Are you there?"

She looked at the radio to make sure she hadn't accidentally switched the channel. The power light was off.

What the...

Crap.

The CB was a handheld model with a charging cradle that, with the help of an instruction manual, they had wired into the bike's electrical system. She snatched the radio out and switched it from external power source to battery.

"...there? Noreen?"

"I'm here. I'm here. What's going on?"

"Hide! Now!"

Noreen looked toward Main Street, almost expecting to see a horde of the undead staggering toward her.

"What's going on?"

Nothing for a second, then Riley said between rapid breaths, "One of them saw us. He...ran back inside to get his friends...and we took off."

"Where are you?"

"No place to hide...getting on our bikes..."

In the distance, Noreen heard their motorcycles roar to life. Then, as their engines idled a bit, a bang.

"What was that?"

"It's okay…we're all right," Craig said.

"Were they shooting at you?"

"Missed us," Riley said.

Hearing motorcycles roar down Main Street, Noreen shot a look at the intersection and was just in time to see Riley and Craig race by. As the sound of their engines began to fade, she heard more bikes coming from the direction of the market.

"They're following you," she said.

Knowing she couldn't be standing there when the other bikes came by, Noreen ducked around the rear of the nearby shop and crouched behind a Dumpster. She could hear three motorcycles race past back on Main Street. A few moments later, a vehicle she guessed was a truck followed.

What was wrong with these people? Why did they care about Riley and Craig?

Staying hidden, she spent the next ten minutes trying to reach her friends.

Finally, Riley answered. "We're okay."

"What happened?"

"We cut up a hill into a residential area. They must have thought Craig had taken the highway north. They sped off that way. We watched them for a few minutes, but can't see them anymore."

"Why did they chase you?" Noreen asked.

"Maybe because we were spying on them?" Craig suggested.

"I guess, but why shoot at you?"

The only reply was silence, but Noreen suspected she already knew the answer.

The rules of life they'd grown up with no longer applied.

RIDGECREST, CALIFORNIA
12:36 PM PST

BEN BOWERMAN HAD checked everyplace he thought

Martina might be.

When he had arrived in her hometown two nights before, his intention had been to head straight to her house. He had been there only once and that had been the previous summer, so he had just a vague idea of its location. If Martina had lived in one of the housing tracts within the city limits, he was sure he'd have no trouble finding her house. But the Gables' home was down a dirt road west of town, where everyone had his or her own few acres of desert.

It turned out there were a lot of dirt roads in that direction, and Ben's search wasn't helped by the sun going down. It took him until almost ten that night before he finally found the house, recognizing it by the large, detached three-car garage with asymmetrical sloped roof.

He felt a rush of hope when he saw Martina's Toyota Corolla parked out front. He jumped out of his car and ran to the front door of the house. It was locked.

"Martina, it's me!" he yelled, knocking loudly.

Nothing. Not even the creak of a floorboard.

He raced around to the back door, but it was also locked.

"Martina! Are you in there?"

He looked up at the darkened second-floor windows but sensed no movement beyond them.

He remembered Martina had said her family kept a spare key in the garage, but for the life of him he couldn't recall where. So he grabbed a log off the firewood pile on the side of the house and smashed it through the window next to the rear door.

"Sorry!" he yelled through the opening just in case someone *was* there. "It's me. Ben Bowerman. Martina's boyfriend."

He reached inside, unlocked the door, and pushed it open.

"Hello?" he called. "Anyone home?"

No answer.

Reluctantly, he stuck his head a few inches inside and sniffed the air. Stale, but no smell of death. Relieved, he stepped all the way inside.

The house was quiet, the same kind of undisturbed silence he'd experienced pretty much everywhere he'd been the last several days. He felt along the wall until he found a light switch and flicked it up. Nothing. He hadn't really expected it to work. He had seen no lights on anywhere else in town. So he returned to his car and retrieved a flashlight from the bag of things he'd been collecting to replace the stuff he'd lost when Iris Carlson stole his Jeep.

Back inside, he methodically worked his way through the house, hoping to find a note or some other indication of where Martina went. It was clear from the open drawers and closets in the bedrooms that the Gable family had left in a hurry, but he discovered no clue about their destination.

He slumped down on Martina's bed, tired and frustrated and depressed. He had been so sure he'd find her here that he hadn't considered what to do if he didn't.

He hadn't intended on falling asleep right there in her room, but that's where he found himself late the next morning when he woke. Still unsure what he'd do, he headed downstairs to see if there was any food left in the kitchen. As he crossed through the living room, he looked out the row of east-facing windows. In the distance, he could see the hill with the large white B painted on it.

B Mountain, Martina had called it. The B standing for Burroughs High School. While the high school was in town, the mountain was located within the confines of the China Lake naval base.

The navy, he thought.

Surely the military had taken some action to try to save people. Maybe it had set up a safety zone within the base. Though Martina's dad was a civilian, he worked for the navy. Wouldn't the navy's first priority be to save its own? Would that include civilian employees and their families?

Yeah. That has to be it.

With renewed purpose, he drove through town toward the base and found the entrance without too much trouble. The guardhouse was unmanned. That was to be expected. If there was a flu-free zone inside, any personnel would most likely be consolidated near it. They'd probably be jumpy, he thought. To be safe, he kept his speed down so he wouldn't look threatening.

He spent the rest of the morning and the whole afternoon driving around the base, checking every building and road. He had been right in one respect. There had been an attempt to consolidate survivors. It had occurred at the airfield in the isolated northern portion of the base.

A series of roadblocks flanked by fortified gun stands had been erected along what appeared to be the only route to the isolated section. None were occupied, though. Because of this, Ben knew what he would probably find, but he had to check anyway so he weaved around the concrete barriers and didn't stop until he reached the airfield.

Hundreds of people had camped out in the hangars— men and women, some in uniform and some not. And children, lots of children.

And every single person dead.

Ben stood frozen outside the main hangar for twenty minutes before he forced himself to grab a hoodie from his bag. Using the arms, he tied the pullover around his mouth and nose and headed into the hangars. He didn't want to walk among the bodies, but he had to know if Martina's family was there.

If *she* was there.

It wasn't long before he lost the small breakfast he had eaten, and by the time he'd confirmed that the Gable family wasn't among the dead, his stomach had revolted twice more.

Weak and in a daze, he had gone back to his girlfriend's house and fallen asleep on her bed before the sun had even set.

When he woke up that morning, he drove up and down the streets of Ridgecrest, honking his horn every once in a while, but the town was as devoid of the living as the navy base had been.

With all options in town exhausted, he didn't know what to do. Martina was still alive. He wouldn't allow himself to believe anything else. But where was she?

A million possibilities raced through his mind before one finally pushed its way to the front.

A survival station.

Would she have gone to one?

Of course. That had to be it. He had assumed that if she was immune like he was, she wouldn't have seen the need of going to one of the stations to get vaccinated, but her family wouldn't be immune so she would stay with them.

Where was the closest one?

He hadn't watched TV in nearly a week, right after the UN secretary general had first come on the air. Survival station locations hadn't been broadcast at that point, and even if they had been, he would have only heard about the ones in the Bay area.

He looked around. He needed to watch the message again.

He ran over to a house half a block away, heaved a potted plant through the window in the door, and let himself in.

He grabbed the remote for the TV in the living room and hit the power button.

The screen remained dark.

He closed his eyes and groaned. In his excitement and hurry, he had forgotten the town was without power.

He closed his eyes and breathed deeply to stem his frustration.

Los Angeles, he thought as he opened his eyes again. There had to be a survival station there.

If the Gables had gone anywhere, that would be it.

With renewed purpose, he headed back outside.

6

AFTER FINDING NOTHING he could use at the port, Robert hopped into the fuel truck and drove through town toward Puerto Moin, the smaller auxiliary port west of the city.

His route afforded him a view of the sea, and it wasn't long before he spotted the ferry meandering along just offshore, heading in generally the same direction he was. He increased his speed and quickly outdistanced the boat.

Puerto Moin was built along a small offshoot of the Caribbean that dead-ended several hundred yards from the sea. The dock took up the entire eastern edge of the miniature bay, allowing ships to pull right up next to the shore.

Currently, two freighters were moored at the southern edge, each looking as though it had been unloading when work was abandoned. The northern end of the port was empty. Robert raced to that end and stopped very close to the edge before hopping out.

Dammit, he thought. On at least two occasions in the past, he'd seen a speedboat tied up to the dock, but it wasn't there now. He looked over at the freighters, thinking one of them might have a smaller vessel on board he could use.

There, mounted on the wall of the pilothouse of the nearest ship, was a Zodiac. The small rubber craft wasn't the perfect solution but it appeared to be his only choice.

He ran over to the ship and up the gangway. As he made his way to the pilothouse, he caught sight of a much smaller dock on the other side of the channel. Lashed to it were three tugboats. He thought they would be too complicated to pilot, but the coast guard skiff moored next to them should be a cinch.

He raced back to the truck and drove around to the other dock, a plan beginning to form in his mind. It would take more time to execute than he'd have liked, but it would give him the best chance of success. Climbing out of the truck, he looked out toward the open water and saw the ferry continuing its trek up the coast.

Good, he thought. He had worried the ship had turned out to sea, that he had lost it.

He hustled down to the skiff and checked the gas tank. It was almost full, but given what he had in mind, he knew it would likely not be enough. He located several spare gas cans in a shed on shore and filled them from the tank on the pickup. Once he'd secured them in the skiff, he checked the craft's built-in storage containers, looking for something he could use as a weapon. He found bottled water, diving gear, a blanket, and a first-aid kit, but no knife or gun.

Another check of the sea showed him that the ferry had moved past the point straight out from the port. In a few more minutes, the trees along the western edge of the channel would block it from view.

He jumped out of the skiff and hurried over to the first tug, where a quick search produced only a long metal pole with a hook on the end. He tossed it into the skiff and moved on to the second tug. Here he had much better luck. First he found a plastic case holding a flare gun and nine ready-to-use flares, and then he hit the mother lode—three identical handguns and two boxes of 9mm ammunition. One of the boxes was half empty, but the other was full.

He knew he should check to make sure the bullets fit the guns, but he couldn't afford to waste any more time. He could check once he was underway. He located a canvas bag and stuffed everything inside before hurrying back to the skiff.

DREAM SKY

The ferry was out of sight now, but that was okay. They couldn't have gone far, and he was sure his little boat would travel a lot faster than the big ship could.

He untied the skiff from the pier and started the engine. The boat was indeed fast, and he was able to zip to the end of the channel in no time and enter the sea.

He spotted the ferry immediately. It was a white blob not much larger than a quarter, off to the left. Once he felt he was far enough from shore, he turned so that he was paralleling the coast on the same line the ferry was traveling.

After that, the hard part was trying not to catch up, his boat wanting to jump across the surface like a skipped rock while the ferry plodded through the water like a blunt instrument. When night fell, that's when he would move in. Until then, he kept a soft hand on the throttle and his prize in sight.

WARD MOUNTAIN NORTH, NEVADA
3:08 PM PST

"THIS STUFF IS useless," Chloe said, tossing the journal she'd been reading onto her bed.

Ash looked over from the chair squeezed into the corner of her small room. "Maybe, maybe not. We need to go through everything."

She glanced at the unfinished pile of journals. "I don't think I can read another word."

"I'll finish them, then," he said.

"Don't tempt me." She picked up the next journal and opened it.

They had been at it for hours, painstakingly going over each page to see if Matt might have written down something that would help them figure out what Augustine dream sky meant. So far, Ash had made a few notes about things that probably had nothing to do with his friend's final words, while Chloe had come up with zilch.

He hoped the answer would be here somewhere, but he was beginning to think Chloe was right. Still, Matt must have felt Ash could figure out the message. Otherwise, he would have tried to give Ash more context, right?

Augustine dream sky.

What the hell did you mean, Matt?

Someone knocked on the door. Chloe jumped up to answer it.

From the hallway, Ash heard Crystal say, "Oh, good. You're here."

"What's up?" Chloe asked.

"Bobby Lion just called in. He wanted to talk to Rachel, but…well, you know. I tried to find Ash, but I'm not sure where he is. Could you talk to Bobby?"

Chloe took a step away from the door. "Ash is in here."

"Oh." Crystal poked her head inside. "Good afternoon, Captain. Bobby Lion needs to talk to someone. Are you available?"

Ash stood up. "Sure."

As Crystal disappeared back into the corridor, Ash set down the journal he'd been reading.

"I'd be happy to talk to him, if you want," Chloe offered.

"What? And stop you while you're on a roll?" He smiled. "I won't be long."

Ash followed Crystal through the maze-like tunnel system to her station in the communications room. Leon and Paul were manning the other two desks, each giving Ash a nod while they continued with the radio conversations they were having.

"Here," Crystal said, handing Ash a headset. She donned a second pair and brought her computer screen out of sleep mode. "Let me get him back."

After she made a couple taps on the keyboard, Ash heard ringing, then—

"Bobby here."

"Bobby, it's Daniel Ash."

"Captain, how are you?"

Bobby and Ash had never met in person, and while Ash had tried to get Bobby to call him by either his first or last name, the former PCN cameraman, like most of the people in the Resistance, called Ash by the rank he'd held in the army prior to Project Eden's test outbreak the previous spring.

"As good as can be expected. How are you guys?"

"Well, it's finally happened. We're jammed."

Bobby and his colleague, Tamara Costello—the PCN reporter he had worked with before anyone ever heard of Sage Flu—were near Washington, DC, at an NSA facility. A few days earlier, they had been able to highjack the signal Project Eden was using to broadcast to the world, and replace it with Tamara telling everyone the truth—that there was no UN left, no worldwide vaccination effort, and the ironically named survival stations were meant to collect and terminate people the Project felt were no longer needed.

"They're back on the air?" Ash asked.

"No. Either they couldn't swing that or decided it wasn't worth the effort. My guess is that they uploaded a virus that shut all the broadcast satellites down. Well, not all of them. We're still broadcasting to parts of eastern Africa, central Asia, and South America. Otherwise, though, we're done."

"No way to get you back up?"

Bobby hesitated. "Hell, I don't know. There might be a way, but my skill level only goes so far."

"We're going to want to get the satellite system working again at some point," Ash said. If nothing else, it would be a good way to get messages around the world in a hurry. "There must be someone here who could figure it out. I'll look into it."

"If you can, that'd be great. What I really called about was to find out what you all want us to do. Stay here or...what?"

Ash glanced at Crystal, raising an eyebrow. She shook her head and mouthed, "Nothing for them right now."

"Bobby," Ash said, "I'll have to look into that, too. For now, why don't you two just hold there?"

"If that's what you want, we can do that."

Ash was about to sign off when he had a thought. He put a hand over his mic and looked at Crystal. "Can you give us a moment?"

"Um, okay," she said, and removed her headset. "I'll, uh,

grab a cup of coffee."

"Appreciate it."

He waited until she was gone before taking her chair and leaning forward so that the computer blocked him from Leon's and Paul's view. In a low voice, he said, "Can you hear me?"

"Yeah, not as good as before but—"

"I want to ask you a question, but I need you to keep it to yourself, all right?"

A pause. "All right. What is it?"

"You and Matt talked a lot, didn't you?"

"On and off," Bobby said.

"Did he ever mention the phrase Augustine dream sky?"

"That's a phrase?"

"Did he ever mention it?"

"I'm pretty sure I'd remember that, which," he said dramatically, "I don't."

Ash had assumed that would be Bobby's answer, but felt it worth a try. "All right. Thanks." Raising his voice to room level again, he said, "You guys rest up. We'll get back to you."

Crystal returned, holding a mug, as he was removing his headset.

"Any problems?" she asked.

"No. Thank you. Sorry I had to kick you out."

She shrugged. "It's not the first time. And quite honestly, I've got enough going on in my head right now, I don't need any more crap crammed in there."

"Fair enough." He paused. "Have you heard from Pax lately?"

"Paul did, I think." She glanced over at the other stations. "Paul?"

His head bobbed up. "Yeah?"

"You talk to Pax today?"

"Yeah, this morning."

"Can we call him back?" Ash asked.

"He's pretty tied up today. They're trying to get everyone off that island and over to the mainland. I could try

65

him, but I doubt he'd answer."

Ash shook his head. "It's okay. I can wait. But if he does call in and has a moment, I'd like to talk to him."

"You got it."

NEAR FORT MEADE, MARYLAND
6:26 PM EST

BOBBY HUNG UP the sat phone and set it in its portable cradle to keep it charged.

He glanced at the computer monitor. It was displaying status readouts from the various satellites. Six still showed the green OPERATIONAL tag. It had been seven before he'd started talking to Captain Ash. If the rate of attrition kept up, all of them would be in the red OFFLINE category by morning.

"So, what's the verdict?" Tamara asked as she walked into the room carrying two microwaved burritos and two cans of soda.

"They're not sure," he said. "I think everything's kind of a mess now that Matt's gone. Captain Ash told us he'd let us know. Until then, I guess we camp out here."

"Well, then, we need to look around for some better food because I swear this is the last of these I'm going to eat." She plopped the burritos on one of the desks. "Beans and cheese? Or cheese and beans?"

"The latter, I think," he said, picking up the one closest to him. After a few bites, he said, "Tam, did Matt ever talk to you about something called Augustine dream sky?"

"Is that a place?"

"I have no idea. Captain Ash asked me about it. Was kind of secretive, too. Told me not to talk to anyone else about it, but I assume he didn't mean you."

"What was it again?"

"Augustine dream sky."

"Augustine...dream...sky," she said, then shook her head. "I've got nothing."

7

PAX ARCHED HIS back and rolled his head side to side. He'd been at the controls of the ferry for hours now, sometimes sitting on the cracked cushion of the raised captain's chair, sometimes standing in front of it, but never traveling more than a few feet away from the controls.

Outside, the sea was getting dark as the sun began disappearing behind the mainland. At least the water had calmed somewhat. For the first couple hours it had been a rocky trip. He'd heard at least two of his kidnappers throwing up over the railing of the passenger deck.

The stairs leading up to the pilothouse creaked behind him. He glanced over his shoulder and saw the fortysomething woman—the older of the two, whom the others called Kat—step into the cabin, carrying a mug of steaming coffee and a bowl of food.

"That for me?" the man leaning against the back wall said. His name was Luke, and he was the guy currently on guard duty.

"It's for Mr. Paxton," she said. "If you want, I can bring you up some, too."

"Or you can give me that and bring him up another."

"Don't be an ass," she said, and carried the food across the cabin to Pax.

"Nice mouth you got," Luke said.

Kat rolled her eyes so that only Pax could see. Then looked over at Luke and said, "I apologize. I'll go get you some food right now."

"Screw that," he said. "Take this and watch him. I'll go get it myself."

As he held out the gun, Pax turned and looked out at the sea again.

"I don't know how to use that," she said.

"Great. Now he knows that."

"If you want to go get food, go. I'll watch him. If he tries to leave, I'll yell. But where would he go? It's getting dark. If he jumped over the side, he might end up swimming in the wrong direction and never make it to shore."

The overhead light in the cabin was enough for Pax to see Luke's reflection in the window. The man appeared to be contemplating the suggestion, then his gaze zeroed in on Pax.

"Hey, you. Paxton."

Pax turned.

"You try anything funny and you're a dead man," the man said.

"Like the lady told you, it's not like I'm going to jump overboard."

Luke narrowed his eyes as if assessing whether or not Pax was lying. Finally he frowned and pushed off the wall. "I'll only be gone a couple minutes."

As soon as he headed down the stairs, Kat placed the bowl and mug on the counter. "It's just some canned beans," she said. "But there was a hot plate down below so they're warm."

"Thanks," Pax said, his voice flat.

They plowed on through the sea, neither saying anything, the food untouched.

There it is again, Pax thought after about thirty seconds.

The sound had come through the open side windows of the cabin, barely audible above the noise of the ferry. It was more an engine whine than a rumble. He'd heard it a few times before, but had thought it was just something wrong with the boat's motor. This time the noise was a little louder, as if the problem was getting worse or the source was closer.

He nudged the throttle up a bit. The decibel level of the engine masked the other sound. He still wasn't sure where it was coming from, but if it wasn't from the ferry, he thought it was probably better if no one else noticed it. He left the engine at the increased RPM.

"I'm…I'm sorry we had to do this," the woman said. "I mean, that they did this. I didn't—"

"You could have just tried talking to me," Pax said.

Pax had been trying to start the bus he found when the guy named Jacob climbed aboard and pointed his rifle at Pax. He ordered Pax to drive to a building in the center of town, where they picked up the others before heading to the ferry.

"I know," Kat said. "I'm sorry. Jacob, he…"

"He's an asshole?"

"He's kept us alive," she said, almost defensively but not quite.

Pax said nothing.

"We were all on the cruise ships. Me and Aiden were on one, Luke and Avery on another, and Jacob by himself. He pulled us together, you know? Helped us to get organized."

"He the one who came up with this brilliant plan?"

"We have to get home."

"Do you really think this thing is going to get you all the way to the States? Do you know how far away it is? I don't even know if we'll have enough fuel to last us past tomorrow morning."

"We'll find more. We'll keep going."

"Maybe. But I've got to be honest, the reality of that happening isn't very good."

"Then we'll get as far as we can," she said, her voice level rising in anger. "We *have* to get home. I have a son. He needs me."

Despite his situation, Pax felt his heart clench. The chance that her son was still alive was minimal at best. He could see in her eyes that she knew it, too, but needed to find out for sure.

If his captors had asked him for help instead of forcing

him to pilot the ship, he would have told them about the plane that would be landing outside Limón in another hour or two, but holding a gun on him from the start had blown any chance of that—not because of some personal retribution, but because he couldn't afford to mix them in with the others.

"I'm sorry," Kat said. "I shouldn't have gotten angry like that."

"Ma'am, I believe everyone who has survived to this point couldn't have done so without building up a lot of anger."

"Have…have you seen others? I mean, besides the friend you were with?"

"I have."

"How many?"

He was saved from answering her question by the creak of the staircase announcing Luke's return.

"All right," the man said, juggling his bowl and mug with his rifle. "I got him now."

Kat took a step back and said to Pax, "There's plenty more coffee if you want some." She looked at Luke. "Yell down when you're both done and I'll come get your dishes."

The man grunted a reply and set to work on his beans.

From outside, Pax started to hear the whine again, so he nudged the throttle forward once more.

TWENTY-FIVE THOUSAND FEET ABOVE NICARAGUA

"EAGLE ELEVEN CALLING Rich Paxton. Pax, do you read?"

Static.

"Eagle eleven calling Rich Paxton. Come in, please."

No answer.

The copilot of the passenger jet heading for the airport outside Limón, Costa Rica, looked at his partner. "I don't like this."

The pilot was silent for a moment before she said, "They're moving a lot of people. Could be they haven't gotten the radio set up yet. Keep trying."

The copilot settled back in his chair and clicked his mic button. "Eagle eleven calling Rich Paxton."

OFF THE EASTERN COAST OF COSTA RICA

ROBERT BEGAN CLOSING the distance between the skiff and the ferry as soon as the sky started to darken. Though he knew he could quickly overtake the larger boat, he approached at a much more gradual speed to minimize the chances of the others hearing him.

As he drew closer, he could see that most of the lights that were on were contained to the front portion of the main passenger level. He was still much too far away to discern any people on board, but he caught a few flickers of light near the front end that he guessed were caused by people moving around. There had been no similar flickers along the stern, leading him to hope no one was back there.

He was about four hundred yards away when the ferry seemed to pick up speed. At first he thought maybe he'd been spotted, but the increase wasn't much, and there seemed to be no change in the activity on the lower level.

A hundred and fifty yards out, it happened again. Reflexively, he eased off the throttle and let the skiff fall back a bit. He scanned the boat, but still picked up no movement indicating he'd been seen.

He increased his speed again, moving past the resort's speedboat that still trailed the ferry, and then eased back a little on the throttle as he inched his way along the towline. When he was only a few feet from the stern of the larger boat, he matched its speed and locked the motor in place to keep his boat from veering off to the side.

Knowing things could go haywire at any moment, he rushed forward, snatched up the line that was secured to the skiff's bow, and jumped over several feet of open water onto the ferry, grabbing tight to one of the posts on the low wall that encircled the stern. He stayed there, crouched on the very edge of the boat, sure that someone would come to see what was going on, but all he could hear was the rumble of the

Albino Mer's engine.

Satisfied that he was at least momentarily safe, he pulled the skiff in close, tied it off, and hopped back on board to kill the motor. He then opened the canvas bag. In the hours he'd spent following the ferry, he'd figured out how to load the guns. He stuck one in the waist of his pants in back, and set another on the deck beside him. Next, he pulled out the flare gun, loaded it, and picked up his pistol from the deck before moving back onto the ferry.

The *Albino Mer* had been designed to comfortably hold a hundred and fifty passengers, and could cram in as many as two hundred in a pinch. The boat had three distinct areas—the main cabin level in the middle, an additional passenger level in the hull below that could be closed off when not needed, and a top deck that went all the way to the pilothouse at the front of the vessel. With the strong breeze helped along by the movement of the ferry, Robert thought it unlikely anyone would be up top.

He carefully scaled the side of the ferry until he could peek onto the upper level. The light leaking out of the side windows of the pilot cabin provided more than enough illumination for him to see he was right. The area was deserted. There were no windows along the back of the cabin, though, so he couldn't see who was inside, but it wasn't a stretch to guess that was where Pax was. At least one of the kidnappers would likely be with him.

Robert set the flare gun on the deck, jamming it between the railing and a box that held life preservers, and lowered himself back down to the main level. Starting only a few feet from where he was and extending three quarters of the way to the front were rows of padded benches. Beyond them was the structure that held the boat's toilets and two sets of stairs—a private one that led up to the pilothouse, and a passenger one that went down to the lower deck. Passengers accessed the top deck via stairways on both sides of the boat.

Painfully aware of every creaking board, Robert moved down the central aisle between the benches until he reached the back wall of the toilets. He took a few deep breaths and brought his gun up to his chest, hoping he wouldn't have to use it.

Sticking tight to the wall, he moved to the corner and peeked around. The bathrooms section blocked much of his view of the bow, but not enough to prevent him from seeing the back of a man standing at the front rail, looking out at the water.

Robert moved over to the other corner and looked around. He could see no one at the bow from this angle.

Five people had taken Pax. One was now at the bow. At least one other would be in the pilothouse. What about the rest? Were they all in the lower passenger area? That would make things a lot easier. All he would have to do was—

A toilet flushed.

Robert pulled back out of sight just as the door nearest him swung open. He heard someone clear his throat and head toward the bow.

"Where's that beer?" a man said.

"Haven't brought it up yet." A different man.

"Hey!" the first one yelled. "Thought you were going to bring up some Coronas!"

"Can't find a bottle opener," a woman answered, her voice coming from the passenger area below.

"Jesus, I got one up here. Come on."

Clop-clops up the stairs, accompanied by the clinking of bottles being carried together.

"Here," the woman said.

"What about Kat?"

"I didn't ask her."

A snicker and the sound of bottle caps being removed.

"Cheers," one of the men said.

So much for most of them being below. Plan B, then.

Quietly, Robert slinked back to the stern and climbed to the upper deck, this time pulling himself all the way up. He retrieved the flare gun and crept over to the pilothouse.

Eyes closed, he tried to remember the layout of the room on the other side of the wall. Carlos Guzman, the *Albino Mer*'s captain, had always invited Robert up anytime he was making the trip between the island and the mainland. But it had been several months since the last time Robert was on board.

The boat's controls, he recalled, were located along a counter that ran across the front of the cabin. There was a stool bolted to the floor in front of the wheel, where Carlos would sit. Behind this was an area big enough for three or four people to stand in. To the right side was the door to the top deck.

No. That wasn't correct.

The door was on the left, while the stairway leading down was on the right. There were some cabinets, a counter, and the boat's controls, but that was about it, he thought. So if Pax was at the wheel, then whoever was with him would be standing in the area behind him.

Robert stepped over to the left corner, crouched, and moved around it. The window in the top half of the door was open. He started to rise so he could peek inside, but stopped before he reached the lower edge when he realized the front window was reflecting an image of the cabin's interior.

He repositioned himself until he had a good view of the reflection. Pax was right where Robert expected to find him, and behind him was the third man of the group. The guy was holding a rifle and leaning against the back wall, looking bored. So that meant the final person, the other woman—Kat, perhaps?—was the only one in the lower deck.

Robert moved behind the pilothouse, aimed the flare gun, and pulled the trigger.

A FLASH OF red light filled the cabin.

"Shit!" Luke said, surprised.

The glow quickly dimmed as a flare flew over the bow and out to sea. As Luke took a step toward the window, something thudded on the top deck outside the cabin door. In the reflection, Pax saw Luke change direction toward the noise.

"What was that?"

"Don't know," Pax said. "One of your friends playing with flares, I guess."

The man pulled the door open. "Who the hell's screwing around out there? You scared the crap out of…" His words faded as his gaze fixed on the deck toward the back of the pilothouse. "What *is* that?"

He stepped through the doorway. The moment he was out of sight, Pax hurried over to the trap door above the stairs, dropped it shut, and rammed the locking bolt into place, sealing the cabin off from below.

AS SOON AS Robert fired off the flare, he tossed the flare gun down on the deck near the back corner of the pilothouse. He had to wait only a few seconds before he heard the door open.

"…scared the crap out of…What *is* that?"

Not Pax's voice.

Robert was a mere two feet from the flare gun, his right hand raised above his head, holding the pistol like a hammer. He heard the man step outside and approach the flare gun without any caution. Robert caught sight of the back of the guy's head as the guy leaned down to pick up the gun.

With only a slight hesitation, Robert smashed the pistol's butt into the back of the man's skull. The guy dropped to the deck and didn't move. Robert wasn't sure if he'd killed the man or just knocked him out, but he wasn't going to waste time checking. He grabbed the guy's rifle and moved up to the cabin door, ready to fight any others who might come up to see what was going on.

But the door to the stairs was shut, and the only one present was Pax.

"Was wondering if you were just going to follow us all night," Pax said.

Robert pulled the second gun from his waist. "Here." He tossed it to Pax. "Are they all armed?"

"Saw four rifles. But I think only the main guy really knows how to use one."

Noise on the stairs below them, then someone knocking loudly on the trapdoor. "Hey, what's going on up there?"

"Can you turn this thing around?" Robert asked.

"I got it this far, didn't I?"

More pounding. "Hey, Luke! Why'd you shoot that flare?"

Another voice yelled, "Open this damn door!"

Pax started turning the wheel.

"What's going on up there? Stop turning! Stop right now!"

"I'll be back," Robert said. "You be okay?"

"I should be asking you that," Pax said.

Robert knew that at any moment the others would come running up the side stairways. He figured his best position would be to get to the rear of the boat before they showed up.

The pounding on the pilothouse door lasted a few more seconds and then there was silence from below.

Robert reached the stern as one of the guys peeked onto the top deck from the stairway and raised his rifle, aiming it at the pilothouse. Robert let off a shot in the man's direction. It flew high, but was enough to make the guy duck out of the way.

"Jacob!" The voice was almost directly below Robert. "There's another boat back here!"

Robert heard someone running below him.

"Son of a bitch!" a second man—must've been Jacob—said. "Gotta be his asshole friend."

"How the hell did he—"

"Shhh."

Robert leaned down to the very edge of the deck, listening. Whispered voices, too low for him to pick up more than a word or two, were followed by the soft padding of feet and creak of the deck. Had they both walked off, or only one?

No way to know. The only thing he was sure of was that the fate of the one hundred and twenty-eight survivors on Isabella Island were in his hands, so he and Pax would either wind up in control of the boat, or he would die trying to make that happen.

Another set of feet slinking away. One of them *had* stayed behind, but he was gone now.

Robert quietly lowered himself over the side.

IF NOT FOR the stars, it would have been impossible to see the coast. Even then, Pax needed to consult the compass to make sure he hadn't overshot the turn and put them on a crash course for the beach. Once he was sure they were headed in the right direction, he straightened the wheel and used the bungee cord system the boat's former captain had created to hold it in place.

The moment he stepped out onto the top deck, a rifle cracked and a bullet slammed through the pilothouse floor, a few inches from where he'd been standing.

"YOU MUST HAVE missed," one of the men whispered from the other side of the toilets.

Robert wasn't sure what they were shooting at. He was only glad it wasn't him.

Bang-bang! Two shots, one on top of the other.

"Dammit!"

Robert sneaked a look around the right side but could see no one. Taking slow steps to prevent the boards from revealing his presence, he slipped past the bathroom door and approached the front corner. As he neared, the back of a man came into view. Robert eased to a stop and put both hands on his gun. When the rifle fired again, he swung out from his hiding place, his gun in front of him. He could see both men now, the one farthest from him aiming a rifle at the roof.

"Drop 'em!" Robert yelled.

The nearest man whirled around and dropped his rifle to the ground the instant he saw Robert's pistol. The other one—most likely Jacob—started to aim his rifle at Robert.

Robert pulled his trigger.

He'd been aiming for the man's shoulder, but the bullet caught the guy under the jaw and exited by the ear. The man grabbed his face as he dropped to the ground, moaning.

"Oh, my God! Oh, my God!" the other guy said. "You shot him! Why did you shoot him?" He dropped down next to his buddy. "Jacob, hold on. Hold on. You'll be okay." He looked at Robert again. "You fucking shot him!"

Robert knew that, knew it to the very core of his soul, but he also knew he would have done it again. "So he wasn't trying to kill my friend?"

The man turned away. "We're just trying to get home, man. We're just trying to get home." He put his hands on Jacob's wounds in an attempt to stop the bleeding, but blood continued to gush. "Oh, God."

Robert took a couple steps closer. "Use your shirt."

He wasn't sure if it would help, but at least it would give the hysterical man something to do. The guy pulled his shirt off over his head and pressed it to Jacob's face.

Robert was about to call up to see if Pax was all right when he heard a loud groan of wood behind him. He turned to see a girl, who couldn't have been more than twenty-five, nearing the top of the steps, a rifle pressed against her shoulder.

When he heard the shot, he flinched, expecting to be hit, but her bullet apparently went wide.

No, he realized as his eyes refocused. It hadn't gone wide because the shot hadn't come from her rifle at all. She was the one hit, the bullet piercing her chest and sending her tumbling back down the stairs.

Robert looked over his shoulder and saw Pax at the other end of the bow, holding his pistol.

"Don't shoot!" a voice called from below. "I don't want any trouble."

A woman, about twenty years older than the girl, appeared near the bottom of the stairs, her hands raised. She looked at the body, then up at Robert.

"I...I...I'm not part of this," she stammered. "I never...never wanted them to do this."

"Come on up, Kat," Pax said as he walked over to Jacob and the other man.

The woman gingerly stepped over the dead girl and hurried up the steps, her hands still high. When she reached the top, she jerked to a halt at the sight of Jacob, but quickly recovered and said, "His own damn fault."

Pax put a finger against the uninjured side of Jacob's neck. After a moment, he looked at the other man. "You can let go now, Aiden. He's done."

The adrenaline rushing through Robert's system finally crashed. That and the knowledge of what he'd done sent him running to the railing just in time to vomit over the side.

PAX AND AIDEN dumped Jacob into the ocean, and then with Robert's help did the same with Avery, the young woman. Luke they left on the top deck with a nasty bump on the back of his head and his hands and feet tied to the railing. They would deal with him when and if he regained consciousness.

Pax knew they wouldn't have any trouble with Kat. She'd only been along for the ride, glomming on to the only survivors she had found. Aiden wouldn't be a problem, either. He was a follower, and with Jacob gone, he might complain a little but he'd do as he was told.

If there was anyone Pax worried about, it was Robert. When he didn't see him for nearly thirty minutes, he put Kat in charge of keeping the ferry on course and headed down to the main deck. He found Robert at the back, looking out at the two boats they were towing.

"Was checking the fuel gauges," Pax said as he walked up. "We've got just under half a tank left. Might be able to make a run at Isabella from here, but I'm not sure. What do you think?"

Robert was quiet for several seconds before saying, "We should refuel in Limón first. Don't want to run out when we're in the middle of the sea."

"Yeah. Pretty much what I was thinking." Pax leaned on the railing next to Robert and watched their wake for a few minutes. Then he said, "Thanks for coming to get me."

Robert made no reply.

"You, um, you going to be okay?" Pax asked.

"I doubt it." A pause. "But who is really ever going to be okay again?"

"True."

Silence.

"Have you ever killed anyone?" Robert asked.

"I have."

"Do you…remember it?"

"Every night before I go to sleep."

Robert nodded. "I guess I have something to look forward to, then."

Pax put a hand on Robert's back. "You did what you had to do. If you hadn't pulled the trigger, he'd have killed you, and then maybe killed me. If that had happened, this boat would still be heading in the other direction."

Robert said nothing for a moment. "What about the plane?" he asked. "It should be there now. What are they going to do when we don't show up?"

"My satellite phone's still on the bus. Didn't want these jerks getting ahold of it. We'll call when we get to Limón. They'll be there."

"What if they're not?"

Pax allowed himself a tiny smile. "They wouldn't dare leave me behind."

It was nearly midnight before they arrived back in Limón and were able to retrieve the sat phone. For a few minutes, Pax received no answer from the plane. Then, after at least a dozen attempts, he was greeted with a groggy, "Hello?"

As he'd hoped, the plane had not left. Pax set a new rendezvous time for late the next morning and signed off.

"Well?" Robert asked as Pax put the phone away.

"Like I said, still here."

They took twenty minutes to motor back to the small tugboat dock at the auxiliary port where Robert had left the fuel truck, but instead of filling up then, they decided to call it a night. They were both exhausted, and didn't think they could make it across to Isabella Island until after they'd had some rest.

They moved the now conscious Luke down to the lower passenger area, where Aiden and Kat were. With Pax holding the gun, Robert untied Aiden from the bench they had strapped him to, undid the bindings around Luke's wrists, then moved back over to the stairs.

"Listen up," Pax said. "We're going to be spending the night here, so that means we're going to lock the stairway door. You all will need to make yourselves comfortable right here."

The two men looked annoyed but not surprised. Kat, on the other hand, looked terrified.

"Please," she said. "Please don't leave me down here."

Her message was directed at Pax.

After a few seconds, he nodded. "You can come with us."

"Thank you," she said, all but jumping up from her seat.

"What the hell?" Aiden said. "If she gets to go up top, we should be able to, too."

"She never held a gun on me. Just be glad we're letting you sleep here and not throwing you over the side."

With that, Pax, Robert, and Kat headed up the stairs. Once back on the main deck, they shut the door and secured it with a rope that even the most talented escape artists would have a problem removing.

Pax pointed Kat to a bench near the rear of the passenger area.

"If you try anything, we will desert you," Pax told her. "Do you understand?"

"I won't. I promise," she said. "You know I won't."

"Good. I just want to make sure we're clear."

"We're clear."

Pax relaxed his stern expression. "I want to trust you, Kat. You know I do. But given what happened, that's something you'll have to work very hard to earn."

She nodded but said nothing, and then sat down on her bench.

Robert and Pax moved to the other end.

"Maybe we should take turns standing watch," Robert said.

Pax glanced back in Kat's direction. "She's not going to be a problem."

"I hope you're right."

Pax lay down on one of the benches and closed his eyes. "Me, too."

January 6th

World Population
798,869,034

8

VAN ASSEN PACKED into two plastic cases the weapons and ammunition that had been stored in the closet next to the senior manager's office. Elsewhere, other Project Eden members cleaned out desks and destroyed equipment that would be left behind after the evacuation.

The order to abandon the Mumbai facility had come down from the new Project leadership twelve hours earlier. Van Assen was surprised it had taken them that long to make the decision. While the Project's operations in Mumbai had worked smoothly through the first few hours of implementation, it had quickly gone downhill after that.

First, senior manager Schmidt had been killed, and a few boxes of vaccine had been stolen by a local Pishon Chem employee who had somehow learned the truth about what was going on. And then, over a week later, that same Indian son of a bitch had returned, freed most of the detainees, and taken the remainder of the vaccine. These events drove Dettling, the new senior manager, to take his own life. In the wake of all this, those who had escaped were probably intercepting any other survivors headed for the facility, because no new survivors had shown up at the station since the breakout.

A complete and total disaster.

As soon as van Assen finished packing the final boxes of the ammunition, he looked down the long hallway and whistled at a group of soldiers at the far end. "Two cases here ready to go."

After the soldiers took possession of the containers, van Assen went up to the second floor.

In the aftermath of Dettling's death, a man named Rainer had been elevated to the senior manager's position. He was even less qualified than Dettling had been, but, in his favor, he seemed to realize this and was more than willing to cede much of the decisions to van Assen. So, in everything but name, van Assen was in charge of the evacuation.

He moved quickly through the management housing area, glancing into each room to be sure they had been cleaned out. Satisfied, he went to check on the rooftop communications center via the narrow staircase that had been constructed in a former closet.

He popped his head and shoulders through the trapdoor at the top and spotted Klausmann sitting at the counter, headphones on.

"Status?" van Assen asked.

Klausmann took a moment before he looked back. "The second plane is in the air. The last is ready when we are."

Van Assen thought something was a little off with Klausmann this morning, but he figured it was probably a reaction to evacuation orders. He would note it later in the man's file, but for now, van Assen had other things to check.

"Tell them we are on schedule, and will be there in forty minutes. Then close up here."

"Yes, sir."

Van Assen headed back down the stairs.

EMERIC KLAUSMANN TURNED back around as soon as that uppity van Asshole disappeared. The bastard was acting like *he* was in charge, but he was no more than an assistant. Which, someone should point out to him, put him a level *below* Klausmann.

He grabbed the bottle of whiskey he'd been drinking right before van Asshole showed up, and took a sip. Thank God for the metal staircase. He hadn't heard the stairwell door open, but he had heard van Asshole clomping up the steps, giving him enough time to hide the bottle.

Who could blame Klausmann for drinking? Things had been screwed up since Implementation Day. Sure, he'd *understood* that a lot of people would need to die for the Project to reach its goals, but actually seeing it happen was something else entirely.

The tipping point for him had come when he was on search duty, tasked with conducting a sweep through the Intercontinental Hotel. Right there in the lobby he'd found an old couple sitting on a couch—European, by the looks of them—leaning against each other. He didn't know how long they'd been dead, a week at least. The worst part was that they looked a lot like his grandparents, both of whom had died years ago.

That's when he started drinking, and had pretty much not stopped since.

He took one more sip of the whiskey, capped the bottle, and set it on the floor next to his bag.

He reactivated the microphone. "Mumbai base to Mumbai Evac Three."

"Evac Three, go ahead."

"On schedule here, at your location in approximately forty minutes."

"Copy, Mumbai base."

"Signing off here. Will see you soon."

"Stay safe."

Klausmann had to put a hand over his mouth to keep from laughing. *Stay safe*? Was that not the most hilarious thing someone could say these days?

He pulled off the headphones and stood up so he could start disabling the equipment. But before he was fully upright, the earth tilted under his feet. If he hadn't thrown his hand out and grabbed the edge of the equipment rack, he would have fallen through the trapdoor.

He hugged the rack until enough of his balance returned so that he could stand on his own two feet. He took several deep breaths, knowing he needed to get himself under control and act sober when he went downstairs with the others. The Project did not look kindly on those not pulling their weight.

Through the windowless walls of the rooftop room, he heard the horns of the waiting trucks, blasting in unison three times.

The ten-minute warning.

Shit. I need to get moving.

Ten minutes to disable the communications room and get his stuff from the barracks was cutting it very close. He couldn't miss the ride to the airport.

He took a tentative step toward the counter and felt his head spin again. Not enough to throw him to the ground, but more than enough to know that picking up the hammer he'd brought with him and using it to smash the equipment would be out of the question.

It's okay, he told himself. The hammer was a fail-safe anyway. There was still the self-destruct.

The incendiary device had been installed in the room when it was set up. All Klausmann had to do was input the code into the activation box and enter the desired amount of delay—twenty minutes, per van Asshole—and voila, the place would go up in flames, eventually taking the entire building with it.

As he leaned down to pick up his bag, another wave of dizziness swept over him. Blindly, he grabbed the straps of his bag and straightened up, forgetting about his bottle of whiskey. After his head stopped spinning, he walked over to the self-destruct box.

Using all of his concentration, he punched in the code. The tiny screen flashed, and two underlined spaces appeared, waiting for him to input the number of minutes to delay. He typed 2 and 0, and smiled at the box.

Perfect.

He headed down the ladder, already feeling a bit more sober.

Nine minutes later, Klausmann hopped onto the back of his truck, taking a seat next to his buddy Gisler. As they started to pull away, Klausmann reached into his bag for the bottle of whiskey. That's when he remembered he'd left it on the floor.

No big deal. He had two more full bottles in his bag. He pulled one out, cracked the seal, and, being the team player he was, passed it around, unaware he had forgotten the final self-destruct step. After inputting the time delay, the ENTER button needed to be pushed, something Klausmann had not done.

So, instead of commencing the self-destruct countdown, the system waited exactly one minute after Klausman entered the length of the delay and then reset itself.

2:03 PM IST

"I THINK WE have waited long enough, yes?" Darshana said.

Arjun studied the Pishon Chem compound. It had been four hours since the last group of trucks had driven away. Forty-five minutes after that, they had seen a third military cargo plane rise above the city and turn north.

Since then, all had been quiet.

He nodded. "We need to be careful, though."

"They are all gone."

"That may be, but think of what these people have done. Think of what they may have left there in case anyone shows up."

"You think they may have contaminated everything?"

"It is possible. We will have to wash down afterward, and destroy any clothes we have on."

They took with them only items they could afford to discard, and left the rest of their things in the building they'd been watching from.

It felt odd to enter the compound through the open front gates. The only other time either of them had come in that way had been in the back of one of the Project Eden vehicles after they were captured in the city. Arjun almost expected guards to rush out of the gatehouse, guns drawn, shouting at them to drop to the ground. But all they could hear were the birds calling to each other high above and the background buzz of insects that seemed to be growing louder.

They knew from what they'd seen in the city that the spray containing the Sage Flu virus left a sheen behind that lasted for several days. But as they passed several of the compound's buildings and dozens of cars that had been left behind, they spotted no sheen.

They came next to the dual holding areas where the people who'd shown up at the survival station had been put— infected in one, uninfected in the other. Both pens were empty, their gates hanging open. And still no sheen.

They moved on to the buildings that had been used as barracks, first by the locals who had falsely thought they'd been hired to help eradicate malaria-spreading mosquitoes, and then by the fake UN soldiers brought in after the outbreak. Once again, no sheen.

"Should we check inside?" Darshana asked. "Make sure no one is here?"

Arjun looked at the building again. He didn't like the idea, but she was right.

With a nod, he approached the door and cautiously opened it. On the other side was a hallway, lit only by the sunlight Arjun had just let in.

"Hold it open for a moment," he said, letting Darshana take the door.

He stepped inside the hallway and searched the walls until he spotted the light switch. The fluorescent tubes flickered for a moment before staying on.

"Come on," Arjun said. "I am not doing this alone."

All they found were rooms that had been abandoned in a hurry. As they stepped outside again, they each sucked in deep breaths, cleansing their lungs of the imaginary bad air they'd been breathing.

Their next destination was the administration building. It was at least four times as large as the barracks, and according to Sanjay, had a living area on the second floor where the bosses of Pishon Chem had resided. As they neared the building, Arjun examined the walls and saw this building had not been sprayed, either. When Project Eden pulled out, they had apparently been too busy to worry about dousing the facility. Either that or, in the chaos of leaving, the thought hadn't occurred to the people in charge.

Arjun opened the door and saw the hallway lights were still on. He exchanged a look with Darshana and knew she was wondering the same thing. Was someone still there?

"We have to go inside," he said.

"I know," she replied.

Neither of them moved.

After a few seconds, Arjun said, "If you would like to check alone, you are more than welcome."

She snorted a laugh, and the tension dropped a few notches.

"Let's get this over with," he said.

Together, they stepped across the threshold.

Sanjay had told them the ground floor was mostly offices and meeting rooms and storage closets. It was also the floor where Sanjay had found the flu vaccine. That was one of the things Arjun and Darshana were supposed to be on the lookout for. Sanjay hadn't thought any would be left behind, but it was best to check.

Their main mission, though, was a little less defined.

"Look for anything that might be of interest," Sanjay had told them over the sat phone after they reported the base was being evacuated.

"Like what?" Darshana had asked.

"If I knew, I would tell you. Information, equipment we can use here, medical supplies. Look around, see what you can see."

Arjun and Darshana made a quick trip through the first and second floors and determined both were unoccupied.

When they discovered a set of stairs leading down to a basement, Darshana said, "I am not going down there."

"Neither am I."

They closed the door and moved a heavy desk in front of it in case someone was down below.

As they began a more meticulous search, it soon became apparent that what equipment Project Eden hadn't taken with it had been destroyed. Monitors and telephones and security cameras and computers had been smashed throughout the facility. As for the medical supply room, the only things left there were empty shelves and trash on the ground.

Arjun was beginning to think the only thing he and Darshana would be leaving with was the knowledge Project Eden was indeed gone, but then they found the narrow staircase in the small room on the second floor, leading up to an unexpected third level. The stairs were not quite vertical but close enough that holding on to the railing was a necessity. At the top was a trapdoor. Darshana, having taken the lead, pushed it up a few inches so she could peek through the opening.

"No one," she said, then shoved it the rest of the way open and climbed out.

Arjun poked his head through a moment later and looked around. At first glance, it appeared to be a single, doorless room, with a chest-high counter running along two walls, and metal racks along the others. Most surprising was that the equipment Arjun could see was still intact.

As soon as he climbed the rest of the way out, Darshana shut the trapdoor to give them more floor space.

"They did not destroy anything," Arjun said.

"I know," she said, as shocked as he was. "But why not?"

Arjun shrugged and turned in a circle, taking in the whole space.

The racks were full of different types of equipment, none of which he could identify. He was an accountant before all this happened, and while he could make his way around a computer, he was not an IT guy. On the counter were a couple of blank monitors, a keyboard, and a headset. Out of curiosity, he walked over and rubbed his finger across the touch pad. Both monitors popped to life, a box in the middle of one requesting a password.

The computers were still on.

Arjun pushed the chair to the side so he could get a better look. There was a thud on the floor as one of the legs hit something. He glanced down and saw a half-empty bottle of whiskey on its side, rolling back and forth. He picked it up so they wouldn't step on it, and set it on the counter.

"Do you know a way around the password?" Darshana asked.

"No. Do you?"

She shook her head.

They left the computer alone and carefully examined the rest of the room. There weren't any windows but there was a door on the back wall. Arjun opened it and took a look outside. It was the roof of the main building, with nothing more interesting that a few vents and a decrepit piece of old machinery.

"What are these for?" Darshana asked.

She was pointing at a group of cables just inside the doorway. While most other wires were on the floor, these ran up the wall and disappeared through the ceiling.

Curious, both Arjun and Darshana stepped outside. They had to move several feet away before they could see what was on top of the room. Two satellite dishes and a heavy-duty-looking antenna. They had seen the equipment from their observation post a few blocks away, but Arjun had paid them no attention at the time.

"This is a communications room," Darshana whispered.

They stared at the dishes as the reality of what they'd found settled in.

"We need to go back for the satellite phone," he said. "Sanjay needs to know about this."

9

"DAD, WAKE UP."

Ash's eyes flew open, his hand already searching for the gun he kept by his side when he was out in the field. But he wasn't out in the field. And his gun was in the cabinet across the room. He was at Ward Mountain.

"I'm sorry," Josie said, keeping her voice low. She hovered over him, dressed in a pair of sweats with her hair in a ponytail. "Crystal says she needs to talk to you."

"What time is it?"

"About twenty 'til one."

Great. Two hours of sleep. Good sleep, too, some of the best he'd had since before he'd been hurt.

He pulled back his covers and slowly swung his legs off the bed. The pain of his injuries was becoming more manageable, but was still a long way from disappearing.

"My shirt," he said, nodding toward the chair.

Josie tossed him the T-shirt and he slipped it on. Before he could push himself to his feet, she was already handing him his pants, her head turned away so she wasn't looking at him.

"Uh, thanks," he said, and pulled them on.

The living space he'd been assigned with his kids consisted of two small studio apartments linked by a door. The bathrooms were located at the front of each room, creating a small hallway that kept the main door separated from the living space.

Crystal was waiting in the public corridor when he stepped outside.

"You're up late," he said.

"We're a little short-handed," she replied, looking tired.

Ash tried to pull the door closed behind him, but Josie had moved in the way.

"Why don't you go back to sleep, honey?" he told her.

"I'm okay," she said.

Realizing he wouldn't be able to get rid of her, he looked back at Crystal. "What's going on? Did Pax call in?"

"He did a couple hours ago, but didn't have time to talk."

"Everything all right?"

She hesitated. "He ran into a bit of a problem, but sounds like it's all okay now. Not why I woke you up, though."

"Okay. Why?"

"It's our new contact in India. Sanjay?"

Ash had been briefed about the group outside Mumbai, so he nodded.

"We've got him on the line, but I think someone a little higher up should talk to him."

"Okay, sure. Want to tell me what's up?"

"Better if you hear from him."

He glanced at his daughter. "I'll be back in a while. Go on ba—"

"I'm coming with you," Josie said, stepping out of the room and pulling the door closed.

He could have argued with her but saw no reason to, so the two of them followed Crystal back to the communications room, where she motioned for Ash to take the seat at her station.

She put on her headset and, after a quick tap on her keyboard, said, "I'm back. Thanks for waiting…Yeah, just a second."

Ash donned the auxiliary headset.

"What about me?" Josie asked.

Crystal looked over at the girl in the station next to hers.

"Hannah, borrow your extra headset?"

After the headphones were secured and plugged into Crystal's computer, she handed them to Josie.

"Sanjay?" Crystal said. "I'd like to introduce you to Captain Ash. He's one of the main people here and works closely with Rachel."

"Pleasure to meet you, Sanjay."

"Are you in the military?"

"Not anymore. As far as I know, there is no military."

Crystal looked at Ash, and, with her mic on, said, "Sanjay's people have found something they thought we might be able to help them with."

"Okay," Ash said. "What is it?"

"Sanjay?" Crystal prompted when Sanjay didn't jump in.

"Are you sure you are not military?" Sanjay asked.

Something was clearly bothering Sanjay, but Ash didn't know what it was, so he decided to give the most honest answer he could. "I was military. I would still be military if not for the Sage Flu. But I'm not anymore. I'm just trying to do my part to keep things from getting worse." When there was no immediate response, Ash said, "Maybe you can tell me what your concern is."

"The only military people we've seen have been the ones who claim to be with the UN."

"There is no UN, and I have *never* been with the people who made that claim."

Another pause. "Of course," Sanjay said. "I was only caught off guard. I apologize."

"Don't. It's understandable," Ash said. "Why don't you tell me what you found?"

"Do you know about the survival station here?" Sanjay asked.

"He's not aware of the most recent update," Crystal interjected. She looked at Ash. "The Mumbai station was abandoned earlier today."

"Everyone's gone?"

"That is correct," Sanjay said. "After the last of these Project Eden people left, two of my friends went into the compound to have a look around. Most of the place has been destroyed, but there is one room that has escaped harm. We think it is a communications room."

Ash's mind was still not completely awake, so it took a few extra seconds for him to process what Sanjay had said.

"Is that right?" he asked looking at Crystal.

As she nodded, Sanjay said, "As far as we can tell, yes."

A communications room. In a Project Eden facility.

"And you're staying it's still operational?" Ash asked.

"I am saying the equipment is still there, undamaged as far as we can tell, and there is power, so it seems to us that everything should still function correctly. We thought it might be helpful to see how Project Eden personnel communicate with each other."

There was no *might* about it, Ash thought.

"Our problem is," Sanjay went on, "we do not know how to make it work."

"We can absolutely help with that."

"I have been told this, but also told that such a thing would need to be approved first."

"Consider it approved." Ash locked eyes with Crystal. "Do whatever you need to do to make this happen right away."

"Of course," she said. "Sanjay, I'll need to get a few things organized here. Can I call you back? Fifteen minutes at the most?"

"I will be here."

As soon as Crystal disconnected the call, Ash said, "Pull whatever resources you need. Make this a priority."

"Yes, sir."

Ash headed for the door, and then stopped. "If they are able to get things working, wake me up again." He paused and looked over at his daughter. "As long as that's all right with you."

Josie gave it a moment's consideration before nodding. "But right now you go back to sleep, okay?"

DREAM SKY

CALEB MATTHEWS STOOD on the street corner in a constant state of anticipation. Every few seconds, he would lift his foot and start to step out, but without fail the black car would screech around the intersection and zip along the edge of the road, forcing him to jump back again.

He only wanted to get across. Why? He didn't know. But the other corner was where he was supposed to be. Again he lifted his foot. Again he inched it toward the street. And again the black car appeared.

"You've got to be kidding me!" he yelled as he pulled away from the curb.

"Caleb."

After the car passed by, he restarted the cycle.

"Caleb."

He lifted his foot. He inched it forward.

"Caleb, get up!"

His eyes flew open as his whole body jerked away from the hand that had been shaking his shoulder. "What? What?" he said, blinking.

Crystal was kneeling next to his bed. "I need you down in communications."

He looked around, half expecting to see the black car heading toward him. As the real world began to embrace him again, he rubbed his eyes and scratched his beard. "Um, what's wrong?"

"I've got a project for you."

"Now?"

With a smirk, she said, "No, I just woke you up for fun."

"Wouldn't put it past you." He started to pull his covers off, but stopped.

"What are you waiting for?" she asked. "We need to go."

"I, um, sleep naked."

"Dear God," she said, standing up and backing toward the door. "I'll meet you down in communications."

"I'll be there in ten minutes."

"You've got five."

CALEB WALKED INTO communications wearing his favorite *Firefly* T-shirt and a pair of jeans that probably should have been in the wash. He hadn't bothered doing anything about his hair so it was still in the same messy state it had achieved while he was sleeping. He had, however, taken a moment to stop by the cafeteria to pick up a cup of coffee and a couple of leftover rolls from the previous night's dinner.

"All right, ladies. No need to worry anymore. I'm here." There were groans from all three of the women manning the stations. "So what earth-shattering disaster do you need me to save us from now?"

"Just sit," Crystal said, pointing at a chair next to hers.

He plopped down and took a bite of one of the buns. It was going stale, but his taste buds weren't really awake yet, so it didn't matter.

"Want some?" he asked, holding out the bun to Crystal.

"No, thanks."

He shrugged and shoved the rest of the bun into his mouth. As soon as he'd swallowed enough of it so he could talk, he said, "So what's the deal?"

Crystal grinned. "I think you're going to like it."

"I doubt it," he said, trying to look skeptical.

"What would you say if I told you we've gained access to an undamaged Project Eden communications hub?"

He leaned back. "Is this a joke?"

Instead of answering, she said, "And what if I told you we don't know how to get it working?"

The corner of his mouth ticked up. "I would say that's because you hadn't talked to me yet. Now please tell me you're not pulling my leg."

"I'm not pulling your leg."

Adrenaline began jolting through his system. "Where is it? When do we go?"

"That's the tricky part. You're going to have to deal with it from here."

"What do you mean?" he said, his growing excitement turning to confusion.

"It's in India."

"India. The country India?"

"Uh-huh. In Mumbai."

"How the hell did we get access to a communications hub in Mumbai?"

She reached for the two sets of headphones on her desk. "There's someone I'd like you to talk with."

10

Robert opened his eyes to a sun barely peeking over the horizon.

As he sat up, he was greeted with the aches and pains from sleeping on a too-thin cushion covering a too-hard wooden bench. He took a few moments to stretch and then rose to his feet.

Pax was still asleep, breathing long and deep. One of the man's arms had fallen off the bench, and his hand now rested on the deck. Robert would be surprised if Pax didn't have a knot in his shoulder when he woke up.

As he stepped into the central aisle, he suddenly remembered Kat had been sleeping up there with them. Apparently she had decided not to slit their throats; that was good. Robert walked down the aisle to check on her, but stopped short when he caught sight of the bench where she'd slept. It was empty.

He hurried back to the front of the boat, not worried so much that the others might have broken out, but more that if they had, they'd taken Robert's and Pax's things with them. The rope holding the stairway door closed was still in place, however, so it appeared Kat had left on her own.

Wanting to get as early a start as possible, Robert hopped off the boat and jogged over to the fuel truck. The tank was less than half full now, but he was confident it would be more than enough to get them to Isabella. The dock was too small for the truck to drive onto it, so he had to pull the hose out to the ferry. By the time the last bit of fuel flowed out of the truck's tank, Pax had begun to stir. Robert pulled the hose back on shore and wrapped it in its holder.

As he walked back on board, someone pounded on the stairway door.

"Hey! You gotta let me outta here!"

"Pipe down," Robert said.

This only seemed to increase the man's anxiety. Rapid-fire thuds, followed by, "You can't leave me down here with him! Come on! Please! Let me out!"

A sleepy-looking Pax came around the side of the toilets. "Our guests are awake, I take it?"

"Jesus, man!" the guy behind the door yelled. "It's inhuman! You can't just leave me here! I don't want to catch it! I don't want to catch it!"

Robert and Pax looked at each other.

"What are you talking about?" Robert said.

"It's Aiden! He's sick! I don't want to be sick!"

Robert looked back at Pax and whispered, "What do we do?"

Pax moved up to the door. "Listen very carefully, Luke. We'll let you out, but only if you promise to head straight off the boat and not touch anything. Do you understand?"

"Come on, open the door! Come on! Come on!"

"We are *not* opening anything until I know you will follow my directions."

"Sure, sure. Whatever. Just open it."

"Not good enough. What are you going to do?"

"What? Uh, uh, walk off the boat."

"Without…?" Pax said.

"Without what?" Luke asked.

"Touching anything."

"Right. Without touching anything. I get off the boat without touching anything."

Pax turned to Robert, and said in a voice loud enough for Luke to hear, "Get the rifles."

"Hey, wait a minute!" Luke said. "What d'you need

rifles for?"

"To make sure you follow directions."

"I'll follow them, dammit! Don't shoot me."

Robert retrieved the rifles and gave one to Pax.

"Tell me again what your instructions are," Pax said

"I, um, I go off the boat and don't touch anything," Luke said.

"Okay. Now you're going to hear some noise around the door, but you hold still until I tell you that you can open it. Got it?"

"No problem."

From deeper in the hold they heard a muffled cough.

Pax whispered to Robert, "You ready?"

Robert pointed his weapon at the door and nodded. After setting his rifle down, Pax untied the rope holding the door closed and tossed it out of the way.

As soon as he was rearmed, he said, "Open it. Slowly."

The handle turned and the door eased out, revealing a terrified Luke standing on the other side. More coughing echoed from below. Luke glanced over his shoulder as if the sound was a monster he could actually see, and then looked back at Robert and Pax, his eyes pleading for release.

"Come on out," Pax said.

Luke stepped through the doorway. Robert and Pax adjusted their positions so they could keep several feet between them and Pax's former kidnapper.

"It's a nice straight shot," Pax said, nodding his head toward the dock. "Keep on going and everything will be fine."

As soon as the way was clear, Robert closed the staircase door.

"I don't want to be sick," Luke said. "I don't."

"Whether you are or not shouldn't be what's worrying you at the moment," Pax said. "Keep moving.

Luke walked across the deck as if his feet weighed a hundred pounds each. When he finally reached the edge of the ship, he stopped and looked back. "What am I supposed to do?" he asked.

"Not our problem," Pax said.

"You can't leave me here. You gotta help me."

"Nope," Robert said. "We don't."

Luke looked at Robert and then at Pax, panicked. "I'm sorry. About the boat, I mean. And…and pointing a gun at you. We were just trying to get home."

"Get. Off," Pax said.

Robert bobbed the end of his rifle to emphasize the point.

"Where's your compassion?" Luke asked.

"I'm about three seconds from pulling this trigger," Pax said.

Luke used the first two to continue to stare before he finally scrambled onto the dock.

"Don't stop there," Robert said, his rifle still aimed at the man.

"I'm off, goddammit. That's what you wanted."

"I said, don't stop."

Luke clenched his jaw, tears gathering at the corners of his eyes. "You can't do this!"

Pax adjusted the aim of his gun from Luke's chest to the man's head. "Move!"

Luke huffed out a breath, whirled around, and started walking toward the street. He only made it about a dozen feet before he stopped, his head turned to the right, looking at something.

Robert followed the man's gaze, and then groaned under his breath.

Kat was standing halfway between the storage building and the boat, cloth bags dangling in both hands. She had obviously been heading back to the *Albino Mer*, but had stopped when she saw Luke being escorted off.

"Keep coming, Kat," Robert yelled. "Don't get anywhere near him!"

Luke shot a quick glance back at the boat and adjusted his course toward Kat.

"Don't even think it!" Pax yelled. "Don't you get anywhere near her!"

Luke slowed but didn't stop.

"What's going on?" Kat asked. She was frozen in

confusion.

"Aiden's sick," Robert told her. "Luke's been exposed! You don't want to get anywhere near him!"

There was a second's hesitation as the words sank in before Kat dropped her bags and began running toward the boat. Luke sped up, undoubtedly thinking he could use her as a bargaining chip to get back on the ferry.

"Luke! Stop!" Pax yelled.

The man was no longer listening.

"Stay away from me!" Kat yelled.

Jumping off the boat, Pax shouted, "Stop now! Last warning!"

Luke was thirty feet away from Kat and showed no intention of stopping. Robert could see Kat was not going to outrun him.

The boom of Pax's rifle echoed across the water.

Luke thrust forward, as if trying to dive the rest of the way to Kat, and smacked into the ground.

With his rifle still tucked tight against his shoulder, Pax rushed over to the downed man, Robert following right behind.

"Get on the boat," Pax told Kat.

She had halted in terror when Luke fell. "Is he…is he…"

"Get on the boat," Robert said.

She looked at Robert.

"Now," he said. "Or stay here. But make the choice."

With a tentative nod, she headed for the ferry.

Pax knelt down next to Luke.

"Is he dead?" Robert asked.

Pax scanned the body without touching it, and then stood back up. "He was dead the moment the virus entered his system." A flash of anger touched his face as he looked at Luke. Without another word, he headed back to the boat.

Robert glanced at the body one last time. The area around Luke's eyes had started to darken, a sure sign the man was getting sick. A part of Robert wished Pax's bullet hadn't killed the man. A suffering death was exactly what Luke deserved.

Another part of his mind tried to protest these thoughts, tried to point out how inhumane they were, that this wasn't the kind of person Robert was, but it faded fast. That may not have been the way Robert was in the Before, but it was clear he couldn't be that Robert anymore.

As he lifted his gaze, he spotted the bags Kat had dropped. Several items had rolled out. Fruit, they looked like.

He jogged over. Papaya and caimitos and even some rambutans. As he put them back into the bags, he discovered Kat had found more than just fruit. She'd also scored two larger packages of cookies, a box of Corn Flakes, and several bags of gummi bears.

Pax was already untying one of the ropes from the pier when Robert returned.

"I take it you fueled us up," Pax said.

"I did," Robert replied as he set the bags down.

Kat was on one of the benches, her arms wrapped tight across her chest. Robert knew he should probably go talk to her, but it would have to wait. He met Pax at the front of the ferry, where a final line was all that was holding them to shore.

"Wait," Robert said as Pax started to release the rope. "What about Aiden?"

"Nothing we can do for him."

"I realize that, but shouldn't we get him off the boat?"

Pax glanced at the door to the down staircase. "I don't have any desire to go down there and carry him out, do you?"

"No," Robert admitted.

"Better if we leave him there, then. There's enough room on this deck and on top for everyone. We don't need the below."

Robert was relieved. While he didn't exactly like the idea of having someone with Sage Flu coughing under their feet, the idea of going down there and helping the man off the ferry was even less appealing.

He took over untying them from the dock so Pax could head up to the wheelhouse. Even though Robert had more experience piloting boats, Pax had become the resident expert of the *Albino Mer*.

Moments later, the engines fired up and the ferry pulled from the dock. Robert watched the expanse of water between shore and boat grow for a few moments before sitting down next to Kat.

"You okay?" he asked.

"No," she said after a moment. "No, no, no. I'm not all right."

He put a hand on her shoulder. "Hey, take it easy. It's over."

She looked at him as if he were crazy. "It's not over. It'll never be over. Everyone's gone. They're all dead." Her voice trailing off, she said again, "They're all dead."

He put his arm around her and pulled her close as she began to cry. He tried to think of something to tell her, to make her feel better.

In the end, he said nothing.

THE JOURNEY BACK to Isabella Island took a little over two and a half hours. As they came out of the channel and into the bay, Robert blasted the ship's horn while Pax guided them toward the dock.

"See anyone?" Pax asked.

Robert was watching the hotel, but had so far seen no movement. He sounded the horn again, his gaze glued to the resort's upper deck right outside the restaurant where they had left the others.

"There!" he shouted as two people ran out onto the deck.

The *Albino Mer* was still too far from shore for him to identify them, but he saw them disappear into the stairwell that would take them down to the bottom of the hotel.

"I'll get the ropes," he said, and headed to the main deck.

He grabbed the line attached to the bow and jumped up on the gunwale, steadying himself against a post to keep from falling into the water. He felt an odd mix of excitement and dread as he watched the dock approach. This island had been his home for a while now and he always enjoyed returning to it. But all the other times he'd come back, there had been people on the beach, Jet Skis on the bay, vacationers on the bar deck. Now the Isabella Island Resort looked deserted. If he didn't know any better, he'd think everyone had died.

Something else added to the eeriness, too. The morning sun glistened off the sheen from the virus solution that had been sprayed over the island, and was still clinging to many of the plants and parts of the building. If it weren't for the death it represented, the sheen would have looked beautiful. Robert wondered how much rain it would take to restore the island to the paradise it once was.

As the boat neared shore, Robert focused on the dock, ready to jump the moment it was within range. When they had closed to no more than fifty feet, he saw Renee and Estella running down the stairs that connected the bar deck to the beach. Though it had been only a day, it seemed he hadn't seen them in forever.

The *Albino Mer* slowed to a crawl, inching forward at a pace Robert suddenly found excruciating.

Come on, come on.

"Robert!" Estella yelled as she and Renee ran across the sand toward the dock.

He waved back and checked the dock again. Close enough.

He leapt over the water and landed with a few inches to spare at the very end of the dock. He moved forward with the boat as it came alongside and tied the line to one of the clamps. As he rose to his feet, Estella raced past Renee and jumped into his arms, hugging him tight.

"When you did not come back last night, I thought...I thought something had happened," she whispered in his ear.

"Well, something *did* happen, but we also came back."

She pulled back far enough so she could look at him. "Are you all right?"

"I'm fine."

She stared for a moment longer before pressing her lips against his.

"So, um, there's a stern line that needs to be tied off,

too," Pax called down from the open window of the pilothouse. "That is, if you don't mind."

Robert reluctantly pulled from Estella's embrace. "We can pick this up in a bit."

"Yes, we can," she told him.

He set her down and took care of the rear mooring line. As he returned to where the bow was tied off, Pax exited the boat.

"It's good to see you two," Renee said.

She hesitated a moment, and then gave Robert a hug.

"Forgive me if I don't put my tongue down your throat," she told him as she pulled away.

As Estella turned beet red, Robert said, "Forgiven."

Renee gave Pax a hug also.

"Glad to be back," he said.

"Have we missed the plane?" she asked. "It was coming last night, wasn't it?"

"It's waiting for us," Pax said. "Which means we should—"

"Who is that?" Renee asked, looking past them at the ferry.

Robert turned and saw that Kat had come to the front of the boat.

"That's Kat," he said. "It's a long story. One I'll be happy to tell you once we're headed to the mainland. Is everybody ready?"

Renee and Estella exchanged a concerned look.

"Most everyone," Renee said.

"What do you mean?"

"Three people came down sick last night," Renee said. "And another this morning. We've isolated them, but…"

Robert turned to Pax. "Everyone was vaccinated. Why would anyone be sick?"

"It happens on occasion, a reaction to the vaccine," Pax said. "Same thing happens with all types of inoculations." He looked at Renee. "I need to see them."

"That may be a bit difficult," she told him.

"Why?" Robert asked.

"When they started getting sick, a few people began to wonder if Pax might have been lying about the shot. That maybe he wanted everyone to get sick."

"That's ridiculous," Robert said. "Everyone saw the spray. If Pax wanted us dead, he would have let us go outside."

"*I* know that. I also know he wouldn't have come back here until we were all dead if that was his plan." With a gesture back at the hotel, she said, "But there's a vocal minority in there that isn't seeing things the same way." She focused on Pax. "You go back in there, you're liable not to come back out."

"I'll talk to them," Robert said.

"They're not particularly pleased with you, either. You did, after all, 'run off' with the enemy."

"All right, enough," Pax said. "We need to get everyone off the island, and we need to do it fast. There's no telling when Project Eden might return."

"I have a feeling some of them aren't going to want to go," Renee said.

"And what?" Robert asked. "They're going to stay here on the island?"

"I'm just telling you what I think, that's all."

"Then they can stay," Pax said.

They all turned to him, surprised.

"Look, every life is important now. And yes, I want everyone on the ferry. But if we have to force some of them to join us, and they end up causing a problem later that might cost others their lives, then it's better if they stay."

"What about the sick?" Robert asked.

"Bring them."

"But they might infect the rest of us," Estella said.

Pax looked out at the island. "So might exposing yourself to all the virus the two of you just ran through." He let his words sink in for a moment, then said, "Round everyone up and bring them down here. We'll give people the choice. But no matter what, this boat leaves this dock in an hour."

11

BEN HAD REACHED the northern edge of Los Angeles right before dark the night before. Knowing it would be easier to find the survival station in the daylight, he'd broken into a diner in Sunland, stretched out in the large corner booth in the back, and fallen fast asleep.

Not long after eleven p.m., he snapped awake to the sound of shattering glass. At first he had thought it was one of the restaurant's windows, but a quick check revealed they were all intact.

Okay, not his building. But one close by.

He made his way to the front of the diner. He was ten feet from the window, buried deep in shadows, when a second crash slashed through the otherwise silent night.

He froze. That had been even closer. A building or two away, at most.

As alarming as the sound was, what followed was truly terrifying.

Laughter. Loud, obnoxious laughter.

And then a second laugh, a different tenor than the first, but no less creepy.

"That one there," a male voice said, his words echoing along the street.

"Easy," another male voice scoffed.

A few seconds of quiet ended with another window shattering and another gale of laughter.

Then footsteps.

Ben dropped to a crouch.

"Okay, my turn," the first one said. From the tone of the voice, Ben guessed the guy couldn't have been more than sixteen or seventeen.

"All right, over there. The one in the middle."

Ben waited for the window of a nearby building to break, but it was the window directly in front of him that exploded.

He barely had time to cover his face before he was bathed in shards. He fell backward onto the floor, unable to hold back the grunt that escaped his lips.

He froze, sure the others now knew he was there. But all he could hear was more laughter and the second guy saying, "Nice one. My turn."

Ben remained on the floor until he could hear them no longer, and then stood up. Glass clung to his shirt and pants. He did what he could to shake it all off, and inspected his arms and hands. He'd been cut in several places, but they were mostly nicks and scratches.

Thinking there might be more glass in his hair, he tilted forward and gave his head a shake. He felt a drip behind his ear, so he reached up and discovered a few inches of hair matted with blood.

He hurried back to where he'd left his things, snagged his flashlight, and went into the windowless bathroom. Holding the light in one hand and using the mirror, he scanned his scalp, expecting to find a big gash. But like the cuts on his arms, the two he located on his head were minor.

The place had no hot water but the faucets still worked, so he was able to wash himself off. In the kitchen, he found a first-aid kit and a shelf full of clean cooking towels. He used several of the towels to dry off and applied some antibiotic ointment to his many wounds. He covered the larger ones on his arms and hands with bandages, and pressed another towel against the cuts on his head.

For several minutes, he seriously considered finding someplace else to spend the rest of the night, but he decided the likelihood of the vandals returning was low, so he went back to his booth bed and tried to fall sleep.

Ten minutes asleep, twenty awake. Thirty out, five awake. Fifteen out, nearly an hour awake. The night went on and on like this. He finally gave up when the first gray light of the dawn leaked into the diner.

He spent several minutes before looking through the front windows at the street to make sure no one was out there. If his experience with Iris hadn't been enough to caution him about other survivors, the window-smashing duo had sealed the deal. The next time he ran into anyone, he wanted it to be at the survivor station. At least there, the UN would make sure everyone acted like human beings.

Satisfied there was no one around, he grabbed his bag and slipped out the back door to the rear parking area where he'd left his car. He still had no idea where the survival station was, but he figured it had to be someplace large enough to accommodate a lot of survivors, given the size of the city.

He found a gas station a block away and went inside, looking for a map. No luck. He tried at two more stations but got the same result. With GPS, maps were something gas stations didn't need to carry anymore, he guessed.

He finally found a map at a motel near the freeway entrance. After studying it for a moment, he figured the most likely places for survival stations would be the area airports. They were big and well known and easy to get to. LAX was the largest, but the Burbank airport was closer to his current location, so he figured he should check there first.

He hopped onto the I-5 and headed south. The first few miles were fine, but right before he reached the Burbank area, he had to slow way down due to the amount of abandoned cars on the road. At one point, the road was so obstructed that he had to exit the freeway and then get back on.

Thankfully, he didn't have to leave the I-5 again until he reached the airport exit at Hollywood Way. He could feel his anticipation growing, sure that there would be people at the survival station, good people who would offer him food and a place to sleep instead of trying to steal his car. And, God willing, Martina would be there, too.

His excitement began to wane as the airport came into view. He'd expected the runways to be full of tents, but they were empty, the whole area quiet.

Perhaps everyone was inside the terminals, he thought.

He continued to the turnoff that would take him into the airport, but there he stopped.

Someone had pounded a makeshift sign into the ground right at the corner. Spray painted across it:

SURVIVAL STATION LOCATED AT DODGER STADIUM

He laughed in relief. He must not have been the only one to think about trying the airport. He pulled out the map and checked it. Dodger Stadium was near downtown. All he had to do was get back on the I-5 and it would take him there.

He made a U-turn and returned to the interstate, feeling that finally things were going right. Once he passed the 134 interchange, the freeway widened by several lanes, but his hope that it would be easy sailing the rest of the way quickly vanished.

The traffic jam started a few hundred yards before the interchange with the 2 Freeway. Ben let his car roll to a stop, then hopped out and climbed onto the hood so he could get a better look. Cars filled both sides of the interstate for as far as his eyes could see, all the vehicles pointed downtown. While most looked empty, a few still had people in them.

If Ben didn't know any better, he would have thought it was just another traffic-filled day in L.A. But from the dust on the cars, he could tell the vehicles had been sitting there at least a week and would probably do so forever—one long monument to the city of cars, a memorial of a world that would probably never be seen again.

Clearly, the freeway was no longer an option.

Ben backed up his car to the previous exit and rolled down the ramp. When he reached the bottom, he found the road as congested as the freeway above.

Where had all these people been going? he thought. He

hadn't seen similar jams in the other cities he'd passed. Having no idea what the answer was, he focused on what he should do next. He could always backtrack to see if he could find another way around, but what if it was just as blocked as this way was?

He knew from some of the signs he'd passed that he was getting close to downtown. If he couldn't drive, he might as well walk.

He put his extra bottles of water into his bag and climbed out. After deciding the freeway would be almost as difficult to travel on foot as in a car, he chose to stick to surface streets. He headed west on Fletcher Drive, hoping to get beyond the hills that paralleled the freeway. It wasn't long before Fletcher fed into a road called Glendale Boulevard, which then veered left and through a mixed area of grocery stores and banks and bars and apartment buildings. When he reached the top of the hill, he caught sight of several high-rises in the distance.

Downtown.

His energy renewed, he headed down the hill and under a freeway overpass into a small valley that he thought opened up at the other end into the L.A. basin.

Smiling broadly, he started jogging down the middle of the road. He knew, just knew he would find Martina at the survival station. The sooner he could get there, the sooner he would see her, and the sooner everything would be all right. They'd have each other. Whatever happened after that wouldn't matter.

GABRIEL DIXON HADN'T meant to finish off both cans of ravioli, but he couldn't help it. He'd been burning a lot of calories these past few days and seemed to be constantly hungry. Still, his little overindulgence came with a price. If he was going to eat again at lunch, he would have to hunt around for something else. Not that doing so would be much of a problem. Los Angeles being a big, empty city meant all he had to do was walk through the front door of any house or apartment or store and he'd pretty much have his pick of food.

Of canned or dry goods at least.

At some point in the past week, the power had gone off in this part of town, so anything kept in a refrigerator or freezer had gone bad. He would have killed for a hamburger at that moment. Ironic, given that he was sitting in a Jack in the Box fast-food restaurant, where hundreds of hamburgers must've been served the day before everything went down.

A fresh loaf of bread. He might kill for one of those, too. Any bread he found now that hadn't gone bad was basically hard as a rock. But that was the price you paid when you were working the front lines.

He brushed the crumbs off the table into a paper napkin and wadded the whole thing up so he could dump it in the trash on his way out. Just because civilization had ended didn't mean he should forget his manners.

Sliding out of the booth, he pulled on his worn leather jacket—careful not to drop the napkin—and donned his pack. After a final check to make sure he'd cleaned up properly, he grabbed his rifle and headed for the door.

It was time to start his rounds.

WRAPPED IN HIS cocoon of hopeful thoughts about Martina, Ben didn't notice the door of the Jack in the Box restaurant open a block ahead. It wasn't until the man wearing the leather coat and carrying a rifle stepped all the way outside that Ben picked up on the movement.

He stopped and slowly lowered himself next to a parked car, hoping he would blend into the background.

The man at the restaurant took another step forward, but then he, too, stopped. In what almost seemed like slow motion, the guy turned to his right and stared down the road in Ben's direction.

For a few seconds, Ben thought the man couldn't see him. But then—

"Hey! Hey, you!"

First Iris, then the two punks the night before, and now this man with a rifle.

"Hey!" the man called again as he started walking toward Ben.

Ben whipped around, looking for a way out. There were no nearby roads leading off Glendale on his side of the street, but there was one almost directly across from him, leading up a hill into what looked like a residential area.

"Buddy, I just want to talk to you!" the man yelled.

Ben shot out from his crouch and ran across the street.

"No, no, no! I don't want to hurt you! Where are you going?"

By the time the man finished asking the question, Ben had reached the other road, and within seconds was hidden from the man's view by the building on the corner. Up the hill he raced, pushing himself hard.

"Hey! Stop!"

Ben looked over his shoulder. The man was at the bottom of the street.

"I can help you! That's what I'm here for! Hey!"

As Ben neared the top, he could see the road he was on ended at a street that appeared to run along a crest.

"Come on! Don't make me go up there!"

Reaching the new road, Ben paused for a second, looking both ways. To his right, the road went back down the hill. To his left, a slight rise.

He turned left, shooting a look down the hill as he did. The man was running up the slope, not quite halfway to the top.

Adrenaline surged through Ben as he sprinted down the middle of the road. When he glanced back again, he saw his pursuer had not yet reached the top of the hill, but Ben knew the man soon would. And when he did, Ben could probably expect a bullet to slam into his back.

He needed to get out of sight before the man could see him again. Hide behind one of the cars? It would be less than perfect, but who knew? Maybe the guy would run right by and not see him.

Just before he decided it was his only option, he came to a gap between the houses on his right, where the slope went

117

down at a steep angle. There was something at the far end that looked like…

…a staircase!

As he veered off the road, he resisted the urge to look back. Either the man would see him or he wouldn't. It didn't matter at this point. Ben had made his choice so he had to go with it.

The concrete stairs consisted of several spans of steps broken up by short, level sections four or five feet wide. Sticking to the railing on the right to avoid the bushes encroaching on the other side, Ben took the stairs two at a time, verging on losing control the entire way down. Scanning ahead, he saw a short road that dead-ended at the base of the staircase. The other end of the road connected to a street that ran through the bottom of a narrow valley. If he could turn down that road before the man knew where he'd gone, he could be free.

He stumbled as he hit the bottom step but righted himself and raced to the end of the street. It wasn't until he started to make his turn that he finally looked back.

The stairs were empty.

THE LAST THING Gabriel expected was to spot a survivor the moment he stepped out of the Jack in the Box. Talk about making things easy for him.

"Hey! Hey, you!"

The man looked scared. Great.

"Hey!" Gabriel said again as he headed toward the man.

The guy suddenly jumped to his feet and raced across the street.

Just my luck. A runner. So much for easy.

"Buddy, I just want to talk to you!"

Gabriel knew his plea was useless. In the five days he'd been patrolling the area, he'd seen two kinds of people: those who were grateful to find him, and those who wanted nothing to do with him. In the latter group, almost to a man, no amount of cajoling would keep them from running away. The only way to bring them in would be by using a more powerful means of persuasion.

Rifle in hand, Gabriel exhaled an aggravated breath and took off in pursuit.

When he realized the man had darted onto a road that ran up the hill, he contemplated letting the son of a bitch go. The guy was in his early twenties at best, and while Gabriel was in good shape, the ten-plus years the kid had on him would likely give the kid an advantage. To catch him, Gabriel would have to outlast the kid. Which meant this pursuit might take some time.

Though he knew it was a waste of breath, Gabriel yelled at the guy again and started up the hill. He wasn't much past the midpoint when the kid reached the top and took off down a road to the left.

The last quarter of the upward slope was the worst. Gabriel's thighs and calves burned from the climb, and his shoulders ached from the pack on his back. Pausing for air when he finally reached the top, he looked down the way the kid had gone.

Shit.

The guy wasn't there.

Gabriel immediately started running again, his gaze swiveling from side to side, looking to see if the kid had hidden somewhere nearby. He didn't stop until he reached the point where the street curved to the left. There, he could see a ways down the new section of road, but it was empty.

How had he lost the kid that quickly?

He looked back, thinking maybe he'd catch the guy jumping out of some bushes and trying to sneak away. Nothing.

He was starting to think the kid was gone for good when he heard the sound of someone sprinting along pavement. It wasn't coming from this road, though. It was distant, off to the side.

He backtracked and tried to zero in on the sound's location. Ahead, there was a section of the road with no houses on the south side. He hurried over, thinking he might be able to see the runner from there.

No such luck on that point, but it didn't matter. There were stairs leading down to the road, from which he could still hear the echoes of running feet.

THOUGH BEN WAS fairly sure he was safe, he continued to move as quickly as possible through the hill, turning down different roads and taking several more of the public stairways that seemed to be abundant in the area.

It wasn't long before he found himself at the bottom of another valley, this one a bit larger than the one at the bottom of that first set of stairs. According to the street sign, he was on Echo Park Avenue.

It had been at least fifteen minutes since he'd last seen the man chasing him. He hoped he'd lost the guy for good but knew he couldn't assume that yet, so he decided it was finally a good time to find someplace to hide. There were plenty of houses around. They dotted the slopes on either side, sticking out between giant old trees and patches of overgrown bushes. Break into one, hang out inside for a few hours, and the coast should be clear.

Then again, if he could make it to the survival station, that would be the ultimate in safety. He allowed himself to slow to a walk as he contemplated his options.

No. No stopping. Keep going. Martina was waiting for him. He didn't want to put off their reunion one moment longer than he had to.

He figured Echo Park Avenue would probably take him out of the valley and put him even closer to downtown than he would have been on his original route. Unfortunately, he thought it might also make it easier for the man to find him.

Perhaps if he kept heading south over the next ridge, he would find another valley. That would probably put him far enough away that he could head into the basin without being spotted.

He began looking for a road or staircase that would take him up the southern slope. At the end of Baxter Street, down a little offshoot road, he found stairs that appeared to do just that.

He adjusted the bag strap on this shoulder and began the ascent. There were more steps than he'd expected, well over a hundred, and by the time he finished the climb, his lungs were burning as much as his legs were.

After he finally caught his breath, he followed the gravel path past a driveway and down to the road along the ridge. He walked down the pavement for a bit until he was able to get a good view of the next valley. Unlike the ones he'd already passed through, this one was not filled with homes. In fact, very few buildings were in it. It seemed to be a park made up of meadows and trees and walking trails.

Ben continued along the road until he spotted a dirt path leading down from the slope into the park. He looked toward the southwest end of the valley, and there, in all its abandoned glory, was downtown Los Angeles. But it wasn't the only thing he saw.

Toward the end of the valley, just beyond the crest of the opposite slope, was a single row of over twenty palm trees, each seventy or maybe eighty feet tall. It was their uniformity that caught his attention. He'd seen them before. Not trees like them, but these very trees, on TV every time he watch his beloved San Francisco Giants play the Dodgers in Los Angeles. The trees were right outside the stadium.

He was almost there.

Feeling excited again, he stepped onto the dirt path.

"Stop right there!"

TRACKING THE KID after having almost lost him had turned out to be relatively easy. The survivor was obviously trying not to be seen again, but he wasn't adept at traveling quietly. Gabriel, on the other hand, had mastered the technique, so he'd been able to follow the kid without letting on he was there.

Gabriel had another advantage, too. In the several days he'd been in the area, he'd scouted most of these streets so he had a good knowledge of the area. When he realized the kid was headed for the stairs that led to the ridge overlooking Elysian Park, he decided to take an easier way up a few blocks west.

He cut down the road behind Elysian Heights Elementary School and turned up the street that would take him to the top. When he reached the end, he stopped behind several bushes and peered up the ridge toward where the stairs let out.

Nearly a minute passed before the kid showed up. After walking about halfway to Gabriel's position, the kid stopped and looked out over the park.

Gabriel eased out from his hiding spot and maneuvered himself into position not far behind the kid.

Raising his rifle, he said, "Stop right there!"

BEN LOOKED OVER his shoulder.

It was the man in the leather jacket, his rifle pointed at Ben's chest.

"All right," the man said. "Here's what I need you to do. Very slowly, turn toward me and set your bag on the ground."

Ben did as ordered. "All yours."

A brief moment of confusion passed over the man's face. "You got me wrong. I don't want your stuff."

A chill ran through Ben. If not his stuff then...?

"I'm trying to help you," the man said.

"I don't need any help, thank you."

"You do. You just don't know it."

Was this guy a psychopath? If so, Ben could imagine what kind of "help" the man wanted to give him.

He glanced at the gun. "You said before that you didn't want to hurt me."

"I don't."

With a nod at the weapon, Ben said, "But..."

After a second of hesitation, the man lowered the barrel, aiming it now at the ground by Ben's feet. "I'm sorry. I need to make sure you come with me."

"Why?"

"Because that's my job."

Ben had heard enough crazy for the morning. If this guy was going to kill him, Ben would prefer that happened while he was trying to get to Martina than after he was taken back to whatever hovel the guy was now calling home.

"Okay. Fine. I'll…I'll go with you," he said, trying to sound defeated.

"Good," the man said. Then, as Ben had hoped, the guy dropped the barrel of the rifle so that it was pointing straight down.

Knowing he might not get a second chance, Ben threw himself backward, hitting the top of the slope on his ass and shoulder, then rolled down the hill, bypassing the path altogether.

GABRIEL WAS GLAD it was over. After he delivered the kid, he might take an hour or two off. Hell, he might even take the rest of the day.

"Good," he said, and lowered his weapon.

He was about to step forward to give the kid a hand with the bag, when the kid leapt toward the slope like he was a wide receiver diving over the goal line.

Gabriel rushed to the edge and watched him roll down the hill in a cloud of dust.

"Whatever you're thinking, it's wrong!" he yelled. "It's safer here with me then where you're headed!"

He half considered running after the kid. The rolling would probably make the kid disoriented for a few seconds, possibly just enough time for Gabriel to grab him. But the ridgeline represented Gabriel's boundary. If he ventured into the park, he would likely be seen and the mission could be blown.

The kid was on his feet now, a bit off kilter as he jogged the rest of the way down the hill.

"You don't know what you're doing!" Gabriel yelled. "There's nothing but death in that direction! We can help you here! We can save you!"

But the kid was having none of it. As Gabriel watched him head toward the center of the valley, he spotted a van with a nice big UN painted on the side heading down the road on the other side of the park.

Goddammit.

Gabriel pulled his radio out of his bag. "L-One, this is L-Four. L-One."

"Go for L-One," Nyla responded.

"Lost one. A runner. Caught me off guard."

A pause. "No chance for retrieval."

"He's already in the park, and they've got a van headed to meet him."

"Copy, L-Four. One lost. Let's make it the last."

"Well, duh," he said, without pushing the talk button.

"L-One out," Nyla said.

"L-Four out," he responded.

12

ASH SENT HIS kids ahead to the cafeteria while he went through his new morning ritual of stretching his wounded muscles. Every day the pain receded more, but not quickly enough as far as he was concerned. He figured he was at about seventy-five percent of his pre-explosion self.

Dr. Gardiner had told him he was unlikely to make it all the way back, which was the motivation Ash needed to push himself to prove otherwise.

Once he was as limber as he would get that day, he took a quick shower, shooed Lucky the cat away from his clothes as he dressed, and went down to join his kids for breakfast.

The mood in the cafeteria was lighter than it had been since Ash had arrived at the facility. Matt's death had been hanging over everyone, but while the loss would be felt by all for years to come, the funeral had given people the opportunity to move forward.

He must have been greeted over a dozen times with "morning, Captain" and "how you doing today, Captain?" and "good to see you, sir." He patted a few backs, shared a few words, and then went up to the counter to get his eggs and bacon and cup of coffee.

His kids had chosen a table at the far end of the room. Ginny Thorton was sitting with them, though her cousin Rick didn't seem to be anywhere around. That wasn't surprising. The kid had pretty much stayed to himself since Ash and his group had arrived in Nevada.

"Hey, Dad," Brandon said as Ash set his plate and mug on the table.

"How are you feeling?" Josie asked.

"I'm fine, sweetie," he said.

"How's the pain?"

"Better."

"Good morning, Mr. Ash," Ginny said as he sat.

"Good morning, Ginny. How's the food?"

"It's okay."

Ash smiled and took a sip of his coffee. Some sort of dark roast today, he realized. Word around the base was that one of the resupply crews had found a whole truck full of premium coffee beans, all vacuum-packed and ready for sale. Someone had said the same type of coffee had not been served twice since they'd been at Ward Mountain.

Ash was almost done with his eggs when he saw Chloe enter the cafeteria, holding one of Matt's journals. She stopped near the doorway and scanned the room. When her gaze landed on Ash, she began weaving through the tables toward him.

"Hi, Chloe," Brandon said as she walked up.

"Good morning, Brandon," she said, then glanced at the girls. "Josie, Ginny, good morning." She then leaned down and whispered in Ash's ear, "I think I found something."

"Your room," he whispered back.

With a nod, she was up and gone.

"What was that all about?" Brandon asked.

Ash set his mug and utensils on his plate. "She needs my help with something."

"What?"

"Nothing that important."

"A secret?"

Ash pushed out of his chair. "That would probably be why she whispered to me." He smiled. "I promise, if it's something you should know, I will tell you."

"SO?" ASH SAID as he entered her room and closed the door.

"Over here," she told him.

She stepped over to the pile of journals on her bed. As Ash sat down beside her, she picked up a journal that had been sitting by itself and began rifling through the pages.

"I missed it the first time," she said, speaking rapidly. "I don't know why. I should have seen it. When I finished everything, I decided to go through them all again. I guess that's why I caught it the second time. I could see the—"

Ash put a hand on the journal, stopping her. "Have you been up all night?"

"What time is it?" she said.

"It's after seven thirty."

"I guess I have been."

"You didn't realize everyone was eating breakfast when you found me?"

"I wasn't paying attention. I went to your room, but you weren't there, then I heard voices coming from the cafeteria so I checked there. If you hadn't been there, I would have—"

"Chloe, take a breath."

So this is how you get the stoic Chloe White to babble— just deprive her of sleep, he realized.

She took a couple of deep, long breaths. "Sorry."

"It's fine. You're kind of fun this way."

"Gee, thanks."

He removed his hand from the book. "What did you find?"

At a more deliberate pace, she flipped through the pages until she arrived at one marked with a piece of string.

"This is from seven years ago."

She turned the journal so it was facing Ash, and pointed at what she wanted him to read.

March 19th

Recruitment: 14 NA, 23 EUR, 33 AFR, 17 ASIA, 2 AUS

DREAM SKY

Check-ins today: C2, C7, and C8. Sched unchanged. Inq re: ds has come up zero. C8 starting to express ser. doubt. Order: contin invest until prove one way or another.

General notes: Structural add at the Bluff should be complete 8 days. GA fac. still a mess. May have to visit. Billy req add med equip should arrive Fri.

Like many of the other entries, it ended in a series of numbers.

00091 56 1226 0783 21274 5 1008

Ash had barely finished reading it when Chloe twisted the journal back around and tapped her finger in the middle of the page.

"It's right there. See?" She began to read, "'Inquiry re: ds has come up zero.' DS. Dream sky."

"Maybe," Ash said. He had noted the initials when he read it. "Could also be a million other things. Like, I don't know, deadlines? Or maybe it's someone's initials. Could be the d stands for doctor and the s stands for a last name."

"Then how do you explain these?" She pulled two more journals forward and opened to pages also marked by strings. "'The ds loc still unknown,'" she read from one, and picked up the other. "This says '7 potential locs ruled out. C8 thinks goose chase, no ds.' And here." She turned to another page in the same book. "'C7 thinks knows where to find info ds.' And this from two days later. 'C7 missed con twice.'" She flipped several pages again. "And finally, 'C8 confirm C7 term.'" She looked at Ash. "Do you see now? *The* ds location still unknown. You don't write the Dr. Smith or the Daniel Stone. It's not a person. It's a place. A place important enough that

Matt was having his inside contacts search for it. According to this, C7 was on to something, but must have been killed trying to access it."

"Yes, apparently something was going on," he said. "But it's a weak connection at best. What about an A for Augustine? That's not there. And besides, it might not be a place at all."

"I realize that," she said. "But how many other potential leads have we found?"

He thought about it then shook his head.

"Exactly," she said. "At least this is something we can look into. Maybe it won't lead us anywhere, but what else are we going to do?"

"You're right," he admitted.

"We should make contact with Matt's people inside the Project. C7 is dead, and as far as we know, C8 is, too." C8 had been the inside man at the New Mexico facility Matt had destroyed right before he died. "But C2 should be around. I also found references for a C9 and an H5. The only question is, how do we get ahold of them?"

It was possible Matt had taken that answer with him to the grave, but if someone did know, Ash had a pretty good guess who it would be.

"I'll talk to Rachel," he said.

"I'll come with you."

"Absolutely not. You'll stay here and sleep."

"I'm fine," she said. "I'll sleep later."

As she started to stand, her hand caught the edge of a stack of journals, sending several of them toppling to the floor.

"Oh, yeah. You're fine," he said. "Get some sleep. I need you sharp."

She frowned, but nodded in resignation. "Promise me if you find out anything, you won't act on it until you talk to me."

"I promise."

DREAM SKY

IT TOOK FIVE knocks before Rachel answered her door.

"May I come in?" Ash asked.

She stared at him for a moment before moving out of the way.

He was pretty sure she hadn't left the room since he'd brought her there after the funeral, but he wasn't about to ask her.

"I won't keep you. I just have a couple of questions I was hoping you could help me with."

"I'll answer what I can," she said with very little enthusiasm.

"Do you know how to reach our contacts inside Project Eden?"

Her brow furrowed. "Why?"

"If we're going to take advantage of the disruption Matt started, we need to get as much intel from the inside as possible."

"Of course," she said, her nod ending with a shrug. "But I don't know how he did it."

"You don't?" he said. "I can't believe he didn't leave some kind of instructions."

"If he did, he didn't leave them with me."

"Then who would he have left them with?"

"If anyone, my guess would be Pax."

"I'll ask him," he said. "One more question. Have you ever heard the initials DS before?"

Again she looked confused. "In what regards?"

"I'm not really sure."

After a moment, she shook her head. "Nothing comes to mind."

THE COMMUNICATIONS ROOM was packed when Ash reached the door. He counted nine people inside a room designed to comfortably hold less than half that number. In addition to Crystal, Leon, and Paul at the comm stations, three others appeared to be dealing with some cables that ran out the room and down the length of the hallway. Two more people were hunched over the back of Leon's station. And presiding over the whole mess was Caleb Matthews.

The Mumbai survival station, Ash realized. He'd almost forgotten all about it.

He squeezed inside and made his way over to Crystal's desk. He nodded toward Caleb and asked Crystal in a low voice, "What's the status?"

"Caleb's trying to get things wired so he can control things in Mumbai without the people there having to do anything," she said. "He's running everything out to one of the communication trailers we used on the trip down from the Ranch. Been a few glitches, but I think he's got things mostly worked out now."

"Has anyone actually tried tapping into their equipment yet?"

"Not yet. Caleb spent a lot of time having Arjun—that's the main guy in Mumbai right now—describe everything in the room so Caleb could figure out what he was dealing with first. Since then, they've been working on this wiring thing. He wants it all in place before they flip any switches."

While it made sense, Ash would really like to know if they could actually listen in on Project Eden's communications. Since there was nothing he could do about it, he moved on to the real reason for his visit. "I really need to talk to Pax. Can we try him again?"

"Sure," she said. "I had a quick talk with him about an hour ago. They're pretty busy down there, but we can try."

As Ash pulled on the second pair of headsets, Crystal dialed the number. It took five rings before it was finally answered, but the voice did not belong to Pax.

"Hello?" a woman said.

Crystal and Ash exchanged a look.

"We're trying to reach Rich Paxton."

"Pax? Hold on. Let me see if I can find him."

They heard boards creaking and a bang followed by the woman cursing to herself.

"It's for you," the woman said, her voice muffled.

A couple seconds later, Pax was on the line. "Yes?"

"It's Ash. Do you have a moment?"

"A moment's about all I got. We're trying to get off the island."

"I'll make it fast." For a second, Ash considered clearing the room, but there was so much activity going on, the only one who could probably hear him was Crystal. He put his hand over his mic and said to her, "I'm sorry. Do you mind if I—"

Already pulling off her headset, she said, "No worries."

She popped out of her seat and moved over to one of the other stations.

Ash said into his mic, "Rachel thought you might know how to get in touch with Matt's contacts inside Project Eden."

Silence.

"You still there?" Ash asked.

"I'm here," Pax said. "I assume there's a good reason you need to know."

"There is."

"I don't know the procedure myself, but I do know where to find the information. Unfortunately, you're going to need to wait until I get back. It's protected by a biometric lock."

"How long will that be?"

"If everything goes right, figure I could make it to Ward Mountain by the morning."

Ash was disappointed by the delay, but at least it wouldn't be long. "Okay, we can make that work. Do you have time for another question?"

"Go ahead."

"Have you ever heard the phrase Augustine dream sky before?"

His answer was quick. "Never. What does it mean?"

"That's what I was hoping you'd tell me. It was one of the last things Matt said to me. It was important to him that I remember it."

"Really wish I had an answer for you."

"Don't worry about it. What about the letters DS together? They sound familiar?"

"Did you say DS?"

"Yeah, as in maybe dream sky."

A long pause. "Son of a bitch."

Ash leaned forward. "What?"

"That's something else you'll have to wait until I get there for."

"You know what it is?"

"I'll get back as soon as I can. Gotta run."

The line went dead.

13

NOAH IS STILL not back. Neither are the other two the guards took out with him yesterday. Last night, when dinner was rolled in, a girl asked the food people if they knew when the three men would return. The workers acted like they didn't know what she was talking about, so she asked a guard. After glaring at her for a moment, he said something like, "It's none of your business. Stop asking."

As I lay in bed trying to sleep, my anger grew and grew. The fact is, we're being treated like criminals, like we're barely worthy of their help. But we all came here because they *told us to. The least they can do is treat us with respect. I finally fell asleep thinking that was exactly what I was going to say when breakfast was brought in, but I didn't have the chance.*

At around 5:30 a.m., the lights suddenly came on, and several voices shouted for us to wake up. We opened our eyes to find at least a dozen guards spaced throughout the building. We were told we had five minutes to get dressed and gather outside.

That might have been fine if it had been a room full of people my age, but we have several older people here—or, I guess I should say, had, but more on that in a moment—and five minutes is not enough time for them pull on their winter clothes and don their jackets. I and several others ended up helping who we could, but it was still nearly ten minutes before we were all outside.

The guards stood in two long rows in front of the gate. Between them and us were three men in parkas. I recognized one as the doctor who'd performed my medical exam, and another as one I'd seen doing the same with someone else. It was the third man, though, who stepped forward.

These weren't his exact words, but as best as I can remember them. "Good morning. We apologized for getting you up so early, but I am sure you will excuse us when you know the reason." He paused, looked at us, and smiled. I think he was trying to appear disarming, but it gave me a serious used-car-salesman vibe, and I instantly didn't like him. He went on: "The time has come to start the vaccination process. We will be taking several of you out now, and more later in the day." That certainly started a buzz in the crowd. Several people shouted that they would happily volunteer to go first. There are assholes in every group, I guess. The man in the parka responded by saying, "Everyone will get their turn. We have prepared a list, so if we call out your name, please step over to the gate."

They called off twenty-seven names. I was not among them, but I was surprised to see that several of the people who had only arrived yesterday were. Also, they took every single person sixty or over. The logical explanation is that the elderly are always more susceptible so it would be in their best interest to be inoculated first.

Still, though I couldn't explain it, it didn't sit well with me.

There was someone else it bothered, too, but for an entirely different reason. A middle-aged guy, one of the people who'd tried to volunteer. He was definitely not pleased to be left off the initial list and made sure everyone knew it. The doctor tried to calm him down and tell him his turn was coming, but the guy wouldn't give up. Finally, after a quick consultation between the three men who seemed to be calling the shots, the main guy said, "I think we can make room for one more."

Smiling like he'd just won the lottery, the complainer quickly stepped over with the others whose names had been called. A few others in our group shouted that they wanted to go, too, but none put up enough of a fight to be included.

After they all left, those of us who remained hurried back inside to get warm. I heard whispered conversations all over the place but talked to no one. I didn't trust my own thoughts on the matter yet.

The second shock of the morning came after the sun was finally up. I was going stir crazy lying there in my bed, so despite the cold, I headed outside. I don't know how long it took me before I noticed—two or three circuits of the fence, at least. Usually I'll spot a few people wandering around the other holding area, but this morning there was no one. Of course, up to now, everyone over there did appear to be sick, so it shouldn't have been too surprising there'd come a time when no one would be out, except for the fact that the door to their dorm building was wide open, letting all the cold air in. I watched for several moments, thinking someone must be right inside and about to close it, but I saw no movement at all. I looked around for a nearby guard so someone could go in and close it. That's when I saw something even more disturbing.

The gate to the other detention area was also wide open. That's why the building door wasn't closed. There was no one there anymore.

Where had they taken the sick? Surely they hadn't died en masse last night.

I'm back in my bed now. I know it only gives me a false sense of security, but at the moment, that's better than none at all.

I don't know what's going on, but if I had to guess, I'd say the people whose names were on the list this morning are not being vaccinated. As for the people from the other area, I don't even want to speculate.

The only thing I hope is that when the men in the parkas return, they don't call my name.

14

"BOGOTÁ CONTROL TO TR117."

"TR117. Go ahead, Bogotá."

"Status?"

"Just completed flyby of Campeche. Twenty-nine bodies sighted. Spotted a few breathers, but they were clearly infected. So that's a confirm endgame in progress."

"Copy, TR117. Campeche endgame in progress."

"Are we cleared to proceed to our next destination?"

"Affirmative, TR117. Proceed to Isabella Island."

"Copy, Bogotá. Setting course for Isabella Island. ETA approximately fifty-five minutes.

ISABELLA ISLAND
10:03 AM CST

IT TOOK MORE than a little coaxing to get everyone out of the restaurant and down to the dock. After all but the sick were present, Robert went up to the *Albino Mer's* pilothouse to let Pax know.

"Ready when you are," he said.

Pax, the sat phone in his hand, didn't move.

Robert walked over and touched him on the shoulder. "You all right?"

He could feel Pax tense before the man looked back at him.

"Sorry," Pax said. "Lost in thought."

"They're here."

"Okay, then." Pax set the sat phone on the counter. "Let's do it."

They went out onto the upper deck of the ferry and moved in front of the pilothouse so everyone could see them. As soon as the crowd realized Pax was there, several people began shouting.

"This is your fault!"

"You're a liar!"

"You knew the vaccine didn't work, didn't you?"

Robert raised his arms, palms out. "Quiet down! Everyone, please!"

While most heeded his words, a few increased their volume.

"You! You! And you!" Robert said, pointing at the offenders. "Shut up now or you will be physically removed."

"What the hell, Robert? Afraid of a few complaints?" one shouted back.

"You can complain all you want once we're underway, but right now I need you all to listen."

"I'm not going anywhere with that killer!" the man—Sebastian something from the UK—said.

Robert opened his mouth to respond, but Pax put a hand on his arm and then stepped to the front railing, the whole time looking directly at Sebastian. "Staying is a choice you have. None of you," Pax said, now scanning the rest of the crowd, "have to go anywhere. But whether you believe me or not, if you stay, you *will* die."

"Bullshit!" someone else yelled. "Your 'vaccine' is what's going to kill us. It's already started."

Some murmurs of support could be heard, but not nearly as many as there had been a few minutes before.

"I don't know how familiar you are with vaccinations," Pax said, "but there's always a small percentage of people who have a reaction."

"You're just making excuses so we don't—"

"Raise your hand if you feel sick," Pax said.

Robert surveyed the crowd. Everyone was looking at each other but no hands went up.

"If there was really an outbreak here, more of you would have fallen ill by now. The even better news is that we've experienced a handful of post-inoculation illnesses in the past, and every single one of those people recovered."

"We don't know if that's true," Sebastian argued.

"You're right, but it doesn't matter. The people here who've gotten sick will survive," Pax said. "The question is, will you? This boat is leaving in fifteen minutes. Anyone not on board at that time will be left behind. We will not be coming back. This is your last chance to get away."

With a nod to Robert, he walked back into the pilothouse.

"You heard him," Robert said. "I need a few volunteers to help bring the sick down. The rest of you who are coming with us can grab your things and board now."

TEN MINUTES WERE still left on the deadline when the sat phone started to ring again. On the display was the number for the airplane crew waiting onshore for the ferry's passengers.

Pax punched ACCEPT. "We'll be underway here in a few minutes. The crossing'll take a couple hours. Probably have to make a few trips with the bus once we—"

"Pax, you might want to think about leaving right now," Donna Jones, the plane's pilot, said. "The watch station in Panama just picked up a plane Caribbean side, heading west-northwest on a line that will take them right over the island."

"We're sure it's not one of ours?"

"It is not."

"All right. We'll see you as soon as we can."

Pax disconnected the call, tossed the phone back on the counter, reached up, and pushed the horn button, holding it down for a full ten seconds. The blast reverberated throughout the resort and bounced back at the bay. After letting the sound die for a few seconds, he pressed the button again. Before he let go this time, he heard someone running up the stairs behind him.

"What's with the horn?" Robert said as he entered the room.

Pax hit the ignition button and the already warm motor quickly roared to life. "We have to leave now."

"The deadline's not even half over. We can't go."

"There's a plane heading in this direction no more than thirty minutes out. We can't be anywhere near the island when it flies by."

"It's them? They're coming back?"

"So it appears. How many people are missing?"

"Twenty-five, maybe thirty."

"Round 'em up. I'll give you five minutes, but can't go beyond that. When I sound the horn again, you'll have sixty seconds."

ROBERT RACED DOWN the stairs and headed for the dock.

"What's wrong?" Estella asked as he passed her.

He grabbed her arm. "Come with me." He explained to her what was going on as they hopped off the boat and ran to the shore.

"Oh, my God," she said.

"We only have a couple of minutes so I need you to help me get everyone down to the boat. But as soon as you hear the horn again, stop and get back as quickly as you can. Understand?"

She nodded.

They sprinted up the staircase to the bar deck.

"You take this level. I'll go upstairs."

Without waiting for her to respond, he ran over to the staircase and headed all the way to the top. His first stop was the restaurant dining room they'd all been living in. He had hoped the majority of the stragglers were there, but the room was empty.

"If you're up here," he yelled, "we've gotta go now!"

He raced around the rest of the upper level but found no one.

One level below was the uppermost guest level. He moved quickly down the hall, knocking on every door without stopping.

"Come on, come on, come on! We have to go! There's another one of those planes heading here *right now*! The boat's leaving in a minute!"

A door near the other end of the hall opened and a woman stuck her head out. "I thought we had at least five more minutes," she said.

"Not anymore."

"But my things."

"Leave them!"

She looked back in her room as if she wasn't sure she could do that.

He ran over to her and yanked her into the hall. "Go! Now!"

Whatever she saw on his face must have convinced her that her life was more important than her suntan lotion and bikini, because she turned and ran toward the stairs.

Robert followed her as far as the end of the hall and then yelled back toward the rooms, "If you think it's better to stay, you're wrong! But don't wait until it's too late to change your mind. We're not coming back!"

He allowed himself a pause, in case any more of the doors opened, but none did. He only hoped that meant no one was left on this floor.

He repeated the run-and-knock technique on the next floor down, rousting three guests. As he started to leave the hall, he heard raised voices coming from behind a closed door near the middle of the corridor. He retraced his steps until he was standing outside it.

One voice was male, the other female, arguing in French. Robert was unable to understand what they were saying.

He pounded on the door. "Open up! The boat's leaving!"

The voices fell silent for a moment, and then the man shouted back, "We are staying!"

The woman started yelling in French again, and the man yelled right back.

Robert recognized the man's voice as belonging to a guest named Bertrand Tailler, which meant the woman was his girlfriend, Aubrey Deniel. The few times Robert had spoken with them, Bertrand had done all the talking, giving Robert the impression the woman was shy, didn't speak English, or was not confident of her skills.

"If you stay, you will likely die," Robert said. "At least this way, you have a chance to get out of here."

"I think it is likely we die if we go!" Bertrand replied.

Robert heard movement, like someone running toward the door, then the woman screamed and Bertrand started yelling at her again.

"Please," the woman yelled. "Please. I…I go!"

Bertrand shouted over her, probably trying to drown her out, but Robert had heard enough. Turning away from the room, he mule-kicked the door a few inches from the knob.

"Leave us alone!" Bertrand yelled. "We are staying! Leave us alone!"

Robert kicked again and heard the doorframe crack. As he cocked his foot back for another shot, the ferry's horn filled the air.

His kick moved the door an inch. Two more hits and the door flew open.

"The boat leaves in one minute!" he yelled as he rushed inside.

Bertrand was near the windows at the other end of the room, his arms wrapped around Aubrey. She looked at Robert, her eyes pleading as she struggled to get out of her boyfriend's grip.

"Let her go," Robert said. "You can stay if that's what you want, but if she wants to go, she goes."

"It is better for her here! Now go! We are staying."

The horn blasted again.

Even if he left at that second, Robert knew making it in time would be a close call, but he couldn't leave the woman like this. In a sudden surge of frustration and anger that had been building for the last couple of days, he rushed forward and sent a punch flying over Aubrey's shoulder directly into

Bertrand's face.

Stunned, with blood beginning to pour out of his nose, the man released his grip and staggered back.

As Aubrey pulled away, Robert turned and put a hand on her back, urging her toward the door. "Run!"

A few feet before she reached the hallway, she glanced back. The fear on her face became mixed with worry and her step faltered.

"Go! Go!" Robert told her.

She looked unsure.

"Now!"

She raced out the door.

Robert, a few steps behind her, stopped just inside the room, intending to give Bertrand one last chance. But as he turned, Bertrand was leaping through the air right at him. There was no question of Robert getting out of the way.

Bertrand smashed into him, sending him falling backward into the hallway with the Frenchman on top of him.

"You bastard!" Bertrand said, swinging his fist. "Everyone will die because of you!"

The blows landed solidly against the sides of Robert's head, until he was able to twist to the side and shove Bertrand away. Like a punch-drunk boxer, Robert climbed awkwardly to his feet and shuffled down the hall toward the stairs.

Bertrand ran at Robert again. His pounding feet gave Robert enough warning and he was able to jerk to the side right before Bertrand would have hit him.

As the man flew past, he flung out an arm and grabbed a handful of Robert's shirt. The yank was hard enough to twist Robert around and knock him off balance. Backward he fell again, his head smacking into the corner where tile met wall.

His whole world went black.

ESTELLA HAD FOUND more than a dozen people gathered in a meeting room just off the bar. It didn't take much to convince them to get on the boat. By the time she finished running through her assigned floor, she had located five others and sent them running for the dock.

She contemplated heading upstairs to help Robert, but worried they might miss each other. She waited for him instead on the sand at the bottom of the stairs to the bar.

When the horn sounded, her already racing heart beat even faster.

"Hurry up," she whispered, her gaze glued to the upper portion of the hotel.

With each passing second, she became more and more worried. Where was he? He should have been back by now.

The horn blared again.

"Robert!" she yelled.

She glanced back at the boat, and then at the resort, then ran up to the bar deck and over to the stairwell. But as she opened the door intending to head up, she heard someone racing down toward her.

Robert, she thought. *Thank God.*

She stayed where she was, holding the door open. But the runner wasn't Robert.

It was a woman Estella had seen around but never talked to.

As the woman rushed through the open door, Estella grabbed her. "Where's Robert?"

Tears were running down the woman's cheeks and she had terror in her eyes. She said something in French that Estella didn't understand.

"Robert," Estella said. "You see?" She pointed at the woman and then at her eyes.

"*Oui*. Robert. Coming."

Estella's relief at hearing this was tempered by the woman's sobs.

"Get to the boat," Estella said, motioning toward the dock. "The boat."

The woman seemed to have stopped listening. She wrapped her arms around herself and squeezed her eyes shut as the tears continued to flow.

Estella realized the only way the woman would be able to get to the ferry on time was if Estella took her there. She looked toward the stairwell.

Robert was coming. The woman had said that much.

It would be all right.

Putting an arm around the woman's back, Estella said, "*Vamos.*"

She quickly led the woman off the deck and across the beach to the dock.

Renee was standing on the gangway to the boat. "Where's Robert?" she called.

"He is coming," Estella said. "He should be here any moment."

She escorted the woman on board, then asked one of the other passengers to help the woman find a seat. Estella returned to the gangway and started to exit the boat, but Renee grabbed her.

"Where are you going?" Renee asked.

"To find Robert."

"I thought you said he was right behind you."

"The woman said he was coming down. I'll go see where he is."

"You do, and you're staying here," Pax called from above.

They looked up. He was leaning over the upper-deck railing.

"I'm sorry, but we have to go now," he said. "Release the lines."

"No!" Estella shouted. "We cannot leave Robert!"

"Believe me, I don't want to leave him, either, but he knew we only had a limited amount of time. And it's already three minutes beyond the deadline I gave him."

"Just a few more minutes," Estella said.

"A few more minutes could get everyone killed. I'm sorry." Pax raised his voice. "Release the lines!"

Someone began untying the stern line, while a man standing near Renee and Estella moved up to the one at the bow.

"I am staying, then," Estella said, trying to twist free of Renee's grasp. "I am not leaving him here alone."

"Don't be an idiot," Renee said, wrapping her other arm around Estella's waist. "The last thing he'd want would be for you to miss the boat."

Of the two small women, Renee was the stronger. As she tugged Estella away from the edge, the rumble of the boat's engine increased, and the ferry began to pull away from the dock.

"Let me go!" Estella screamed. "Let me go!"

But Renee didn't heed Estella's request until long after the boat had passed through the channel and into the open sea.

FIFTEEN THOUSAND FEET ABOVE THE CARIBBEAN SEA
THIRTY-SIX MILES EAST OF COSTA RICA
10:44 AM CST

THE PILOT OF TR117, a Learjet 31A/ER Project Eden scout aircraft, checked the GPS and then tapped his radio switch. "Bogotá, TR117."

"Go, TR117."

"Commencing descent to five thousand feet. ETA Isabella Island eleven minutes."

"Copy, TR117. Descending to five thousand feet. Eleven minutes out from Isabella Island."

As the pilot signed off, the copilot looked back into the small cabin.

"Wake up, Freddy. Showtime."

The technician—Freddy Marquez—opened his eyes and blinked a few times. "Already?"

"Sorry to disappoint."

"How much time?"

"Ten minutes."

The technician stretched his arms above his head, bending them at the elbows so that he didn't smash his hands against the ceiling like he'd done before. He then unbuckled his belt and moved over to the equipment that would allow them to get a close, detailed view of the ground from thousands of feet in the air.

Though he'd just used the system when they'd flown over Campeche, procedures dictated that he check everything again to make sure it was all working properly.

Once he'd done so, he said, "Good to go."

ISABELLA ISLAND
10:46 AM CST

ROBERT'S RETURN TO consciousness started with a low groan. This was followed by a slow turning of his head, which stopped only when his right cheek came into contact with a hard surface. His eyelids fluttered before finally opening all the way.

In those first few seconds, he had no idea where he was. He lifted his arm to rub his head, but his hand bumped into something. He jerked in surprise before realizing he was lying right next to a wall.

As he inched away, pain radiated from the back of his head.

What the hell?

He gingerly felt the spot, half expecting to find it wet with blood. No blood, but a nice bump that stung even though he barely touched it.

Things started coming back to him. The resort. A woman shouting. A man, too. Bertrand. Aubrey.

Robert's eyes widened.

The boat!

Doing his best to ignore the pain, he scrambled to his feet and raced into the stairwell. Down he flew, two, sometimes three steps at a time. When he reached the bottom, he shoved open the door and ran out onto the deck surrounding the bar.

The ferry was gone.

He scanned the bay and the channel and the sea on the other side, but saw no sign of it.

How long had he been out?

He turned quickly to check the clock behind the bar, but had to squeeze his eyes shut for several seconds as a combination of pain and dizziness hammered down on him. For a moment, he thought he was going to throw up, but soon the nausea and vertigo subsided enough so that he could open his eyes again.

According to the clock, it was nearly 10:50. He tried to remember when the boat was going to leave. Pax had given Robert a five-minute deadline. That had been when? Ten fifteen? Ten twenty?

The boat had been gone at least thirty minutes.

Panic began to build in his chest. He'd been left behind. He was going to die here. He had screwed up and had no one to blame but—

Relax, a voice in his mind said. It had sounded very much like his own. Not the crazy, concussion-addled Robert who was on the brink of freaking out, but the calm, in-control Robert who had emerged over the last few weeks to lead the others in their struggle for survival.

Calm down.

After a few long, deep breaths, his panic diminished to a more controllable level.

Think, the voice said. *The boat being gone is a good thing. The others are on their way to safety. But it doesn't mean you're stuck here.*

More of the haze that had been clouding his mind began to part.

It would take the ferry no less than two hours to get back to Limón. That meant it still had somewhere between an hour and an hour and a half left to go. There were several boats on the island that could make the trip in less time. The other speedboat would get him to the mainland ahead of the ferry, and even one of the scuba boats, if he left soon, would get him there about the time the others reached the port.

He ran toward the stairs to the beach. As he reached them, he noticed someone sitting at one of the bar tables.

Bertrand. On the table in front of him was a bottle of Jack Daniel's and a nearly empty glass.

The Frenchman sneered and raised his drink. "*Salut.* It looks like you and I are the only ones who will not die today. You should thank me." He took a sip.

Though Robert was loath to talk to the man, he said, "Everyone else got on the ferry?"

DREAM SKY

"You are the only other person I have seen, so it would seem so." He poured himself another drink. "Grab a glass and join me."

"I don't think so."

Bertrand's laughter followed Robert as he ran down the steps and across the beach.

The speedboat was tied to a buoy in the bay, about a hundred feet from shore.

Robert stripped off his shirt and kicked off his shoes, then ran into the warm water until it was deep enough for him to swim. It took only ten overhead strokes for his head to start spinning again. He quickly switched from freestyle to breaststroke. It didn't completely quell the disorientation, but he was able to keep moving. Upon reaching the boat, he grabbed the railing and hung there for a moment, letting the spinning pass.

That's when he heard a distant drone.

He looked around, thinking maybe the ferry had come back. But the sea was empty. Odd, because the noise was getting louder. It sounded like—

Oh, God.

He looked up and scanned the sky.

There, almost due south, he spotted a small jet airplane.

Project Eden had returned, just like Pax had warned.

Robert watched as the aircraft approached the island. According to Pax, the Project would be checking for signs that the spraying had worked.

Thank God, the ferry had left. If it was still in the bay, crowded as it was with survivors, there was no telling what those evil bastards would do. Pax had said most likely this plane would be merely reconnaissance, but deadlier aircraft could be called in quickly if needed.

Robert hoped the *Albino Mer* had been able to get far enough away that it wouldn't be noticed, or, if it hadn't, that the watchers' focus would be solely on the island, and they wouldn't notice anything in the ocean around it.

Which begged the question, how would they react when it appeared no one was on the island?

Wait, he thought. *Not no one.* Bertrand was sitting on the deck looking very much alive.

He eyed the shore, wondering if he could get there in time and at least lie on the sand and pretend to be dead, but there was no way he could make it in time. His best bet was to keep the boat between him and the plane.

And hope he wasn't spotted.

FIVE THOUSAND FEET ABOVE ISABELLA ISLAND
10:55 AM CST

MARQUEZ MONITORED THE camera feeds on three separate screens. On the center screen was the view of the island via a high-resolution video camera. Video could go only so far, though. That's why on the screens to either side were feeds from ultra-high-res digital cameras similar to those used in satellites orbiting the planet. From a paltry five thousand feet up, they could zoom in tight enough to discern the pattern of a butterfly's wing.

The system was fully automated, so the technician's job became one of merely looking for anything out of the ordinary. The system was also programmed to note discrepancies, so Marquez took it as a point of pride to try to discover things before the computer did. Since they'd started doing flybys a week earlier, the results had been forty-sixty in the computer's favor. Given the sophistication of the code, Marquez took that as a win.

"There," he said, pointing at the center screen a half second before the computer *donged*, indicating it had also made the discovery. He turned on his mic. "We've got a breather."

"How many?" the pilot asked.

"Only one so far."

"Bodies?"

Marquez made a quick check of all three screens. "None yet."

As soon as the plane passed over the rest of the island, he quickly ran through the captured footage again. It was a pretty damn nice resort on a beautiful bay, with a few boats anchored just offshore. It didn't take an expert to see the boats were all empty so he didn't bother zooming in on them. Instead, he did so with the man sitting at the table on the hotel deck. The guy did Marquez the favor of looking up at the right moment.

Caucasian. Late twenties. Brown hair and a couple days' growth of beard. On the table was a square bottle. Looked like a Jack Daniel's bottle to Marquez, a guess reinforced by the glass in the guy's hand filled with brown liquid.

The guy didn't look sick, but he was very much alone.

"Tally?" the pilot asked.

"Just the one breather and no bodies."

They all knew what that meant. Anytime no bodies were spotted, a second flyover was required to make sure survivors hadn't decided to hide during the first pass.

"Hang on," the pilot said, as he began to bring the plane around.

ISABELLA ISLAND
10:57 AM CST

THE MOMENT THE plane moved beyond the hotel and became hidden behind the palm trees edging the bay, Robert pulled himself into the boat.

He checked the fuel gauge and saw it was sitting a hair below a quarter tank. Better than nothing, but he would have to add to it.

The fuel supply line was over by the dock, so Robert untied the boat from the buoy, started the engine, and raced over. After lashing a line around one of the posts, he jumped up on the dock and retrieved the end of the hose. He hooked it up to the speedboat and flipped the pump switch, hoping there was enough still in the reserve tank so he wouldn't have to go around siphoning fuel from the scuba boats.

The moment he heard the jet's engine again, he knew he was screwed. Sure, there was always the chance the people in the plane wouldn't notice a boat that had been anchored by itself minutes before was now tied to the dock, but really, how would they miss that?

The only thing that might make it worse was if they saw him on the dock, he thought. The boat with no one around? A head scratcher. The boat with him standing beside it? A problem.

He jumped into the water and swam between the hull and the pier. From there, he watched the plane fly overhead once more.

FIVE THOUSAND FEET ABOVE ISABELLA ISLAND
11:03 AM CST

AS THE CAMERAS started snapping away again, Marquez focused all his attention on the hotel. He figured if people were still around, that's where they'd be, and given that this was the plane's second flyby, someone might get curious enough to peek out a window or stick a head out a door. But the only person he saw was the man sitting at the table, his glass still in his hand.

"Anything?" the pilot asked.

"No. Looks like we're clean."

"Copy that. What's next on the list?"

The question was for the copilot, so Marquez took off his headset and put his equipment back in sleep mode. Hopefully, there would be enough time for a little longer nap than the one he'd just had.

He leaned back in his chair and closed his eyes. It wouldn't be until he landed back at the base again and was reviewing the footage in preparation for writing his report that he would notice the boat in the bay had moved between passes. He would zoom in on the hi-res image and carefully look for signs of anyone else. He would find none, but would discover that the boat was tied to the dock during the second flyby.

For several minutes he would sit staring at the screen as he contemplated the possibility they had missed something. That *he* had missed something.

But it was only one small boat, he would tell himself. And after checking the photos again for any changes in the footprints on the beach, he would note there was no evidence of more people moving around.

Despite the fact it would have taken impossibly fast currents to get the vessel around to the far side of the dock, Marquez would convince himself this was exactly what happened, and that the man on the deck had gone down to tie it up before returning to his drink. In his gut, Marquez would know this was a lie, but a minor one. Better this than to admit his mistake and be punished, maybe even with exile.

ISABELLA ISLAND
11:19 AM CST

ROBERT DIDN'T WANT to get fooled again, so he remained in the water for a full fifteen minutes after the plane had flown by the second time. Even then, he worried the plane would fly by a third time and catch him out in the open, but he knew he couldn't afford to wait any longer. His speed advantage over the ferry was quickly dwindling.

He pulled himself up onto the dock and removed the hose from the fuel tank. At some point during the flyover, the pump had automatically shut off. He hoped it was because it had filled the boat's tank to the brim, but a check of the gauge showed it was only sixty percent full. That had to mean the reserves were gone. Still, as long as he didn't go full out the whole way, he probably had enough to get to Limón.

He hesitated as he was about to climb back into the boat, and looked to shore.

Bertrand was still on the deck, drinking his whiskey.

Robert knew he should leave the asshole, but he couldn't bring himself to do that. Annoyed, he jogged onto the beach and over to the deck stairway.

"I'm leaving," he called up.

There was a delay before Bertrand turned and looked down. If he wasn't drunk already, he was well on the way.

"Come with me," Robert said. "You don't want to stay here alone."

"Fuck you."

"Last chance."

Bertrand raised his glass. "Did you not hear me the first

154

time? Let me tell you again. Fuck you." He laughed and took a drink.

Knocking the guy out with a punch to the jaw was easy. It was dragging the asshole to the boat that Robert hoped he wouldn't regret.

LIMÓN, COSTA RICA
10:57 AM CST

AFTER RENEE RELEASED her, Estella spent the rest of the voyage slumped against the outside wall of the bathroom, staring aimlessly out at the sea.

All she could think about was Robert. What had happened? Why hadn't he shown up? Why couldn't the boat have waited a little bit longer?

She hadn't known Robert for a long time, and they had only become close within the last week. But the intensity of the new world they found themselves in made those few days feel like so much more.

She didn't even realize they were nearing shore until the rumble of the engine revved down to a low growl. Commands were shouted across the deck as the ferry slowed and then gently bumped against the dock.

While the boat emptied, Estella remained where she was.

As the last few passengers were trickling off, someone touched her arm. "Let me help you."

Renee was hovering beside her, holding out a hand .

Estella wanted to stay on the deck, but before she could say this, Renee grabbed her arm and gently but firmly lifted her to her feet. Renee then guided Estella off the boat to where the others had gathered.

Pax arrived a few moments later.

"All right," he said, loudly enough for everyone to hear. "I only had time to get one bus yesterday, so if we crowd in we can do this in two trips."

"Couldn't we find another one?" someone asked.

"Won't save any time. Airport's not that far away." Pax paused. "Let's divide right down the middle. Group closest to me, you'll go first."

"Let's get you in the first group," Renee whispered to Estella.

"No," Estella said. "Please. Not yet."

Renee frowned but didn't push.

It took twenty minutes for Pax to return after taking the first group to the plane. When the bus doors opened, those in the second group started climbing on board. Estella and Renee took seats about a quarter of the way back, Renee at the window. As soon as the last person squeezed into the aisle, Pax shut the door and put the bus in gear.

The murmur started in the rear, and then more voices joined in as the mumbling moved forward through the bus. Renee looked toward the back.

"What is it?" Estella asked.

"I'm not sure," Renee said.

A voice from the back shouted, "Is that a boat?"

As Renee looked out the window, Estella leaned across so she could see, too. Cutting through the water around the easternmost arm of the port was a speedboat.

"Stop!" Estella yelled, jumping up. "Stop the bus!" She forced her way through those standing in the aisle. "Stop!"

Pax hit the brakes a little too hard, rocking everyone forward and nearly sending Estella sprawling.

"What is it?" Pax said as she reached the front.

She swung around the metal pole and toward the exit.

"Open the door! Open the door!" she yelled.

Pax pressed the release. As the door started to open, Estella pushed against it until there was enough room for her to squeeze through. She jumped out and ran back toward the dock.

The speedboat arrived there before she did, stopping on the far side of the ferry, out of sight. As she neared she got a view of the smaller boat, but no one was in it anymore. Then she saw him moving across the main passenger area of the ferry to the gate on the railing.

Robert.

She sprinted and reached him just as he stepped onto the dock. They threw their arms around each other.

"You missed the boat," she said.

"So I found out," he replied.

Renee and Pax arrived a few moments later.

"Glad to see you could join us," Renee said.

"Thanks," he said.

Pax looked uncomfortable. "Sorry we didn't wait."

"It's good that you didn't. A plane flew over about a half hour after you left."

"Did it see you?"

"Not me," Robert said in a way that made it clear the plane had seen someone. He nodded back toward the boats. "I could use a hand."

"There's someone with you?" Renee asked.

"Bertrand."

"Is he all right?"

"Nothing he won't recover from."

15

BEN HAD NEVER felt as much relief as he did when saw the United Nations van heading down the road toward him. Two men smiled as they climbed out, but their good cheer quickly disappeared when Ben told them about his pursuer.

He was quickly ushered into the van and they sped back the way they'd come. A screeching turn to the left took them up the south side of the valley. As they crested the hill, Ben could see that instead of more parkland ahead, there was a giant, nearly empty parking lot, and in the middle of all that asphalt—Dodger Stadium.

He had made it.

Traveling through the lot, his anticipation of seeing Martina exploded. He was sure she was here. It was the logical place for her to go. His smile was so wide his cheeks hurt, but he barely noticed.

"How many people are here?" he asked.

Without turning to look back at him, the man sitting in the front passenger seat said, "They'll give you all the information inside."

It was an odd answer, but Ben was too excited to give it too much attention.

The van drove counterclockwise around the stadium until it passed the narrow end—the home-plate end, Ben guessed— then turned down a smaller section of the lot, lined on both sides by trees. Unlike the rest of the parking area, this section was full of vehicles: more vans with the letters UN on the side, at least twenty sedans of various makes, and nearly as many military-grade trucks and Humvees.

The driver stopped next to an entrance under a blue awning. Immediately, the door swung open and four people—two male soldiers and a man and a woman, both in white lab coats—exited.

"What's with the soldiers?" Ben asked, his excitement dimming slightly.

"Standard procedure," the man in the passenger seat said. "Not everyone who comes here is cooperative."

"They're not? Why?"

"Beats me." He turned and looked at Ben. "Hop out. The counselors will escort you from here."

"Oh, okay." Ben opened the side door. "Uh…thanks for picking me up."

As soon as he exited and shut the door, the van pulled away.

"Welcome to the Los Angeles survival station," the man in the white coat said. "My name is Dr. Rivera and this is Dr. Lawrence." He motioned toward the woman. "If you will come this way, please."

Ben followed the doctors into the stadium, the two soldiers falling in silently behind him. Their footsteps echoed off the dark, polished concrete as the group proceeded down a wide walkway. It was walled off on both sides, preventing Ben from seeing the interior of the stadium.

Dr. Rivera stopped at an unmarked door, pulled out a key.

"This way," he said, unlocking the door and holding it so that Ben and Dr. Lawrence could pass through first.

Ben had been expecting some kind of office, but found himself in a stairwell.

"We're going down," Dr. Lawrence said with a smile.

As they headed down the steps, Ben said, "Where are you taking me?"

"Processing," she said. "We need to get information

about you, where you came from, what you were doing before the outbreak, that kind of thing."

"Oh," he said. That made sense.

"Tell me," she said. "What's your name?"

"Ben. Ben Bowerman."

"Nice to meet you, Ben." She offered him her hand.

As he grabbed it, he realized she was wearing a latex glove. He looked down at it, then at her, confused.

"Just a precaution," she told him.

"Do I look like I have the flu?"

"It's not the flu that concerns us." She paused. "Of course the flu would concern us, but we've all been vaccinated, so if you had it, we wouldn't get it. There are, unfortunately, other things out there."

At the bottom of the stairs, they entered another concrete hallway, only this corridor was considerably smaller.

"Are you feeling at all ill?" Dr. Lawrence asked him.

"No. I feel fine."

She smiled. "Excellent. You're one of the lucky ones, then."

"Well, I—" Before he could share his theory that he'd become immune to the Sage Flu, Dr. Rivera stopped at another door.

"Here we are," the man said as he pulled it open.

The area beyond had obviously once been used for business. There were several cubicles in the main area, with doors to other offices lining the back wall. Most of the cubicles were occupied, and Ben could see someone in at least two of the offices.

The doctors led him to a windowless room at the far left side. It had been set up like an examination room, complete with scale, exam table, jar of tongue depressors, and several pieces of medical equipment Ben couldn't identify.

"On the table, please," Dr. Lawrence said.

"I told you, I'm feeling fine," Ben said.

"I'm sure you are," Dr. Rivera said. "But I'm equally sure you can understand our need to check."

While Ben did understand it, he felt uncomfortable about

it.

The sooner you get through this, the sooner you can find Martina, he told himself.

He sat down on the table.

They checked his pulse, his blood pressure, his temperature, his throat, his ear, and his nose. Dr. Lawrence probed the glands along his neck and in his armpits, while Dr. Rivera looked into his eyes. They even had him strip down so they could scan what seemed like every inch of his skin.

And the whole time they asked him questions.

Where are you from?

San Mateo.

Why didn't you go to the survival station in the Bay Area?

I was looking for my girlfriend.

Where is she from?

The desert. North of here.

So you didn't come straight here?

No. I went to her home first. When she wasn't there, I assumed she came here.

How old are you?

Turned twenty-one last month.

How many sick have you been around?

My parents. My sisters.

How many sisters?

Two.

Is any of them still alive?

No.

What was your job prior to the pandemic?

I didn't have a job. I was going to school.

Where?

Santa Cruz.

What were you studying?

Anthropology.

How did you find out about the survival station?

The message on TV. From the secretary general.

When was the last time you saw the message?

I don't know. A week ago?

You haven't watched TV since then?

No. Should I have?

Why do you think you're still alive?

I think I'm immune.

Ben immediately regretted saying it.

Both doctors stopped what they were doing and looked at him.

"Why would you think that?" Dr. Rivera asked.

As the interrogation progressed, Ben's uneasiness had increased considerably. Now, with both doctors staring at him, he felt almost scared.

Something wasn't right.

"I, um, just assumed I was," he said. "I mean, I took care of my family when they were sick. I fed them and cleaned them up. Sometimes they coughed on me. But...but I'm still here."

All of that was true, but it wasn't the reason he knew he was immune. That, he decided, he'd wait to tell them after he felt more comfortable with his surroundings.

While Dr. Lawrence smiled and said, "Of course, that's only natural," Dr. Rivera continued to look at Ben as if he were expecting more.

After a few seconds, Ben said what he thought someone in his position would say, "Makes sense, though, right? Why else wouldn't I be sick?"

Dr. Rivera finally looked away. "There could be many reasons," the man said. "It could be that you have a tolerance for the disease. But I would caution you on believing that you are immune."

"But that doesn't really matter anymore, right?" Ben said.

"What do you mean?" Rivera asked.

"The vaccination. That's why you're here, isn't it? Once I have that, I *will* be immune."

There was an almost imperceptible hesitation before Dr. Lawrence said, "Right. Exactly."

Her pause had been long enough to send Ben's concerns rocketing skyward.

"So, do I get that now?" he asked.

"The procedure is a waiting period of two days before you are given the inoculation," she said.

"Waiting period?"

"Everyone has to go through this," she said, her tone reassuring. "We need to make sure you aren't sick."

"I told you, I'm not."

"Just because you aren't showing the signs," Dr. Rivera said, "doesn't mean it's not gestating in your system."

"But it looks like you're right," Dr. Lawrence said, continuing to play the good guy. "The waiting period merely gives us time for some observation and to run some tests on your blood. After that, when we know everything is fine, as I'm sure we will, you'll receive the vaccine."

"So what am I supposed to do until then?"

"We have an area set up here where you will wait. You'll have a bed, warm food, entertainment if you'd like. Two days will be over before you realize it."

The examination went on for another ten minutes, but the questioning seemed to be done. After they finished, Ben was turned over to the two guards who had accompanied the doctors earlier. They escorted him through the interior of the stadium, then down a corridor glowing with sunlight from the far end.

As they exited the corridor, Ben saw they had come out into one of the dugouts inside the stadium. The dugout was two tiered. The tier the tunnel opened onto was the lower one and covered by the dugout roof. The second tier was more a series of steps and a few flat areas right up against the railing that lined the ball field.

Beyond the field, he could see grandstands full of empty seats rising high into the sky, but it was the field itself that held his attention. Where before there had been base paths and chalk lines and grass and a pitcher's mound, there now were fences and posts and razor wire, all strung together to form enclosures. He couldn't tell how many, but definitely more than one.

"What is this?" he asked the guards as they guided him

up the stairs to the field.

"Holding areas," one of them said. "Keeps you isolated and safe from exposure. Only a precaution."

The words would have been more comforting if they hadn't sounded so rote.

When he was standing at field level, he could see two enclosures. The nearest ran from about midway between what had been home plate and third base—where it was narrowest—out a good hundred feet into left field, where it widened to about another hundred feet. A giant triangle. The second enclosure was similar, the only difference being it ran up the first-base side.

The guards led him to the gate of the nearest enclosure, opened it, and motioned him in.

"Am I the only one here?" Ben asked, looking around.

"Haven't had a lot of people come in the last few days," the guard closing the gate said. "There are four others." He nodded his chin toward the building at the back of the enclosure. "Probably in the dorm."

"So I'm just supposed to stay here?"

"For your protection."

The guard snapped the lock closed, then he and his buddy headed back toward the dugout.

Ben stared after them until they disappeared, then he did a three-sixty and took in his surroundings. The first thing he noticed was that the grandstands surrounding the field weren't as deserted as he'd originally thought. Spaced all the way around the stadium were ten armed soldiers. The second thing he noticed was that the fence surrounding his enclosure was not only on top of the ground but had been buried into it. That, combined with the three strands of razor wire running along the top, sent the clear message that attempting to leave was not encouraged.

Yes, he could understand precaution. Yes, he could understand the need for isolation. But what he couldn't understand was the need to treat him like a prisoner. Because that's what he felt like. Thirty minutes earlier he had been so elated. Now the hairs on his arms were standing on end.

Martina. He had come here for Martina. It didn't matter if they locked him up. As long as he could find her, everything would be okay. Before he realized it, he was running toward the dorm building, thinking one of the four people inside might be her. When he reached the door, he flung it open and raced inside.

The large main room was lined with triple high bunks running down both sides. At the midway point was an open area where a few tables and some chairs were set up. The four people the guard had mentioned were sitting in the chairs facing one of the walls, with the distinct glow of a television falling on them. Instead of looking at the TV, though, they had all turned toward the door when Ben rushed in.

One man and three women, none of whom was Martina.

THEIR NAMES WERE Ava, Grace, Melody, and Diego. None had known each other before the outbreak, though Ava and Grace had found each other prior to making the journey to the survival station.

Diego had been there the longest, ten hours shy of two days. The women had all arrived a day later, Melody first, then Ava and Grace a few hours after that. Diego said there had been six others in the holding area when he arrived, but when he woke after his first night, they were gone. The person who brought the food told him all six had cleared their quarantine period, been inoculated, and sent on to one of the UN safe zones.

"The six who were here—was one of them a girl, about eighteen, named Martina?" Ben said.

Diego shook his head. "There were only two women. One was probably around forty, and the other had to be in her seventies."

Ben felt defeated. He had been so sure he would find her here. Of course, if she had come as soon as the survival stations opened, she could have already moved on to this safe zone.

"Are there people in the other fenced-in area?" he asked.

"I saw someone in the big one next to us last night," Grace said. "He didn't look well, though."

"I've seen a couple there, too," Diego said. "None of them looked too good."

"Makes sense," Ben said. "Separate the sick from the healthy."

"Don't know about the small holding area, though," Diego said.

"Small holding area?" Ben asked. He had only seen the two.

"It's out in center field, but the fence is covered with a tarp so you can't see in."

"I've heard some voices from over there," Melody said. "Couldn't understand anything, though."

"How many voices?"

"Three or four maybe."

"Male or female?"

"Female, I think, but I can't be sure."

Though he knew he was grasping at straws, Ben couldn't help but feel a resurgence of hope. "Have any of the guards told you what that area's for?"

"They don't say much. I was lucky just to get one of them to tell me what happened to the people who left," Diego said.

"Have any of you tried to get out?" Ben asked.

"Get out?" Melody said. "Why would we want to get out?"

"Doesn't it seem kind of weird for them to lock us up like this?"

"They're trying to keep us safe," Ava said. "After we pass our two days, we'll get the shot and we can go."

"But if they're really trying to make sure we aren't sick, wouldn't they put each of us in our own room?" Ben said, adding, "If one of us turned out to be sick, we could infect the others. So what good would that do?"

He could see none of them had thought about it. Confusion began leaking into their expressions.

"No," Ava said. "I'm sure they know what they're doing.

It's the UN, for God's sake. They're trying to keep people alive, so why would they do something that would harm us?"

"I don't know," Ben said.

"Exactly my point. We just need to do our time and everything will be fine."

The thought had come to Ben as he was sitting there, and he wasn't sure he was right so he decided not to push it any further. Still, it troubled him.

The conversation fell into stories about what each of them had gone through to get there. After a while, Ben said he wanted to stretch his legs and went outside.

He walked slowly around the perimeter of his holding area. When he reached the point closest to the smaller enclosure out in center field, he stopped.

Like Diego had said, the fence was covered with a green tarp. Ben was willing to bet it'd been cut from the covering that was once used to protect the playing field from rain.

He turned his ear toward the other area but could hear no voices.

Facing the tarped enclosure once more, he cupped his hands around his mouth and said, "Martina?" Even as her name left his lips, he knew he wasn't speaking loudly enough. He tried it again, raising his volume a bit. "Martina?"

No response.

"Martina?" he said, louder.

Nothing at all.

He was tempted to shout, but didn't know how the guards would react if they heard him. Until he discovered otherwise, drawing attention to himself didn't seem like a good idea.

"Martina," he said one last time.

Silence.

16

CALEB'S FIRST ATTEMPT to remotely control the equipment at the abandoned Mumbai survival station failed miserably.

"Son of a…" He looked back at Jesse, Devin, and Mya. "What the hell did you forget?"

"We didn't forget anything," Devin said.

"Well, that's obviously not true or it would be working, wouldn't it?"

"Maybe you messed up the schematic," Jesse said.

Caleb leveled his gaze at him. "Not possible."

"Who's got it?" Mya asked. "Let me see it again."

Devin retrieved the plans Caleb had sketched out and gave them to her.

She looked at it, following lines with her finger. She moved over to the equipment rack they'd put together and glanced from the paper to the actual item and back.

"Looks good to me," she said, holding out the paper to Caleb.

"Of course it does," he said, snatching it from her, sounding more confident than he felt.

"Must be on Arjun's end," Jesse said.

The Mumbai side of things *was* the weak link, Caleb knew. Unfortunately, he'd only been able to talk the Indian man through what to do and couldn't see the work.

Caleb opened the phone application, switched on the external speaker, and dialed.

"We're having a problem," he said once Arjun was on the line.

"What type of problem?" Arjun asked.

"I'm not able to connect into the system there. I'm going to have Jesse talk you—"

"One moment, please," Arjun said. "Are you saying you tried already?"

"Well, yeah," Caleb said.

"The computer would then have to be on, yes?"

Caleb groaned and looked up at the trailer's ceiling. "Yes, of course. Are you saying it's not?"

"Naturally."

Caleb could feel his frustration surge, but before he could say anything, Arjun spoke again.

"You were the one who told me to leave it off until you gave me the go-ahead. You have not done this yet."

A laugh burst out of Devin, while Mya slapped a hand over her mouth, trying to contain her amusement.

"Oops," Jesse said.

"I am sorry," Arjun said. "I do not think I heard that correctly."

"It was nothing," Caleb said quickly. "I want you to go ahead and switch on the computer."

"Stand by, please."

"Nice one," Devin whispered, holding out his hand like he wanted to give Caleb a fist bump.

Caleb glared at him. "Fine. I'm not perfect."

"I'm sorry," Mya said. "I don't think we heard that correctly. Can you repeat that?"

"Go to hell. All of you." He turned back to his terminal.

A few moments later, Arjun said, "The computer is cycling up, and...there we go. It is on and asking for a password."

"All right. Let's see if this thing's working." Caleb reinitiated the link between the systems.

Three seconds passed, then the message on his screen

changed from ESTABLISHING CONNECTION to CONNECTION SUCCESSFUL.

Caleb and his team shouted in triumph.

"The password box has disappeared," Arjun said. "Does that mean it is working now?"

"Damn straight, it does," Caleb said. "Great job, Arjun. Thank you. I'm going to hang up, but I need you to keep your phone with you in case anything comes up."

"If I do not answer, Darshana or Sanjay will."

"Sanjay's there now?"

"He will be soon. He wanted to see for himself."

CALEB SPENT THE next hour familiarizing himself with the Project Eden operating system. When he finally felt he had a handle on things, he decided to see what else was out there.

"They're definitely using encrypted voice transmission and e-mails. Looks like there are also some password-protected document-sharing sites." He hunted through the code a bit more. "Oh, looks like they use a lot of video transmissions, too. There appears to be several conversations going on right now. Let's see if we can eavesdrop on one, shall we?"

He clicked his tongue against the roof of his mouth as he attempted to gain access to the video feed. He managed to break in, but the image was far too scrambled for him to make anything out, and the audio was nothing more than pops and electronic echoes that were impossible to decipher.

"Let me take a look at that," Devin said.

While Caleb thought highly of his own skills, he was well aware there were people far better at certain tasks than he. When it came to hacking through scrambled signals, few on the planet—even when there had still been seven billion others around—were better than Devin.

Caleb scooted out of the seat and Devin moved in.

After studying the signal for nearly a minute, Devin looked back at Mya. "Can you get me my laptop? My backpack's over by the door."

When she returned with it, he launched a program that looked a lot like a recording studio audio board, and then used the Bluetooth function to sync with Caleb's machine. As he adjusted the sliding levers on the laptop, the video image began to come into focus.

There were two images side by side. A graying man with a mustache on the right and another man, perhaps ten years younger, on the left.

"That's good enough for the video right now," Caleb said. "Try fixing the audio."

Devin changed a setting at the top of the laptop screen and manipulated the sliders again. At first there was little change, but then sounds much more human than the digital noise from before began to seep out. Finally—

"…tons per hundred," the older man said.

"That syncs with what I have here," the younger one replied. "Column B?"

"Second quarter. Four hundred thirty-five metric tons per hundred. Eighty-two-point-seven-five metric tons per hundred. Nine hundred twenty-three-point-two-five metric tons per hundred. Four hundred seventy-one—"

"Sounds like someone's doing inventory," Mya said.

"Let's check some of the other signals," Caleb said.

They eavesdropped on several other equally boring conversations for thirty minutes before hitting on one that sounded more interesting. It was between an older, distinguished-looking woman and a young, well-coiffed man.

"What is that?" Mya asked. "German?"

"Dutch, I think," Jesse said.

"Do you understand it?" Caleb asked.

Jesse shook his head.

"Do any of you?"

More shakes.

To Caleb, this conversation sounded more important than a discussion about how many sacks of flour were sitting in a particular warehouse.

"We *are* recording this, right?" Caleb asked.

"Every second," Devin said.

The conversation went on for another three minutes, then both parties signed off and the signal ended.

Caleb thought for a moment before turning to Mya. "Think you can find someone who can translate that?"

"I can try. Devin, put a copy in my dropbox."

"Will do."

As soon as Mya left, Caleb said, "All right. Let's see what else we can find."

MYA THOUGHT IF anyone knew about a Dutch speaker among the Resistance at Ward Mountain, it would be Crystal, and, sure enough, she did. There were two Dutch speakers at the base—a German man named Jans Stephan who also spoke Dutch, and a Belgian named Ilse Vanduffel who spoke Flemish, which, according to Crystal, was a Dutch dialect.

Mya decided to seek out Ilse since she would be the native speaker. The woman was part of the Resistance's security forces. Mya tracked her down in one of the workout rooms, where hand-to-hand combat training was taking place. When Mya entered, those inside stopped what they were doing and looked over at her.

"Sorry to interrupt," she said. "I'm looking for Ilse Vanduffel."

A tall, lean, muscular woman with short brown hair broke from the crowd. "I'm Ilse."

"I have a translation job I need your help with."

Ilse looked a bit put out. "Is it urgent?"

"Very." Mya wasn't sure she had the authority to make that call, but what the hell?

After a nod from the man who appeared to be in charge, Ilse said, "What is it I can help you with?"

THEY FOUND A computer in an unoccupied office down the hall from the workout room. Mya accessed her internal network dropbox and opened the video.

"What is this?" Ilse asked before Mya hit PLAY.

"A video call between two Project Eden members."

Ilse's eyes widened. "Are you serious?"

"Yes."

Mya clicked the arrow to start the video. She had expected Ilse to start telling her what was being said, but the woman silently watched the entire conversation, her expression unchanged throughout.

When it was finished, Mya said, "Well? It is Dutch, isn't it? You understood it?"

Ilse continued to look at the screen for a few more seconds before she looked over. "I understood it." She wet her lips. "Where is Captain Ash?"

"I don't know exactly. Somewhere around.

"We need to find him."

SINCE CALEB WOULD want to know what was going on, Mya decided they would gather back in the communications trailer. She sent Ilse ahead and went in search of Captain Ash, finding him at a back table in the cafeteria, hunched over a couple of open books with Chloe. When Mya explained the situation, they both came with her.

"Finally!" Caleb said as Mya, Ash, and Chloe entered. He gestured toward Ilse, who was sitting on a chair against the trailer wall. "Will you tell this woman it's okay to share with us what she knows?"

"Your charm didn't work on her?" Mya asked, smirking.

"All she said was that she'd come to tell us what the message meant, and then she promptly sat down and shut up."

"She told me Captain Ash should hear it, too."

Caleb spread his hands, palms up. "And telling a story twice has never happened in the whole history of mankind?"

"Cool it," Ash said. "I'm here now, so we can get on with it."

"Ilse," Mya said. "Go ahead."

Ilse stood up. "Can we play the message here?"

Mya shot a look across the room. "Devin?"

"Two seconds."

DREAM SKY

The trailer had no large screen like in the comm room, but there was a medium-sized HD monitor at the empty station next to where Devin was sitting. Within seconds, it filled with a still image of the recorded video conversation.

Before Devin could click PLAY, Ilse said, "One moment." She walked over to the screen and pointed. "This man is Dutch. If I have to guess, I would say he was from Amsterdam or very nearby. The woman refers to him as van Assen. That would be his surname. She never says his entire name. The woman is not Dutch nor is she Flemish. While she speaks Dutch very well, it is not her native language. By her accent, I would say she is possibly English, but more likely American or Canadian."

"Is her name mentioned?" Ash asked.

"He calls her only Director." She looked at Devin. "Please start."

As the video played, Ilse gave a running translation.

DIRECTOR: ...as you promise.

VAN ASSEN: So my file?

DIRECTOR: Contains a commendation for your work in Mumbai, and clears you of any responsibility for what occurred.

VAN ASSEN: I very much appreciate that, Director. Thank you.

DIRECTOR: You earned it, so no need for any thanks.

VAN ASSEN: My new assignment starts in a few hours, so I won't bother you any longer.

DIRECTOR: There has been a change of plans.

VAN ASSEN: Change?

DIRECTOR: You will not be joining the transition division in Madrid.

VAN ASSEN: I won't? Then where do I report?

DIRECTOR: You will be reporting directly to me.

VAN ASSEN: Oh. Thank you, Director. I'm honored. I will arrange transportation and can be there as early as tomorrow.

DIRECTOR: Hold on. You will be reporting to me, but you will not be coming here. I'm sending you back to India.

VAN ASSEN: What?

DIRECTOR: There is a new…structure in place. One I am part of. But if I am going to do my job effectively, I need to keep an eye on my colleagues. You will be my eyes in Jaipur. You are to proceed to NB551, where you will fill an opening on Director Parkash Mahajan's staff. While you carry out your daily duties for the director, you will keep me informed on the director's activities. I assume this is not outside your abilities."

VAN ASSEN: Not at all, Director. It would be an honor to serve you.

DIRECTOR: Then I would say you have a very bright future in the Project.

"YOU CAN STOP now," Ilse said.

As the image paused, Ash said, "Is there more?"

"They talk for another few minutes. Details that I can translate and write down, but the main focus of the conversation ends here."

Ash looked back at the screen. *Director* was a term used at many different levels within Project Eden—department directors, facility directors, division directors, to name a few. The woman could have been any of these. But from the way she and this van Assen were talking, and the scant description of Director Mahajan, Ash had the sense the woman was much higher up in the organization. Wanting to keep tabs on another director not stationed anywhere near where she was could mean her position was right near the top, if not within the innermost circle itself.

Since the death of the previous principal director in the destruction of NB219, Project Eden would have quickly moved to fill the leadership vacuum. But without access to Matt's contacts within the Project, the Resistance had yet to learn who or what filled that vacuum. Was this conversation a clue to that?

Ash looked over at Mya. "Can we bring up our database in here? I want to see what we have on this Parkash Mahajan."

She scanned the room, but before she could answer, Devin said, "I can bring it up on my laptop."

"Do it."

Less than a minute later, Ash, Chloe, and the others were huddled behind Devin. On the computer screen was the Resistance's information sheet on Parkash Mahajan. There weren't as many details as Ash would have liked, but enough to show Mahajan was indeed high up within the Project Eden leadership structure. The most recent information listed him as possible regional director of Southern and Southeast Asia.

"If he's a regional director, then the woman must be at least that level, too," Ash said. "Is there a way to bring up a list of other presumed regional directors?"

"Let me see," Devin said.

He ended up having to cobble it together, so it took him a few minutes, but when he finished, he had a list of eleven names.

"That can't be all of them," Chloe said.

"It isn't," Devin said. "But it's as complete as I can get."

There were several regions not listed but must have had directors: western Africa, the Middle East through the area around the Black Sea, Northern Europe, Australia and New Zealand, and the Pacific Islands area, though the last may have been covered in full or in part by the western South America director or the East Asia director.

Ash scanned the list and zeroed in on two names—Marlene Lee, who was thought to be in charge of the southern

Africa region, and Celeste Johnson, in charge of the eastern half of North America. Both were names that could have easily been found in the States.

"Are there any photos of these people?" he asked.

"I doubt it," Devin said.

"Can you check? I'm interested in Marlene Lee and Celeste Johnson."

Devin set up the search, then shook his head. "Nothing on Celeste Johnson." He switched the parameters to Marlene Lee and studied the results. "This might be something." He clicked on the link.

Ash stared, surprised, when the picture appeared on the screen. It was a candid shot of a group coming out of what appeared to be a conference room. Most of those in the image were men Ash had seen before, though they were not as old as when he had been in their presence.

"The pre-flu directorate," he said.

He could feel Chloe tensing next to him, and knew she recognized the men, too. These were some of the Project Eden leaders who had died at Bluebird, the Project's base on Yanok Island, from where the pandemic had been initiated.

Devin pointed at the screen. "According to the photo tag, that's Marlene Lee."

The woman he indicated was half turned away from the camera, and mostly blocked from view by the others. But there was enough detail to see she was Asian, not Caucasian like the woman on the video call.

"All right. At least we know the woman's not Marlene Lee," Chloe said.

"Doesn't tell us if she's Celeste Johnson, though," Devin said.

"No, it doesn't," Ash said. "But I'm willing to bet it's her. Do we have a location on Ms. Johnson?"

Devin checked the database and shook his head. "It says here that she is probably located at one of the Project's facilities on the East Coast, but it doesn't say which one."

"Van Assen said New York," Mya said.

"That might be as close to a confirmation as we can get,"

Chloe said.

Ash leaned back, thinking.

After he's gone, we'll go after the next set of leaders and the next and the next. Each time we succeed, the Project becomes more unbalanced.

Matt's words, said after he'd told Ash and Chloe he was going after Principal Director Perez. A keep-knocking-them-down-until-they-stay-down strategy. It was as sound a plan as the Resistance could hope for.

"Maybe there's someone who can pinpoint where Director Johnson is for sure," Ash said. "We can look into that in a bit. In the meantime, we do know where Mahajan is. NB551 in Jaipur." He looked around. "Do we have anyone near there?"

He was greeted with blank faces.

"We don't handle that," Caleb said. "Operations would know, or the comm center."

Ash looked around at all the equipment. "I assume you can connect me from here."

Twenty seconds later, he was talking to Crystal.

"The closest people we have are in Thailand and Singapore," she said, her voice coming out of the speaker on Caleb's computer. "But they're pretty tied up."

"There's no one in India?"

"We had three teams there. But two had to be diverted to help out in southern China, and the third's been sent to deal with a sizable group of survivors in Sri Lanka."

Ash pressed his lips together, annoyed.

"I'm open to suggestions," he said.

"I would have to check on statuses, but I might be able to free up someone in a few days."

Ash didn't like the delay, but it was better than not sending anyone at all. "All right. See what you—"

Mya said, "What about Sanjay's people?"

Ash looked over at her.

"I mean, they're in India already," she said. "I don't know how far Jaipur is from where they are, but they've got to be able to get there sooner than a few days, right?"

She had a point.

"Can someone tell me how far it is?"

"Checking," Devin said. "Um, it's not exactly close. Seven hundred thirty-five miles or thereabouts. Maybe sixteen hours of driving?"

As Mya said, still sooner than a few days.

"Can we get Sanjay on the phone?" Ash asked Crystal.

"Actually," Caleb said, "we can do it from here. If he's not at the Mumbai survival station yet, he should be soon."

"Get him on the line."

17

A LOUD RING jerked Arjun awake. He blinked and looked around, surprised to find he was sitting in the communications room chair. He had meant to stretch out on the blanket he'd spread on the floor, but he seemed to have fallen asleep right there at the desk. No wonder, though. It had been a long night.

A ring again, off to his left. As he twisted to see where it was coming from, he winced. His less-than-optimal sleeping posture had left a kink in his neck. As he rubbed the sore muscle, there was another ring.

The sat phone.

Answering it, he said, "This is Arjun."

"It's Crystal," the woman said. "Has Sanjay arrived yet?"

"Uh, I am not sure. I have not seen him yet. Give me a moment and I will check. If he is here, I will have him call you."

"Thank you. As soon as possible."

Arjun made the journey down from the rooftop room into the main building, and hunted around until he heard voices coming from the dining hall on the ground floor. There he found Darshana, Sanjay, Kusum, and Prabal drinking tea.

"Ah," Sanjay said. "You are awake."

"Awake? I was…working," Arjun said. "I was not asleep."

"So you have mastered the art of working with your eyes closed?" Darshana said, an eyebrow raised.

Apparently someone had paid him a visit while he napped. "Okay, okay," he said. "Perhaps I was asleep for a little while."

Sanjay smiled. "You should not worry. You have to sleep sometime, my friend. Come, have some tea."

"Actually, Sanjay, I have—" Arjun stopped as he accidentally turned his head a millimeter the wrong way, sending a shockwave of pain down his neck.

Darshana stood up. "Are you all right?"

He held up a hand. "I am fine. Just a muscle pull."

"May I suggest you use a bed next time you want to sleep?" Kusum said.

There were smiles all around and a few chuckles.

Arjun glared at all of them before allowing himself a small grin. "I would laugh with you, but it would hurt too much." He pulled the sat phone out of his back pocket. "Sanjay, the Americans would like to talk to you."

"About what?" Sanjay asked as he took the phone.

"I did not ask."

Sanjay pressed the preset they'd assigned to the Americans' number, then put the call on speaker so his friends could all hear.

The voice that answered belonged to the woman named Crystal.

"I understand you are looking for me," Sanjay said.

"Oh, Sanjay. Great. Hold on."

The line went silence for well over a minute before a new voice said, "Sanjay, it's Daniel Ash."

"Hello, Captain Ash," Sanjay said.

"Good morning, I guess. It is morning there?"

"Yes. It is."

There was a pause. "First, I want to thank you and your friends. What you've found there and helped us gain access to is vitally important. We've already learned quite a bit."

"I am pleased to hear that."

"There's something we've discovered that…well, we

could use your help on."

"Of course. We are not technicians, but we will do what we can."

"This actually has nothing to do with the equipment or anything there in Mumbai."

Sanjay exchanged a surprised look with his friends.

"Then what does it have to do with?" he asked.

"Something that involves a trip." Ash told them about the intercepted message and learning about a potential Project Eden leader working out of Jaipur. "What we would like—if you're willing, of course—is for one or two of your people to go there and quietly survey the area so we can determine if there's a way to exploit the situation."

"You want us to find this Director Mahajan?"

"We haven't been able to obtain a picture of him yet. Besides, he's likely to stay inside the base, out of sight. You might, however, have the opportunity to spot the man whose conversation we overheard. He's lower level, so he might venture outside on occasion. From the information we have here, the base is located within blocks of the Jaipur survival station. Unfortunately, we don't have the exact coordinates of the base. But there will likely be some back and forth between the two facilities, so if you spot this guy at the station, he should be able to lead you to the base. He's Caucasian, and I couldn't tell for sure from the video, but think he's about five ten, maybe six feet." Ash's voice became muffled as he asked a question to someone on his end. When he came back on, he said, "That's a hundred eighty or a hundred eighty-two centimeters, or thereabouts. We're all but positive he's Dutch. I'll have someone grab an image from the video and send it to you."

"What happens after we find this man or the director?" Sanjay asked.

"Good question. The way we see things is that if we can keep them off balance, we might have a chance to defeat them. So, depending on the situation you find there, if there's a chance we can take the director out, we'll send some people over to do that. That isn't a problem for you, is it?"

"Absolutely not."

IF SANJAY HAD his way, he would undertake the spy mission on his own, but Kusum was not about to let him go off alone.

"All right, all right," he said, knowing it was an argument he would never win. "I'll take Arjun with me."

"Arjun has been working with the Americans the most. He should stay."

"Okay," he said, knowing she was right. "You and I."

"And Darshana," she said.

"Why Darshana?"

"It is a long trip, so I assume we will take a car and not our motorbikes. With three drivers we will not need to rest. Or, if you prefer, we could take Prabal instead of Darshana," she suggested.

"No, no. Darshana is fine."

Prabal had made quite a mess of things here in Mumbai before the survival station was abandoned, and while he'd been trying hard to rectify his actions—actions which, admittedly, worked out for the better in the end—Prabal was a bit of a walking disaster, so taking him along was not an option Sanjay wanted to consider.

Sanjay located a Toyota dealer on Lal Bahadur Shastri Road, picked out a brand new Land Cruiser, and returned to the survival station, where he, Kusum, and Darshana loaded enough supplies into the back to sustain them for several days. When they were done, they went inside to let Arjun and Prabal know they were leaving.

Both men were up in the communications room, so Sanjay called up the stairwell, "We are all set. Our satellite phone will be on if you need to reach us."

"Wait!" Arjun said.

He climbed down the ladder, still clearly bothered by the pulled muscle in his neck. When he reached the bottom, he pulled a smartphone out of his pocket.

"Here," he said, handing it to Sanjay.

"What do I need this for?" The regular cellular system had gone out of commission only a few days after the outbreak started.

"The picture. I put it on there."

"What picture?"

"From Mr. Ash. Of the Dutchman."

Right. In his rush to leave, Sanjay had forgotten. He put the phone in his pocket and held out his hand to his friend. "If you have any problems, let us know."

"Same for you," Arjun said. "And whatever you do, do not let them see you."

18

DR. LAWRENCE RAN the test a second time, but the results were exactly the same. She hurried over to the lab door and stuck her head out into the main medical room.

"Dr. Rivera, can you come here for a moment?"

Not waiting for a response, she returned to the workstation, where the results of the two separate tests run on Ben Bowerman's blood were displayed side by side on the computer monitor. As she checked them again, she heard Dr. Rivera enter the room.

"What is it?" he asked. "Is he sick?"

There was no need to indentify the detainee he was talking about. Bowerman was the only intake they'd had all day.

"Not sick," Dr. Lawrence said. "Immune."

"Are you sure?"

"He has the antibodies. He's had KV-27a."

"But he doesn't look like he just got over it," Rivera said. "He looks fine."

She locked eyes with him. "I don't think he had it recently."

The corner of his mouth rose as he realized what she meant. "Another one?"

"Yes."

"Incredible."

"Isn't it?"

THE STADIUM LIGHTS lit up the field, holding back the night.

Outside, a whistle sounded twice.

"Finally!" Diego said.

"What's that mean?" Ben asked.

"Dinner," Melody told him.

They walked outside into the cool but not uncomfortable evening.

"We wait here," Diego said, after taking only a few steps from the building.

"Why?" Ben asked.

"It's what we're supposed to do."

It wasn't much of an answer, but before Ben could pursue it further, the gate on the other side of their yard opened, and a guard entered, his rifle held high against his chest. He was followed by two men, each carrying a pair of individually wrapped trays. They set them on the ground, exited, and then one returned with an additional tray.

As soon as they had all left and the gate was closed, Diego said, "Okay."

They retrieved their food and took it back into the building, taking seats around the tables in the central area. The sound of crinkling aluminum foil filled the room for a moment as they removed the covers from their food.

Dinner consisted of salad, fried rice with chicken, and sliced fruit. There was also a bottle of water and a small piece of cherry pie. Ben picked up the plastic fork and wondered if those in the sick holding area received the same food.

He froze, a forkful of rice inches from his mouth.

The other holding areas.

He dropped the utensil on his plate and shot out of his chair.

"Where you going?" Ava asked.

Without answering, he ran outside. If he hadn't already missed it, he thought this might be his opportunity to see into the tarp-covered area, when the guards opened the gate to deliver dinner.

He hustled around to the back corner of the fence. The third enclosure looked unchanged from the last time he'd checked it out. Had dinner been delivered?

He studied the fence, and then groaned. Of course. There was no break in the fence that he could see, so the gate must have been on the backside, out of his view. He pushed away from the fence and headed back around to the dorm entrance.

But as he came around the corner, he stopped dead in his tracks. The gate to his holding area was open again. This time there were four guards—two by the opening, and two accompanying Drs. Lawrence and Rivera as they walked toward the dorm.

Seeing him, they too stopped.

After a moment of confusion, Dr. Lawrence smiled and said, "Mr. Bowerman. Excellent. We were looking for you. Please, come with us."

"Come with you where?"

"Please," she said, motioning him to join them.

In contrast to Dr. Lawrence's friendly demeanor, the two guards stared at him, as if ready to swing their rifles around and shoot him at the slightest protest.

"Mr. Bowerman?" Dr. Rivera said.

Knowing he had no choice, Ben nodded and walked over.

"Thank you," Dr. Lawrence said as they escorted him out of the pen. "We'll go over here for a moment." She gestured to the third-base-side dugout.

After they took the steps down, Dr. Rivera pointed at the bench. "Have a seat."

Ben did as asked. "What's going on? Is something wrong?"

"Not at all," Dr. Lawrence said. "We just need to draw a little more blood. Our fault. We had a problem with the earlier sample."

Quickly and efficiently, they poked his arm and filled another vial.

"That's it," Dr. Lawrence said, placing a bandage over the puncture wound. She turned to the guards. "All yours."

"Up," one of the guards said to Ben.

They led him back onto the field, but instead of heading to his holding area, they took him to the left along the outside of the fence. When they reached the corner out in left field, they veered right toward the tarp-covered enclosure.

"What's going on?" Ben asked.

"You're being relocated."

"Why?"

"I don't have that information."

As much as Ben wanted to see who was inside the mysterious pen, he couldn't help feeling nervous as he approached it.

"What's this area for?" he asked.

The guards said nothing as they took him around to the side that faced the center-field wall. There, as he'd already guessed, was the gate. After it was unlocked and opened, Ben was pushed firmly, but not unkindly, inside.

The gate closed behind him and the lock clicked into place.

What the hell just happened?

He turned in a circle, assessing his new surroundings.

Like in the other areas, there was a building here, though it was only about a third the size of the dorm he'd been in, leaving an outside area that wasn't much bigger than his parents' yard in San Mateo. The tarp was attached to the outside of the fence and blocked some of the stadium lights, creating areas of shadow here and there.

As he turned to look at the building, he saw a woman looking out one of the windows at him. He headed over and pulled the door open.

"Hello," he said, stepping inside. "Didn't mean to scare anyone. Guess I've been assigned here."

There were bunks here, too, but they were only two high. As he came around the set nearest the door, he saw at least a dozen people sitting on chairs in a small open area at the far end, all staring at him. They were men and women ranging anywhere from late teens to probably mid-fifties.

As he started walking toward them, a teenage girl rose out of her chair. "Is Martina with you?"

Ben jammed to a halt, his breath gone. "Martina?"

The girl took a few steps toward him. "You're Ben, Martina's boyfriend, right? I remember you."

"From where?"

"Cryer's Corner. You…you were there with us."

Cryer's Corner? That was where he'd met Martina, where they had both been exposed to the—

He took a hard look at the girl. "You were on the softball team with her."

"Yeah. I'm Jilly."

"Right. Jilly. I remember."

Out of habit, he held out his hand to shake, but instead of taking it, Jilly threw her arms around his neck.

"You're alive! She said you would be!"

He pushed her back. "Why did you think she'd be with me? Isn't she here?"

"No, of course not," Jilly said, looking confused. "She went looking for you. Didn't she find you? Isn't that why you're here?"

"I haven't seen her since before the flu hit."

"Oh," Jilly said, concern creeping into her voice. "But…oh, no."

"Do you know where she went to look?" he asked.

"She didn't say. I assumed she was going up north. That's where you're from, right?"

He could feel the blood draining from his face, as he realized they must have crossed paths and missed each other. She was still out there somewhere, looking for him. He should have never come here. He should have known she'd look until she found him.

"When did you see her last?" he asked.

"New Year's Eve."

Five days ago. Five whole days!

Someone—Jilly probably, but in his daze he wasn't sure—led him to the seating area and eased him into one of the chairs. He didn't know how long he was lost in thought, but when he finally regained some sense of his surroundings, he saw that everyone was gathered around, watching him.

"You all right?" a man of about forty said. "You're not going to throw up or anything, are you?"

"No," Ben said, his voice low. "I'm not going to throw up."

Jilly knelt next to him and put a hand on his arm. "I'm sure she's all right. Martina's pretty good at taking care of herself."

"But she's still out there. How am I ever going to find her?"

"You don't have to. She'll come here eventually. That's what she said she'd do after she found you. When she doesn't, she and the others will probably show up."

"Others?"

"Noreen and Riley and Craig went with her."

Ben didn't know who Riley or Craig were, but he knew Noreen. She was one of Martina's best friends. At least Martina wasn't out there alone.

All right, he told himself, *she'll be okay. Jilly's right. Martina can take care of herself.*

His panic subsiding a bit, he allowed himself to take a good look at the others in the room. "I recognize some of you from the softball team," he said, "but the rest of you weren't at Cryer's Corner."

"No," a woman said. "I'm from Sage Springs. So's AJ over there." She nodded toward another woman.

"I'm from Victorville," said the man who'd asked if Ben would throw up. "In fact, we're all from the high desert."

"You're all from the desert?" Ben said. "Nowhere else?"

"Well, you're not," Jilly said.

"You're right. I'm not." Ben fell silent for a moment before it hit him. "But I was there during the first outbreak. I caught the flu before. So did you girls." He looked at those who hadn't been at Cryer's Corner. "Did you all get it, too, last spring? You were all sick?"

Nods and a few uh-huhs.

Everyone.

Holy shit. "Were there others?"

"What do you mean, others?" another man asked.

"In here with you guys when you were first brought in," Ben said.

One of Martina's old teammates snorted a laugh. "This place wasn't here before us. One morning there was nothing but grass, and by the end of the day, our new home. That evening they moved us all in."

"And no one else," he said.

"No one," Jilly said.

Ben did not like where this was going. "Did any of you tell them that you had the flu before?"

Most of the people who hadn't been on the Burroughs High School softball team answered yes.

"We didn't," Jilly said. "We were afraid they wouldn't give us the vaccine if they knew."

"Apparently they figured it out anyway," Ben said. "You all had your blood tested, right?"

They all had.

"I don't understand why the UN would put us by ourselves," a girl said.

"Maybe so they can use our blood to make more vaccine," someone suggested.

One of the members of Martina's softball team—Valerie, if Ben remembered correctly—rolled her eyes and said, "They already *have* a vaccine, remember? That's why we came."

"If you ask me, these people aren't with the UN," a ponytailed girl said.

"What makes you say that?" Ben asked. Though he'd been thinking the same thing, he hadn't been here as long as the others so he'd thought he might be overreacting.

"Well, for starters, that message we saw on TV said that everyone who showed up would get the vaccine. When we were still in the other area, not one of the people in there had been given it."

Ben said, "The people I talked to who are in there right now told me there was a two-day waiting period, and then after you were inoculated, you were sent to a safe zone where everyone's being gathered."

"Maybe," the ponytailed girl said. "But we all know how the guards look at us. They pretty much act like we're cattle. If this was really some kind of UN humanitarian operation, they'd treat us a hell of a lot better, no matter how bad things have become." She smirked. "I'll tell you something else. If the UN was really running things, there'd be a whole lot more problems, don't you think?"

"Problems?" Jilly said.

"Sure. Operation this size, presumably worldwide, pulled together a matter of days after the outbreak of all outbreaks, would be bursting with screwups. They couldn't avoid it. The world is falling apart. There would at least be some chaos. But we arrived the first day this place opened, and it's been operating like they've been doing this for years."

"The rest of you feel the same?" Ben asked.

"I hadn't thought about it that way, but Ruby's right," Jilly said. "Things have been too well organized."

"You guys are overthinking things," one of the men said. "If you're looking for problems, I'd bet there are plenty. We just haven't seen them."

A few of the older adults mumbled agreement.

"Besides," the guy said, "if they're not UN, who are they?"

No one had an answer for that.

Soon most everyone wandered off to bed, leaving only Ben and the girls from Ridgecrest still awake.

Ben asked them what had happened after the virus was released, and how they got there. As the girls talked, they all began hearing snores and deep breathing from the beds.

Ruby was in the middle of describing the day they left Ridgecrest when she shot a look back at the bunks, leaned forward, and whispered, "I think we should get out of here."

"Oh, really?" Valerie said. "And how do you expect us to do that? If you haven't noticed, they've got us locked up tight."

Ben broke the silence that followed. "Actually, there is

one potential weak point."

"And what would that be?" Valerie asked.

"This holding area is built near the center-field wall. The gap between the gate and the wall is no more than twenty feet, and the enclosure fence blocks some of the stadium lights back there. So it's darker than the rest of the stadium."

"And what good is that supposed to do us?"

"It also blocks the view of most of the guards."

"You're sure?" Jilly asked.

"Pretty sure."

"All right, smart guy, two problems," Valerie, Miss Negativity, said. "So how do we get on the other side of the fence, and if we do, what happens then? Correct me if I'm wrong, they may not see us at first, but they'll see us for sure if climb over the outfield wall."

"Jesus, Valerie, do you expect all the answers right off the bat?" Jilly said, glaring at the girl. "Yeah, those *are* problems, but it's at least worth thinking about, right? Unless you want to just sit here and see what happens."

Valerie's cheeks reddened as her eyes narrowed. "Don't you dare talk to me like that. I'm in charge here. I decide what we do."

The other girls started shifting uncomfortably in their chairs.

"Excuse me?" Jilly said. "I don't recall you being appointed dictator."

"You are a hair's width from crossing the line."

"That's too bad. I was hoping I'd already jumped over it. Want to know what I really think?"

"No, I don't."

"I think we should have all gone with Martina. I think it was a mistake to follow you here."

Valerie jumped out of her chair, looking as if she wanted to launch herself at Jilly.

Ben rose quickly to his feet. "Whoa. Let's all calm down. We're just talking here."

"Shut the fuck up. You're not part of this," Valerie said, then looked at the others. "This kind of bullshit fantasy talk isn't going to get us anywhere, so I think it's time we all got some sleep."

She headed down the aisle toward one of the bunks near the door. No one moved for several seconds, then the tall blonde girl mumbled, "Good night," and headed off for bed. Slowly, the others did the same, until the only ones left were Ben, Jilly, and Ruby.

"What was that all about?" Ben whispered.

"If you weren't Martina's boyfriend, I think she would have been more open to the idea," Ruby said, her voice as low as his.

"What does Martina have to do with it?"

"It's stupid," Jilly said. "Not even worth talking about. Let's just say they've been butting heads for a very long time."

"To hell with her," Ruby said. She looked at Ben. "I say we figure out a way for us to escape. The others will come."

"Count me in, too," Jilly said.

Ben smiled. "I don't think we have to figure anything out."

"What do you mean?" Ruby asked.

"Didn't you guys ever watch the Dodgers play?"

Jilly shrugged. "Sometimes."

"Well, I watched them every time the Giants were down here," he said.

"Oh, wonderful. A Giants fan," Rudy said, feigning disgust.

"You should be happy you have a Giants fan here because I happen to know a little fact about the part of the center-field wall right behind us."

"And what's that?" Ruby asked.

"It swings open."

19

OMEGA THREE TOOK a drag on his cigarette as he began another three-sixty scan of the town.

It wasn't a large place, so he could see pretty much everything from his post on the roof of the three-story school. Power to the town had been out for nearly two weeks now, but unlike other places in the world, this had not been due to system failure or emergency shutdown. The electricity here had been intentionally terminated within minutes after the Implementation Day go signal was received. The purpose had been twofold: first, killing the lights made it possible for those on sentry duty to use night-vision gear after sunset, greatly decreasing the chances of missing unwanted visitors; and second, cutting the power ensured the town's native population would die faster.

It had been six days since the last resident was seen on the snowy streets. A thorough check three days later confirmed no one remained alive—an assignment Omega Three was glad he hadn't drawn.

The town tonight was as quiet as it had been on all the other nights. The only signs of life he'd picked up were those of Omega One, Two, and Four, all of whom were at their assigned positions.

"Omega team, this is Tau One." The earpiece of Omega Three's comm gear was so high quality, it almost sounded like Tau One was standing right next to him.

"Tau One, this is Omega One," the Omega team leader replied. "Go ahead."

"Tau team deploying now."

"Copy, Tau One."

Omega Three turned his attention toward the northern edge of town, and immediately spotted the glowing green blobs of the four-man Tau team. He followed its progress, and watched as every few blocks one member would peel off onto a different road. The last man headed straight for the school. Omega Three tracked him until he entered the building.

One minute later, at exactly fifteen seconds before eleven p.m., the roof door opened and the Tau team member stepped out.

When the man reached the lookout position, he said, "Tau Two reporting. You're relieved."

Omega Three stepped back and pulled the goggles from his eyes. "Thank you. All quiet. Have a good evening."

As Tau Two moved into place, Omega Three headed for the door.

Retracing the path the relief crew had taken, he met up with the other members of Omega team. Like always, no one said a word as they walked out of town, passed the dead-end barrier that marked the end of the road, and into the snow-covered field. Sitting in the center of the clearing was a five-by-four-foot, concrete-sided building. To the casual observer, it looked like nothing more than a pumping station or perhaps a utility hut. It had a single door and no windows, and was painted a light shade of gray.

What the casual observer would not notice, even if he or she had moved in for a closer examination, were the micro cameras fitted into the eaves on all sides. They looked like nothing more than holes where screws were embedded.

And while there was a dead-bolt key slot on the door, it was only for show. The real lock was triggered by those on the inside.

Omega team trudged across the field to the building and stopped five feet in front of the door, as they'd been trained to do. For several seconds nothing happened, and then there was a faint click.

Omega One grabbed the handle of the door and pulled it open. One by one they filed inside the twenty-square-foot room, the last, Omega Four, securing the door behind him.

There were no pipes on the walls, no electrical junction boxes, no pumps, no transformers, no telecommunications switches. There were simply a light in the ceiling that came on when the door was closed, and a round metal cover on the floor.

Several more seconds passed before the hatch lifted soundlessly, revealing the forty-foot vertical tunnel that led to Project Eden's most secret base.

To home, as Omega Three had come to think of it.

To Dream Sky.

January 7th

World Population
786,910,553

20

THE CLOSEST AIRPORT to Ward Mountain large enough to accommodate the Boeing 757 carrying the survivors from Isabella Island was in Salt Lake City. Unfortunately, with no one working maintenance, the runways at SLC were buried under several feet of snow, rendering them unusable. The next closest airport was in Las Vegas.

The plane was met there an hour after it landed by three tour buses driven by Resistance members. The first stop was a restaurant on the edge of town, where other Resistance members had been dropped off earlier to prepare dinner for everyone.

There was little talk as the island's survivors ate and then climbed back on the buses. Within a few miles after hitting the road again, most were asleep.

Pax wasn't one of them. As the bus headed north, he rose from his seat and moved to the front. There, he took a spot on the exit stairs, leaned against the wide dash, and stared at the road ahead.

His was the first of the three buses, so the headlights lit up only asphalt and dirt and brush. He wasn't looking at any of it, though. No longer needing to worry about keeping Robert and his people alive, he was finally facing something he'd been trying hard to ignore.

Matt was dead.

That didn't seem possible. He desperately wanted

someone to tell him Matt's death had been a trick, that when he reached Ward Mountain, Matt would limp out to the bus to greet Pax, a stupid grin on his face.

Pax couldn't picture how they would move forward now. Matt had not only been the brains of the Resistance, but also the soul. How could that void ever be filled?

And then there was Billy, too, the Ranch's former doctor. It had been less than three weeks since he'd died in the explosion in Cleveland.

Pax's two best friends in the world—gone. Both died because of the Sage Flu, but neither from it.

Memories of conversations and trips and projects they had all been a part of spun through his mind, until he forced himself to stop. He started to think about the future, about what they were going to do, but that just circled him back to the loss of Matt and Billy and so many others.

What finally saved him was focusing on what Captain Ash had asked him about.

What about the letters DS together? They sound familiar?

Pax had never heard the phrase Augustine dream sky before, but the letters DS? Definitely. From Matt himself, years ago.

Could what Matt had thought they represented be true?

As the bus suddenly came to a stop, Pax blinked and looked around. They appeared to be in a town.

He turned to the driver—Juliana Herbert—and said, "Is something wrong?"

"We're here," she told him.

"Here where?" This wasn't Ward Mountain.

"Ely," she said. "We cleared out a couple of hotels. There's a La Quinta right over there." She pointed to her left and then gestured to the right. "And a Motel 6 half a block that way. There'll be some sharing, but there are more than enough beds."

Of course.

If he'd been thinking clearly, he'd have realized there wasn't enough room for everyone at Ward Mountain. The facility could accommodate less than half the personnel the Ranch had been able to house.

"We're not leaving them alone, are we?" he asked.

She shook her head. "We've got people to help with logistics, and a couple of medical folks to tend to the sick and anyone who needs attention. Ward Mountain will also be in constant touch, so if need be, we can get people over here in a hurry."

Pax could hear some of the people stirring behind him. He was about to go back and wake Robert when a van pulled to a stop next to the bus. The two occupants jumped out, opened the side cargo door, and started pulling out armfuls of what looked like cloth bags.

After each man was loaded up, the newcomers approached the bus door.

"You're going to want to get back," Juliana said.

Pax moved into the central aisle but stayed near the front.

When the doors opened, a blast of frigid air rushed inside. The two men from the van hurried in, and Juliana quickly closed the door again. The damage was already done, though. The temperature—at least at the front of the van—had dropped a good fifteen degrees.

"How many you have in here?" one of the men asked Juliana.

"Forty-eight," she replied.

"Here," the man closest to Pax handed him the items in his arms. "We need to get a few more."

Coats, Pax realized. The subzero type skiers used.

The second man set his pile at Pax's feet, then he and his partner headed back out. As more cold air rushed in, Pax started passing out the jackets.

"I'm going to wish I stayed on the island, aren't I?" Robert said when Pax reached his seat.

"Don't worry," Pax said. "It'll probably hit thirty degrees here in a day or two."

"Celsius or Fahrenheit?"

Pax tossed him a coat and moved on.

After he passed everything out, he returned to Robert and

said, "Can I borrow you for a second?"

"Sure." Robert looked over at his seatmate, Estella. "Be right back."

Pax led him outside and explained the lowdown on the living situation.

When he was through, Robert asked, "What about the ones with the flu?"

"Medical team on site."

"Are you staying?"

"Wish I could, but I've got work to do. Our facility is just over the hill, not more than twenty minutes away. If you need to talk to me, grab one of our people and they'll get me on the line."

Robert seemed disappointed, but said, "Okay."

"I realize this isn't the perfect situation, but—"

"No, it's all right. Really. We're all just glad we're still alive. Someday it would be nice to go somewhere warm again, but for now this will do fine."

"Glad to hear that."

From down the street came the rumble of a powerful engine. Pax turned toward the noise and saw it belonged to a dark-colored Mustang. As it neared the buses, the vehicle slowed to a crawl.

The window rolled down.

"I thought you might need a ride."

Pax smiled and rushed over to the car, giving Chloe a hug through the opening.

"I do, indeed," he said. As he stood back up, he looked over at Robert. "I'd like to introduce you to Chloe White. She's, uh, one of our frontline people."

Robert walked over and held out his hand.

"Chloe, this is Robert Adams."

Her eyebrow shot up as she grabbed his palm. "The savior of Isabella Island. Nice to meet you."

"Uh, I'm not...no...there was a lot of..."

Chloe laughed. "Hold on to that modesty. It's attractive."

Robert's mouth opened a couple of times, but nothing came out.

Pax slapped him on the back. "I gotta go. But I'll see you again soon. I promise."

"Okay," Robert managed. "Be safe."

WARD MOUNTAIN NORTH, NEVADA

ASH HAD INTENTIONALLY fallen asleep on top of his covers, fully clothed.

He had argued a bit with Chloe about who should pick up Pax, but in the end she won. Thankfully.

He'd stretched out after dinner, thinking he'd sleep for only an hour or two, but when he looked over at his clock again, it was nearly two a.m.

A jolt of adrenaline shot him out of bed and into the public corridor outside his family's rooms. He made a beeline for the comm center, where he found three women he didn't know by name manning the stations.

"Does anyone know if Chloe or Pax is back?" he asked.

The closest comm tech turned toward the door, her eyes widening when she saw who he was. "Captain Ash," she said. "Um, no. They're on their way. Should be here any minute."

"Thanks," he said.

He hurried to the main entrance, grabbed a coat off one of the pegs, and stepped outside.

The moon was low on the western horizon, the stars packing the rest of the sky, leaving only small pockets of black unfilled. At first there didn't appear to be anyone on the road leading to the highway, then twin beams of light popped up from a dip about two miles out.

Ash stomped around, trying to keep warm. He knew he should go back inside but he was too keyed up. He couldn't help but feel a sense of urgency about figuring out the meaning of Matt's message. Add to that the potential of striking another blow at the Project Eden directorate and it was a wonder he wasn't running down the road to meet the car halfway.

Finally, the dark Mustang pulled under the camouflage netting that covered the base's parking area, and stopped. As

Ash jogged over, the doors opened and Chloe and Pax climbed out.

This was the first time the two men had seen each other since the hunt to find Bluebird to stop the Project from releasing the virus, so they threw their arms around each other in a bear hug.

"So good to see you, Captain," Pax said.

"Likewise," Ash told him.

As soon as they parted, they started walking toward the base entrance.

"Chloe filled me in on what's going on in Mumbai," Pax said. "She also said Rachel's basically removed herself from things."

"Only temporarily, I'm sure," Ash said. "You might be able to bring her out of it better than any of us."

"I don't know about that, but I'll give it a try when I get a moment." Pax glanced at Chloe then back at Ash. "So the one thing Chloe and I didn't discuss is this issue you asked me about on the phone."

"DS," Ash said.

"Yeah."

"What do you think the letters mean?"

Pax grimaced. "There's no easy answer."

"So we've gathered."

Pax rubbed the arms of his coat. "Do you mind if we get inside first? I've been down in the tropics for a few days. Think my blood's gone thin."

They entered the base and went straight to Chloe's room. It had been crowded when it contained only Ash and Chloe. With Pax there, they barely had enough room to breathe. Ash let the other two have the bed, and he took the chair by the door.

Pax spoke first. "Augustine dream sky. You're sure that's what he said?"

"One hundred percent," Ash said.

Pax frowned, thinking for a moment before shaking his head. "Like I told you on the phone, I'd never heard that phrase until you said it to me."

"But DS means something to you," Chloe said.

"It does."

When he didn't go on, Ash said, "Are you going to make us drag it out of you?"

"Sorry. Was just...remembering," Pax said. "The truth is, I don't know what the letters specifically stand for, and as far as I know, Matt didn't, either. What I do know is that Matt was obsessed with those two letters for several years, and was sure they referred to a secret Project Eden program."

"What kind of program?" Chloe asked.

"I wish I could tell you, but I don't know. There were times when it seemed Matt thought finding out about DS was almost as important as figuring out how to stop Implementation Day. He told me once if the Project was able to release the virus, DS might be the key to their ultimate success."

"What the hell does that mean?" Ash asked.

Pax shrugged. "He kept this one pretty tight. I think Billy and I might have been the only ones he ever talked to about it. I knew he grew frustrated when his contacts couldn't come up with anything more solid. After a while, he seemed to give it up, or maybe he just stopped talking about it, I don't know. Felt to me like he was chasing a ghost."

"Do you think DS stands for Dream Sky?"

Pax grunted a humorless laugh. "Who knows? Seems kind of a stretch to me. But it was the last thing he said, so I guess you have to give that theory some weight."

"Maybe even more than you think," Ash said. "Right before he said those words, he'd been with one of his inside contacts. That's how he got into the Las Cruces base."

Pax's eyebrows furrowed. "I didn't know that. Do you know which one?"

"C8."

"C8? Are you sure?"

"That's what he told us," Ash said.

Pax blew out a breath.

"Why?" Chloe asked. "What's the significance?"

"C8 was one of Matt's oldest contacts, one of his

deepest. He was someone Matt had been close to when he was still in the Project." He paused and looked at Ash and Chloe. "And he was the one Matt got the original info from about DS."

No one said anything for a moment.

"That's a pretty strong connection," Chloe said.

"Still might be nothing," Pax cautioned.

More silence.

"What about Augustine?" Ash asked.

"Doesn't mean anything specific to me," Pax said.

"There was an Emperor Augustine, wasn't there?"

"Augustus," Chloe corrected.

"Right. Augustus," Ash said. "Another form of the same name, though. Let me see, there was a St. Augustine. A city in Florida named after him. Isn't it the oldest European-founded city in the US? Maybe that's important."

"There's got to be hundreds of things the names could point to," Chloe said. "I'd kill for Google right now."

Pax tilted his head. "How many letters long is it? Nine?"

Ash ran the word through his mind again. "Yeah. Nine."

"I need paper and something to write with," Pax said in a burst of energy.

Chloe pulled a pad and a pen from inside the top drawer of her dresser, and handed them to him. He created a square three-by-three grid and wrote letters in each space—A-U-G in the top row, U-S-T in the middle, and I-N-E along the bottom. He then made several more grids, using different combinations of the letters in each. When he was through, he stared down at the paper.

"I'm not as good at this as Matt was," he said.

"Is that a code?" Ash asked.

"A key. I think." He patted the air above the pad with both hands. "It's here somewhere. I'm just not seeing it."

"May I?" Chloe asked.

Pax passed her the pad. "Have at it."

While she examined it, Ash asked, "How do you know it's a code?"

"Matt kept things with his Project Eden contacts to

himself most of the time. I think he was afraid one of us might get captured with the info. Felt the best way to protect those inside was to share only when absolutely necessary. I can probably count on one hand the number of times he showed me a communication he received."

"You said you knew how to get ahold of them, though."

"No. I said I knew where the information was that would tell us how. Unfortunately, it's at the Ranch, in the Bunker. I'm the only one who knows the combination to the safe, and I sure as hell wasn't going to give it to you over the radio."

Ash couldn't help but feel disappointed. Retrieving the information would mean a trip back to Montana, something none of them could afford to do right now.

"Tell me about the messages you did see," he said.

Pax closed his eyes for a second. "On the surface, each seemed like a note or letter you might receive from an old aunt or someone like that. Nothing really there. But every single one of them would begin with a nine-letter word, a decoder. Once you figured it out, you could use the result to pull the real message from the note."

"So how do you decode the word?"

Pax looked pained. "That's the problem. I saw Matt do this once, and that was years ago. I'm not the dumbest guy around by any means, but when it comes to this kind of thing, I just might be. I remember the squares. I remember him putting the letters in. I don't remember how he figured it out, though. Or how the code then unlocks the message. I missed something."

"But if we do figure it out, this…key will show us what dream sky really means, right?"

"Maybe. I don't know."

Chloe looked up from the pad, frowning. "I got nothing."

Ash took the pad and gave it a quick examination. He didn't expect anything to jump out at him, and he was right.

"Is there anyone here who might be good at this kind of thing?" he asked.

Chloe said, "Yeah. There is."

CALEB FINALLY ACKNOWLEDGED that he and his team were not superhuman and could not stay awake indefinitely. So a shift system was put in place that would allow each of them a generous six hours of sleep in the sectioned-off portion at the front of the trailer, always leaving three of them awake and working.

Caleb was about as deep into the unconscious world as one could get when Mya shook his shoulder.

"Hey, Caleb. Wake up."

Reluctantly, he opened his eyes. "What?"

"Get up. We've got company."

He looked at his watch and realized it hadn't been six hours yet. It had barely been two and a half.

"Why did you wake me up?"

"I told you. We've got company."

He angrily pushed himself up on an elbow. "What company?"

"Higher-up type of company. They want to talk to you."

"Did you tell them I was *asleep*?"

"I sure did."

He started to throw off his blanket, but halted and looked at Mya. "A little privacy?"

She rolled her eyes as she walked back around the partition.

Alone now, he hopped out of bed and pulled on his CAL TECH sweat pants and HAN SHOT FIRST T-shirt. He then headed into the main area like a bull entering the ring,, intending to give these higher-ups a piece of his mind. He figured it was probably someone from communications, or, more likely, the engineering department. The latter was ticked off at him for all the resources he'd been using since the India project had begun.

"Whatever the hell it is you want, it could have—"

His guests were not from engineering.

"Sorry to get you up so early, Caleb," Pax said. "I understand you've been working very hard."

Pax wasn't the only one who was there. Chloe and

Captain Ash were with him.

"Mr. Paxton, Captain Ash, Ms. White, I'm, uh, sorry. I didn't realize it was you." Caleb shot a quick glare at Mya.

She gave him an exaggerated shrug, like she had no idea why he'd be upset.

Forcing a smile, he said, "What can I do for you?"

"We have a puzzle we were hoping you and your team could solve for us."

"What kind of puzzle?"

Chloe set a pad of paper she'd brought with her on a desk. "Easier if we show you."

21

"GABRIEL, ARE YOU up?"

As he always did before he went to sleep, Gabriel had turned the volume down on his radio and tucked it in next to the pillow. He was not asleep, however, when Nyla's voice trickled out of the earpiece. He was simply lying there, eyes closed, performing his morning meditation.

"Gabriel?"

With a sigh, he grabbed the radio, stuck the receiver in his ear, and clicked on the mic. "Morning, L-One."

"Time to get up, big boy. L-Seven spotted someone heading down Sunset Boulevard but lost them in Silver Lake."

"Copy, L-One. Should be able to get to the Alvarado intersection in five."

"Copy that."

So much for a shower, Gabriel thought as he rolled out bed and pulled on his clothes.

He'd stayed at the same house on Scott Street for the last three days. It was near the middle of his assigned area and met his basic requirement of being dead-body free. The bonus was the bed. It had one of those mattresses made out of a material that conformed to his body. The damn things were so expensive, he'd wondered why anyone would spend money on them, but not anymore. He was sold. Good thing the prices had dropped.

He grabbed a couple energy bars from his pack before he slung it on and headed out the door into the still-dark morning.

Jogging most of the way, he reached the corner of Alvarado Street and Sunset Boulevard ahead of his promised time, and moved over to a small building housing a takeout place called Burrito King on the northwest corner. Standing at the front edge, he stopped and listened for footsteps.

All was quiet.

He thought about radioing Nyla and asking how long ago L-Seven had spotted the survivor, but decided it wasn't worth the effort. If the person was heading toward Dodger Stadium, Sunset Boulevard would be the logical route from Silver Lake. All Gabriel needed to do was wait.

He was starting in on his second energy bar when he heard the faint echo of a step. He put the bar away and leaned around the building to look west on Sunset. No one there, but the road bent to the right about seventy-five yards away so he couldn't see that far. He could hear more steps, though— rhythmic, unhurried, and definitely heading his way.

He considered moving down the road so he could get a better look, but his encounter with the runner the day before was still fresh in his mind, so he didn't want to be seen until he was ready to be. Besides, his position at Burrito King was about as good as he could get. It would hide him from the approaching person, even as the person passed by.

He stared down the road, his mind registering all the unmoving shapes, waiting to see one in motion. When the human silhouette finally moved into view, he ever so slowly eased his head back around the corner of the restaurant.

There was no change in the sound of the steps, only the continuous *thud-thud-thud* of rubber meeting asphalt.

As the person came abreast of Burrito King, Gabriel tensed, his eyes on the road. The moon had already dipped below the horizon, so the stars provided the only light. That was more than enough for him to get a good sense of the walker.

It was a guy, medium height, wearing a light jacket and

213

baseball cap. No backpack, though, which was kind of odd. Most of the people Gabriel and the rest of the team had come across had been carrying things.

He was concerned that maybe this wasn't a regular survivor, but one of Project Eden's people on patrol. But the unease lasted only a second because he had never seen one of them out alone, and he'd certainly never seen any of them unarmed, like this guy appeared to be.

So how are we going to handle this?

Get over to the guy before he realized what was going on?

Call out to him?

Or follow him for a bit and make sure he wasn't Project Eden?

The last seemed the most prudent. The guy was heading toward Nyla's position anyway. Worst case, she and Gabriel could close in together.

He let the survivor cross the Alvarado intersection, then he followed.

A block down, Sunset took a slight southeast turn, so Gabriel cut the gap between them to prevent losing sight of the guy. As he started to slow back down, the toe of his shoe tapped a discarded screw and sent it skittering across the road.

The man whipped around. "Who's there?"

Dammit!

"Sorry," Gabriel said, holding his hands out to show they were empty. "I didn't mean to scare you."

"Wh...why are you here? Are you following me?" the guy was clearly scared, his voice raised.

"Yes, I mean, it's not what you think. I'm here to help."

The guy started to back away from him. "I don't need your help. Thank you. Now leave me alone. Please."

There was a click over the receiver in Gabriel's ear. His eyes flicked past the man, down the street. Though he saw no one there, he knew the click meant Nyla was somewhere nearby.

He took a step forward. "I'm not going to hurt you."

"Good!" The man started to turn away.

"But if you're headed for the survival station, the people there will."

As the man looked back, Gabriel realized the survivor wasn't a man at all, but a young woman.

"What do you mean?" she asked.

"They aren't who they claim to be."

"What are you talking about?"

"The UN doesn't exist anymore. The people at the stadium are only taking in survivors so they can get rid of them."

"Get rid of them?" A look of total disbelief flooded her face. "You mean kill?"

"Yes."

"I don't believe you. You're…you're just saying that because…because…"

She turned and began running down Sunset.

"I'm not lying," Gabriel said as he took off after her. "I just want to talk to you."

His thighs ached, still remembering the chase from the day before. The runner had gotten away then, but Gabriel had no intention of letting it happen two days in a row. It wasn't easy, but he was starting to gain on the woman.

As the road took another bend to the right, Nyla rushed out from behind a car, reaching the middle of the road moments before the survivor got there.

"Whoa, whoa, whoa," she said, holding out her arms.

The woman tried to alter her course to go around Nyla, but she reacted too late and Nyla was able to grab her waist and hold on tight.

"Let me go!" the woman yelled, squirming.

She almost broke free, but Gabriel arrived in time to grab one of her arms.

"Calm down," he said. "I told you, we're not going to hurt you."

The woman continued to struggle.

"Relax," Gabriel said.

"We're trying to save your life," Nyla told her.

Whether it was Nyla's words or because the woman was

losing strength, she finally stopped struggling. Eyes narrowing, she said, "I don't believe you."

"We're telling the truth," Gabriel said. "The survival stations are really death traps. If you go in, you don't come out again."

"Why would they do that?"

"Because the people who are running them are the same ones who planted the shipping containers full of Sage Flu around the world. This is their way to finish what they started."

The woman looked stunned. "How can you know this?"

"We've been trying to stop them for a long time," Nyla said.

"You didn't do a very good job, then."

"No, we didn't."

"You want me to believe you," the survivor said, "prove it."

This was not the first time someone had said this, so Gabriel and Nyla were prepared.

"I'm going to pull my phone out of my pocket," Nyla said. "Okay?"

The woman nodded.

Nyla retrieved her phone, pulled up the video shot a few days before on a scouting trip to the stadium, and turned the screen so the man could see. On the trip, the closest she and Gabriel had been able to get was a hill right beyond the parking area, straight out from the back end of the stadium. This was the only part of the structure where there was no double-deck seating, just two sets of much smaller bleachers, one behind left field and one behind right.

Though the angle of the video was a bit acute, it clearly showed two large fenced-in areas on the playing field, with several people in each.

Nyla said, "We know from information gained about other survival stations that those are detention areas. They place people who are obviously sick in one, and those who are not in the other."

"But isn't that what they should do?" the survivor asked.

"Hold on." Nyla sped up the image until it zoomed in on a portion of the grandstands, and then she let the video play again. The picture moved around some because the zoom was so extreme, but there was no mistaking the man holding the rifle, facing the field. "Separating the ill and the non-ill does make sense, but putting them behind locked fences with razor wire on top and surrounding them with well-armed guards doesn't. The survivors go to these stations of their own free will. They *want* the help. They're not going to put up a fight, so why treat them like they would?"

"I…I don't know. But they must have their reasons."

"Then how about this? No survivors have left the stadium, and yet the amount of people in each detention area has dropped dramatically."

"That's not proof," the woman said. "You could be making that up."

"True," Nyla replied. "And there are other things I could tell you that you may or may not believe."

"Did you see the video on TV?" Gabriel asked.

"Why do you think I'm here?" the woman responded.

"I don't mean the video that claims to be a message from the UN. I'm talking about the one that went up several days go from that reporter who used to be with PCN."

"I don't know what you're talking about."

Nyla was already shuffling through her phone. She found Tamara Costello's video and hit PLAY.

The woman watched, rapt, as Tamara explained what was really going on.

When the video ended, she stared at the screen for several seconds before saying, "I don't know. I don't…"

Nyla watched her for a moment, then glanced at Gabriel and nodded. They both took a few steps back, giving the woman space.

"If you want to continue on, we won't stop you," Nyla said.

The woman shifted her gaze between the two of them.

"My…my friends are there," she said. "We were supposed to meet there. I…I…"

Gabriel's chest tightened. "When did they go there?"

"New Year's Eve."

A week before.

Gabriel wanted to say something comforting, but he thought the woman's friends were likely dead.

She stared at the ground, and when she looked up again, her eyes were hard and determined. "Can you show me?"

"That's probably not a good idea."

"You want me to believe you? Show me."

Nyla considered the request. "Gabriel can take you."

"Thank you."

"If it saves your life, we're happy to do it." Nyla held out her hand. "I'm Nyla."

The woman shook it. "Martina."

MARTINA GABLE DIDN'T know what to think. Were Nyla and Gabriel telling her the truth? Was it possible the UN message had been a fake? That its purpose had been to take even more lives? Only a few short weeks ago, that would have sounded like conspiracy-theory bullshit. But a few short weeks ago, there hadn't been survival stations and the release of a virus that had killed who knew how much of the human race.

And then there was the video from that Tamara Costello. Martina had seen the reports the woman did during the spring outbreak. The news said the woman had died during the mini-epidemic, but clearly she had not. Her words, more than anything else, were what kept Martina from marching up to the front door of Dodger Stadium right then.

Until she had more proof, she'd keep her guard up, something she'd stopped doing the last few days.

When she had finally caught up to the woman driving Ben's Jeep, and been told Ben was dead, Martina had slipped into a state of despair. She still couldn't remember where she had gone or what she had done in the forty-eight hours that followed. Her family, most of the people she knew, and then Ben. It was too much.

After she finally began to pull out of her funk the day before, she'd found herself near the ocean in Santa Monica. She had wandered out onto the pier, passed the arcade games and amusement-park rides, to the very end, where she leaned against the railing and stared out at the vast, empty sea.

She knew she had a choice: she could either give up or take control again and live. In the face of all the loss caused by the pandemic, could giving up be considered a weak decision? She vacillated on the answer for a while, but as more of the fog lifted from her brain, she saw the truth. Giving up *would* be weak. She had to live. If not for herself then for those she knew who had died. Besides, she still had friends who were alive. Friends, she realized, who were not far from where she was at that very moment.

Her first thought, of course, had been of Noreen and Riley and Craig, but she didn't know where they were. What she did know, though, was where they would eventually go, if they hadn't already—the survival station at Dodger Stadium.

She figured the stadium couldn't have been more than ten or fifteen miles away at most, so that afternoon she had walked off the pier and headed east, deciding to go on foot and use the time to fully clear her mind. She grew tired not long after sunset, so she found an apartment free of the smell of death and collapsed onto a couch in the living room.

It was as dark when she woke as it had been when she'd lain down. She checked her watch and saw it was about ten minutes to one in the morning. There was no question of going back to sleep, though. The anticipation of seeing her friends again would not allow it.

She hit the road and walked alone through the darkened streets. Alone, that was, until she'd heard Gabriel behind her.

Now here she was walking beside him into a hilly neighborhood north of Sunset Boulevard.

"I thought I was closer to the stadium than this," she said after they'd been hiking for a while.

"You were, well, are. It's over there." He pointed to the right. "We're going around to the backside. Same place we shot the video. Best view."

The sun began to rise as they headed up a ridge road. The left side was lined with homes, and the right with a narrow valley filled mostly with trees and grass.

They continued until the valley began to close.

"Going off road now, so watch your step," Gabriel said.

He led her down the slope, staying under the trees to avoid the open grass areas. At the bottom, they came to a four-lane street.

Gabriel paused under the trees and scanned the road before whispering, "Quick across."

In a sprint, he led her to the other side and up the eastern slope. At the top, they crossed a smaller road and moved rapidly through a cluster of buildings. A sign identified the area as the Los Angeles Police Academy. Unlike most of the other places Martina had seen, the parking lot was jam-packed with cars gathering dust. She guessed they belonged to recruits and active officers who had been called to a duty they never completed.

She and Gabriel moved down the edge of a clearing, then along a trail that paralleled the main road, and passed another building complex before finally stopping.

"We'll cross here and go up that hill," he whispered, pointing at the land on the other side of the road. "Follow exactly where I go, and if I motion for you to get down, don't hesitate."

"I won't."

He checked the road in both directions, and then sprinted across. Martina followed right behind, matching Gabriel step for step. Once more under the cover of trees, they climbed the small slope and headed south until the hill began to descend again. Through the branches, she could see glimpses of the large parking area and the stadium, but her view was too obstructed for her to make out many details.

Gabriel knelt and removed his pack. From inside, he pulled out a pair of binoculars and motioned for Martina to follow him. Staying in a crouch, they worked their way to the right until most of the foliage in front of them cleared away, and then stretched out on the ground.

There it was. Dodger Stadium, the banks of seats brightly lit by the morning sun.

Gabriel looked through the binoculars, adjusted the magnification, and handed them to Martina.

She raised the glasses to her eyes.

"Concentrate on the center," he instructed. "Over that black barrier separating the two outfield bleachers. Like I said before, the angle isn't perfect, but...well, just look."

The eye line he suggested allowed her to see a portion of the outfield area and all of the infield, or at least where they used to be. Now, like she'd seen on the video, there were fences cutting across the grass and dirt, with posts hammered into the field.

"They look empty," she said, taking in the two larger areas.

"What do?"

"The...detention areas? Is that what you called them?"

"The first few days they were pretty full, but after Tamara's video knocked that phony UN message off the air, the number of new arrivals decreased considerably. Out of those who still came, we've been able to get to most of them first." He paused. "Now look around the grandstands. Lower deck, top end, right before it disappears."

Martina focused in on the seats and slowly began to pan across the stadium. "What am I looking—" She froze.

"You see them?"

"Yeah."

Dead center in her binoculars, facing the playing field, was a soldier with a rifle. She searched some more and found others, all facing the field. It was all exactly as Nyla and Gabriel had said. Granted, none of it proved this wasn't a UN operation, but her doubt was beginning to fade.

She refocused back on the field and noticed something she'd missed before. "There's another fenced-in area in the outfield."

"As far as we can tell, it's a special holding area. It went up a few days after the survival station opened."

"Why is it covered like that?"

"We're not sure. Maybe so people in the other enclosures can't see inside."

"Maybe my friends are in there," she said.

"I don't want to get your hopes up," he said. "It's more likely they were put in one of the other two. If any of them were sick, they would have been in the one to the left, the rest in the other."

"They're immune so they wouldn't have been put in the sick one," she said.

He silently cursed Nyla for putting him in the position of dealing with this. "Most of those who have survived are simply lucky, not immune."

"I realize that. But we're all immune. We had the flu."

His eyes narrowed. "Excuse me?"

"We were all sick, you know, during the outbreak last spring. I'm pretty sure it made us all immune."

"How many friends are we talking about?" he asked.

"Well, there were nine of us, but me and three of the others headed north to look for my boyfriend."

"Your boyfriend?"

"He had the flu, too."

"And you know for a fact he's still alive?"

Water glistened in her eyes. "He was. He'd left messages for me on my phone. But..." She fell silent, remembering what the woman on the road had told her.

"These five other friends of yours," Gabriel said after a moment. "They're the ones who went to the survival station on New Year's Eve."

"Yes."

He stared out at the stadium, then whispered, "Is that what it's for?"

"What are you talking about?"

He looked at her as if he hadn't realized he'd spoken out loud. "The special enclosure. I was just...well...see, none of the other survivor stations have reported a similar space. But that would make sense, wouldn't it? Los Angeles is the closest station to the spring outbreak. If those who had survived the spring outbreak are actually immune, this would be the station they would come to. So once Project Eden realized it, I would think they'd want to separate them from the other survivors."

"Who is Project Eden?"

"That's the people running the stations."

"So you're saying you think my friends *could* be in there."

He hesitated, and then nodded. "I think it's a possibility."

She lowered the binoculars, but kept her eyes on the stadium. "We have to get them out."

"I might be wrong. There's a good chance they aren't there. Besides, there are only eight of us here. That means those guys with the rifles outnumber us more than two to one."

"Not eight. Nine. You're forgetting about me."

22

SURVIVAL STATION, CHICAGO, ILLINOIS
FROM THE JOURNAL OF BELINDA RAMSEY
ENTRY DATE—JANUARY 7, 8:00 AM CST

THE DOCTORS DIDN'T come back until this morning. Woke us up again just like yesterday. They read more names. Sixteen. This time no one else volunteered to join them.

I don't feel like writing anything more.

23

NEITHER SANJAY NOR Kusum had ever been so far outside Mumbai. In fact, until the outbreak, neither had ever ventured more than a few miles from the city. That had changed when they moved to their new home at the former boarding school. As for Darshana, she had been to Goa several times to visit family, but nowhere else.

The thing that felt the strangest was being so far from the ocean. It had always been there, a constant in their lives even if they didn't see it every day. Now it was growing farther and farther behind them, the distance feeling somehow suffocating.

They took the expressway, most of the time surrounded by kilometers and kilometers of untended fields, some barren and waiting to be planted, some fully grown and waiting for a harvest that would never come. There were few cars on the road, so for the majority of the trip, they were able to maintain a steady pace.

The tense moments came as they skirted around larger cities like Akota and Ahmedabad and Udaipur. At least Mumbai was a city they had known. These others were masses of unfamiliar buildings and homes where millions had once lived. Ahmedabad was the worst. The wind was blowing in such a way that even with their windows rolled up, they could smell the death.

It was almost a blessing when night fell and all they could see was the road in front of them. But that brought its own sense of eeriness. A land of over a billion people being so dark and unpopulated seemed impossible, as if someone had built giant blinders along the sides of the road to keep the normal life beyond out of view.

A sign ahead announced Jaipur was only fifty-four kilometers away. Forty minutes and they would be there.

"Would you like me to drive now?" Sanjay asked Darshana. He had taken the first shift that morning, driving for nearly six hours before turning over the duty to Kusum. Five hours after that, Darshana had assumed the driver's seat.

"I'm okay," she said. "But thank you."

Sanjay glanced into the back to check on his wife. She was lying across the backseat, but her eyes were open.

"We are almost there," he said.

"Finally." She stretched her arms and sat up. "What time is it?"

"Almost midnight."

He held out his hand and she put hers in it.

"Did you sleep well?" he asked.

"Do I look like I slept well?"

"You always look beautiful to me."

She frowned, but squeezed his hand.

"What is that?" Darshana said.

As Sanjay turned around, Darshana flipped off the headlights and took her foot off the accelerator.

The white glow of bright lights rose like a halo beyond a rise in the road ahead.

"Is that the city?" Kusum asked, peeking between the seats.

"No," Sanjay. "I do not think so."

The glow seemed to be coming from just beyond the crest, far too close to be from Jaipur. It was also too concentrated to be coming from something more than a single building, and unless the highway curved drastically on the other side of the hill, it appeared to be right in the middle of the road.

About a hundred and fifty meters from the top of the rise, Darshana let the car come to a stop without her touching the brakes. She moved the transmission into PARK and killed the engine.

"Shall we take a look?" she asked.

When they opened their doors, the interior dome light came on. All three reached up quickly to turn it off, but it was Kusum who got there first. They had to allow their eyes to readjust to the darkness before climbing out.

There was a thin, shoulder-high barrier running along either side of the expressway, and down the middle a shorter metal railing dividing the two directions. They moved along the side barrier until they reached a break and were able to hop down off the expressway onto the local road that paralleled it.

They crossed the blacktop to a row of dark shops and stands, and used them to conceal their presence as they continued up the rise.

Nearing the top, the glow grew considerably brighter, making Sanjay sure its source wasn't much farther beyond the crest. He noticed something else, too—the light seemed to be accompanied by two distinct noises, a low hum and even lower rumble.

Ten meters from the apex, he tapped the two women's shoulders and motioned for them to follow him around behind the roadside restaurant they were about to pass. From there they were able to get over the crest unobserved, and then found a gap between the next two buildings wide enough for them to take it back to the other side. At the end of this alley, they peeked across the road at the expressway.

Sanjay had been right. The source of the lights was nearby.

Perhaps another fifty meters down the highway was a set of portable lights raised at least five meters into the sky. They were so intense that the road below them was lit up like day. Right in front of the lights, several cars had been moved into the lanes to prevent passage. There was a gap wide enough for only one vehicle to pass through. Parked in the gap was a military truck, and standing guard on either side were soldiers in all-too-familiar UN uniforms.

A roadblock. Similar to the ones they'd seen in Mumbai. The only difference being that this one was several kilometers outside the city. Could that have had anything to do with this Director Mahajan? Did he need extra protection?

The three spies retreated to the back of the building.

"How are we going to get into the city?" Darshana asked.

"They will only be guarding the major roads," Sanjay said. He looked around at the back of the buildings. "Somewhere around here there must be a map. We find one and pick out the least likely route to be guarded."

They decided to hunt for one back on the other side of the rise, and found a whole stack of maps in a little market. They were able to identify four routes not too far away that they thought would give them the best chance of avoiding Project Eden soldiers.

With the Land Cruiser's engine off, Sanjay and Darshana pushed on the back as Kusum steered the vehicle in a U-turn. The downhill slope of the road was enough that the SUV started to gain a little speed as it came out of the turn, forcing Sanjay and Darshana to hop in on the run.

The first turnoff came to quickly for them to take, but the second was far enough away that they thought they could use the brakes without the brake lights being seen. After they were off the expressway, they started the engine and, keeping their headlights off, worked their way past fields and small villages until they found the road they were looking for.

The gamble paid off, and soon they entered Jaipur.

As much as they all would have liked to get a look at the survival station, the tension of the last fifty minutes had added to their exhaustion. They found a small hotel down a dark, narrow street and, at Kusum's suggestion, used one of the rooms with two beds so that Darshana would not be alone.

As Sanjay emptied his pockets onto the tiny round table by the bed, he pulled out the phone Arjun had given him. He had totally forgotten about it during the journey. Curious, he touched the button that brought it to life, but never having had a smartphone himself, he was unsure how to access the picture his friend had put on there.

"Problem?" Darshana asked. She was sitting on her bed while Kusum was down the hall using the toilet.

"The picture from the Americans is on here. I don't…" He paused, embarrassed. "I don't know how to look at it."

She stood up. "May I try?" He tossed her the phone, and within seconds she said, "Here we go."

A moment after she handed it back, Kusum returned, but Sanjay barely noticed. He stared at the phone.

"Sanjay?" Kusum said. "Is something wrong?"

It took a moment for him to realize she was talking to him. He turned the screen so she could see.

"The man they want us to watch for, he was Director Dettling's assistant in Mumbai," he said. "It is van Assen."

EN ROUTE AMSTERDAM TO JAIPUR
FOUR AND A HALF HOURS FROM DESTINATION

WILLEM VAN ASSEN finished the last of his coffee and carried his empty cup to the galley. Though he had his pick of first-class seats, there were no flight attendants.

A shame, really. There was nothing like having all your needs taken care of while you were whisked across the globe.

He peeked through the closed curtain into the business-class section. The plane, an Airbus A330-300 with a capacity of carrying 295 people, had only fourteen other passengers on this flight. Thankfully, they were all security team members. By Project regulations, this meant they were assigned to the economy section or, if available, business class, but never first.

Technically, van Assen wasn't supposed to be using first class either, but no one was more senior than he on the flight, so he had taken the liberty and assigned himself to the foremost cabin. As he'd expected, no one had questioned him.

Most of the security team appeared to be asleep, though a few people were either reading or watching a movie on the video system. No one had told van Assen why the others were on the plane, but it was easy to guess. Director Mahajan's status within the Project had just been elevated to the very top. Increasing the security around him would be a natural consequence.

Van Assen let the curtain fall back into place and returned to his seat, hoping to get a few hours of rest before they arrived.

As he closed his eyes, he thought once more about his situation within the Project. His new position was definitely a step in the right direction, so why was he feeling uneasy?

The simple answer would have been because he was heading back to India, where things hadn't gone so well on his last assignment. But that wasn't it.

The truth was harder to pinpoint. It was more a sense, really, a feeling that something was off within the Project itself. Not the goals or the steps being taken to achieve them—those were rock solid, as far as he was concerned—but more with the actual membership.

He had noticed it first with Senior Manager Dettling in Mumbai after the prisoners had escaped. It was a loss of confidence, as if the faith Dettling had had in the Project was crumbling.

After van Assen realized this, he began to see the signs in others. Little things—missed details, far-off looks, drifting attention spans, and perhaps not verbal but visual signs of second-guessing.

Was he reading too much into things? And if he wasn't, did any of it really matter?

Probably not. The Project was on the proverbial rails and could not be stopped now.

Still, the unease wouldn't go away.

He'd have to keep an eye on things, and if need be, act decisively.

For the Project.

And, maybe a little bit, to help his own rise to the top.

It was this last thought, this comforting vision of a future where he had a say in decisions, that finally relaxed his mind enough for him to fall asleep.

24

"I DON'T CARE, Dad. You've still got a long way to go before you're better, and getting only a few hours of sleep every night isn't helping. You're going to lie down now."

Josie had given Ash that little speech right after they finished breakfast. She and Brandon had then escorted him back to their quarters and waited until he climbed into bed.

"We're going to be standing outside the door to make sure no one bothers you," Brandon told him. "So don't even think about sneaking out."

"Wait," Ash said. "If something comes up, I need to—"

"Dad, you *need* to sleep," Josie said. As if she could read his mind, she grabbed the stack of Matt's journals on the shelf by the bed and added, "There'll be no pretending to sleep, either. We'll be checking."

He lay back on his pillow. "Okay, fine. Whatever you say, warden."

He had thought he'd rest his eyes for maybe twenty minutes, a show of good faith, then he'd get up and they would let him out. But, like his nap the night before, when he opened his eyes again, hours had passed.

Apparently, his honor guards had decided they were no longer necessary because they were gone when he exited the room.

Anxious to find out if Caleb had made any progress, Ash made his way back to the comm trailer. As he entered, Mya and Devin looked over from the terminals they were using.

"For God's sake, shut it," Devin said, shivering.

Ash stepped inside and closed the door.

"Oh, sorry, Captain. I didn't realize it was you."

"Yeah, he's a dick to most other people," Mya said to Ash.

"How's it going?" Ash asked, walking over to them.

"We've recorded forty-seven video conversations and nearly three times as many audio," Mya said.

"Anything of interest?"

"You'll have to ask Crystal. She's set up some people to go through them all. It's taking all our effort just to keep up with the volume. No time to listen in."

"I'll check with her, then."

"That's not the best part, though," Mya said.

"Is that right? Then what is?"

She looked at Devin. "It's your thing."

Devin grinned but said nothing.

"You're not getting a drumroll, if that's what you're waiting for," Mya said. "Just tell him."

Devin shot her a quick, dirty look before saying to Ash, "I've been able to tap into their computer system."

Ash stared at him. "Are you serious?"

Before Devin could answer, Mya said, "Not to take all the wind out of his sails, but some of the credit goes to Arjun and Prabal."

"They only did what I told them," Devin argued.

"And if they didn't, you wouldn't have gotten in."

"True. I'll admit that. They do deserve some credit for helping."

"Look," Ash said sharply.

Mya and Devin turned to him, startled.

"No one's handing out medals at the moment, so for now it doesn't matter who gets credit. What I want to know is what kind of access we're talking about. Just basic or can you dig through everything?"

Devin looked a bit uncomfortable. "I'm still in the middle of mapping the system, but given what I've seen so far, I'm confident we'll have access to whatever we want."

This was more than Ash could have hoped for. Being able to peruse the Project Eden database would be a huge game changer.

"You're sure they don't know we're inside?"

"Positive. It's not the first system I've hacked."

A sound from beyond the racks at the other end of the trailer reminded Ash why he was there. "Is that Caleb back there?"

"No," Mya said. "Jesse. Caleb's inside the base."

"Communications?"

Mya shrugged. "He's been working on that code of yours all morning." She nodded at a counter space covered with sheets of crumpled paper. "Chloe came in a while ago. They talked for a few minutes, then all of a sudden Caleb jumped up and the two of them ran out."

"Do you know what they were talking about?"

She shrugged. "No clue."

Devin shook his head.

Ash spotted a handheld radio and snapped it up.

After tuning in to the band Chloe would be on, he pushed the talk button and said, "Ash for Chloe. Come in."

Static.

"Chloe, where the hell are you?"

Still no reply.

He switched to the comm room's band.

"Comm, this is Ash," he said. "I'm looking for Chloe White. Have any of you seen her?"

A pause, then—

"Leon here. I saw Chloe about thirty minutes ago, heading toward residential section A."

"Was she with Caleb?"

"Didn't see him."

"Okay. Thanks, Leon."

Ash thought for a moment. Chloe could have only been passing through that area on the way to engineering or medical or one of the storerooms. But he had a pretty good feeling none of those was her destination.

He set the radio down. "Get ahold of me the moment you've finished your assessment," he told Devin as he headed for the door.

RESIDENTIAL SECTION A was beyond the weapons training room in the northeastern portion of the base.

As he headed down the hallway toward it, a voice called out behind him, "What are you doing up?"

Josie.

Turning, he said, "It's okay. Only woke up a few minutes ago."

She stared at him as if wondering whether to believe him or not.

"You were right. I needed it. I feel better now. Thanks for making me do that."

"You shouldn't be running around."

"Honey, I have work to do. You know that."

A quiet second. "Have you eaten lunch?"

"Not yet."

"I'll get you something. Where are you going?"

"Um, I'm looking for Chloe. I'll, uh, stop by the cafeteria in a bit."

"Dad…"

"I promise." Before she could say anything else, he said, "I'll see you later," and continued on his way.

When he reached Matt's room, he stopped and listened at the door. Voices inside, Chloe's and Caleb's. As soon as he knocked, they went quiet.

"Chloe, it's Ash. Let me in," he said after knocking again.

The door jerked open.

"Finally," Chloe said. "Do you have them?"

"Have what?"

"The journals. I sent Brandon to tell you we needed them ten minutes ago."

"I must have missed him. I went out looking for you guys."

"Then how did…never mind." She grabbed Ash's arm and pulled him inside.

Caleb was sitting on Matt's never-used bed, several of the journals spread out around him, open. Among them were a laptop, several wadded up pieces of paper, and a small stack of paperback books.

As Chloe shut the door, she whispered, "He's cracked it."

"Augustine?" Ash asked.

"Uh-huh."

"So does that mean we also know what dream sky means?"

Without looking up from the pad of paper in his lap, Caleb said, "Dream sky means Dream Sky."

Ash said, "But I thought the key word translated the message."

"It does," Caleb said. "But Dream Sky wasn't the message it was intended to be used on."

"Then what message does it translate? And what the hell is dream sky?"

"Okay, question two, I'm almost positive Dream Sky is a place," Caleb said. "And, question one, that's why I need those other journals."

"So you don't know for sure the code works?" Ash asked.

"When did I say that? I never said that."

"You just said you need the other journals to see what it translates."

"What I need the other journals for is to get the full picture of the message."

"It's spread out," Chloe said. "It appears to be an ongoing conversation."

"We both read the journals," Ash said. "We didn't see any kind of conversation."

Chloe picked up one of Matt's notebooks. "The numbers at the end of the entries," she said, opening the book and pointing at a page. "That's the conversation."

Ash took the book from her and stared at the number.

After a moment he said, "So Augustine translates all of these?"

"Not Augustine per se," she told him. "It's kind of—"

"A mind blower if you really think about it," Caleb said, unable to contain his excitement. "They used a combination of methods. I have no idea how Matt received the numbers, but at some point he would also receive a key word of nine letters." He flipped through some pages on his pad, found what he wanted, and turned it so Ash could see. It was a table with the letters of the alphabet across the top, and below, the numbers 0-9 repeated until each slot was filled. "With the key word they used a modified Vigenère cipher."

Caleb turned to the next page. Here there were dozens more tables, each with the alphabet across the top, but with the numbers in various different arrangements. The number one was circled several times.

He tapped the circled one. "This is it."

"How do you know?"

"I didn't at first," Caleb said as he set the pad down and pulled one of the paperback books from the stack. "There was a lot of hit and miss. Hell, I wasn't even sure it *was* numbers at first, but…" He turned the book over and held it out to Ash. "Here. Read that back to me." He tapped the white box near the bottom of the cover.

"US six dollars and ninety-nine—"

"No, no, no. That!" Caleb pointed again.

Ash read the number aloud.

"Now look at this," Caleb said as he picked up the pad again and turned to the next page.

Here there was a single, nine-letter string, A-U-G-U-S-T-I-N-E, and underneath, numbers in a seemingly random order.

It wasn't random.

Ash looked back at the book and then at the number. "It's the same except for the first digit."

"First digit doesn't matter. For book ISBN numbers, the first just indicates what language it's in. Since they were dealing with English, which would either be a zero or a one, they didn't worry about that." He took the book from Ash.

"Now this is the real key. Get it? The nine-letter word would point Matt at which book he needed, then he'd use that to decipher the previous message."

"What if he didn't have the book already?" Ash asked. "That might take a day or two or more to track it down."

"It would also depend on how quickly he received the key word after getting the original message," Caleb pointed out. "The thing is, we know from Matt's journals that he was receiving other messages from his contacts inside Project Eden, ones he could read right away. This special number method"—he held up the book—"was limited to a very specific topic."

"Which was?" Ash asked.

"DS," Chloe said.

He looked at the back of the paperback again. "I don't understand how—"

"Aha!" Caleb said. "You're wondering where that book came from, aren't you?"

"I am." If Matt had been passed the code word in Las Cruces, he shouldn't have had the book that matched up to Augustine since he had died right after.

"I found it," Chloe said. "Used bookstore in Ely, while you were sleeping."

There was a knock at the door.

Chloe answered it, then looked back and said, "Ash."

His kids were standing in the doorway, Josie carrying a sandwich on a plate, and Brandon holding the requested journals.

Caleb rose from the bed. "Are those what I think they are?"

Ash put a hand on Caleb's chest, stopping him. "I'll get them."

"I thought you said you were going to stop in the cafeteria," Josie said.

"I was. I just haven't had time yet."

She grunted and shoved the plate toward him. "Here."

Ash had no choice but to take it. "Thanks. I'll eat it all."

"I know you will. I'm going to watch."

"Uh, no, you're not."

"Yes, I am."

She tried to enter the room, but Ash moved into her way.

"I'll make sure he eats," Chloe said, moving up behind Ash. "I promise."

Josie didn't look happy but she stopped protesting.

"Are those the books?" Chloe asked Brandon.

"Yeah," he said, and handed them over.

"All right," Ash said. "We need to get back to work. I'll check in with you both later."

As he closed the door, Josie said, "Every crumb."

Caleb took the journals from Chloe, carried them over to the bed, and began rifling through them.

"How long will it take?" Ash asked.

"Depends. If all the books are here, forty-five minutes, maybe an hour."

"More than enough time for you to finish that sandwich," Chloe said.

"If you want to know the truth, I'm not hungry."

He'd barely gotten the words out when there was another knock. His immediate thought was that Josie had been listening at the door and was not pleased with what he'd just said. Only it wasn't his daughter, but one of the women who usually worked the nightshift in the comm room.

"Captain," she said. "Sorry to intrude, but you're needed in communications."

25

MARTINA HAD BEEN so desperate to know if anyone in the third detention area was one of her friends that Gabriel allowed her to stay in their lookout spot for over an hour, but when he heard the snap of a branch, he regretted the decision.

The sound had come from about fifty yards away, down a dip that led to a private parking area.

He motioned for Martina to stay quiet as he grabbed the binoculars from her.

From observations that he and his team members had made, Gabriel knew that in addition to the jeeps that patrolled the parking lot and streets around the stadium, there were also the occasional guards on foot. These patrols averaged two a day but, as far as he could tell, had no set times.

He wondered if the sound came from one of those sweeps, or had he and Martina been spotted and a patrol sent out specifically to capture them?

A crunch of leaves, a bit closer than before.

Gabriel scanned the area around their position. They were under the trees but there was little ground cover. The closest was a dense patch of brush ten feet behind them.

He pointed at it, making it clear they had to move silently.

In a crouch, they circled to the backside of the group of bushes and discovered a spot where the branches rose off the ground about two feet, creating a tunnel to what looked like a larger clear area in the middle of the brush. If they could get in there, they might be all right.

Gabriel put his mouth right up next to Martina's ear. "Crawl through. I'll hand you my pack and then follow."

After Martina snaked under the bushes, Gabriel passed the bag to her and began to crawl through himself.

Before he reached halfway, he heard the footsteps, two pairs at least. They couldn't have been more than twenty-five feet away. He stopped where he was, pulled his knees to his chest, and hoped to God his feet were far enough in.

For over a minute the footsteps moved through the area, coming very close to the clump of brush multiple times but never stopping.

"Must have been bullshit," a male voice said. "Probably just testing us."

"Rodney was sure he saw a glint off something," another guy said.

"Probably an old beer bottle or something. I'm telling you, there's no one here."

More moving around.

"I've got footprints over here," the second voice said.

"So what? There are footprints all over the place. They could be from weeks ago."

"They look fresh."

"It's dirt. They'll look the same until it gets windy or rains."

"I don't know. Maybe."

"Well, do you see anyone around?"

A long pause.

"No. I guess you're right."

"I'm always right, you know that."

There was a snort. "Only in your head."

The steps started to move away.

"Oh, like you're right all the time."

"Not that we're keeping score, but more than you."

"Oh, really. What kind of faulty calculations are you…"

The voices and steps began to fade.

Gabriel held his position for several more minutes before

pulling himself all the way into the center of the bushes with Martina. Silently, they waited there another hour before he decided it was safe to move again.

Fearing the patrols would still be out, Gabriel plotted a course that avoided all but the most necessary open areas. This took them on a wide loop that went all the way to the edge of the I-5 then over to the 2 Freeway, where they finally headed southwest again.

When they reached Sunset Boulevard, Gabriel led Martina into Mohawk Bend, a restaurant half a block down from Alvarado, and radioed Nyla.

"I was beginning to worry about you guys," Nyla said.

"Sorry, we were…delayed. Listen, can you come over here?"

"Why?"

He hesitated. "There's something we need to talk about. Better in person, I think."

When Nyla arrived forty minutes later, Gabriel and Martina were sitting at the long central table between the bar and the kitchen, eating a lunch of crackers and cheese and dried salami from the supplies Gabriel had in his pack. They were washing it down in style. The restaurant had a large selection of beers, and days ago Gabriel had taught himself how to tap into the kegs. Right now they were enjoying a lukewarm Racer 5 IPA.

"Can I pour you a pint?" he asked as Nyla walked in.

For a second it looked like she was going to chastise him for drinking, but then her frown faded and she said, "Sure."

Nyla took a seat across from them. Gabriel filled a glass and put it in front of her.

"So you're going to tell me why I'm here," she asked.

"We need to get those people out," Martina said.

"What people?"

"The ones in the third enclosure," Gabriel said.

Nyla frowned. "You know we don't have the resources for that."

Gabriel glanced at Martina and then back at Nyla. "Then we need to get them."

"What the hell's going on here?"

"I think I know why this is the only station that has a third enclosure."

Nyla raised an eyebrow. "Really? Okay, then. What's your theory?"

"Immunity."

DR. LAWRENCE COULD not believe how lucky she was. Initially, she had been assigned to the station in St. Louis. But for whatever reason—the rumor was the suicide of another Project doctor, though she had yet to confirm it—the rosters were shuffled, and her name was moved onto the personnel sheet for Los Angeles.

How boring would St. Louis have been? Sure, they would have probably found one or two people with a natural immunity to KV-27a, but for the most part, they would've been dealing with people who had either been lucky or had strong enough immune systems to keep them alive to that point but no true immunity. There, the decision on the life or death of a survivor would be made by other departments, who would base it on whether or not the individual was someone the Project could use.

But here in Los Angeles, she and Dr. Rivera had been presented with a surprise treasure trove. Of course, it shouldn't have been a surprise. Someone in research should have anticipated this exact event happening, but maybe it was good the ball had been dropped. Perhaps if it hadn't been, a more senior doctor would have received the L.A. assignment, and she would have been stuck in St. Louis or God only knew where else.

Twenty-three immune survivors.

Twenty-three.

And not one of them had inherited the resistance to Sage Flu. They had developed it because they'd been among the final wave of infected during the test outbreak, the wave that had survived. When she and Dr. Rivera had realized that, they knew if there were twenty-three at the station here in Los

Angeles, there had to be hundreds more scattered throughout the high-desert region of southern California. Which was why, come the next morning, she would be part of an exploratory group heading out to look for them.

Until then, she and Dr. Rivera had time for a little experimentation. It was important to know exactly how strong the immune systems of these special survivors had grown.

"How about him?" Dr. Rivera said, pointing at one of the twenty-three photographs laid out on the table.

She studied the image, then shrugged. Really, what was the difference? "Works for me," she said.

Dr. Rivera picked up the photo and handed it to the guard who had been waiting patiently to the side. "This one. As quickly as you can."

WHILE MARTINA'S FRIENDS were all in favor of trying to get out, most of the others being held with them did not seem as open to the idea. Ben had been careful about what he said as he spoke to them, trying to gauge their thoughts on the situation without going into any details. The only people he shared more information with were a man named Preston Campbell from Barstow, who was in his mid-thirties, and a woman named Ivy Morse, who was probably closer to sixty and from Sage Springs.

As Ben had pointed out from the beginning, getting out of their detention area would be the easy part. All they would have to do was scrap enough grass and topsoil away to slip under the gate. It wouldn't be easy but very doable, especially if they waited until night. The trick was getting the center-field wall open.

Ben was huddled with Jilly, Ruby, and Preston, going over ideas on how to do just that, when the compound gate opened and five guards entered. All conversation ceased as the guard in front looked at a piece of paper in his hand and then scanned the survivors.

When his gaze landed on Ben's group, he pointed. "You. Come here."

No one moved.

"Blue shirt, let's go," the guard said.

Ruby was the one in blue. "Go where?" she asked.

"The doctors want to see you."

"What for?"

"You'll have to ask them. Come on."

Ruby glanced nervously back at the others. "What do I do?" she whispered.

"Let's move it!" the guard yelled.

"It'll be okay," Jilly said.

None of them believed that.

The guards started walking toward them. Ruby said to her friends, "Don't leave me," then turned and walked toward the gate.

"How long will she be gone?" Ben asked.

Without answering, the guards formed a circle around Ruby and led her out of the detention area.

As soon as the gate was closed, Jilly said, "What the hell?"

"The sooner we get out of here, the better," Preston said.

"But not without Ruby." Jilly looked at Ben. "We can't leave her."

"We won't," he said, with no idea how he'd keep that promise.

THE DOOR TO the lab opened and the test subject was escorted in.

"Have a seat..." Dr. Rivera looked down at the file. "Ruby."

With a wary glance back at her guards, the girl sat down. The subject's apparent agitation surprised Dr. Lawrence.

She looked at the lead guard. "Was there a problem?"

"No. Why?" the guard asked.

Instead of answering him, she switched her attention to the survivor. "You appear upset. Is something wrong?"

"I just...I want to know why I'm here."

For a brief second, she thought maybe the girl had

realized what they were going to do, but that wasn't possible. Her nerves must have been on edge from being locked up for so many days.

She gave the survivor a disarming smile and said, "We realize this has been an ordeal for you and the others. Know that we're only doing what's necessary to keep people alive."

Out of the corner of her eye, she saw Rivera preparing the syringe.

She looked over at the lead guard again. "Thank you. That will be all." After the guards retreated and shut the door, she said, "Due to the nature of the…emergency, we haven't always been able to get the best help. The men on sentry duty are good men, just a little rough around the edges at times, so I apologize if their behavior's disturbed you."

When the test subject relaxed a little, she knew she had guessed right, that the guards had somehow spooked her. Lawrence made a mental note to have a discussion with their boss later. Things would go much more smoothly, especially when the exploratory group went out in the field, if everyone projected an aura of understanding and sympathy. Flies to honey and all that.

Rivera stepped next to the girl and said, "Please roll up your sleeve."

The survivor looked at the syringe. "What's that?"

Rivera looked a bit confused, so Lawrence jumped in. "The vaccine. You've passed the incubation period, so it's time."

Rivera gave her an admiring nod.

"Vaccine?" The girl looked surprised.

"Yes. It's why you came here in the first place, isn't it?"

The subject looked as if she were having some kind of internal debate. Finally, she started to roll up her sleeve. When her bicep was clear, Rivera stuck her with the needle and pushed down on the plunger, sending a mega dose of active KV-27a virus into the girl's arm.

As soon as the needle was removed and a small bandage applied, the survivor reached over to roll her sleeve back down. "Hold on," the doctor said. "One more."

"One more?"

"Yes. As you can imagine, this is a very special virus," Lawrence said, improvising again. "We've developed a, um, two-injection method to combat it."

"I've never heard of anything like that before."

"We had to work in a hurry," she told the girl, her confidence building with every word. "Two separate teams have come up with different variations. Both methods work, but some people react better to one than the other. So by injecting both, we're giving you a much better chance at survival."

The survivor considered her explanation, and then nodded. Rivera, on the other hand, was staring at Lawrence with what appeared to be a new level of respect.

"You may give her the second vaccine now, Doctor," she said to nudge Rivera out of his trance.

Rivera blinked, then, somewhat embarrassed, grabbed the syringe containing the sedative. After he had given the injection and applied another bandage, he said, "You can pull your sleeve down now."

"It will be a full day before the vaccine is truly effective," Lawrence said, enjoying playing the part of the kind doctor. "So we're going to put you someplace where you can rest and wait. It's only a few doors down. After twenty-four hours have passed, you will be free to leave."

The girl blinked a few times. "Or...or...go to the safe...zone."

"I'm sorry?" Lawrence said, momentarily confused. Then she realized what the girl had meant. "Right. Of course. If you so choose, you can join the next group heading for the safe zone. It's definitely the choice we recommend."

The survivor blinked again, her lids closing for a second before popping back open. Lawrence could tell she was confused by the response, but the drug was hindering her thought process.

"How...long...does...does..."

Her head drooped forward before she could finish the question, the sedative knocking her out even faster than the

246

doctor had hoped.

Together, Lawrence and Rivera moved their test subject into the small office just off the lab. They had earlier removed all the furniture and replaced it with a single metal cot. They had covered the walls and ceiling with plastic and made sure the seams were sealed tight. Next up had been replacing the door with one from down the hall. It had a window taking up the top half and a square vent on the bottom. It had taken a little work, but they had created a space in the vent through which they could pump in whatever they wanted.

A tidy and safe observation room.

Once they had the girl on the cot, they closed the door and sealed off the joints along the frame with more plastic. Rivera walked over to the set of valves they'd mounted to the wall and activated the oxygen tank. He then skipped the middle two valves, neither of which was connected to a tank, and turned on number four, sending a fine mist of concentrated Sage Flu virus into Ruby's room.

Perhaps it was overkill to inject KV-27a into the subject *and* the air she would breathe, but the first thing they wanted to know was if the acquired immunity was a hundred percent or not. If the girl caught the disease, they could then use the other subjects to find the borderline of where the immunity stopped working. If the girl didn't, well, then, that would be something else, wouldn't it?

Dr. Lawrence tingled with anticipation of the outcome, wondering which would prevail. She didn't have a preference, of course. She never did.

It's what made her such a good researcher.

26

SINCE LEAVING TEXAS, Curtis Wicks slept only when he absolutely had to. Otherwise he kept heading northeast.

The route was nowhere near as straight as he would have liked. Avoiding permanent Project facilities and locations where survival stations had been set up was a priority, so that meant detouring onto smaller highways that were often littered with accidents and abandoned vehicles.

And then there were the blockages like he encountered on the Kentucky side of a bridge over the Ohio River. He was on one of his detours at the time, avoiding the survival station in Cincinnati. The accident was in Maysville at the mouth of the two-lane suspension bridge that he'd planned on using to enter Ohio.

Even on his motorcycle he couldn't get around the problem. Several cars had been deliberately jammed between two concrete columns to bar any vehicles from passing.

Deciding to walk across and find another motorbike on the Ohio side, he climbed over the cars and hopped down on the other side. More cars were strung out on the bridge, sitting sideways to the lane markers. It looked like there had also been a car fire or someone had tried to burn down the bridge near the center; the metal railings and concrete sidewalk were scorched black. Why someone thought they could burn down the bridge, he didn't know. What he did know was that with all the obstacles, it would take him forever to get to the other side. There had to be a better way.

He decided to see if there was another bridge close by he could try. When he turned to climb back over the main roadblock, he stopped in his tracks.

Painted on each concrete pillar was a message that clued him in to what had happened here.

STAY OUT. GO BACK. VIOLATORS WILL BE SHOT.

A last stand. The police or desperate locals trying to keep the outbreak from crossing the river. And perhaps they had succeeded, but unfortunately for them, the Sage Flu had been coming from all directions, not only the north.

He located another bridge a few miles north, but it too turned out to be a bust. While the side railings were still there, someone had blown a twenty-foot hole in it near the center. Perhaps that explained the burn marks on the other bridge. Maybe someone had tried to blow it, too, but failed.

Wicks did finally find his way across, one that allowed him to keep his ride, but it was only after traveling more than fifty miles east to South Portsmouth. That had been the previous evening, and since it was already dark by the time he crossed and he was bone tired, he stopped not far north of the border and slept dreamlessly until that morning.

When he sat down to plan that day's route, he realized he needed to take several factors into consideration. The first was NB191, the Project Eden facility right outside Columbus, Ohio. Like the majority of other facilities, its main function was that of a warehouse and would have only a small staff. Still, he wanted to keep away from it. The second issue would be the survival station in Pittsburgh, Pennsylvania. Again, avoiding the city altogether would be the best course.

If not for the third item, he would have passed Pittsburgh to the south and cut north through the center of the state into New York and then on to his final destination. But the third item necessitated turning north prior to Pittsburgh, then heading east through the middle of the state. Unlike the others, it was a stop he had to make.

Heading out, he saw patches of snow here and there that spoke of severe weather sometime in the not too distant past. Though it had warmed at bit since then, Wicks was freezing, even with his jacket zipped all the way up and his scarf wrapped tight around his neck.

He couldn't help but smile when he reached the I-80 north of Pittsburgh. It had been years since he was last in this part of the country. When he was a kid, he used to visit often. It had been a magical place of trees and farms and streams and secret paths through the woods. The people who had lived there were all gone now, many dying naturally as they grew older, but the majority taken by the flu.

That thought forced him to the side of the road, the bike skidding a bit on a patch of ice as he stopped. He pushed out the stand and was barely able to get off before the tears flooded his cheeks.

Safe inside Project Eden's facilities, he'd been able to distance himself from what was happening to the world around him. He'd even told himself, because he passed on information to Matt and the Resistance, that he was on the side of good.

But for the last few days, he had driven through the silent towns, passed over the deserted roads, smelled the rotting corpses. And now here he was, a few miles away from a town where he'd known people.

He could distance himself no longer, nor could he disavow his part in the horror.

He fell to his knees, his hand covering his face, and sobbed.

There was nothing he could do to make up for what had happened.

Nothing.

He had killed them.

Killed them all.

Even after his tears ran out, he knelt there, staring at the ground.

His soul was not lost. He knew exactly where it was—in the lowest pit of hell, irredeemable.

When he rose to his feet, he was no longer shaking. Since leaving Texas, he had feared what might happen to him on the mission he was undertaking, but no more.

The damned have nothing to fear, he realized.

He took the Allegheny Boulevard exit in Brookville ten minutes later, and soon was turning off Jenks Street onto Cemetery Road. He slowed as he passed between the two columns that had flanked the entrance since long before he was born. Carved in relief in the capstone on the left was BROOKVILLE and the one on the right CEMETERY. No fancy names here, just telling it like it was.

He had no problem finding the headstone he was looking for. It wasn't ornate or as high as many of the others, but even if a hundred years had passed, he would have found it just the same. It was his grandfather's, a humble monument Wicks had helped his mother pick out.

The gravestone was a five-inch-thick slab of granite that rose a foot into the air from a wide base flush to the ground. He squatted next to it and brushed away a crusty chunk of snow from the bottom.

He'd always loved his family's trips here to visit his grandfather, had loved playing in the sweet old man's barn, and walking with him through the fields. Wicks had been fourteen when his grandfather died, and—until he'd come back seven years earlier for a short, purposeful visit—the man's funeral had been the last time Wicks was there.

He ran his palm across the front of the stone, outlining his grandfather's name before moving his hand to the very top of the monument. As much as he would have liked to spend hours cloaked in the good memories, that was time he did not have.

He gripped the stone with the other hand and yanked it forward. The first jerk barely moved it, but with each back and forth motion, the marker tilted more and more until finally it tipped over onto the grass and snow.

Moving around behind it, he reached into the hole where the base had been. After clearing away some clumps of dirt, he found the box and pulled it up. The container was made from a hard, durable polymer that was guaranteed to last a hundred years. It probably did not gain the favor of the ecologically minded but was exactly what Wicks had wanted. With the exception of being a little dirty, the box looked like new.

He twisted the top counterclockwise and looked inside. It was still there, like he knew it would be. He closed the top, set the box to the side, and tilted the marker back into place.

"Thank you," he said, looking down at the grave.

His grandfather would be shocked at what Wicks had been a part of, but he hoped the old man would at least be supportive of what he was trying to do now.

He picked up the box as he stood. The container felt so light for something so important.

Please still work, he thought. *Dear God. Please.*

27

"HERE," CRYSTAL SAID, handing a headset to Ash. She then donned the second set and clicked CONNECT.

The line rang only once before it was answered. "Nyla."

"It's Crystal. I have Captain Ash here."

"Afternoon, Nyla." Ash had met her in passing, but had never really talked to her.

"Hello, Captain," she said. "We have a situation here we need some guidance on."

On the way to the communications room, Crystal had briefed Ash on Nyla's assignment in Los Angeles, but had no details on why the woman wanted to talk to him.

"All right. I'll do what I can," he said.

"I think it's probable we have a unique group of survivors here."

"Unique in what way?"

"Sir, we believe they are immune."

"You mean they've been vaccinated?" It had happened in India, so it wouldn't be completely surprising if the same situation had occurred here.

"No. Not vaccinated. Immune."

Ash knew a few people with a natural immunity were to be expected. He and his kids were examples of that. "How many are we talking? Two? Three?"

"At least twenty. And, if I'm right, there's probably

many times more than that."

"Start at the beginning," he said.

She had barely begun when Pax entered the room.

"Nyla, hold for a moment," Ash said. He motioned for Pax to join them and then touched Crystal on the shoulder. "Put her on speaker."

"What's going on?" Pax asked.

Instead of answering, Ash said, "Nyla, Rich Paxton is here with me now. Do you mind starting over?"

"No problem."

She told them about Martina Gable and her friends, all of whom were survivors, and all of whom had been stricken with the flu the previous spring. She described the special holding area at the Los Angeles survival station, and that a head count of the people inside was larger than the group Martina had been with.

"The other holding areas have been pretty much emptied out," she said. Though the pattern was sporadic at the moment, teams had reported similar purges at other stations. They all knew this meant Project Eden had begun eliminating the survivors they'd collected. "Thankfully, we've had a drastic reduction in the number of new arrivals here since Tamara's message started playing, and out of those, we've been able to get to most before they reached the station. What I'm concerned about is what the Project's going to do about this immune group." She paused. "Sir, I'm tired of watching people die. We need to get them out."

"How large is your team?" he asked.

"Eight."

There was a voice in the background. Ash couldn't understand what was being said, but it was clearly defiant.

Nyla said into the phone, "Nine, if we count Martina."

"And how many people does the Project have there?"

"Rough estimate, twenty-five to thirty guards and a couple dozen ancillary personnel."

"Give us a moment here, okay?" Ash said.

"Sure," Nyla replied.

Crystal muted the call.

"Do we have anyone we can send out there to help them?" Ash asked.

As Crystal thought about it, her face was already projecting the answer. "We're stretched thin. We've got teams at only ten percent of the survival stations as it is. We could maybe break one of them free, but that would compromise the location where they're working."

"No. I don't want to do that. What about here at the base?"

"We're already operating at bare bones," she said. "I'm sorry. We don't have anyone left."

"Actually, we do," Pax said.

They both looked at him.

"We have a hundred twenty-nine people just sitting around over in Ely."

"The Isabella Island group? But they're just…tourists," Ash said. "They're not trained to do anything like this."

"None of us are really trained for this," Pax said.

"You know what I mean."

"I do, but what choice do we have? Besides, they might have been tourists when they went to the island, but they had lives before that. Who knows? Some might even have a military background." He shrugged. "It's the end of the world, Captain. All hands on deck."

Ash considered it for a moment and then nodded. "All right. We can at least ask them."

"Exactly what I was thinking."

"Put her back on," Ash said to Crystal. He glanced at Pax and grinned. "If you recall, I was army, not navy. So next time I'd prefer a more appropriate metaphor."

CALEB STARED AT the pad of paper.

"I got it. I…got it!" He looked up. "I got…"

His words cut out as he realized he was alone in Matt's room. Last he remembered, Chloe had been there, too. He had no idea if that had been ten minutes ago or two hours.

He looked down at the pad again and rechecked his final

bit of decryption. Those extra numbers in several of the sets had been the biggest trouble, but everything had finally clicked, making him feel like an idiot for not figuring it out sooner. Of course, he still needed to check it on a computer, but as far as he was concerned, that was only a formality.

He grinned at his handiwork. Breaking into Project Eden's communications network by night, solving encrypted messages by day. Damn, he was good.

Chloe. I need to find Chloe.

As he shot off the bed, several of Matt's journals and dozens of pieces of paper tumbled to the floor. Ignoring them, he crossed the room and yanked the door open.

"Chloe!" he yelled as he entered the hallway. "Chloe!"

He heard a door behind him open. He swung around.

"What's going on?" Not Chloe, Rachel.

"Oh, um, I'm sorry, ma'am," Caleb said. "I didn't mean to disturb you. I'm, uh, looking for Chloe."

Rachel stepped into the hall. "Why would Chloe be—" She stopped as her gaze fell on the open door to her brother's suite. "Were you in Matt's room?" She walked quickly to the doorway.

"I was just…I…I gotta find Chloe." He whipped back around and started jogging down the hall.

"Caleb! I want to talk to you!" Rachel called after him.

He kept going, not allowing himself to breathe until he turned down the hallway to the main portion of the base.

He found three people in the cafeteria.

"I'm looking for Chloe. Have you seen her?"

Head shakes.

He was about to ask the same question when he reached the comm room, but a quick look through the door told him everyone was busy.

He almost ran past the gym without stopping, but the rhythmic bass throbbing from inside made him stutter step and return to the door. As he opened it, he winced at the music blasting from inside. Chloe was the only one there, keeping pace with the drumbeat on a stair-step machine in the corner.

Afraid his eardrums would burst if he took a step inside, he yelled her name. He might as well have been running around naked in a pitch-black room for all the good it did. Bracing himself, he took a step over the threshold and yelled again, this time waving the pad of paper in the air. That did the trick.

She hopped off the machine, picked a remote off the ground, and hit a button. The music cut out.

"Are you done?" she asked, using a towel to wipe the sweat off her face as she walked over.

"Uh-huh."

She motioned at the pad of paper. "That it?"

"Uh, yeah."

Holding out a hand, she said, "Let me see it."

"There's, um, something you might want to deal with first."

THEY FOUND RACHEL kneeling on the floor of Matt's room, picking up the journals. All the wads of paper had already been tossed in the trash.

"Rachel?" Chloe said.

Rachel turned. "What the hell is going on here? These are Matt's personal journals. Who gave you permission to go through them?"

Chloe stepped toward her. "Rachel, it's okay."

"It's *not* okay," Rachel said, slamming the journal she'd been holding onto the bed. "These are my brother's things! This is his room! You have no right to be in here!"

It took all of Chloe's will to maintain her cool. These were not the kind of situations she'd ever been very good at. "We had no choice. We had to come—"

Pushing herself to her feet, Rachel said, "You *what*? Coming in here was *not* a choice! You didn't even think to ask me?"

"You needed your rest."

Rachel looked between the two of them. "I want you and Caleb to confine yourselves to your quarters. You will—"

257

"Caleb had nothing to do with this. He was doing what Ash and I asked him to."

"Captain Ash is in on this, too? What has happened to all of you?"

"What has *happened*," Chloe said, her jaw tensing, "is that Matt left us a message and we've been trying to figure out what it means. I realize that his death has been very difficult for you, but we couldn't just stop doing anything until you were ready. We are in the middle of a war we are losing badly. We need every advantage we can get, and if your brother's message points us toward something that will help, then we need to know what he meant." A brief pause. "I'm sorry we did not ask your permission, but we didn't do anything wrong. Matt is dead. There is nothing that will change that. But there are people out there who need our help to stay alive. So, no, we will not detain ourselves in our rooms. And, no, we will not stop looking at your brother's journals."

Rachel stared at Chloe, stunned.

"Actually," Caleb said, "I don't think we need the journals anymore. I've figure out the—"

"Shut up," Chloe said, her words meant for Caleb but her gaze still on Rachel.

Rachel's lips parted. After a few false starts, she said, "What message?"

ELY, NEVADA

PAX HAD CALLED ahead, so when he and Ash arrived at the hotel, Robert had already gathered everyone in the largest meeting room available. There were some handshakes, a lot of hellos, and a few inevitable grumbles of dissatisfaction with the living arrangements. As the others took their seats, Pax and Ash moved to the front of the room.

"Well, as I warned you on the plane, the weather here's only slightly cooler than what you'd been experiencing back on the island," Pax said.

A smattering of laughter.

"Can't say it'll be getting much warmer anytime soon," he said. "But the good news is, you are all safe."

A few people clapped.

"How long are we going to have to stay here?" someone shouted.

Several others said, "Shhh."

"It's all right," Pax said. "A natural question. First off, you can leave anytime you want. There are cars on every street. All you have to do is get in one and drive away. No one will stop you, but if something happens to you, no one will be around to help you, either. For those who choose to stay, I'm not going to lie to you and give you any kind of time frame. Truth is, we have no idea when you'll be able to get out of here. We do plan on finding someplace more permanent, but other matters are taking precedence right now."

He looked around the room before launching into what he'd really come to say. "Without outside help, none of you would be alive today. I'm not saying that to gain a cheap pat on the back. I'm saying it because it is a fact. It's also a fact that others like you are out there. We have people scattered around the globe trying to help them, but we can't be everywhere." He could see he had everyone's full attention now. "I'd like to tell you about one of the survival stations and what's been happening there…"

PAX'S STORY ABOUT Los Angeles was greeted with shocked stares and more than a few tears. Even though Robert and his fellow Isabella Island survivors had seen firsthand what Project Eden could do, it still seemed so incredible, so unbelievably horrible.

Robert could barely hold in his own emotions upon hearing about people who had voluntarily gone to the station, thinking they were going to get help, only to have their lives taken. Estella was a wreck, leaning against him, her wet cheeks pressed against his arm.

When Pax finished the story, he said, "I tell you all this because we have an opportunity here to do something right.

DREAM SKY

At least twenty people are still being held there that we can get out. We have some people on the ground keeping an eye on things, but there are too few of them to make a move. What we need is help, and that's why I've come to you."

"Wait, are you—what do you call it?—forcing us into your army?" The question came from Bertrand Tailler, the same asshole who had almost made Robert miss the plane. He was sitting alone in the back corner.

"No, not at all," Pax told him in a much calmer voice than Robert would have used. "What I'm saying is, we need volunteers. Military training is a plus, but it's not necessary. If you don't want to volunteer, that's completely fine. No judgment. Any questions?"

There were a few, mostly about the danger involved.

"Yes, there's a chance someone will get hurt." Pax said. "Will anyone die? It's a distinct possibility. This isn't the old world anymore. Our lives will never be as comfortable as they used to be."

"You expect people to volunteer to die?" Bertrand said. "Good luck with that."

"Thank you," Pax said, ignoring the sarcasm. "Anyone else have something they want to say?"

A few indistinct whispers, but no more questions.

"All right, then. We'll do this the simple way. If you're willing to volunteer, raise your hand."

No hands shot up.

Robert looked around, wondering what was wrong with these people. Pax and his friends had saved them. If the Resistance needed help, they should get it.

That's when he realized he had yet to raise his own hand. He lifted it into the air. He didn't know how much help he could be—he'd been scared to death when he went after the hijackers on the *Albino Mer*—but he figured he could do something.

Estella sat up straight and raised her own hand.

ASH WATCHED AS hands rose like a reverse game of

tumbling dominoes. Even two of the people who'd become sick after receiving the vaccine, but had improved enough to come to the meeting, volunteered. Pax thanked them but excused them from service.

Ash and Pax had been hoping for fifteen people. The final tally was thirty-seven.

They gave everyone time to gather their things, then loaded the volunteers onto one of the buses that had ferried the group up from Las Vegas. With Pax behind the wheel, they headed for Ward Mountain, where everyone would be equipped as best as possible before heading for the airplanes that would take them to Los Angeles.

A few miles out of Ely, Pax reached under his seat and pulled out the bag he'd brought along. "Sat phone's ringing," he said, tossing the pack over to where Ash was standing.

Ash pulled the phone out and hit ACCEPT.

"This is Ash."

"What the hell happened to you?" Chloe did not sound happy. "I've been trying to call you for like an hour."

"Is something wrong?"

"Not wrong," she said. "Caleb's decoded the entire message."

"Fantastic. What's it—"

"Do you want to know the best part?"

"Is that a trick question?"

"Fine, I'll wait until you get back. You are coming back, aren't you?"

"What's the best part?"

It wasn't hard to imagine the sly smile on her face as she said, "I said when you get back."

"Chloe!"

"Okay, okay. We know where Dream Sky is."

WARD MOUNTAIN NORTH

WHILE ASH HAD expected Chloe to be with Caleb when he and Pax entered the conference room, Rachel's presence was a surprise.

261

He almost asked if she was all right but stopped himself. Instead, he said, "I'm glad to see you."

She nodded, a quick, humorless smile gracing her lips.

Pax walked up to her and put his arms around her, whispering something Ash couldn't hear.

When they parted, she said, "Thank you." In a louder voice, "We should start."

Chloe looked at Caleb. "Tell them."

"Right. Okay, so some of the messages were confusing the hell out of me," Caleb said as he grabbed one of the journals on the table. He flipped through a few pages, then turned the book so everyone could see. It was one of entries that had a sequence of numbers at the end. He pointed at the numbers. "Every once in a while when I decrypted one of these, there would still be a few numbers left. Anywhere from one to three digits. At first I figured they were placeholders and concentrated on the bigger messages."

"And?" Ash asked.

Caleb traded the journal for a well-used legal pad. "I've got all the messages right here." He tossed it into the center of the table. "It's one sided, though. Just the responses Matt received. As far as I can tell, he didn't keep a record of his side of things. Still, you can pretty much figure out what they were talking about.

"The earlier messages all concern the what and where of DS. And before you ask, he never says Dream Sky, only uses the initials and sometimes not even that. At one point, C8 says he thinks it might be a secret supply dump. Later he suggests it's a weapon of some kind. He throws out a bunch of other possibilities, too. Apparently Matt had an idea of what it was, but C8 didn't agree. He kept saying things like there was no way Matt was right, and he could find no proof of Matt's theory, and even went so far as to tell Matt that he had to be wrong and they were wasting time pursuing the idea. They did agree that from the secrecy surrounding it, it seems to be a key to the Project's success. They don't mention why they believe this, but if you read between the lines, it's pretty clear it's based on something Matt had known when he was still on the inside. Which, by the way, still blows my mind that he was part of them. How could he hide it from—"

"Stick to the subject," Chloe told him before Ash could say something similar.

"Oh, right." Caleb glanced at Rachel. "Sorry." He took a moment to regain his composure before restarting. "Several years ago, C8 changed his tune, and began saying that they'd been wrong. That DS didn't exist. I mean, he really tried to sell Matt on it. It was like something spooked him and he didn't want any part of it." He smiled. "Interestingly, it was around this time he started including the odd stray numbers in his messages." Caleb gestured at the pad. "Matt asked him about the extras and why they didn't work into the code. C8 played them off as nothing important, which, as I was first going through them, was exactly what I was thinking."

"But they weren't filler," Rachel said.

Caleb grinned again. "No, they were not. But I wouldn't have figured it out if it weren't for the message Matt passed on to Captain Ash. Well, the Augustine part, anyway. It unlocked that last set, where I discovered four more strays. That really bothered me. That was more than any of the previous messages had had. So why were there so many now? I was having a hard time continuing to think they were simply filler. I was missing something. So I put all the strays on a single piece of paper."

He pulled a sheet out of his pocket, unfolded it, and laid it on the table. On it were two rows of eight numbers each. The first started with 43 and the second with 73.

Caleb smiled at everyone expectantly, but after no one responded, he said, "Don't you see it?"

"See what?" Pax asked.

Caleb rolled his eyes and groaned. He pulled a pen out of his pocket and inked a period after both the 43 and the 73. He then drew a minus sign in front of the seven.

"How about now?" he asked.

"GPS coordinates," Ash said, surprised. He'd seen plenty of similar numbers while in the army. "Are you sure?"

"Am I sure?" Caleb scoffed.

He grabbed a shoulder bag off the chair closest to him and pulled out a laptop. After placing it on the table, he typed something in and turned the screen toward them. On it was a mapping application showing a wide view of the planet. In the text box at the top, Caleb had input the two sets of numbers. He gave them all a second to look at the screen and then pressed ENTER.

The map zoomed in until a blue arrow appeared, pointing at the center of what looked like a very small town. In a floating box above the arrow were the coordinates.

"Where the hell is that?" Pax asked.

Caleb widened the shot back one step and the name of the town appeared.

"Everton?" Ash said. "Everton where?"

Caleb zoomed out until state lines began to show. "This one's in Vermont."

Ash studied the map for a moment. "Okay. I'll give you that C8 was pointing Matt here for some reason, but it doesn't meant that place is Dream Sky or whatever DS stands for."

"That's the same thing I told him," Chloe said. "As strong as it was circumstantially, it could still mean anything."

"Which pissed me off," Caleb said. "I mean, it's *obvious*. But I get it. God forbid we assume anything, right?

Chloe and Caleb shared a conspiratorial smile.

"What?" Ash asked.

"Devin used the link into Project Eden's computer network to confirm that there *is* a Project base at the coordinates," Chloe said.

"Again, not proof," Ash said.

"No," she agreed. "But what he was unable to find probably says the most."

"What do you mean?"

"She means," Caleb said, sounding like he felt he should be the one driving the conversation, "that he checked dozens of other facilities in the system, all of which had abundant, accessible information. The base at these coordinates"—he pointed at the map—"had nothing. Not even encrypted info."

"Then how did you find anything on the base in the first place?" Ash asked.

"Devin was able to locate a map in an old archive that had the base marked. But it's not on later editions of the same map. Okay, so maybe it's not Dream Sky, but whatever it is, it seems pretty damn important."

"Or maybe it's not there at all," Ash said.

"C8 was pointing at something," Chloe said. "Something he felt was important enough to tell Matt about. And Matt felt it was important enough to tell you before he died. We need to check it out and see for ourselves."

As Ash opened his mouth to respond, Pax said, "Captain, maybe it is something else entirely, but if there's a chance this place is Dream Sky, and taking it out would severely cripple the Project, how can we pass up the opportunity to at least check it out?"

The room fell quiet.

"He's right," Rachel said. "We have to check. We have to check *now*."

Again there was silence.

Ash finally broke it. "Caleb, thank you. If we have more questions, we'll come and find you."

Caleb looked confused for a moment before his eyes widened in understanding. "Oh, okay. Sure. Um, they probably need me back at the trailer anyway."

After he was gone, Ash said, "If we're going to do this, we need to do it right."

"We can't afford to waste time," Chloe said. "The longer we wait, the more entrenched the Project will become. At some point we won't be able to topple them."

"I'm not talking about waiting. If this *is* as important as we think it might be, then I'm talking about being ready so we can take advantage of the situation right now."

28

TERRELL FISHER SHOVED his hands into his jacket pockets so Diaz wouldn't see them shaking. Not that Diaz would have noticed anyway. Terrell was pretty sure the guy was dealing with his own internal repercussions for what they were doing.

"Think we can fit the last two in," Diaz said, stepping off the back of the truck onto the loading dock. "You get the gurney."

"Sure," Terrell said. "Right behind you."

He waited until Diaz started walking toward the warehouse door before pulling his hands out again. The empty gurney made an awful racket over the uneven concrete floor, but he definitely preferred it to the muted *clackity-clack* it made when it was loaded.

The warehouse was on the eastern edge of Project Eden's Chicago survival station. All of the offices—medical, processing, security—were located in the building. The holding areas had been constructed in the large parking area that separated the warehouse from a twin building a few hundred yards away. When the Project had first arrived at the facility to begin the conversion, the lot had been full of semis and trailers. Terrell's first assignment here had been to help move the vehicles out.

Diaz held the door open and allowed Terrell and the gurney to pass through first. They were basically on autopilot as they headed down the hallway. Someone—a Project psychologist, probably—had labeled their destination as the Reassignment Room. This wasn't the name by which Terrell thought of it. In his mind it was the Kill Room.

The room was large enough to hold up to fifty people at one time. Five rows of ten chairs faced a wall where a video projector would play a message from Gustavo Di Sarsina, supposed Secretary General of the UN, talking about what survivors should expect when they arrived at the safe zone.

This was also the product of the head doctors, telling Terrell and the others that feeding into the survivors' sense of hope as the gases were introduced made everything humane. The doctors even pointed out that the survivors were really the luck ones. In place of a painful death at the hands of the flu, they would be drugged to sleep before a second, toxic gas was added to the room to ensure they would never wake again.

People were going to die. That was basic knowledge if you were a part of the Project. What Terrell had not thought through before Implementation Day was how it would truly feel to be alive with so many dead filling the world. When he'd begun seeing the bodies on TV, knowing it was real, he'd gone numb. But what was infinitely worse, what had never ever crossed his mind, was that he would have an active hand in eliminating those who had survived the flu but did not fill a need within the Project.

For days they had been killing survivors. Hundreds, thousands—he wasn't sure anymore how many. He and Diaz and the others escorted people into the airtight room, waited for the cycle to pass, then transported the bodies to the mass grave outside of town.

Despite what the doctors said, it wasn't humane. The humane thing would have been to let people know what was going on, give them a chance to fight for their lives. The stories, the double dose of gas—that was for the psyche of Project Eden personnel, Terrell had finally realized.

Grasping this allowed him to see the truth.

He was a killer.

"Hey, watch out," Diaz said.

Terrell looked up and straightened the gurney right before it would have hit the wall. "Sorry."

A few minutes later they reached the Kill Room. Quickly they loaded up one of the two remaining bodies and headed back into the hallway.

They hadn't gone far when a voice called out behind them. "Are you almost done?"

They stopped and looked back. Walking toward them was Theo Gates, head of processing.

"One more after this," Diaz said.

"Is there a problem?" Ward asked.

Diaz looked confused.

"No, sir," Diaz said.

"Then do you want to tell me why you aren't already at the dump site?"

Dump site, Terrell thought. The words hammered home the utter disgust he was feeling, but he appreciated that Ward wasn't covering it up by calling it the safe zone like they were suppose to.

"We should be on the road in ten minutes," Diaz said.

"You're behind schedule. We'll be bringing in another group in four hours, so I expect you to be back and everything ready by then."

"Won't be a problem," Diaz said. He looked at Terrell. "Let's move."

As they headed down the hallway, faster than before, all Terrell could think was, *Another group.*

29

BOBBY COULD HEAR the sat phone ringing as he exited the bathroom. He figured Tamara would answer it, so he made no effort to hurry back to the surveillance room. Then he heard the toilet flush in the women's bathroom.

In a burst of speed, he ran down the corridor, his shoes squeaking loudly as he skidded around the corner into the big room. He paused inside the doorway, unsure where he'd left the phone. Another ring solved his dilemma.

"Hello?" he said, even before he had it pressed against his ear.

"Bobby? It's Leon."

By the time Bobby hung up the phone, Tamara had returned.

"Pack up," he said. "We leave in ten minutes."

"Leave? Where are we going?"

He smiled. "We have an assignment."

SANJAY SAT UP with a start. He blinked as he looked around.

Kusum was still asleep beside him, and while the room was still dark, he could see the unmoving lump of Darshana on the other bed.

Had a dream woken him? He could feel his heart racing so he assumed the dream had been a pretty wild one. As he took a deep breath to calm down, he heard a buzz behind him. Looking back, all he saw was the dark form of his pillow. And then he remembered.

The phone.

He had switched it to vibrate and put it under his pillow to prevent anyone outside the building from hearing it ring. He pulled it out and hit CONNECT.

"Yes?" he whispered.

"Is this Sanjay?"

"Yes. Who is this?"

"Crystal. I know it's early for you, but do you have a moment?"

"Hold on."

He carefully climbed out of bed and exited the room into the nearly pitch-black hallway. "Okay," he said. "We can talk now."

He returned to the room four minutes later.

"Kusum, Darshana, you need to wake up."

The women stirred but neither opened her eyes.

Sanjay walked over to his wife and kissed her on the forehead. "Wake up, my love."

A low grunt escaped before her eyes finally fluttered open. "Sanjay? What's going on?"

"Time to get up."

She looked confused. "It is still dark."

"There are things we need to do."

He straightened up and turned to wake Darshana, but saw her eyes were already open.

"Are you going to kiss me, too?" she asked.

"Don't count on it."

ELY, NEVADA
3:50 PM PST

THE RUNWAYS AT the Ely Airport had not been long enough for the plane that had flown north from Isabella

Island, but the largest was long enough for the Gulfstream G550 executive jet that was on its final approach from San Francisco. This was the first of four such aircraft that had been called in from Resistance locations on the West Coast. The other three would be arriving within the hour.

Ash, pensive, looked at the jet's lights.

"Now would be a hell of a time to second-guess yourself," Pax said.

"Tell me this is going to work and I'll stop," Ash said.

"Whether it works or not doesn't matter," Chloe threw in. "If we wait we'll definitely fail."

"I'm pretty sure whether it works or not is going to matter," Ash said.

"You know what I mean."

He gave her a half smile. "I do."

A screech of rubber announced the jet's touchdown.

"I believe your ride is here," Pax said.

Ash watched the plane for a moment longer, then turned to his friends. "Call us as soon as you have a feel for the situation," he said to Pax. "Crystal should have everything set by then, but if you need to act, don't wait."

"Don't worry about us," Pax said. "We'll handle our end."

"I don't doubt that for a moment."

Pax looked over at Chloe. "Watch out for him. He's liable to forget he's still injured."

She hugged him. "I'll do my best."

The two men shook hands.

"Good luck," Ash said.

"You, too, Captain."

ROBERT AND THE other volunteers were waiting in the small terminal building. If any of them was regretting raising his or her hand, no one was saying anything.

"Freshen up your coffee?" he asked Estella.

"No, thank you," she said, setting down her nearly full cup.

271

"How about you?" he said to Renee.

"I'm with Estella," she replied. "I think if I actually drink any of this, I'm going to throw up." She put her cup down next to Estella's.

Robert was having the exact opposite reaction. Drinking the coffee was keeping his nerves settled. He was about to go for a refill when the outer door opened and Pax, Captain Ash, and Chloe came in.

"My group up and ready," Ash said. "Our plane just landed."

Robert felt Estella slip her hand into his and squeeze tight. They, along with Renee, were three of the eight who would be accompanying Ash and Chloe east. The rest would take the later planes and head to Los Angeles with Pax.

"If anyone needs to hit the toilet, now is the time," Chloe said.

It was as if all the coffee he'd been drinking had suddenly made it through his system at once. Clenching, he whispered to Estella, "I'll be right back."

Several others made the trip to the bathroom with him, and by the time he returned, the jet had pulled up next to the building.

"Come on," Estella said, taking his hand again.

They picked up the duffel bags they'd been assigned and headed outside. Each bag contained winter gear, two handguns, ammunition, and, in Robert's case, four stun grenades. Ash and Chloe were waiting outside the plane's door.

"You're in 2A and B," Chloe said to Robert and Estella.

After all the volunteers were inside, Ash and Chloe climbed in and closed the door.

Standing at the front, leaning a bit forward so that his head didn't hit the roof, Ash said, "If any of you would rather stay, this is your last chance to back out."

Robert turned in his seat to see if anyone would take the captain up on his offer, and was pleased to see no one did.

"All right, then," Ash said. "You should try to get some rest. It might be a while before you get another chance. If you need a sleeping pill, talk to Chloe." He swiveled around and said to the pilots, "Let's go."

LOS ANGELES, CALIFORNIA
4:22 PM PST

"YOU ASK ME, looks like they're planning some kind of trip," Gabriel said, his eyes tight to his binoculars.

He, Nyla, and Martina had carefully worked their way around to a tree-covered hill east of Dodger Stadium. Parked in the lot closest to the entrance Project Eden used the most were three trucks and two Humvees. Two of the trucks were troop carriers, while the third was a red delivery truck with a logo on the side for La Brea Bakery. It was into this last vehicle that supplies were being loaded.

"Yeah," Nyla said. "But where?"

"Maybe they're closing up shop," he suggested.

"Why would they do that?" Martina said, concerned.

"It's happened at a few other stations already. Probably because they're not getting the intakes they expected."

"But if they leave, what happens to my friends?"

It took all of Gabriel's effort not to cringe. There was still no proof her friends were in the special area. "The plan is to get everyone out before that happens."

"Maybe…maybe we should do something now."

Nyla set her glasses down and looked over at Martina. "The only things that would be accomplished by going in now would be to get us killed and tip them off that something was up. They'd likely kill all the prisoners, too."

"But if we do nothing, and they kill them before the others get—"

"What?" Nyla asked. "Should we just die with them?"

"Yes! It's better than sitting here and watching!"

Gabriel put a hand on Martina's back. She flinched but he didn't move it away. "It's not, and you know it. Look, we realize there might be people you care about in there. We want nothing more than to get them out, but until we're ready, anything we do would be suicide. And that's not going to help *anyone*."

Before Martina had a chance to argue again, the sat phone buzzed. Nyla answered it.

"Yes…uh-huh…okay…okay…great, thanks." When she hung up, she looked over at the other two. "Time to go. The planes are on the way."

NEW YORK STATE
8:18 PM EST

WICKS WAS REALLY flying now. The only place he'd had to be careful about since leaving his grandfather's grave was Scranton, where there was supposedly a satellite survival station tasked with sending survivors to the three much larger ones in the New York City area.

Other than that, he'd been able to drive at a pretty constant eighty miles per hour and had already blown past Binghamton, New York. If he kept up this pace, he'd get there before midnight.

The sooner the better, he thought.

WARD MOUTAIN NORTH, NEVADA
5:23 PM PST

"THAT WAS BERLIN," Crystal said as soon as she disconnected the call. "They're ready."

"How many is that now?" Rachel asked.

She had been in the comm room since Pax and Ash left with their teams for the Ely Airport. The emptiness she'd been feeling since the death of her brother was still there, but she was no longer ceding control to it. With Pax and Ash and Chloe all away, someone needed to run things here. There was no time for a spiral into despair.

"Seventeen," Crystal said.

"Eighteen," Leon shouted. "Just confirmed with Johannesburg. Said it won't be that much, but I told them whatever they can do will help."

Eighteen. That was good, Rachel thought, but would it be enough?

She gave Leon a nod and said, "We need more."

274

30

THE VAN NUYS Airport was located in the San Fernando Valley portion of Los Angeles. While there were landing strips closer to Dodger Stadium, those would increase the likelihood of the jet being seen as it descended. Van Nuys was hidden by the hills and just far enough away that the plane would hopefully touch down unnoticed.

Still, Pax couldn't help consider the possibility of a rocket knocking them out of the air as they headed toward the runway. When they were finally on the ground, he relaxed enough to unbuckle his seatbelt and push himself up.

"All right," he said, looking at everyone as the plane taxied across the tarmac. "We're going to be met by some of my people here. It is very important that you all follow any directions we give you from this point forward. Not doing so could result in serious injury or...or worse." He caught the eye of a man two rows back. "Duncan, you're going to be squad leader of the people on this plane." Duncan was one of the volunteers who had served in the military, a four-year stint with the British army.

"Yes, sir," Duncan said.

"Anyone have any questions?"

A hand belonging to a dusty blonde woman near the back went up.

"Yes?" Pax said, pointing.

"Well, um, I've never even hit anyone before. How am I

supposed to shoot at someone?"

A few others mumbled the same concern.

"It's not an easy thing to do, but if you're looking for motivation, then let me remind you that the people holding the survivors are the same people responsible for killing nearly every person you know. Your acquaintances, your friends, your *family*—these are the people who took their lives."

The whole plane stared back at him, unmoving.

He gave it a few seconds before he said, "Any other questions?"

There were none.

The moment the plane pulled to a stop, Pax opened the door, allowing the outside air in. It had a long way to go to match the balmy, tropical heat he'd experienced on Isabella Island, but the temperature was at least fifty degrees warmer than Ely had been when they left.

He lowered the steps and climbed out to find six people standing next to several vans a few dozen yards away.

"Nyla," he said, smiling broadly as the group approached.

"Good to see you, Pax."

After they shook hands, she presented the rest of her team to him, most of whom he'd already met.

"We have three more who are keeping eyes on the station," she said, and then turned to the only person she had yet to introduce. "This is Martina Gable."

Pax held his hand out toward her. "The immune girl," he said.

She looked a bit self-conscious as she shook his hand. "Good to meet you." She glanced at Nyla. "Can we go now?"

"You're anxious about your friends, aren't you?" Pax said.

Martina nodded. "If we wait too long—"

Pax held up a hand. "I understand." He thought for a moment and then said to Nyla, "The other planes should be only a few minutes behind us, but there's no reason to hang out until they get here. We'll take this first group now and see what we can figure out."

"Of course," Nyla said. She pointed. "We'll take that van." She turned to the man next to her. "Gabriel, you drive, and I'll fill Pax in on the latest. The rest of you will bring the others the moment they're on the ground, got it?"

"Yes, ma'am," the rest of her team said.

Pax looked back at the volunteers, all of whom were off the plane now, and motioned at the van. "Load up. Time to go."

As he turned back around, Martina was looking at him.

"Thank you," she mouthed.

He dipped his head slightly and put a hand on her back. "Let's see what we can do."

THEY TOOK THE 101 Freeway from the Valley into Hollywood and approached the stadium from the basin side. Gabriel, clearly knowing where all the jams were, exited at Gower and turned down Hollywood Boulevard, heading east.

"Any theories on where this convoy might be going?" Pax asked when Nyla finished her brief.

"No idea," she said. "Unless they're all leaving."

Pax frowned. "The reports I heard said the other places that have bugged out usually had a stream of trucks moving from the station to whatever airport they were using."

"Could be they're getting ready to do that."

"Could be," he said. "But from the way you described it, it sounds a little bit different."

"If it's not that, I don't know what it is."

Eastern Hollywood gave way to Los Feliz and then Silver Lake.

"We're getting close," Nyla said. "We'll stop about a mile and a half out and hike in from there. Any closer and they might see us."

When they reached Alvarado Street, Gabriel pulled the van into the gas station on the northeast corner.

"The hike's a little hilly," Gabriel explained as they climbed out. "But the good thing is that so far we haven't seen any patrols at night. Hopefully that pattern will hold."

Duncan organized everyone into two parallel lines, and told them to keep their pace steady while watching out for the person in front of them.

Pax noticed a few of them pulling their guns out of their bags. "Hold on," he said. "Best if you keep those stowed for now. Nobody's got holsters so you'd have to hold them, which means you might accidently pull the trigger. I've done it myself and let me tell you, it's the last thing we need right now."

There was reluctance from a couple of people, but in the end they all put their weapons back in their bags.

"Everyone ready?" Pax asked.

There was no dissent.

Looking at Nyla and Gabriel, he said, "Lead the way."

LOS ANGELES SURVIVAL STATION
5:40 PM PST

DR. LAWRENCE WAS looking through the window when the subject regained consciousness. The girl lay there for several seconds, staring up at the ceiling before she finally sat up.

Immediately, she placed her hands over her eyes and winced.

Lawrence pushed the intercom button. "Ruby, are you all right?"

The girl moved her palms far enough apart to squint at the door. "What happened? Why am I in here?"

Lawrence clicked the button again. "You had a reaction to the vaccine that caused you to lose consciousness. How are you feeling now? Are you ill?"

The girl looked around. "What is this place?"

"Isolation chamber. Merely a precaution."

Turning back to the door, the survivor said, "Precaution for what?"

"As I told you, you had a reaction to the vaccine. It's standard procedure in such circumstances to isolate the patient until we are sure everything is okay. Now, please answer my question. Are you feeling sick?"

The girl blinked a few times. "My head hurts."

That symptom could have been as easily caused by the sedative as the virus.

"Anything else?" Lawrence asked. "Do you feel...congested? Any difficulty breathing? Aches? Pains?"

"Just the headache."

Interesting. The doctor noted it on her tablet.

"How long do I have to stay in here?" the girl asked.

"Overnight, at least. You will hopefully be able to leave tomorrow."

The answer didn't seem to please her. "Can you at least turn up the air conditioner in here? It's hot and..." She touched her arms. "I'm sticky."

"Why don't you try to rest more and I'll see what I can do."

As Lawrence stepped away from the door, Rivera asked, "So?"

She grinned. "Nothing yet."

BEN WAITED UNTIL twenty minutes after the kitchen crew collected the dishes before he headed for the dormitory door. He only went a few steps, though, before Jilly ran up behind him and grabbed his arm.

"Where are you going?" she asked.

"You know where," he said.

"But we can't leave Ruby."

Ben had known since Ruby had been led away that this discussion was coming. Jilly had pretty much spent the rest of the day sitting in the yard, watching the fence in hopes her friend would come back. Any attempt to discuss the escape plan had been shut down. Ben and the others knew, however, they couldn't wait.

"No one said anything about leaving her," he said, "but we can't do anything for her from in here. After we get out, we'll figure something out."

"Like what?"

"I promise. We're not going to just disappear. We'll get her."

"What if they bring her back right after we leave?"

He grabbed her by the arms and locked eyes with her. "Jilly. We *will* get her out. But we need to get out of here first. Do you understand?"

She blinked several times, fighting back tears. "We can't leave," she whispered.

"You can stay here if you want, but if you choose to come, you have to do everything I tell you."

"I'll...I'll come."

"You're sure?"

"Yeah."

He smiled as he gave her arms a squeeze. "You'll be number one behind me, okay?"

"Okay. But don't forget your promise."

"I won't."

When he let go of her, he glanced at Preston, who was standing only a few feet behind them. Preston gave him a shallow nod, indicating he'd heard the conversation and would keep tabs on Jilly when Ben couldn't.

Ben made his way outside, strolled over to the fence, and dropped down. Crawling along the narrow shadow at the barrier, he worked his way around to the gate.

Close up now, he examined the grass. What was amazing to him was how uniform and tightly woven it all was. His father had always prided himself on the grass in their yard but it was nothing like this. This was a work of art.

He almost felt guilty as he dug his fingers through the blades, grabbed the roots, and pulled. As he'd hoped, a large chunk of grass came free in a single piece. He set it aside and began removing more and more grass, creating a lane about two feet wide and three long all the way to the gate. Once the grass was out of the way, he began digging through a layer of sand that came out a lot easier than he'd expected.

"How's it going?" The half-whispered question came from behind him.

He looked back and spotted Preston standing a dozen

feet away, facing the side so he wasn't looking at him.

"Faster than I thought," he replied.

"It's going to work?"

"I think so."

A foot down would probably be enough, but he went farther just in case. They certainly didn't want anyone getting stuck trying to get out. After about two feet, he hit a layer of black plastic that he realized must be part of the irrigation system. That was fine. The trench was more than deep enough.

After he had it cleared all the way to the gate, he stopped. They would dig out the other side when it was time to go.

Though the sand he'd removed was all in the shadows, he covered it with the pieces of grass to cut down any chance the lighter colored material would be noticed. After examining his handiwork and determining there was nothing else he needed to do, he retraced his path along the fence and returned to the dorm.

Those who were with Ben on trying to escape were gathered around one of the bunks near the door. The others were in the seating area, unaware what Ben had been doing.

"So?" Jilly asked.

"All done. Five minutes to clear the other side and we're out."

"Except for the center-field fence, and the guards, and who knows what else," Valerie said. She had reluctantly joined their escape plan, but still wasn't above pointing out at every opportunity why it wouldn't work.

"Yeah, except for that," Ben replied, choosing not to engage.

"How long should we wait?" Preston asked.

Ben shot a look toward the back of the building. "Until the others fall asleep, and then we go."

"WHAT THE HELL is he doing?" Nyla said.

"Who?" Pax asked.

"In the special holding area."

Pax had been studying the guards in the stadium bleachers. He refocused his binoculars on the area within the tarp-covered fence. "I don't see anyone."

"That's what I'm talking about," she said. "He came out of the building and walked over to the fence, then I lost him."

"You sure he didn't go back inside?"

"Yes, sir. One hundred percent."

Pax scanned the fence all the way to the gate, searching for a tear in the tarp that might give him a view inside, but found none.

"Could be he just needed some time away from the others," he suggested.

"I guess."

"Keep an eye out for him. I'll be back in a minute."

He crawled backward from the crest of the hill and made his way to where the others were waiting.

When Martina saw him, she stood up. "Are they still there? Please tell me they're still there."

"The lights are on in the building, and Nyla saw at least one guy," Pax said. "So someone is."

She frowned. "A guy? Not any of the girls?"

Gabriel stepped over. "They usually stay inside after dinner, so that's probably where they are."

"'Probably' doesn't mean they are."

"Martina," Pax said. "I understand what you—"

"No, you don't. You don't understand. I should be—"

"We have *all* lost people. Many, many people. So when there's someone close to us still here, still breathing, we want to do anything we can to keep them alive. I get it. More than you can ever comprehend." He paused. "My aim here isn't to sound mean, but if you want to help us free your friends or whoever it is being held over there, then you need to get your head on straight and focus. If you can't, if you'll run off on your own and not follow directions, then I can't have you coming along. And worse, I'll have to task someone to stay here with you to make sure you don't do anything rash."

She hugged her arms across her chest and looked away.

After a moment, she nodded. "I get it. You're right."

"So are you in or out?"

"I'm in," she said, looking at him again. "Definitely."

"And I can trust you won't do anything stupid?"

"I'll do whatever you want me to do."

He held her gaze for a second before he smiled. "Never doubted you would. Wanted to make sure you didn't doubt, either." He turned to Gabriel. "The others?"

"Second team's in place," Gabriel said. "Team three's hiking in, but should be in position within thirty minutes."

"Good."

"Do we have a plan yet?"

"I got an inkling of something. It'll be a little risky."

"At this point, what wouldn't be?"

"You're right about that." He glanced sideways at Martina, who was still standing nearby. To Gabriel, he said, "Walk me back."

They headed up the slope toward the lookout point.

After they were out of range of the others, Pax said, "I'm going to need two people. Preferably a man and a woman. Gotta be people who are willing to act without hesitating. You got anybody like that in your squad?"

"Sure. Nyla and I."

The same as Pax had been thinking, but no way would he risk them both on what he had in mind. "I'll give it a little more thought and let you know what I decide."

"I'll be ready for whatever you need."

"Thanks."

Gabriel turned back when they reached the point where Pax had to drop to a crawl.

After Pax rejoined Nyla, he whispered, "Your guy show up again?"

Still looking through her binoculars, she nodded. "A moment ago. Popped up same place where he disappeared, then walked inside the building."

"Just getting air, I guess."

"Not sure about that. Take a look at the gate."

He raised his binoculars. "What am I looking for?"

"On the ground right outside."

He adjusted his angle.

"You looking?" she asked.

"Uh-huh."

"Just off center to the right."

He looked where she directed. "What the hell is that?"

"I'm not sure. But it slid out from under the fence a few minutes before I saw him again."

"Is that…dirt?"

"Could be."

"So he scooted a handful of dirt under the fence? Why?"

"No idea."

Pax searched the area around the dirt, but there was nothing else to see but grass. Whatever the kid was doing, they couldn't figure it out from where they were.

Putting it out of his mind, he refocused on the bleachers. "Let's take another count of the guards to make sure we haven't missed anyone."

31

ASH LOOKED OUT the Gulfstream's window at the world below. During the flight, he had seen lights on the ground in a few places, small pockets of false hope where the electricity had yet to fail. But as they descended toward Albany, New York, all lights were off.

Behind him, Ash could hear the others stirring in their seats, everyone awake and nervous about the unknown barreling toward them.

As the plane continued downward, Ash tried to get a sense of how much farther they had to go, but the darkness made it nearly impossible to judge. An exclamation of triumph from one of the pilots drew his attention to the cockpit. He leaned into the aisle to get a better look, and smiled when he saw what all the excitement was about. Out the front window were two rows of dim lights marking the runway.

Ash looked out the side window as the wheels touched down, and noted the landing lights weren't the ones affixed to the runway, but portable lamps with wires running between them.

The plane slowed and then taxied toward a hangar, where someone was waving more lights. When the G550 pulled to a stop, three people jogged toward it from a large helicopter parked nearby.

Ash unbuckled his belt and stood up. "Everyone hang

where you are for a moment. I'll be right back."

He motioned for Chloe to follow him, and headed over and opened the door. By the time he hopped off the steps, the three people were there.

A big man with a wide smile stepped forward. "Are you Captain Ash?"

"Ash is fine."

He held out his hand and the man took it.

"Edward Powell," the guy said. "Philadelphia team."

He turned to his two companions. "This is Omar Gamin, also Philadelphia."

"Omar," Ash said, shaking.

"And this is Tamara Costello."

As Ash shook her hand, he said, "We all enjoy your work."

"Thank you," she said, looking a bit embarrassed. "Really, all I do is stand there and talk. It's my partner Bobby who does the real work."

"The cameraman."

"Among other things."

Ash looked past them toward the helicopter. "Is he here?"

Powell shook his head. "He's on the recon team."

It had been Ash's idea to send an advance team to the coordinates so it could report back if something was there or not. He didn't know why Bobby was on it, though. The cameraman and Tamara had been brought into the mission so they could get some footage that, if there was a chance to broadcast it, would show people what was really going on.

Tamara apparently sensed his confusion. "Trust me, you'll be glad he went. Let me show you."

They walked quickly to the helicopter, where Tamara grabbed a laptop sitting inside and woke up the screen. She worked the keyboard and cursor for a moment, then said, "Bobby?"

A whisper came back. "Here."

"Captain Ash has arrived. Can you show him?"

"Hold on. Repositioning."

Tamara turned the computer around so they could all see the screen. Filling it was a green-tinted moving image. When it settled a few seconds later, Ash could make out three men crouching behind some trees. Beyond them was a black void.

The image zoomed into the darkness. As it passed the last of the trees, the area beyond began to take shape. It was a shallow valley with several buildings sitting squarely in the middle, lit only by moonlight.

A dead town.

"Everton, Vermont," Tamara told Ash.

"Changing lenses," Bobby whispered.

The picture went blurry for a moment before sharpening again and focusing on a brick building, large for the area, probably three stories high.

"On the roof," Bobby said. "Give it a second."

Scattered across the roof were several exhaust vents and a small, hut-like structure that Ash figured provided access to the inside of the building. Nothing unusual.

For several seconds the scene remained unchanged, and then, in a flash of brighter green, something moved out from behind the hut. Not something. Some*one*.

The person was carrying an M16A4 rifle, and decked out in the same military-style winter gear Ash had seen Project Eden soldiers wear that night in Las Cruces. He watched as the guard moved deliberately along the retaining wall at the edge of the roof.

No question. He was a lookout.

"Are there more?" he asked.

"We've ID'd two more guards so far, but the guys with me figure there's probably more."

"What about ones not obviously on watch?"

"No. Town's quiet otherwise."

"Do you know what they're guarding?"

"Haven't found it yet. But we haven't completed our loop. There has to be something."

Powell said, "I told them to do a full circuit of the town without getting too close."

Ash nodded, then said to Bobby, "When you finish,

return to whatever you deem the best spot for observation and hold there."

"Will do."

"And try not to get caught."

A low, nervous laugh from the other end, then, "Yeah, that's pretty high on my priority list."

As Tamara ended the communication, Ash glanced at Chloe. "You saw it, didn't you?"

"The uniform."

He nodded and turned to Powell. "How long will it take to get there?"

"I can fit your whole team in the helicopter. We can go as far as Rutland. Made the trip already when we dropped the others off. That's about twenty miles from Everton. Flight time just over thirty minutes."

"All right. Let's move."

As the team transferred to the helicopter, Ash called Ward Mountain.

"This is Leon."

"I need to talk to Rachel," Ash said.

"Hold on."

The delay was brief.

"Captain?" she said.

"There's definitely something there," he said.

A beat. "So we're on."

"Yes. Expect the go from me in the next few hours."

BOBBY LION AND the team from Philadelphia walked as silently as possible through the woods and around to the east side of the village. All this activity was a huge change over Bobby's past few days of lounging around the NSA facility.

First he and Tamara had raced up the highway from DC to right outside Philly, where they hooked up with Powell and his men at a private airfield. From there, they had flown north to Rutland in a surprisingly luxurious Sikorsky S-92 helicopter. The initial intention had been for only Powell's people to head up to Everton, but during the flight, Bobby had opened his big, fat mouth and mentioned the specialized gear he had in his bag, and how it might be a good idea if he went with them.

He didn't regret suggesting it, but there had been moments since they arrived on scene when he questioned his sanity. So far, though, the worst part was the cold.

They were walking across the side of the hills surrounding the valley, right around the midway point to the summit. For the most part, the walking was easy, but occasionally a slope forced them to lean to the side so they wouldn't lose balance.

After several more minutes, Marcos, the head of the team, motioned ahead at an opening in the dense forest, and made the signal Bobby had learned meant it was time to take another look around.

They stopped just inside the tree line at the top edge of the clearing and took a preliminary look at the town. Bobby was surprised by how close they were now. One of the homes on the outskirts of the village was maybe a hundred yards away, at the base of the hill. He had a sudden urge to turn and run but he held it together.

Marcos caught his eye and nodded, indicating Bobby was up.

With the help of one of the other men, Bobby removed his pack and pulled out the camera. As before, he started off with the small zoom lens and did a sweep of the valley. The man on top of the three-story building was still doing his slow rounds of the roof. One of the others Bobby had spotted earlier was also still in position, standing on a lower roof to the south.

He turned the lens to the north, and stopped. There was a third man, but not the one he'd seen earlier. That man was out of sight on the other side of town.

"Another one," he whispered.

"Where?" Marcos asked.

Bobby handed him the camera. "Two blocks this side from center. On the roof of the gas station."

Marcos searched for a moment, then nodded. "That's four."

He handed the camera back to Bobby, who continued his check. He spotted no more men, only a few additional buildings he hadn't been able to see before, and a nearly empty field just north of Everton, with what looked like a small pump house or storage hut in the middle.

He switched to the bulkier lens, once more needing assistance to hold the camera steady. He hit RECORD and repeated his sweep, spending a few extra seconds on the newly discovered guard before continuing north and ending when he reached the field.

He clicked the camera off and lowered it. "All set."

Less than a minute later, they were on the move again.

WICKS BARELY HAD time to drop to the ground before the patrol in the woods came into view. He froze, hoping they weren't wearing night-vision goggles. If they were, he was dead for sure.

Where the hell had they come from? He'd been watching Dream Sky for over an hour, and not once had there been any patrols this far out of town. Had he tripped some sort of sensor? There had been no mention of any in the information he'd culled about the place over the past few years.

He tilted his chin up enough so he could watch the patrol as it snaked through the trees and passed by less than thirty feet away. Five people in all—three men and two women, though he could have been wrong about that. Four of them were carrying rifles, while the fifth—definitely a man—carried a large pack on his back, but no obvious weapon.

That was strange enough, but what was even odder was that none of them were dressed in the typical Project Eden security outfits. The guard Wicks had seen in town was properly dressed, so why wasn't this patrol?

Once they passed out of sight, he rose to his knees and looked out at the field and the utility hut that was not a utility hut, then back in the direction the patrol had gone.

"Dammit," he whispered.

He climbed to his feet and headed after them.

32

Pax DECIDED HE and Nyla would execute his little ruse, while Gabriel remained with the others to take charge if something went wrong.

"You ready?" Pax asked her.

With a wicked smile, she said, "You bet I am."

He clicked the radio. "Everyone stand by. We're moving."

As he put his arm over Nyla's shoulder, she threw hers around his back.

"Lean into me," she said.

He did. "How's that?"

"Fine."

They moved along the edge of the stadium parking lot, Pax practicing his limp.

When he felt like he had it, he said, "Let's do this."

They turned onto the asphalt and headed straight for the stadium. The lot was largely dark, only the lights nearest the ballpark were on, so it wasn't until they'd stepped into the illuminated area that they earned the reaction they'd wanted.

"Car," Nyla whispered.

The sedan appeared around the corner to the right, coming fast. Pax and Nyla kept walking toward the stadium as if they hadn't seen it.

"Here we go," she said a few seconds later.

The car slowed to a stop directly in their path. Pax and Nyla halted, looking appropriately dazed. The two people inside climbed out and clicked on flashlights, shining them in Pax's and Nyla's faces.

Pax raised his free arm in front of his eyes and said in a weak voice, "Can you lower that, please?"

The beam tilted downward.

"Thank you."

"Evening," the driver said. "You two look like you've been through hell."

"Have you been out there?" Nyla said, a tremble in her voice. "It is hell."

"Of course," the other man said, his voice more soothing than his partner's. "But you've made it, and you're going to be fine now."

"So, this is the survival station?" Pax asked.

"Yes, sir."

"Thank God."

"I do need to ask," the nice one said, "are either of you sick?"

"No," Nyla said.

"You, sir?"

"I don't feel great," Pax said. "But it's because of my ankle. Think it might be busted."

The man smiled. "Not to worry. Our doctors can take care of that. Hop into the car. We'll give you a lift the rest of the way."

"That would be great," Nyla said.

With a nudge from his friend, the driver helped Nyla guide Pax to the vehicle.

"Best if we put your backpacks in the trunk," the nicer man said. "It'll be a tight squeeze otherwise."

"Oh, um, sure." Nyla peeled off her pack. "Here, Mr. Paxton, let me help you with yours."

After the bags were loaded up and Nyla and Pax were sitting in the backseat, the two men climbed in.

"You two know each other from before?" the nicer man asked as the driver started the car.

He never received his answer. Before the driver could drop the car in gear, Pax and Nyla placed guns—previously strapped to their legs—against the backs of the two chairs and pulled the triggers. They had chosen smaller-caliber pistols so the sound would be minimal. The choice also meant the Project Eden men had a higher chance of survival, but with the guns pressed against their backs, neither had a chance.

As soon as Pax and Nyla were sure the men were out of commission, they reached up front and hauled the driver into the back. Nyla slipped behind the wheel, while Pax ran his hand across the top of the backseat until he found the latch that allowed him access to the trunk.

Seat lowered, he pulled their bags through, dug out his radio, and clicked the talk button.

"Go!"

BEN TIPTOED THROUGH the building, checking the other bunks. On his last pass, two of the others had been awake, but now they too had drifted off. When he reached the girls and Preston, he nodded, put a finger to his lips, and headed over to the door.

As soon as they'd joined him, he pointed at each of them in the order they would follow him, starting with Jilly. He slipped out the door and along the building to the shadow by the fence. He was already on his way toward the gate when he heard the faint sound of the door opening again as Jilly came out, followed immediately by Preston.

At the gate, he crawled into the short ditch and began scraping away at the dirt on the other side, temporarily leaving the grass above it. He only had to clear away enough so they could scoot under and up, maybe two feet out at most.

Every third or fourth time he pulled the dirt under the gate, he glanced up to check on the others. Like they had discussed earlier, they were lining up in the shadow along the fence, waiting until the hole was done.

The farther he went, the more the layer of grass drooped. Once he felt he'd gone far enough, he moved back inside the enclosure and whispered, "Get ready."

Going under the gate on his back this time, he worked his fingers up through the grass and began pulling it down until the playing field tore loose at the edges. He ripped most of it out in a single large section and cleared away the rest, then pushed all the grass under the gate, knocking it out of the hole with a flick of his feet.

He stared up at the night sky. Things had gone well so far, but from this point forward everything would be improvisation. He lifted his head above the level of the grass and looked both ways. No one in sight.

He could feel his heart thumping, knowing the next step would put his life in serious danger.

It's better than staying here, he told himself. *You stay and you* will *die.*

He counted to three and pulled himself the rest of the way under the gate and out of the hole. He got up into a crouch and took another look around. No sign of any movement.

Something scraped below him, then the chain link on the gate rattled momentarily. He shot a look down. Jilly was part of the way through, her hand holding the gate in an attempt to stop it from moving.

"Quiet," he mouthed.

Her eyes were wide and scared, but she nodded. Slowly she let go of the fence, and relaxed when there was no more rattle.

Ben held out his hand, telling her to wait in the hole. He crept over to the outfield wall, which was covered by large blue sections of padding. Between the two mats at the very center was a crack through which he could see beyond the wall. He'd been right. It did open.

The problem was, how?

He ran his finger along the crack but found no release. He would have to go over, which meant he'd be in sight of every guard in the place. Maybe if he went quickly, he could—

A double *pop*.

He dropped to the ground.

The sound hadn't been loud, but it had been unusual. He looked back toward the stands and realized he had just enough of an angle to see part of one guard. The man was leaning against a pole as if nothing had happened.

Had he not heard the noise? Or was it a normal sound around here that Ben hadn't noticed before?

"What's going on?" Jilly whispered, her voice barely drifting out of the hole.

He crawled over. "Did you hear that noise?"

"I heard something. Thought you made it."

"Uh-uh."

"What was it?"

"Don't know."

He looked back at the fence.

"Are we going to go or not?" she asked.

"Hold on. Let me—"

The sound of running steps stopped him. Not on the field, but farther away in the stands, and…receding.

He cautiously rose back to his feet and inched out until he could see the guard he'd noticed before, but no one was there. He inched out a little farther, checking to see if the guy had repositioned. He found that not only was the guard missing, but the next guard down was gone, too.

Emboldened, he continued pushing the boundaries until he was standing free of the holding area's cover.

All the guards in the stands were gone.

For a full two seconds, he didn't move.

Then he turned toward the center-field wall and ran.

MARTINA WAS NOT happy.

Gabriel had decided she would be on lookout, meaning she had to stay on the hill and report what was going on instead of being with everyone else headed to the stadium.

"You promised you would do what we told you," he reminded her when she protested the assignment.

She hated him in that moment for reminding her, but she

had taken the binoculars and remained behind.

From her vantage point, she was able to watch while Pax and Nyla were stopped in the parking lot and put in the car. Moments later, there was a bright flash from the interior, followed by the soft echo of the bullets.

Then Pax's voice came over the radio. "Go!"

Martina moved the lenses from the car to the trees where group one was gathered. Seconds after Pax's command, the group moved into the parking lot in a loose line. Though she couldn't see them from here, she knew the other two groups were also making their way toward the stadium.

She switched her view to the interior of the stadium, focusing on the detention area she was sure her friends were in. Her brow furrowed.

What the…?

Someone was outside the gate, kneeling next to…a hole in the ground? Not only that, apparently someone was *in* the hole.

Oh, my God, she thought. *They're breaking out.*

The person who'd been kneeling suddenly shot up and looked inward at the stadium. She raised her glasses, trying to see what had drawn his attention. For a moment she couldn't figure out what it was, then she realized the guards were gone.

She trained the glasses back on the guy on the field. He had moved away from the hole and was stepping slowly from the shadows into the lit open area to the right of the fence.

It wasn't very long before he seemed to realized what she'd already discovered, because he turned and started running toward the back of the field.

Martina gasped.

As the man turned, his face had come into view.

Ben.

He was *alive!*

Without another thought, she jumped up and began running down the hill.

BLEEP-BLEEP.

Bleep-bleep.

Dr. Lawrence looked up from her desk, unsure where the noise was coming from.

Bleep-bleep.

Bleep-bleep.

Dr. Rivera grabbed the radio off the central table. He twisted a dial on top and the sound decreased.

The general alarm, Lawrence realized. It had been tested once when they first arrived but hadn't been used since.

Suddenly the *bleeping* was replaced by the voice of Brooks, station director. "All security personnel report to entrances one, two, and four. Multiple individuals approaching."

"Multiple?" Lawrence said.

"I repeat," Brooks said. "All security personnel report to entrances one, two, and four. Multiple individuals approaching. Intake officers report to your stations."

"That's us," Lawrence said, standing.

Rivera looked annoyed. "The others can handle this."

"I'll let you explain that to the director when she comes asking where you were."

"Fine." He pushed up.

On the way to the door, Lawrence swung by the observation room. The subject was stretched out on the cot, staring at the ceiling. Lawrence activated the intercom. "Ruby, how's your headache?"

"Gone."

"Excellent news."

"I take it you are still feeling no other symptoms?"

"You take it right," the girl said, not hiding her displeasure.

"Don't worry. In the morning this will all be over," Lawrence said with a smile before heading for the door where Rivera was waiting.

"Still no sign of infection?" he asked.

"None."

WHILE THE TEAMS drew the attention of the security personnel, Pax and Nyla drove over to the back of the stadium and hopped out of the car.

"Martina," Pax said into his radio. "Have they pulled the guards from inside the stadium?"

No answer.

"Martina? Do you read me?"

He turned and looked toward the hill where she was supposed to be stationed.

"Martina?"

He saw someone enter the parking area from the base of the hill, running.

"Who the hell is that?" he said.

Nyla followed his gaze. "I'm not sure."

"Is it Martina?"

"Could be."

Two armed men ran out from the east side of the stadium, on an intercept course for the person Pax had spotted.

"Son of a bitch," Pax said.

If it was Martina, there was no one around to help her.

"Come on," he told Nyla as he headed back out into the parking lot.

"STEADY," GABRIEL SAID just loudly enough for the others in his group to hear.

They were walking at a normal pace, hopefully projecting a sense they were not a threat. Their weapons, though, were all close at hand.

Ahead, five Project Eden soldiers were approaching. They, of course, were not even attempting to conceal their firepower. Each carried a rifle, the barrels angled at the sky.

When there were only about fifty feet between the guards and Gabriel's group, one of the guards shouted, "Please hold right there."

"Are we in the wrong place?" Gabriel said. "Isn't this the survival station?"

"Yes, sir, it is, but we need you and the others to stop so we can talk with you."

"Oh, sure. Everyone, it's okay."

The group came to a staggered halt, while the guards continued forward until they were only a few yards away.

The guard who'd spoken said something softly into a mic attached to his jacket. When he looked back at Gabriel, he said, "You're a pretty big group."

"Picked up people here and there on the way," Gabriel said.

"What about the others?"

"What others?" Gabriel asked, feigning confusion.

"Got a couple other groups about the same size as yours coming in on the other side of the stadium."

Gabriel made a big show of sighing in relief. "I'm so glad to hear that. I thought we'd lost them."

"They're with you?"

"Yes. We got separated once we reached the city. I'm glad to hear they're okay." Gabriel stuck his hand out and stepped forward. "I'm Gabriel."

The move took the man off guard. He hesitated, then removed his hand from the stock of his rifle and shook Gabriel's.

Gabriel had the man's rifle before the guy had a chance to react. The main guard grabbed for his radio, but Gabriel smashed the butt of the gun into his hand, batting it away and breaking bones in the process. He looked over and saw the rest of his team, led by Resistance security members, had disarmed the other guards.

"Ramon," he said. "Please take possession of this man's radio."

As Ramon removed the device, the guard said, "What the fuck? This is not the way to get our help."

"That's funny," Gabriel told him. "I hadn't realized Project Eden was in the business of helping."

The guard stiffened. "Who are you?"

As tempted as Gabriel was to answer with another thrust of the rifle butt, he motioned to the others that it was time to move. Keeping the guards between them, they hurried the rest of the way to the stadium.

Gabriel took a quick look around, and then pointed at a metal pipe railing meant to protect the public from a sunken drainage intake. "That should do nicely," he said.

They secured the guards to the railing with zip ties.

"Whatever you're planning," the main guard said, "do you really think you're going to get away with it?"

Gabriel plucked his own radio off his belt and clicked the SEND button. "Team B?"

The delay was barely a second. "Team B secure."

"Team C?"

Again, a brief pause. "Team C secure."

"Anyone have any problems?"

"Negative."

"None here."

"Stand by," Gabriel said. He looked at the guard. "Actually, I think we've already gotten away with it."

Hypodermics were produced, and before the guards realized what was going on, they were each injected with enough sedative to knock them out for at least twelve hours.

Gabriel raised the radio again. "Phase two."

33

THE REASSIGNMENT ROOM was back in order—the chairs in straight rows, the body fluids cleaned up, and the smell of sweat and fear filtered from the air.

Terrell had felt like a robot as he helped Diaz and the others get things ready for the next group. When he and Diaz had hauled the bodies out of town, Terrell had considered slipping away and disappearing forever. But that would have been the cowardly choice, a selfish act no better than if he were pushing the button to activate the gas.

So he had returned and done what he had done so many times before.

"Better be the last group today," Diaz whispered to him as they waited outside the room for the guard detail to return with the next batch of survivors. "By the time we get back from the dump, it'll be almost three a.m., and if I don't get some sleep I might start bashing in heads myself."

Terrell knew he should respond with some witty comeback—that kind of banter made up most of their communication—but all he could manage was a small nod and barely audible "yeah."

Diaz frowned. "What's wrong with you? You've been acting weird all day."

"Sorry. Just...tired," Terrell said, seizing on to Diaz's

own admission.

"Lightweight," Diaz said.

Terrell forced a smile. "Better a lightweight than a dumb shit like you."

If Diaz noticed Terrell's less than smooth delivery, he made no mention of it. Instead, he seemed to take Terrell's jab as a sign that everything was okay. He grunted a laugh and said nothing more.

FROM THE JOURNAL OF BELINDA RAMSEY

I HAVE BEEN trying to sleep for the last two hours, but the buzzing in my head refuses to go away. So I've decided to write a bit and hope that getting some of my thoughts down will clear my mind.

The doctors and their soldiers came a total of three times today, taking more of us with them each time. Our holding area is no longer crowded. No one needs to share a bed anymore. In fact, there are several empties around.

No one who had been taken away has come back. Not a single person. But the things they arrived here with, the things they'd been allowed to bring with them into the holding area, are all still here. Someone, I'm not sure who, has moved all the missing people's possessions to the back of the room. Why? I don't know. I just know that I don't like it. When the others do come back, they are going to wonder why someone touched their things.

All right, all right, I know. Maybe the others aren't coming back. It still doesn't mean we have the right to displace their things so quickly.

I think I'm going crazy. I think I'm focusing on things that aren't important, but what else can I do?

Where have the others gone? Why won't the doctors tell us what's happening? Why are they—

I hear the gate opening.

They're calling for us to come out again.

More later.

TERRELL HEARD THE footsteps long before the procession came into view. As usual, Drs. Harvell, Wilhelm, and Yang were in front, followed by the survivors—twenty-one this go-around—and then the guards.

The first few groups that had been escorted in had been full of hope and excitement, while those that followed were progressively less so. The new group looked as if nearly everyone's hope was gone.

Terrell tried not to glance at any of their faces for more than a second, but then a girl near the middle of the pack locked eyes with him and he could not look away. She was maybe twenty, with an intelligence in her gaze that reminded him of a girl back in high school. Lindsey, two years ahead of him. She had always been kind, even helped him study on occasion.

The girl being led to her death continued to stare at him all the way into the room, and for a moment he thought, *She knows. She knows what we're about to do to them*. But that was impossible. She was just tired like the others, he told himself, done in by the ordeal of survival and the wait for the promised vaccine.

"Please, everyone, move all the way to the end of the rows and take a seat," Dr. Wilhelm said as the survivors entered.

Terrell and Diaz followed the last of the guards in, stopping next to the door as they'd done at the start of each previous session.

After everyone was seated, Wilhelm said, "Let me be the

303

first to say congratulations. You have all cleared the quarantine period, and in a few minutes you will be administered the Sage Flu vaccine."

There were murmurs of relief and even a few smiles, the dark mood lifting a little.

"First, though, we will be showing you a video that explains the safe zone you'll be taken to after you get inoculated. So please relax and we'll get it started."

Several hands shot up.

Dr. Harvell took a step forward. "We understand that you have a lot of questions. Some of those will be answered by the video. If you still have questions after, we'll be happy to answer them then."

Though Terrell had heard the words before, their true wickedness hit him hard this time. They were for the doctors' benefit only, so that they wouldn't have to face any longer than necessary those who were about to die.

The survivors lowered their hands. As Terrell was about to look away, he saw the girl again. Unlike the others who were watching the doctors, she was looking at him. It was almost as if she were trying to see into him to find the truth.

He blinked and tore his gaze away as the lights began to dim.

The doctors and guards made their way out of the room, then Terrell and Diaz grabbed the double doors and began to close them. As he swung his half around, Terrell tried to resist the urge to look back at the girl but failed. She wasn't looking at him anymore. Her eyes were on the screen, and he could see the faintest bit of hope on her face. His breath caught in his throat.

Click. The doors sealed shut.

Click. A switch flicked on inside him.

Per routine, the doctors headed back to their offices. They would stay there until twenty minutes later, when they would be needed to verify everyone was dead. All but two of the guards also left. The two who remained took up positions in front of the airtight doors while Terrell and Diaz made their way to the control room.

"Evening, guys," Harris said as they entered. He was the board operator and had been the one who'd dimmed the lights.

A wide-screen monitor on the front wall displayed a feed from inside the room. A few of the survivors were fidgeting in their chairs.

"Showtime," Harris said as he hit a button that dimmed the lights the rest of the way.

A second button started the video projector, and on the screen in front of the survivors, the image of Gustavo Di Sarsina appeared. As the man started speaking, Diaz stepped over to the controls that operated the gas. A turn of the key and a tap of the switch would set things in motion.

Terrell watched as his partner removed the safety guard and reached for the key.

"Wait," Terrell said. "Can I?"

Diaz raised an eyebrow. He'd always been the one who had to perform this task.

"About fucking time," Diaz said.

He stepped away and made a grand motion of ceding control.

As Terrell stepped into place, Diaz said, "You know what to do?"

"I know what to do."

Terrell placed his hand on the key, feeling the curved top and the hole where a ring would go through. Just turn and push the button and they would all die.

"Anytime now," Diaz said, a laugh in his voice.

Enough.

The key slipped out of the slot surprisingly easily.

Diaz was still grinning as Terrell whirled around and jabbed the jagged piece of metal into his neck. Though unintentional, the aim had been perfect. Blood pumped from Diaz's carotid artery, gushing down on the counter and covering the touch screen.

"What the fuck?" Harris said, turning at Diaz's gargling sound.

Terrell launched himself forward and slammed into

Harris, ramming him back against the other counter. There was a loud *smack* as Harris's torso connected with the sharp edge. He screamed as his face twisted in pain. Terrell jammed the bloody key into the man's neck. Unfortunately, he was a little off this time, and had to dig around for a second before ripping open the artery with the uneven edge of the key.

Harris dropped to his knees, clutching at his wound.

Terrell leaned against the wall, hyperventilating as the reality of what he'd done hit him. Both men were on the floor, unmoving. Unconscious or dead, he didn't bother to check.

Keep moving! he told himself. He was all in now.

He ran over to the control room door and inched it open. He could see the two guards down the hall in front of the sealed doorway.

He opened the door a bit more and said, "Excuse me." The guards looked over. "Could one of you come down here? We've got a piece of equipment malfunctioning and need to move it. Could use some help."

As soon as the nearest guard was headed his way, Terrell pulled back.

This was going to be trickier, he knew. A guard wasn't a defenseless tech, and wasn't likely to allow a key to be shoved into his neck. Terrell grabbed an unused laptop off the table near the door. It was the only thing near him with any heft to it. He then moved to the other side of the door.

As soon as the guard entered, Terrell pushed the door closed and brought the edge of the laptop down onto the back of the man's head.

The guard buckled but didn't fall. As the man put a hand over where he'd been hit, Terrell brought the computer down again, and again, and again. Finally, the guard joined the others on the ground.

Working quickly, Terrell retrieved the guard's rifle and returned to the entrance. He cracked the door open and peeked outside, expecting the other guard to still be back at his station, but the man was heading toward the control room.

"Everything all right?" the guard asked.

Terrell widened the opening. "A bit more trouble than

we thought. Sorry."

The guard was about a dozen feet away now, his eyes narrowing. "What's that on your face."

Terrell lifted a finger to his cheek and felt a drop of something sticky and wet. Blood, he realized.

The approaching guard seemed to sense something was up a half second after Terrell realized his ruse had run its course, but he had enough time to raise his rifle and pull the trigger before the other man could do the same.

As the guard dropped to the ground, the echo of the shot reverberated down the hall. Knowing it wouldn't be long before someone came to investigate, Terrell raced out of the room, snatched up the other man's rifle, and ran to the Reassignment Room door.

The rubber seals sucked loudly as he pulled the doors open.

When he rushed into the room, several of the survivors screamed, and all jerked back as if he were about to attack them. Which, he quickly realized, was what barreling in there with two rifles probably looked like.

"It's okay. It's okay. I'm not going to hurt you. I'm here to get you out. We need to go now!"

No one moved.

He searched out the girl and spoke directly to her. "Please. If you stay here, they will kill you."

"Who will?" the girl asked.

He gestured with the rifle back toward the rest of the warehouse. "Everyone!"

She stared at him, confused.

"Don't you understand?" he said. "We didn't bring you in here to vaccinate you. We were supposed to gas you."

Shock and terror rippled through the room.

"Come on," he said. "There's no time!"

He turned for the door, hoping they would follow.

The girl was the first to get up. "He's right. We all knew something was wrong. We need to leave."

"What if it's a trick?" someone argued. "What if he kills us out there?"

"Here. There. What does it matter?"

The girl ran toward the door. Before she reached it, the others were up and following.

Terrell moved into the corridor and checked both ways. No one was there yet. Perhaps the others hadn't heard it, or maybe had been behind closed doors and hadn't registered what the noise meant. If so, it was a blessing, but one that would last only until someone noticed the guards weren't where they were supposed to be.

He held the extra rifle out to the girl.

"I don't know how to shoot."

"Point and pull the trigger. Anyone you see who is not in this group will want to kill you."

As soon as she took it, he led the group down the hallway toward the loading docks. It wasn't the closest exit, but he thought it would give them their best chance to get away.

The girl stayed with him step for step. After a few moments, she said, "You're not the UN, are you?"

"No. No one here is."

"The others who were locked up with us and taken out earlier?"

"Don't ask me that."

She was silent for several seconds. "Why are you doing this?"

"Don't ask me that, either."

Five yards ahead, another hallway branched off to the right. Terrell held up his hand, telling everyone to stop, then proceeded to the intersection alone and took a look around the corner.

Shit.

A couple of techs were standing outside a door maybe twenty feet down, drinking coffee and talking. Worse, a dozen feet farther down the hall, a guard was heading toward them on rounds. If it had been only the techs, Terrell and the survivors could have waited a few minutes and hoped the two men went inside the room. The guard, though, would come all the way to the end of his hall, turn the corner, and see them standing there.

Terrell leaned against the wall, unsure what to do.

Who's more important? a voice in his head said. *The three people in the hall who work for the organization responsible for more human deaths than ever in the history of the world? Or the innocents behind you?*

He cursed to himself and then took a deep breath. Gripping the rifle in his hands, he pushed himself from the wall into the middle of the intersection.

The only one to notice him was the guard, but the man only had time for a puzzled look before Terrell squeezed the trigger.

The burst of bullets filled the hallway, cutting down all three men. Off to Terrell's side, several of the survivors screamed.

"That way!" he yelled, waving down the hallway past him. "Go! Go!"

"WHAT THE HELL was that?" Evie Ruiz asked.

The unmistakable sound of gunfire had come from the warehouse.

Alonzo Knox moved his binoculars back and forth as he examined the building. "Don't see anything."

"That wasn't one of ours, was it?" She brought up her radio. "Blue One to all. Who fired that?"

Her three satellite teams all reported back that it wasn't them.

"And none of you are receiving fire?"

None.

Had someone been doing target shooting inside the building? Seemed a little late at night for that.

As Evie started to bring up her own binoculars, more shots rang out, at least two different guns, maybe three.

"Sounds like a firefight," Alonzo said. "Should we do something?"

Evie grimaced. They were supposed to do nothing until told otherwise.

She grabbed her pack and pulled the sat phone out of the main compartment. She hesitated a moment before punching in the quick-dial number.

"Ward Mountain."

"Ruiz. Chicago."

"This is Leon. Go ahead, Evie."

"Think we might have a situation here," she said.

"Explain."

She told him what she'd heard.

"No visual sign of activity?" he asked.

"None yet. But I'm wondering if this is something that we should take advantage of."

"Hang on for a sec."

While she waited, she looked back at the building. She and her team had been given the task of creating a disruption at the survival station once they were given the go signal. It would be part of a coordinated effort with teams all over the world, so she was pretty sure what the decision was going to be.

When Leon came back on, he said, "We'd like you to hold for now. But keep monitoring the situation. If things change and you have enough time to report back, do so. Otherwise you are free to make the call. Just be sure to let us know as soon as you can after."

The hold was what she'd expected, but the flexibility was not. "Got it," she said. "I'll keep you posted."

After she hung up, Alonzo said, "So?"

"For the moment, we wait."

TERRELL STAYED AT the back end of the group, constantly looking over his shoulder for the counterattack he knew would be coming.

"Where are we supposed to be going?" the girl shouted from up front.

"Loading dock. Straight ahead," he said just loudly enough for those around him to hear.

They passed the message forward.

He was starting to think they might make it to the dock unmolested when a burst of bullets raked the wall only ten feet behind him. The shots came from a hallway they'd passed seconds before. He couldn't see the shooters but returned fire anyway, hoping to keep them tucked back around the corner.

He chanced a look ahead, and saw that the girl was nearing the warehouse door. There shouldn't be anyone on the other side but that wasn't a guarantee.

"To the side," he said as he ran through the group, arriving at the door a moment after the girl did. "I'll check."

He eased the door open and let his gun lead him through. The truck they used to transport the dead was backed up to the dock where they'd left it, waiting for its next trip. Otherwise, the area was empty.

"All right," he said. "Quick. Into the truck."

He held the door open as wide as it would go so they could pile past him.

"Get in the cab," he told the girl. "The keys are in the ignition. Start it up. I'll be right there."

She nodded and took off around the side of the truck while the others climbed into the back. He couldn't help but think about the fact the truck had been waiting for those people, only they weren't supposed to be still breathing when they boarded it again.

After the last person raced by, he slammed the door closed and jammed a shipping dolly under the handle to slow down their pursuers.

As he was turning to run for the truck, bullets punched through the metal door. At first he thought a piece of the door had torn free and hit him in the back. He stumbled a few steps but righted himself. That's when he realized he was bleeding, not only in back but in front, too. A bullet had passed through his right shoulder just below his clavicle.

He gritted his teeth against the pain as he hopped off the dock and moved quickly to the cab of the truck. He jumped on the running board outside the driver's door and saw the girl in the passenger seat.

"You're going to have to drive," he said through the open window.

"What? Why?" Then she saw his shirt. "You've been hit."

"You can do it. It's an automatic. Pretty much like any car." He motioned at the other end of the loading area, where the overhead cover ended. "Hang a left and that'll get you to the main road. From there go south as fast as you can. There are several car dealers that way. You can't miss them. There are trackers in this truck so you need to switch vehicles."

"You're not coming with us?"

"Don't worry about me! You need to get out of here! Whatever you do, avoid big cities and any survival stations. Hurry!"

As she crawled into the driver's seat, another salvo of bullets ripped into the metal door and flew through the dock, barely missing the truck.

"Go!" he said, stepping to the ground.

More gunfire poured out of the building. The girl stepped on the accelerator and the truck jerked away from the dock.

Terrell glanced back at the now perforated door, knowing members of the security team would come charging through it at any moment. He aimed his rifle at it and let off several warning shots, in hopes of delaying them for a few more seconds, and then took off running after the truck.

He reached the vehicle right before it cleared the covered area. He jumped onto the rear bumper, and could see those he'd rescued huddled together in the back, their eyes wide with fear. He wanted to say something to comfort them, but no words came.

As the truck turned for the main road, he saw the shipping dolly give way and the door fly open. He didn't bother aiming when he fired off three more shots as the dock disappeared from view.

Turning onto the main road, the truck started to pick up speed, so Terrell hopped off while he still could and ducked behind an abandoned VW van at the side of the road. He watched the truck race away, and then turned his attention back to the warehouse, hardly believing what he had done.

THE GUNFIRE WAS now coming from the loading dock area. Evie had her binoculars trained on the entrance, but so far had seen nothing.

She snapped up her radio. "Everyone stand by."

A truck rumbled out of the dock area, the same one they'd seen go in and out several times, always with a male driver. This time, the driver was a young woman, her face tense and scared.

As the truck took a right turn onto the main road, an armed man hopped off the back and ran behind a van like he was trying to hide from anyone still at the survival station.

She couldn't comprehend what she was seeing.

"Evie," Alonzo said, slapping her arm. "In the back of the truck."

She swung her binoculars around and looked inside the vehicle's cargo area. There were people there, fifteen or more. Old and young, men and women, and none dressed in Project Eden uniforms.

For a second, she simply stared, unable to move as she realized what was going on.

"Go," she said to Alonzo. "Follow them. Take Gage with you. Those are survivors. They're escaping!"

TERRELL KNEW THE Project would never let the detainees escape unchallenged, so he would have to try to stop them.

He had no idea how many shots he had left. He would have to make the remaining bullets count.

Yeah, and then what?

And then…well, he would deal with *then* when it came.

He had expected to see security rush out of the loading dock, but instead a Jeep came racing along the back of the warehouse.

As it turned onto the main road, Terrell took careful aim and squeezed the trigger. His bullet pierced the windshield and entered the driver's head. With a sudden swerve to the right, the Jeep jumped the curb and plowed head on into the side of a plumbing supply building.

While the men in front were clearly dead, the two in back pulled themselves from the wreckage and staggered to the sidewalk. Terrell recognized them as two of the men usually tasked with watching the holding areas, but he didn't know their names.

The one in the lead raised his rifle and scanned the street.

It would have been an easy shot for Terrell, but he hesitated. Taking out the Jeep that could have easily caught up to the truck was one thing. Shooting an injured man standing still was something else altogether.

Terrell crept back behind the van so that he wouldn't be seen, but as he stepped over the curb, his foot slipped on a patch of ice and he instinctively slapped his hand against the vehicle to steady himself. The man in the street whirled around at the *whap* of metal. He pulled his trigger and held it down, burning through the whole magazine.

The vehicle shuddered under the barrage. Terrell wasn't sure at what point the bullets struck him, but it didn't matter. He deserved it.

With what strength he had left, he pulled himself out from behind the van.

"You?" the security guard said, surprised.

The man's expression transitioned into one of pure fury. He clicked a new magazine into place, raised his rifle, and aimed it at Terrell's head.

Go ahead, Terrell thought.

The blast from two shots filled the street. But neither hit Terrell. Instead, the guards dropped to the ground.

EVIE WATCHED IN near disbelief as the guy who'd hopped off the back of the truck took out a Jeep full of soldiers with a single shot.

When the two guards who'd survived climbed out, she expected the man behind the van to shoot them, too. Instead, one of the soldiers shot first, strafing the van until his rifle clicked empty.

Evie missed the next few seconds as she reached back for her rifle. When she looked at the road again, the man had crawled out from the van's protection, his clothes covered with blood. The soldier in the street had just finished reloading his rifle and was bringing it up to shoot again.

Evie aimed her weapon and squeezed the trigger, taking out the soldier, then quickly moved the barrel and eliminated his partner.

She picked up her radio. "Everyone, now!"

Before she could even get to her feet, explosions started going off all around the perimeter of the survival station. She pulled out her own remote and set off her charges. The first was a hundred yards down the street, in a car parked next to the warehouse. The concussion ripped a whole in the side of the building.

Her second bomb was the one she was most proud of. She had been able to place it outside the loading dock area. When it went off, the entire covering collapsed, rendering the dock inaccessible and blocking the access road that the Jeep had used along the back of the building.

As she made her way off the roof and down to the street, more bombs went off, some merely adding to the chaos, some doing actual damage to the building. Explosions were timed to continue for the next hour, with the occasional lull built in to achieve the maximum amount of terror.

She stopped when she reached the sidewalk and checked to make sure the street was clear. Then, keeping low, she headed down the block. In the gutter, she found the man who'd been hiding behind the van, lying on his back and blinking at the sky.

She knelt beside him and said softly, "Hi."

With much effort, he turned his head enough to see her. "Who…who are…you?"

"A friend."

"I don't…remember you."

One look at his wounds told her all she needed to know.

"What happened in there?"

"I'm sorry," he said. "I...couldn't do it...any...more. I know I broke...the promise...but we...we were..."

"Don't worry about the promise. I don't care about that. Who were those people in the truck?"

He closed his eyes for a moment. "I couldn't kill anyone else...I just couldn't. I'm sorry. But can't you...let this group go?"

She smiled. "You have my word. No one will harm them."

He looked at her as if unsure he could believe her. "You're just saying...that."

"I'm not."

Whether she convinced him or not, she would never know. He exhaled a breath and never drew in another.

She stayed with him for another few seconds out of respect for what he'd done, and then hurried back to grab her things and get out of there.

34

BEN LEAPT AS he neared the fence, grabbed the top, and pulled himself up and over.

No yells for him to stop. No bullets hitting the ground around him.

He'd been right. For the moment, no one was watching.

He examined the back of the fence, found the latches holding the two sections together, and unhooked them.

As soon as the wall parted, he said, "Jilly, now!"

She climbed out of the hole and sprinted over to him.

"Stay here until everyone is through," he said. "The instant the last person comes out, close the gate."

"What are you going to do?"

"Figure out where we go from here."

WHEN DR. LAWRENCE and Dr. Rivera entered the room used for large group intakes, they expected all the other administration personnel who usually helped out to be there. Surprisingly, only two others were present.

"Are we in the wrong place?" Lawrence asked.

Dieter Schneider, the man in charge of survivor viability assessment, shrugged. "I just got here myself, but I do not think so."

"Then where is everyone?" Rivera asked.

The girl sitting in one of the chairs said, "There were more people here, but the director got a call and she took them with her."

"When was this?" Lawrence asked.

"About two minutes ago."

"Did she say what we were supposed to do?" Schneider asked.

"The only thing anyone told me was to say here."

They were probably up in the director's office, Lawrence thought. She turned for the door.

"Where are you going?" Rivera asked.

"Well, I'm not staying here. If something's going on, I want to know what it is."

Apparently so did Rivera and Schneider. They followed her upstairs and found the others not in the director's office, but in the security monitoring center down the hall. Formerly a conference room, it was now equipped with dozens of monitors, each showing feeds from different cameras around the stadium. The director and the rest of the management team were gathered in front of two of the biggest monitors.

Lawrence walked up to the group. "What's going on?"

"Problems," Hughes, head of supply, whispered.

"What problems?" Lawrence asked, looking at the monitors.

Each displayed a lit-up slice of the parking area surrounding the stadium. One was completely empty, while in the other was a large group of people talking to seven members of Project security.

"Just watch," he said.

"Is this live?"

He shook his head. "Happened a few minutes ago."

Except for the size of the survivor group, it seemed no different than other encounters Lawrence had witnessed. If all stayed to form, within a few minutes the guards would be escorting the survivors to the stadium for processing. But things did not stay to form.

Before she realized what was happening, several of the survivors had weapons in their hands. Others grabbed the guards, stripping them of their rifles. One of the guards struggled free and tried to make a run for it, but the man who'd taken his rifle smashed it into the guard's back, knocking him to the ground. The guard tried to rise but the man hit him again, this time in the head. The guard collapsed and stopped moving.

"Oh, my God," Lawrence said. "Who are these people?"

"We don't know," the director said. "Three large groups arrived at once. We sent teams to intercept each, but we've lost contact with all of them. This is the only one we have on camera, but I assume the others have met with the same fate."

"A coordinated attack?" Schneider said. "Why?"

The director turned and looked at him. "Let me take a stab in the dark. Perhaps they've discovered the true nature of our business here?"

"How...how could they possibly know that?" he stammered.

"At the moment, I don't care. I'm more concerned about the safety of this facility."

"How many guards are missing?" Lawrence asked.

"Nineteen."

The facility had a twenty-five member security force. Six was not nearly enough to guard the stadium.

The director was clearly on the same wavelength. "Have everyone in your departments report to the armory immediately," she said, scanning the managers assembled behind her.

Hughes grimaced and said, "But they don't all have training for—"

"I don't *care* what they've been trained for," she said. "Go! Get them—"

"Director!" Rivera shouted from the back of the pack. "The detainees!"

They all turned toward him. He was pointing at a small monitor that showed a wide shot of the stadium's interior from the press boxes above home plate. All three holding areas could be seen in the image, but everyone was looking at the gap in the center-field fence. They watched as two people ran out from somewhere behind the immune compound and through the opening.

"Goddammit!" the director yelled. "How many?"

"At least three," Rivera said. "Shouldn't the guards have…" He stopped, obviously realizing no guards were currently inside the stadium."

"What are you all standing here for?" the director asked. "Go!"

MARTINA RACED TOWARD the back of the stadium, her legs aching from her days of walking. But it was easy to ignore the pain.

Ben was *here*.

She was so focused on her destination that she didn't see the two soldiers running toward her until they shouted at her to stop.

She nearly tripped over her own feet, and had barely stopped when two gunshots rocketed across the parking lot. The uniformed men dropped to the ground.

Seconds later, Pax and Nyla ran up, rifles in their hands.

"What are you doing?" Nyla shouted.

"I…I…"

"You need to get back to your post," Pax said.

"No! I can't. Ben. He's there. I saw them."

"Your boyfriend?" Nyla said. "I thought you told me he was dead."

"I was wrong. He's alive. He's inside!"

She stepped to the side to get past them and head for the stadium, but Pax snagged her around the waist.

"Let me go!" she yelled. "Let me go! It's Ben!"

"It's too dangerous," he told her.

She twisted and turned but couldn't break his grip. "Let me go. Please! He's there. He's trying to get out! I need to help him."

"What do you mean, trying to get out?" Nyla asked.

"I was watching the stadium and saw that they've dug a hole under the gate of the tarped area. Someone was standing outside. When he turned, I saw it was Ben."

"Are you sure?"

"Absolutely."

"And you think he was trying to get out?"

"Yes! Yes! Now please let me go."

Nyla and Pax shared a look.

"All right," Pax said. "We'll go together. But you need to stick with us."

"Sure, sure. Whatever. Come on!"

WITH NO STAFF assigned to the medical assessment department other than the two of them, Lawrence and Rivera were the first to reach the armory. Rivera used his code to get inside, and they each selected a pistol because, like most non-security Project personnel, it was the only type of weapon they'd been trained on.

As they exited, Rivera turned in the direction of the lab.

"No. Follow me," Lawrence said as she started jogging the other way.

"Where are you going?"

Without stopping, she said, "I don't know about you, but I'm not about to lose a whole group of potential test subjects!"

KEEPING AS CLOSE to the stadium as possible, Gabriel led his team to a ticket-holder entrance along the third-base side. The gates were solid on the bottom, but the tops were covered with heavy wire mesh. As expected, all gates were locked, but Gabriel's team had come prepared for that.

He nodded at Cahill and Walker. They ran up to the nearest gate and pulled out the reciprocating saws they'd been carrying on ropes under their jackets. Each was equipped with a blade intended for metal use. While the two men went to work cutting through the mesh, the others split their attention between watching the parking lot and keeping an eye on the inside area beyond the gate.

"We're at our entrance now," Gabriel said into his mic. "Team B and C, status?"

"Team B, at our gate, almost through."

Gabriel waited. After a few seconds of silence, he said, "Team C?"

"Sorry," the leader of Team C said. "Had a little problem with one of the guards. Taken care of now. We're still on the way to ours, but should be there in the next two minutes."

The basic goal of the mission was to free the prisoners and cause Project Eden as much trouble as possible. The wish-list goal was a complete takeover of the facility. The next several minutes would decide which one they'd accomplish.

"Done," Cahill said.

He and Walker pulled out the freed section of mesh and dropped it on the ground. Two volunteers from Isabella Island hoisted another former island resident—a short and sinewy woman—through the hole to the other side. Once she was clear, one of the saws was passed through, and she made quick work of the chain holding the gate closed.

As Team A hurried into the stadium, Gabriel tapped his mic again. "We're in."

BETWEEN THE TWO sets of outfield bleachers was a wide concrete wedge running from the center-field wall to the outer wall of the stadium. Ben crossed it in no time and moved along the perimeter fence, looking for a way out.

The only gates he found were locked solid. He spent a few precious moments searching for something to pry one open, but there was nothing in his immediate vicinity.

They would have to go over the top. Not the ideal situation, but better than staying here.

As he turned to head back to the others, a gunshot boomed across the playing field.

DR. LAWRENCE WAS the first out of the dugout and onto

the field. Not waiting for Rivera to catch up, she raced past the non-sick holding area and into the outfield. As soon as she hit the end of the fence, she angled her path toward the back of the immune pen.

When she spotted the ditch dug under the gate, she muttered, "Unbelievable." She turned toward the outfield wall just in time to see the two sections of walls pushed shut. She raised her 9mm pistol and pulled the trigger twice. Thankfully, no screams came from the other side. She needed the prisoners alive.

She ran to the wall and shoved the left half open. In the lit up area beyond the gate, she could see the immune survivors running toward the back fence. If they made it over, her chances of getting them all back would be slim.

She sprinted through the opening, halted ten feet in, and pointed her gun at the escapees. "Stop where you are or I will shoot!" she yelled.

Only those in the back heeded her order.

She moved her barrel just left of the runners and fired off a shot, then quickly did the same on the right.

That stopped them. Even the guy straddling the top of the fence froze, looking at her.

Ben Bowerman, she realized. Their newest inductee.

"Mr. Bowerman, I advise you to climb back down. On *this* side of the fence, please. If not, one of your friends here will pay the price."

The kid hesitated for a moment before pulling his leg back over and dropping to the ground.

"Thank you," she said.

Behind her, she heard Rivera arrive, breathing heavily. "You got them," he said, sounding both surprised and pleased.

"Why are you doing this?" one of the girls asked. "You're supposed to be helping us."

Lawrence smirked. "If you're running then you already know that's not true. So let's not pretend anymore." She raised her voice. "Everyone line up! Now!"

"What are you going to do with us?" another girl asked.

"You're lucky we haven't killed you on the spot," Rivera

said. "Now do as Dr. Lawrence said. Line up!"

"YOU SEE THIS?" Cahill asked.

"Yeah. I see it," Gabriel said.

THE FAILED ESCAPEES began forming a single line. All except for Bowerman. He walked toward the two doctors and didn't stop until he was only ten feet away.

"Please, let us go," he said. "We're a small group. We promise we'll disappear and never cause you any problems."

"Really?" Lawrence said. She nodded past him at the fence. "I believe you and your friends out there already have."

He looked confused. "What friends?"

"That's enough. Get in line."

"No, wait. At least let them go. I'll stay. It was my idea to try to escape."

"Is that so?" she said. "Under normal circumstances, that might have changed things, but unfortunately we need more than one test subject."

"Test subject?"

She smiled and raised her pistol, pointing it at Ben's head. "But I guess I don't need all of you."

She was going to pull the trigger, knew that beyond a doubt, had even started to apply the pressure. But the next thing she knew she was on the ground, trying to fill her lungs with air, but unable to do so. The pain came next, a visceral, scorching pain.

Her hand found the wound on her chest and came away covered with blood.

How...? What...? Tired. So damn tired.

She remembered the prisoners and tried to grab for the gun that seemed to have fallen from her hands. All she could manage, though, was to twist enough so she could see Rivera. He, too, was on the ground, but the top of his head seemed to be missing.

So tired.

She closed her eyes, thinking she'd rest for a second, regain her strength so she could…figure out…what…had…hap—

GABRIEL MOVED HIS eye from his rifle's scope and patted Cahill on the back. "Nice shot."

"Thanks," Cahill said. "You, too."

Gabriel frowned. "I was trying for her head."

"Close enough."

As they rose to their feet, Walker asked, "We go after them?"

Gabriel scanned the back of the stadium, and saw that the group that had been fleeing was heading once more for the fence.

"They'll be fine. We go inside."

AT THE SOUND of the first two shots at the back of the stadium, Martina increased her speed, getting almost all the way to the wall by the time the second pair of shots went off.

She raced along the wall, looking for a way in as she tried not to think about the possibility that one of the bullets had hit Ben, but all the gates were locked.

She screamed in frustration.

"Over here!" Nyla yelled from along the fence behind her. "Boost me up."

Martina raced back. "I'll go."

"No. I will."

"No way!"

"Martina, which one of us is armed?"

Martina almost said to give her the rifle, but she knew Nyla was right. Martina had no firearms experience.

She laced her fingers together. As soon as Nyla stepped into the cradle, Martina thrust up her hands.

"Hurry," she said as Nyla dropped out of sight. "Please hurry."

325

BEN HAD BEEN sure his life was over. But then the doctor had collapsed. Before her colleague could react, he was down, too.

There were shouts of surprise. Ben thought one of them had been his, but he quickly pulled himself together and said, "Come on!"

He raced back to the outside fence and was about to start climbing when he noticed movement to the left.

A woman with dark brown skin stepped from the shadows, a rifle in her hands.

As soon as the others saw her, they stopped in their tracks, a few raising their hands in surrender.

"Drop your weapons!" the woman said.

"We're not armed," Ben told her.

"We heard gunshots," she said.

He couldn't help but flick a gaze at the two dead doctors. When the woman looked, too, he said, "We didn't do it. Someone else shot them. I don't know who."

The woman sidestepped over to the bodies. She poked a foot against Dr. Lawrence but didn't bother with Dr. Rivera. When she seemed satisfied, she lowered her weapon.

"You're the prisoners?" she asked.

"Um, yeah, I guess we are," Ben said. "Who are you?"

"Let's just say I'm not with them," she said, nodding toward the bodies. "Any of you know how to shoot?"

No one moved.

She picked up the pistols the doctors had been using. "Anyone?"

Still no response.

She tossed one pistol to Ben, and the other to Jilly. "You'll figure it out. Now come on. Let's get you out of here."

She led them behind the left-field bleachers and showed them how to help each other over the fence.

"There are more people still in the detention area," Ben said. "And another inside somewhere. We can't leave them here."

The woman thought for a moment. "It's Ben, isn't it?"

He was surprised, but didn't think he had time to ask how she knew. "Yeah."

"Good to meet you, Ben. I'm Nyla. Show me where these others are."

TEAMS B AND C each reported successful entry into the stadium. All three teams made their way into the interior and headed toward the home-plate end of the structure.

Here and there they encountered sporadic gunfire, but most of the shooters appeared to have very little idea about what they were doing and were subdued with little effort.

"Gabriel?" Anton Helms's voice said over the radio as the teams did a final sweep.

"Go for Gabriel."

"Something here you need to see."

"Where are you?"

Following Helms's directions, Gabriel made his way to a set of rooms that appeared to have been converted into a medical facility. Helms and two others were standing by a windowed door.

"So?" Gabriel said.

"Over here."

Gabriel walked over and looked through the window. A girl who couldn't have been much more than eighteen was standing a few feet inside, staring back with fear in her eyes.

"Please, let me out," she said, her voice coming out of an intercom on the wall. "Please."

Gabriel glanced at Helms. "What's going on?"

Helms shrugged. "We just found her like this. Said they stuck her in here earlier today after giving her an inoculation."

"Double inoculation," the girl corrected.

"Right, double. Apparently they told her she had to wait twenty-four hours to make sure it took."

"Uh, and why would that be?" Gabriel asked.

Helms turned off the intercom and motioned for Gabriel to follow him. About ten feet over was a set of valves mounted on the wall, with one set of hoses leading to the door of the room the man was in, and another set leading to several metal tanks.

He touched the first. "This one's on and hooked up to a couple of tanks marked O2." He skipped the two middle ones and pointed at the fourth. "This one? Well, come here."

He traced the hose back to a single tank. On the outside was stenciled KV-27a.

Gabriel gaped. They'd all heard the code before. It was Project Eden's designation for the Sage Flu virus.

"They're pumping virus into her room?" he asked.

"Pumped," Helms corrected him. He easily picked up the tank with two fingers under the valve. "It's empty."

Gabriel shot a look back at the room. "Why?"

"You got me."

They walked back over.

"Can you at least tell me what's going on?" the girl pleaded.

"You're going to be okay," Gabriel said, hoping that was true. "The people who were running this place are no longer in charge."

Her eyes widened. "Oh, God. We were right, weren't we?"

"Right about what?"

"Some of the others and I were starting to think the doctors and guards weren't who they claimed to be. And that they didn't really plan on helping us."

"No, ma'am, they didn't."

"Are you the UN?"

"The UN died with everyone else."

"Then who are you?"

"We're the ones who are going to figure out how to keep you alive."

PAX AND MARTINA heard the sound of running steps just inside the stadium, and then voices. A few seconds later something pounded against the fence and a head poked over the top.

"Jilly?" Martina said.

The girl looked down. "Martina?" She turned so she could glance back on the other side. "Martina's here!"

Jilly swung over the top and dropped down. She hugged Martina so tight it hurt, but neither seemed to care.

"Oh, my God. Oh, my God," Jilly said. "You came for us!"

Four more came over, including a man Martina didn't know, but the others were from her old softball team. She and Valerie even hugged, whatever problems between them forgotten for now or maybe forever.

When the last person dropped down, Martina stared expectantly at the top of the wall. "Where's Ben? I saw him. He's with you, isn't he?" She moved up to the fence and yelled, "Ben!"

"He went back to the enclosure with that woman," Jilly said.

"What woman?"

"The one with the gun. I thought she was with you."

"Nyla?"

Jilly shrugged. "I guess."

"Why would he go back?"

"There were others locked up with us," Jilly said. "And Ruby…they took her somewhere early today."

"All right," Pax said. "We're not safe here. I want you all to head across the parking lot to those trees over there and wait. Martina can show you where."

"I am *not* going anywhere," Martina told him.

He frowned but said, "Okay. The rest of you go. We'll be there as soon as we can."

"We're not leaving, either," Jilly said.

"Definitely," Valerie agreed.

"You've got to be kidding me," Pax said. "Did you hear those gunshots?"

"We saw two people killed in front of us," Jilly said. "So, yeah, we heard them. And we're staying."

It was another four minutes before they heard people

arriving on the other side again.

"Stand back!" Nyla yelled.

Everyone moved away from the fence.

A rifle blasted and the fence shuddered. There was the rattle of a chain, and then a gate a few feet away swung open.

The rest of the survivors swarmed out.

And at the very end came Nyla and Ben.

Martina rushed forward and threw her arms around him. At first he didn't seem to realize who she was. He pushed her back enough so he could take a look, and then his breath caught in his throat.

Their kiss was infused with relief and joy and longing.

It didn't matter what happened now.

She had found him.

January 8th

World Population
701,217,009

35

"I SEE HIM. I see him," Darshana said over the radio.

Sanjay looked west toward the building she was on, though he couldn't see her from where he was. "What's he doing?" he asked.

"Talking to another man. It looks like they are walking back to the car."

"This other man, what does he look like?"

"Tall. Maybe forty. Short hair."

"European or Indian?"

"European."

Sanjay frowned. Not Director Mahajan. At least they still had eyes on van Assen.

"Kusum, are you ready?" he asked.

"Ready," she responded.

Two hours earlier, van Assen had shown up at the survival station, alone in a car. Hopefully his next stop would be NB551. Sanjay and Kusum were both waiting on motorcycles, ready to take up pursuit.

"Van Assen's getting in the car," Darshana said.

"The other man going with him?"

"No. He's alone." Several seconds, then, "He's leaving. Turning…east."

Kusum's route.

"I'll catch up," Sanjay said. He kicked his bike to life.

DREAM SKY

The people in America had called early that morning with the request for him and his friends to prepare to create some chaos in Jaipur. Since there were only the three of them, it was understood the chaos wouldn't be much, but they were told whatever they could do would help.

To that end, the first thing they'd done that morning was locate a fireworks factory on the edge of town, where they obtained several small barrels of powder and reels of fuses. They hid the kegs around the perimeter of the station, ganging fuses so several could be lit at the same time. Darshana was staying behind so that if the call to act came while he and Kusum were following van Assen, Darshana could light them up. The makeshift bombs wouldn't do much damage, but they would be unnerving.

Sanjay caught up to Kusum five minutes later on the street paralleling the one van Assen was using.

"Keep on him," he told her over the radio. "Tell me every time he turns. I am going ahead."

"To where?"

"I have an idea. Just do not lose him."

Sanjay twisted the accelerator and raced away. He didn't want to share his plan with her, knowing she would try to talk him out of it, but if it worked, they might be able to provide the Americans with more than the distraction from a few barrels of gunpowder.

Using Kusum's directional information, he tried to stay at least two blocks ahead of van Assen. One time he screwed up and fell behind, but quickly made up the distance. Finally, when it seemed the Dutchman was going in one steady direction, Sanjay increased his distance to four blocks, then five, then six.

As they neared what appeared to be a warehouse district, he thought they must be getting close to van Assen's destination, so he decreased his speed.

Two streets down and to the left, he saw it. Thankfully, it was far enough away that the guard at the gate didn't see him. Even if there wasn't a guard there, he would have pegged the place for a base. The array of satellite dishes and antennas on the roof was incongruous with the rest of the buildings in the area, and while the structure itself appeared appropriately worn, he would swear it was designed to look that way.

He turned the bike around. "Where are you?" he asked.

Kusum gave him a location that was only two and a half blocks away. He moved up to the end of the street and laid his bike down in the middle of the road, making it impossible to drive around it. Then he hid in the shadows of the building on the corner.

Twenty seconds later, van Assen's car appeared on the road. When it neared the bike, it slowed. Van Assen had two choices: get out of the car to move the bike, or back up to use a different street. Sanjay wasn't about to leave things to chance.

A second after the car stopped, he sprinted toward it, and was only a few meters away when the driver's door started to open.

Perfect.

Sanjay leapt forward and grabbed the door. Van Assen yelped in surprise.

"Good morning, Mr. van Assen," Sanjay said. "So nice to see you again."

MADRID, SPAIN
8:08 AM CET (CENTRAL EUROPEAN TIME)

LALO VEGA SILENTLY worked his way around the Madrid survival station, checking on each of his people.

He sure as hell hoped this wouldn't be for nothing. Putting all his people on the line like this felt like a disaster in the making. But the Resistance leadership back in America assured him his team wouldn't be the only ones out tonight. It was a worldwide effort, they had said. The big push.

Despite his concerns, he put on a brave face as he made sure everyone was set.

"Any time now," he told them. "Wait for my word."

DREAM SKY

THIS WAS GOING to be something to see, Raheem Bahar thought with a smile. The Cairo survival station would not know what had hit them.

During the first days of the epidemic, Rahim and his people had cleaned out five army ammo depots, moving the munitions to a centralized location for later use.

When the request from Resistance headquarters had come through, he knew the time had come.

They had to temper their initial plan for fear of harming the survivors in the detention areas, but their effort would still pack more than a simple punch. Because Rahim had no intention of only putting a scare into Project Eden personnel at the station.

He and his people would destroy them.

GUANGZHOU, CHINA
2:09 PM CHINA STANDARD TIME

"YOU GOING TO be all right?" Pieter Dombrovsky asked.

Megan Zhang nodded. "I'll be fine."

Whether she would be or not didn't matter. The call would come soon and they would go into action, despite her nerves.

She had always known that by joining the Resistance, there was a good chance she'd be involved in a mission like this. She had done what she could to lessen the potential trauma, and had volunteered for the Guangzhou contingent so that she wouldn't be faced with seeing the death of anyone she knew back in Hong Kong.

Then stupid Pieter had volunteered to come with her. Now she had to worry about him.

She tightened her grip on her rifle, hoping to quell her shakes.

Pieter must have noticed, because he pried one of her hands loose and put it in his. "No one will see us up here," he told her. "We'll set off the charges, fire off a few shots, and before you know it, it'll be over."

Unable to help herself, she flung her hand around the back of his head and pulled his lips to hers, kissing him for the first time ever.

"Don't you dare die on me," she whispered.

"I won't if you won't."

"Deal."

TOKYO, JAPAN
3:09 PM JST (JAPAN STANDARD TIME)

THE CHOICE OF the location for the Tokyo survival station had been a poor one on Project Eden's part. To be fair, it was impossible for anyone to know about all the tunnels that ran under the city, whether new or long abandoned.

It was one of the forgotten tunnels that would be the station's downfall, at least if Toshiko Nagawa had anything to do with it. The tunnels allowed her team to get right under the facility and place remotely detonated explosives below the administration building.

Now all she had to do was press a button when the call came, then walk in and free the detainees.

As her college roommate back at Berkeley used to say: Done and done.

36

CELESTE JOHNSON STOOD in the back of the comm room, eyes narrow. "Well?" she asked.

"Still nothing, ma'am," the comm operator said.

Less than an hour earlier, they had received a message from the Los Angeles survival station that said a large number of survivors had shown up. L.A. was supposed to have reported in with a follow-up thirty minutes ago, but none had come, and all subsequent attempts to reach the station had gone unanswered.

Chicago was another matter altogether. While the station was still in contact with New York, it had been attacked in a coordinated effort to free a group of survivors scheduled for elimination. One of those in the attack had apparently been a Project Eden technician, a traitor within their organization. He was killed as he led the survivors out of the facility, but others on the outside had used explosives and gunfire to create diversions that allowed the prisoners to get away.

Of course, neither event was the first time a station had experienced difficulties. There had been minor flare-ups here and there, and, most spectacularly, the escape at the Mumbai station that had necessitated the closure of that facility.

Celeste was tempted to send out a general warning, but she wouldn't allow herself to imagine either event as something significant. She decided that in the morning, she would send a team to Chicago to find the troublemakers and destroy them.

As for Los Angeles…

"Keep trying," she instructed the operator.

37

"WE HAVE TWENTY-NINE locations ready to go," Crystal said over the phone. "A few won't be much more than window dressing, but the others should more substantial. Just waiting for your go."

"Very soon," Ash said. "Don't stray too far away."

"Glued to my chair."

Ash hung up and walked back over to the others. "So?"

Without looking back, Bobby Lion said, "Give me a few more seconds."

They were in a hollow behind some rocks on a hill a quarter mile east of the town. Bobby and the people he'd arrived with had set up a monitoring station with four five-inch screens sitting on a crack in one of the boulders. They were being fed by cameras placed around the town, and all monitors were in night-vision mode.

Right around midnight, not long before Ash, Chloe, and their group had arrived, Bobby had spotted someone walking through the streets. At first he had thought it was one of the guards he'd already identified, but all four were still in place. He tracked the silhouette all the way to the location of guard number three, where some kind of conversation occurred. The new arrival apparently took over guard duty, while the man he replaced headed through town the way the other man had come.

Unfortunately, at that point, only four cameras had been up and running, and Bobby had lost the guard as the man reached the north end of the village. Since then, Bobby had been trying to figure out where the guy went. One of the team members had been sent out with a camera and was moving around the town at Bobby's direction, trying to pick up the guard's footprints in the snow.

When Ash had gone to take Crystal's call, Bobby had traced the path through several streets but still had no end point.

"I need you to move fifty feet to your left," Bobby said into his radio. "Then aim along that road leading out of town....Yeah, the one that dead-ends."

Ash leaned over Bobby's shoulder as the feed in monitor five repositioned. The road in question was a flat expanse covered with snow.

"Zoom in," Bobby instructed. "Slowly. Eastern edge."

The picture darkened as it pushed in, the tighter angle cutting down on the amount of ambient light the lens could pull in.

"Stop," Bobby said. "There." Bobby pointed at the monitor.

Along the edge of the road was a depression in the snow, almost a trough. It appeared to be…

"A path?" Ash asked.

Bobby grinned. "That's what it looks like to me." He switched back to his mic. "Marcos, you see that dark line on the edge of the road?…Right, that one. Follow it out. Let's see where it goes."

OMEGA THREE WALKED over to his bag and pulled out his thermos of coffee. With a clear sky, the temperature was a lot lower than it had been in the last week, so staying warm was going to be a challenge. He really should have brought two thermoses. He'd have to remember that for tomorrow.

God, he hated the graveyard shift, he thought as he sipped some of the warm liquid.

DREAM SKY

The teams rotated on a weekly basis. Tonight was Omega team's first night back on the eleven p.m. to seven a.m. shift. What he wouldn't give to be in his bed, under his blankets, fast asleep. Maybe he should have done what Omega Two had done and feigned illness. Not that Omega Two wasn't sick, but Omega Three couldn't help but feel envious the guy had spent only an hour on duty.

Have to remember that trick.

He finished his coffee and pushed all thoughts of his bed out of his mind. It would only make him crazy.

His thermos back in the bag, he returned to his post, and once more took up scanning the ghost town below.

THE GROUP WICKS had been following was clearly not the Project Eden patrol he had thought it was.

Instead of entering the town, the group went around it, leaving behind what he'd discovered were cameras at strategic points, each covering a different portion of Everton. Leaving the cameras in place, he continued to follow the patrol to the eastern hill, where the team set up camp.

Then, within the last hour, the patrol had swelled in number with the arrival of a larger group. If not for the cameras, he might have thought these people were a band of survivors who'd come together and were looking for someplace safe to stay. If that had been the case, he would have moved on long ago. But they obviously weren't simply a group of survivors, so he thought it best to figure out what they were up to, make sure they wouldn't mess up his plans.

Very carefully, he worked his way through the trees so he could get close enough to their camp to hear what they were saying.

CHLOE HEARD A subtle crush of snow. It had come from up the hill to the left.

She took a quick head count, thinking someone might have wandered off to take a leak, but everyone was there.

342

Another crush, slight and slow, like someone taking a long time to lower his or her foot.

As casually as possible, she moved behind the group, going right, away from the noise. After she was out of the hollow, she angled up the hill fifty feet before coming back across to the right. There she paused and scanned the hillside between her and the others.

It wasn't long before she spotted the shadow among the trees, creeping downhill, right where she thought it would be.

WICKS STOPPED, KNOWING he had gone as far as he dared.

For several seconds there was silence. Perhaps they were whispering, in which case he wouldn't be able to safely get close enough. Then a voice, not loud, but enough for him to hear.

"What is that?"

Another voice. "I don't know. A storage building? Whatever it is, that's where the trail leads."

The third voice did not come from in front of him. It came from behind.

Right behind him.

"Don't move."

He could feel the breath of the words on the back of his neck. He wanted to turn and see who it was, but what did it matter? He was caught.

"On my command, you'll stand up. Nice and slow. You try anything and my knife will cut through you before you realize it. Nod if you understand."

Wicks nodded.

"Good. Up."

He rose.

"Now walk forward."

ASH HEARD A murmur from the back of the crowd and turned to see what was going on. Out of the trees, a man emerged with Chloe tailing him, holding a knife.

"What's going on?" Ash asked.

"We have a visitor," Chloe said. "He seemed very interested in what we were doing."

The man appeared too old to be a sentry, but that could have been Ash's bias. As Ash walked over, he couldn't help but notice the man was staring at him, almost gawking.

"Who are you?" Ash asked.

The man didn't appear to hear him. Chloe poked the tip of her knife into his back. He winced then blinked several times.

"I know you," the man said, still looking at Ash.

"I don't think so."

"Las Cruces. You were there."

Ash narrowed his eyes. "Who are you?"

"You were kneeling next to Matt. You were with him when he died. I saw you. You're with the Resistance, aren't you?"

Ash couldn't stop himself from grabbing the man's shirt and pulling him forward. "Who *are* you?"

"My...my name is Curtis. Curtis Wicks."

"I don't know you," Ash said. "I've never seen you before. How do you know Matt?"

"He was my friend. He was..." The man was quiet for a moment. "Maybe you know my code name. Matt called me C8."

Ash let go of the man's shirt and took a step back.

"C8 died in the explosion at NB219," he finally said.

"I didn't. Obviously. Matt warned me about what was going to happen. I was up in the warehouse when the blast went off, and was able to get out before everything burned down."

His anger growing, Ash said, "If you saw us, why didn't you join us?"

The man looked as if he were searching for the right words, but ended up saying nothing.

"If you're really C8," Chloe said, "then you know why we're here."

"Matt told you, didn't he?" the man said.

"Told us what?" Ash said.

The man looked from him to Chloe and back. "Dream Sky. It could be the only reason you're here."

The skin of Ash's arms prickled.

"What is it?" Ash asked. "What is Dream Sky?"

Through trembling lips, the man said, "Everything."

"That's a little broad for my taste. What is it?"

The man stammered but made no answer.

"Whatever it is," Chloe said, "once we destroy it, it'll bring the Project down, won't it?"

The man's eyes widened. "You can't destroy it!"

"Why not?" Ash said. "Isn't that what Matt wanted to do?"

"No. He wanted to take it," the man said. "You *need* it. We all need it if we're going to start over. It's a repository of irreplaceable knowledge!"

"Are you telling me it's a library?" Ash asked.

"No. Not a library. People."

38

AFTER ALMOST DYING at the survival station, Belinda Ramsey is not sure if she and her fellow survivors should be trusting these people who found them not long after they went on the run, but there was little choice. She and the others were both physically and emotionally exhausted, and the promise to help them get far away from the Chicago survival station was all it took.

The bus is headed west to where they've been told other survivors are gathering. It sounds suspiciously like the safe zones the UN people, or whoever they were, talked about. But these new people have already treated Belinda's group much better than the others back at the station. Food and clothes and medical attention have all been offered.

Belinda is hopeful and at the same time scared to hope.

The only thing she regrets about leaving the survival station is that her journal is still sitting on her bunk. She must have said something to someone about it, because when they take a break at a large truck stop, one of the new people brings her a pen and a blank diary from the store.

"In case you get the urge," the woman says, placing it on the seat next to Belinda.

Belinda at first isn't sure she'd ever have the urge to write again, but after a while on the road again, she realizes that's not true. There is at least one thing she has to write.

She picks up the book, opens it to the first page, and begins:

I don't know what his name was. I don't know what happened to him. I don't know where he is. All I know is that if not for his actions, we would all be dead. Since there is no way I can thank him, all I can do is tell you what happened.

Last night, after eleven p.m., my name was finally called...

PAX ISN'T SURE exactly what it is he's feeling. Satisfaction for taking over the Los Angeles survival station? A bit. Relief that they were able to save Martina's friends and the other detainees? Sure. Revulsion at what was done to the girl named Ruby? Absolutely. All these thoughts and more race through him, making it impossible for him to hold still for more than a moment.

The amazing thing is that the Campbell kid isn't sick or dead. He appears completely unaffected by the virus, only agitated at being cooped up. Why the virus didn't make him sick is something Pax will let others work out. For the moment, he's strictly concerned with getting all possible intel out of the facility, then getting out of there before Project Eden sends people in to find out what happened.

As soon as he finishes searching the facility director's office, he picks up his radio and says, "Finish up whatever you're doing and get to the main entrance. This is the fifteen-minute warning."

MARTINA WILL NOT leave Ben's side. He doesn't seem to mind, though, and appears just as glued to her. They are waiting in the back of one of the troop trucks at the stadium, told that after their rescuers finish what they're doing at the station, they'll head out. The rest of her friends are also in the truck, with the exception of Ruby, who is still in isolation. Martina was able to visit her before leaving and was happy to see her friend's spirits were up and that she looked perfectly healthy.

Now, all the others are asking her questions about where she's been and who their saviors are.

She answers as best as she can.

Then Jilly asks, "What about Noreen and Riley and Craig? Where are they?"

Until that moment, Martina was pretty sure she's never been happier, but the mention of her missing friends dampens her mood. It's her fault they're not here. She raced off, focused solely on Ben's Jeep, and lost them.

"We'll find them," she says. "Tomorrow, first thing."

Ben squeezes her hand. "Absolutely."

NOREEN ISN'T SURE if Craig is dead or only unconscious. If she could check, she would, but her hands are bound behind her and tied to a pipe running up the wall of the mostly empty room. Craig is slumped to the side ten feet away, similarly bound to another pipe. She watches his chest to see if he's breathing, but in the dim light it's hard to tell.

Where Riley is, she has no idea. It was Riley's turn to gather food for dinner, so she wasn't there when the men they saw in Cambria returned and sneaked up on them. Thankfully, Riley took her motorcycle with her. Otherwise the men wouldn't stop looking until they find out who it belongs to.

Noreen doesn't know what's going to happen, but she's sure it won't be good.

"Craig," she whispers for about the millionth time. "Craig, can you hear me?"

ROBERT AND ESTELLA have been given their assignment. They wait with four others in the trees at the western edge of town. They can't see the guard with whom they're supposed to make contact, but they know where he is.

The only question Robert has is, will the guard shoot first or wait until it's too late?

It's a huge risk, but no bigger than some of the stunts

he's pulled lately.

At least that's what he tells himself.

KUSUM SITS BEHIND the wheel of the car. Sanjay and van Assen sit in back.

When Sanjay confronted him at the makeshift roadblock, van Assen tried to grab Sanjay, probably intending to knock Sanjay's head into the car. Sanjay batted away van Assen's hands and kneed him in the gut.

Now, as they sit in the backseat, van Assen lunges at Sanjay as Sanjay is talking to Kusum. The Dutchman is able to get in a few jabs, but fails at wrestling away the gun Sanjay procured from the trunk of the vehicle. Sanjay slaps the weapon against the side of the man's head, causing a trickle of blood to run from his ear.

If the man tries anything again, Sanjay is prepared to shoot him, first in the foot, then, if necessary, the knee, and then the hip. He doesn't think pulling the trigger will be needed, though. He is pretty sure van Assen has received the message, but Sanjay will stay vigilant nonetheless.

After he resumes his conversation with Kusum, he glances occasionally at the sat phone sitting in the front passenger seat, knowing that at any moment, the call will come.

RACHEL PUTS A supportive hand on Crystal's back. "You doing all right?"

"Fine," the girl says.

"And we're all set?"

"As set as we can be."

Rachel smiles. "Good."

She knows the girl, like most of the others present, is running on adrenaline, having already put in more than twenty hours straight. Soon Crystal can rest, but not yet. There is still work to do tonight.

Help me give them strength, Rachel thinks, hoping somewhere her brother hears her.

She is still shattered by his absence, but she's learning to cope with it, if barely.

She walks over to Leon and puts the same hand on him. "Hanging in there?"

CELESTE JOHNSON'S ANNOYANCE is growing with every minute the Los Angeles survival station remains silent. She decides to dispatch a squad from the Bay Area to get eyes on the ground, and is told they will arrive within ninety minutes.

With nothing else to do and the hour growing extremely late, she decides the best thing she can do now is get some sleep.

ASH EYES THE concrete building in the middle of the snow-covered field. So unassuming, so easy to dismiss.

C8 has confirmed it's the entrance to the facility.

To Dream Sky.

Ash looks over at Powell and whispers, "Are we all in position?"

"Yes, sir," the man responds.

Ash turns to Chloe and notices a far-off look on her face. "You okay?"

She jerks a little in surprise and then tries to smile. "Yeah, yeah. I'm good. It's just…"

"What?" he asks.

"I feel like I've been here before."

Ash waits, but nothing else comes. "You want to sit this one out?" he asks.

A sneer leaps onto her face. "No way."

That's good enough for him. He reaches into this coat pocket, pulls out the sat phone. The number for Ward Mountain is waiting for him on the screen.

He looks again to Powell. "Group one, go."

As Powell raises his radio to his mouth, Ash moves his thumb over the SEND button.

It's time.

The Project Eden saga returns later in 2014

Made in the USA
Las Vegas, NV
31 July 2021